AGENT GATES

AND THE SECRET ADVENTURES OF DEVONTON ABBEY

(A PARODY)

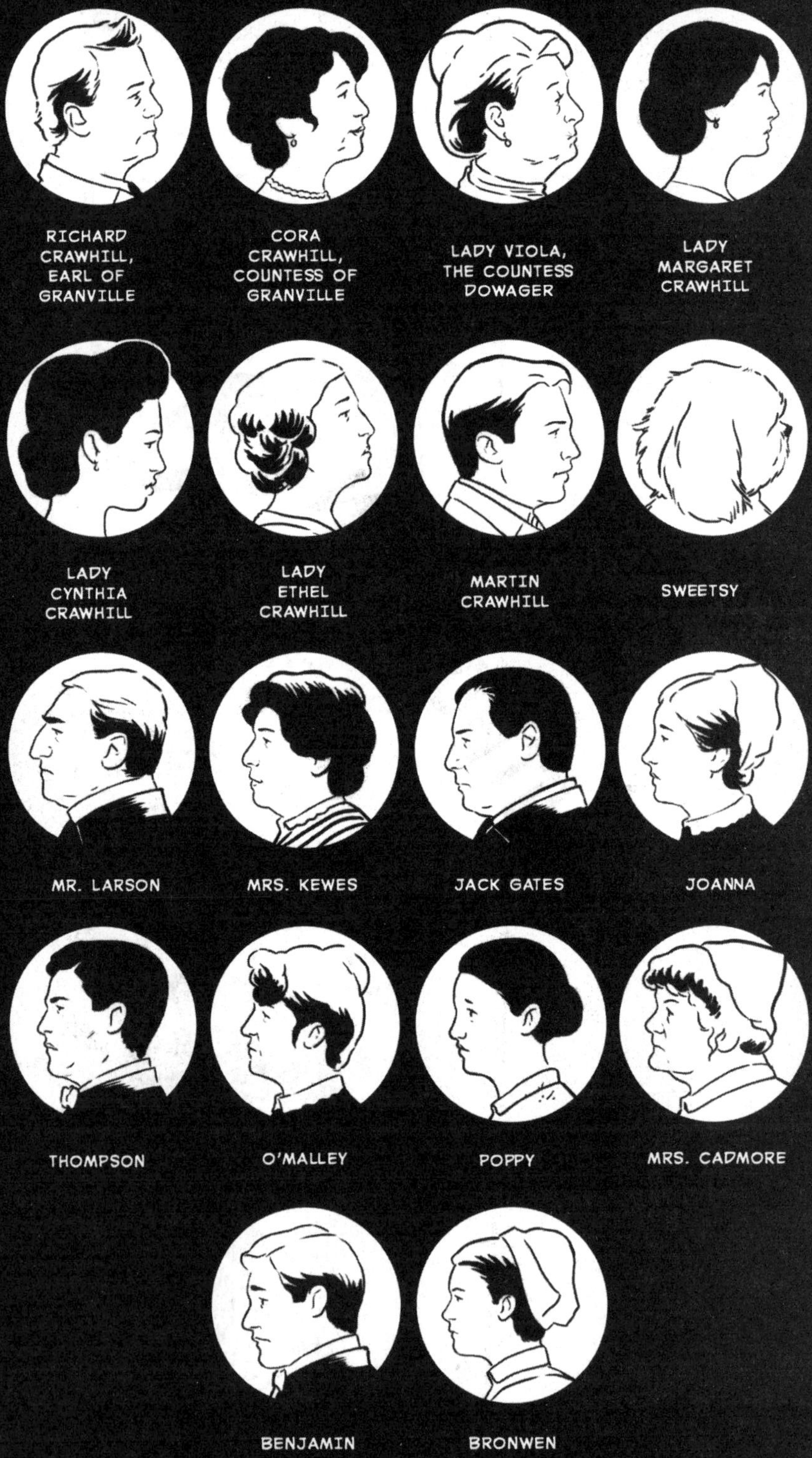
RICHARD CRAWHILL, EARL OF GRANVILLE
CORA CRAWHILL, COUNTESS OF GRANVILLE
LADY VIOLA, THE COUNTESS DOWAGER
LADY MARGARET CRAWHILL
LADY CYNTHIA CRAWHILL
LADY ETHEL CRAWHILL
MARTIN CRAWHILL
SWEETSY
MR. LARSON
MRS. KEWES
JACK GATES
JOANNA
THOMPSON
O'MALLEY
POPPY
MRS. CADMORE
BENJAMIN
BRONWEN

AGENT GATES

AND THE SECRET ADVENTURES OF
DEVONTON ABBEY

(A PARODY)

WRITTEN BY
CAMAREN SUBHIYAH

ILLUSTRATED BY
KYLE HILTON

**Andrews McMeel
Publishing, LLC**
Kansas City • Sydney • London

CHAP

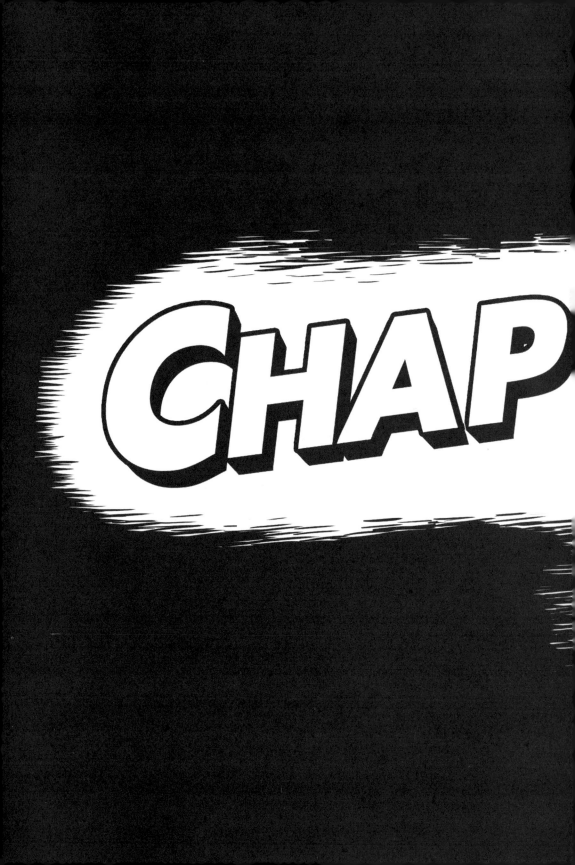

TER ONE

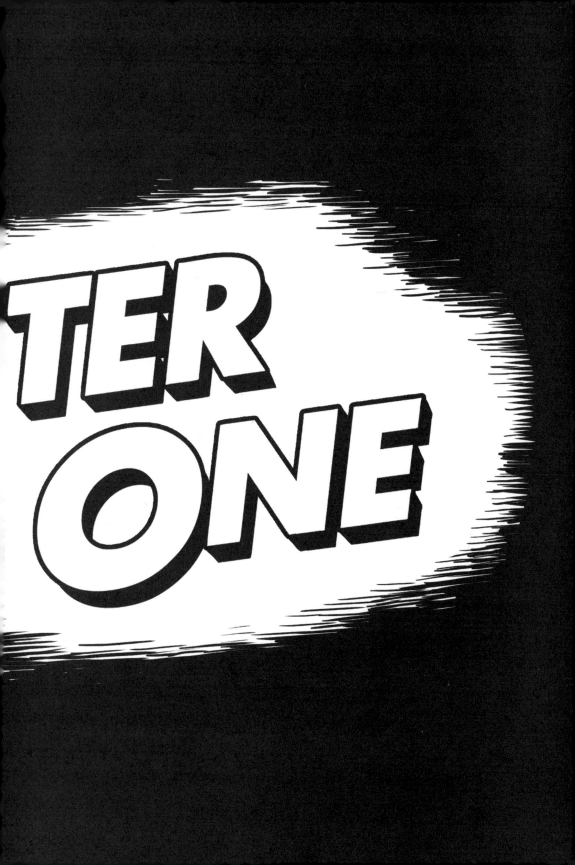

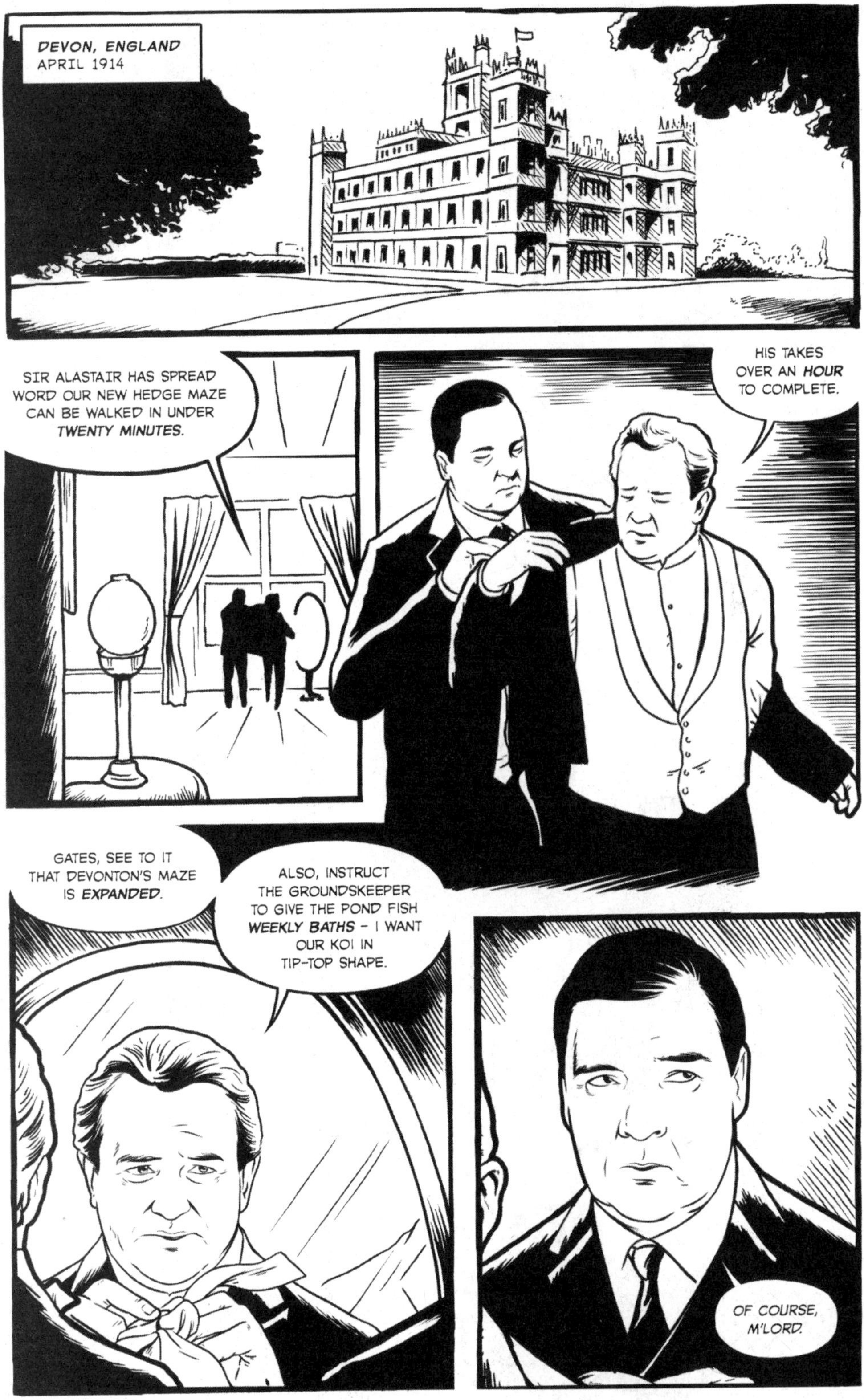
DEVON, ENGLAND
APRIL 1914
SIR ALASTAIR HAS SPREAD WORD OUR NEW HEDGE MAZE CAN BE WALKED IN UNDER TWENTY MINUTES.
HIS TAKES OVER AN HOUR TO COMPLETE.
GATES, SEE TO IT THAT DEVONTON'S MAZE IS EXPANDED.
ALSO, INSTRUCT THE GROUNDSKEEPER TO GIVE THE POND FISH WEEKLY BATHS - I WANT OUR KOI IN TIP-TOP SHAPE.
OF COURSE, M'LORD.

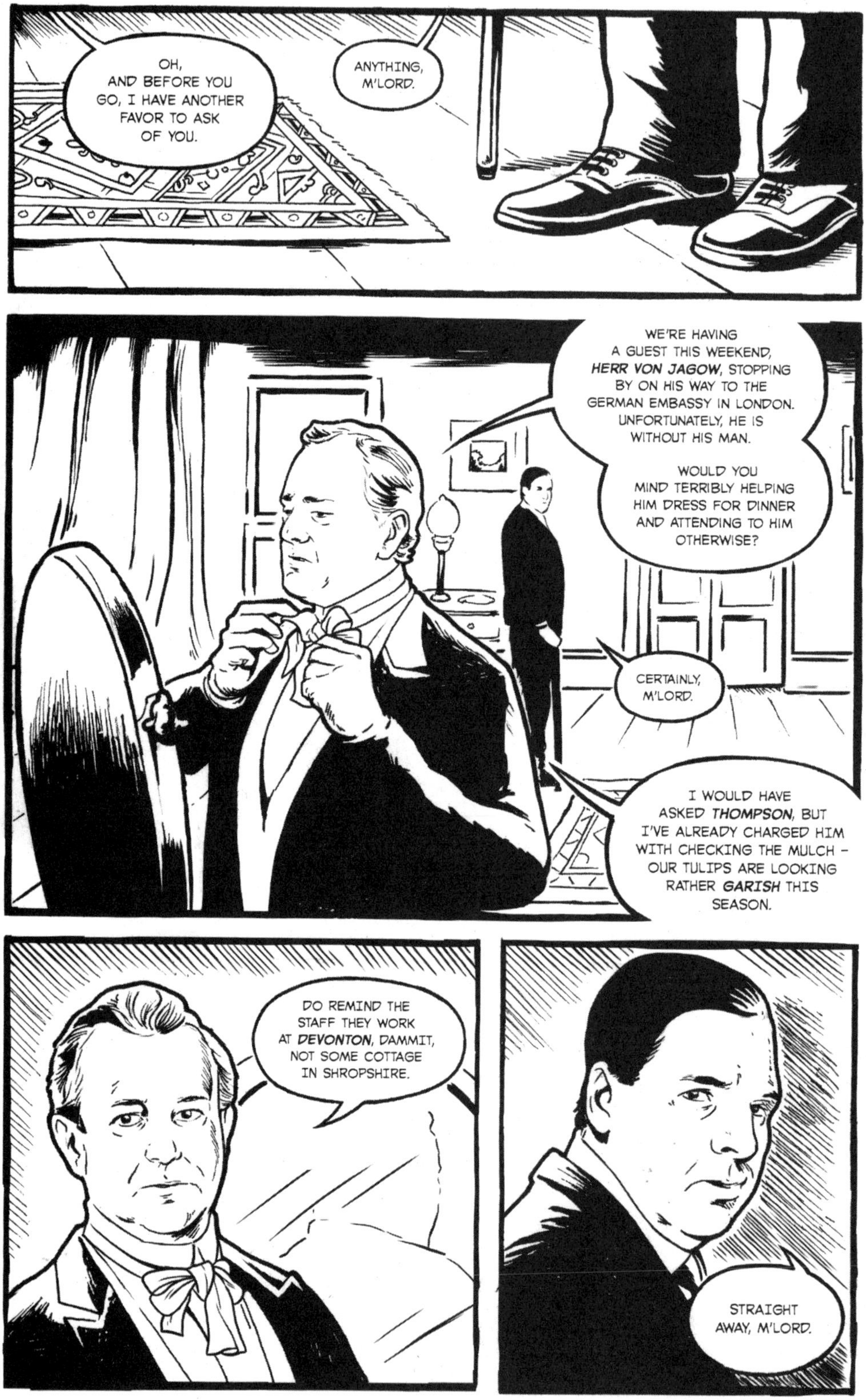
OH, AND BEFORE YOU GO, I HAVE ANOTHER FAVOR TO ASK OF YOU.
ANYTHING, M'LORD.
WE'RE HAVING A GUEST THIS WEEKEND, **HERR VON JAGOW**, STOPPING BY ON HIS WAY TO THE GERMAN EMBASSY IN LONDON. UNFORTUNATELY, HE IS WITHOUT HIS MAN.
WOULD YOU MIND TERRIBLY HELPING HIM DRESS FOR DINNER AND ATTENDING TO HIM OTHERWISE?
CERTAINLY, M'LORD.
I WOULD HAVE ASKED **THOMPSON**, BUT I'VE ALREADY CHARGED HIM WITH CHECKING THE MULCH – OUR TULIPS ARE LOOKING RATHER **GARISH** THIS SEASON.
DO REMIND THE STAFF THEY WORK AT **DEVONTON**, DAMMIT, NOT SOME COTTAGE IN SHROPSHIRE.
STRAIGHT AWAY, M'LORD.

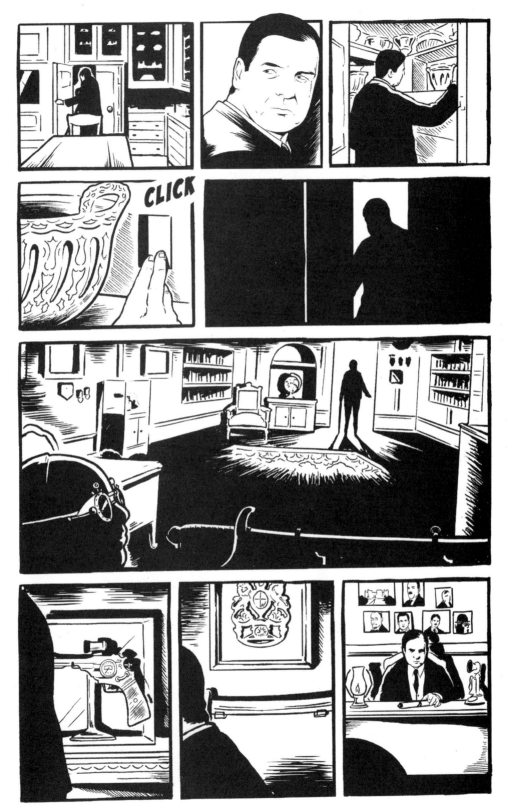

CLICK

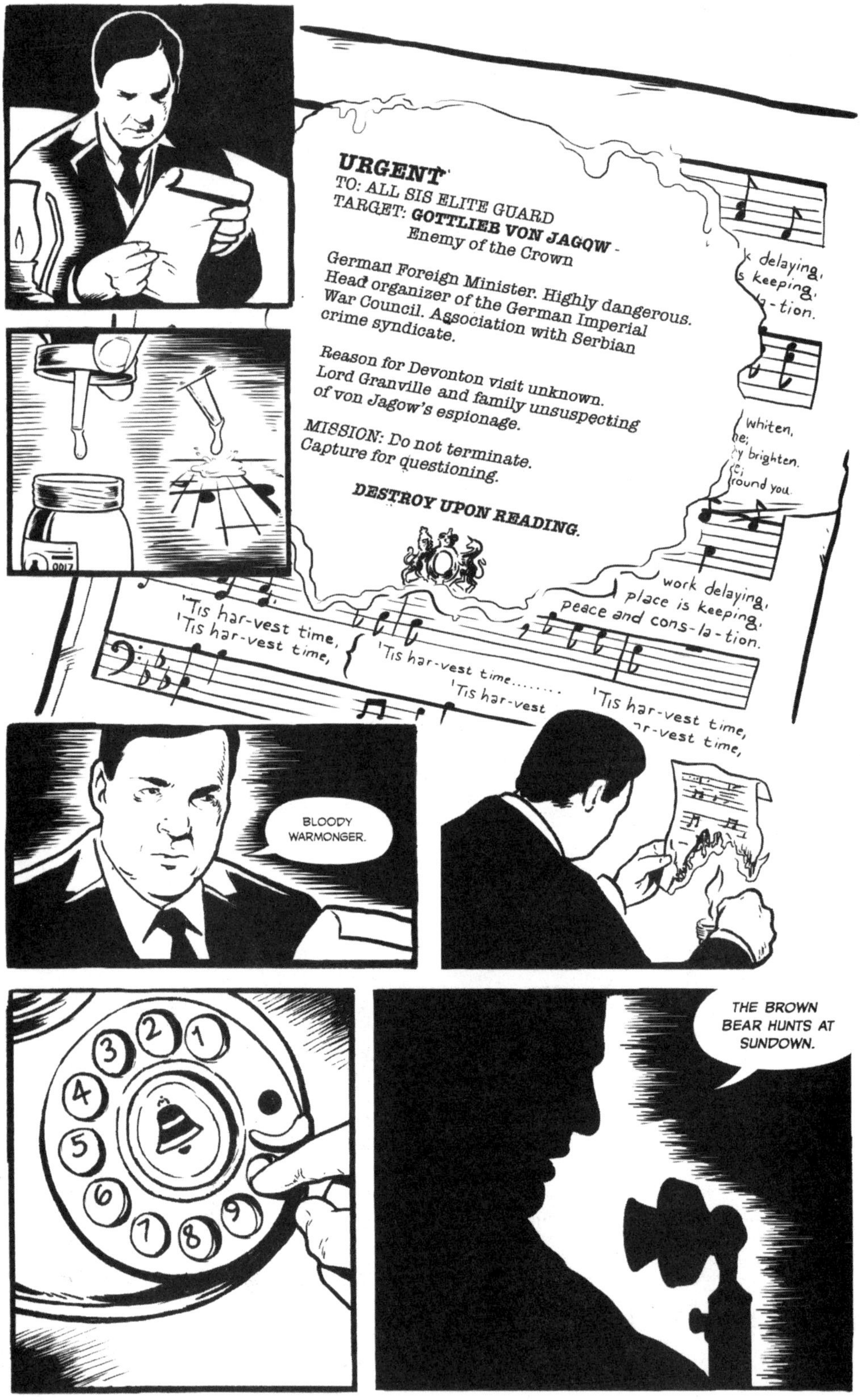
URGENT
TO: ALL SIS ELITE GUARD
TARGET: GOTTLIEB VON JAGOW - Enemy of the Crown
German Foreign Minister. Highly dangerous. Head organizer of the German Imperial War Council. Association with Serbian crime syndicate.
Reason for Devonton visit unknown. Lord Granville and family unsuspecting of von Jagow's espionage.
MISSION: Do not terminate. Capture for questioning.
DESTROY UPON READING.
work delaying,
place is keeping,
peace and cons-la-tion.
'Tis har-vest time,
'Tis har-vest time,
'Tis har-vest time........
'Tis har-vest
'Tis har-vest time,
BLOODY WARMONGER.
THE BROWN BEAR HUNTS AT SUNDOWN.

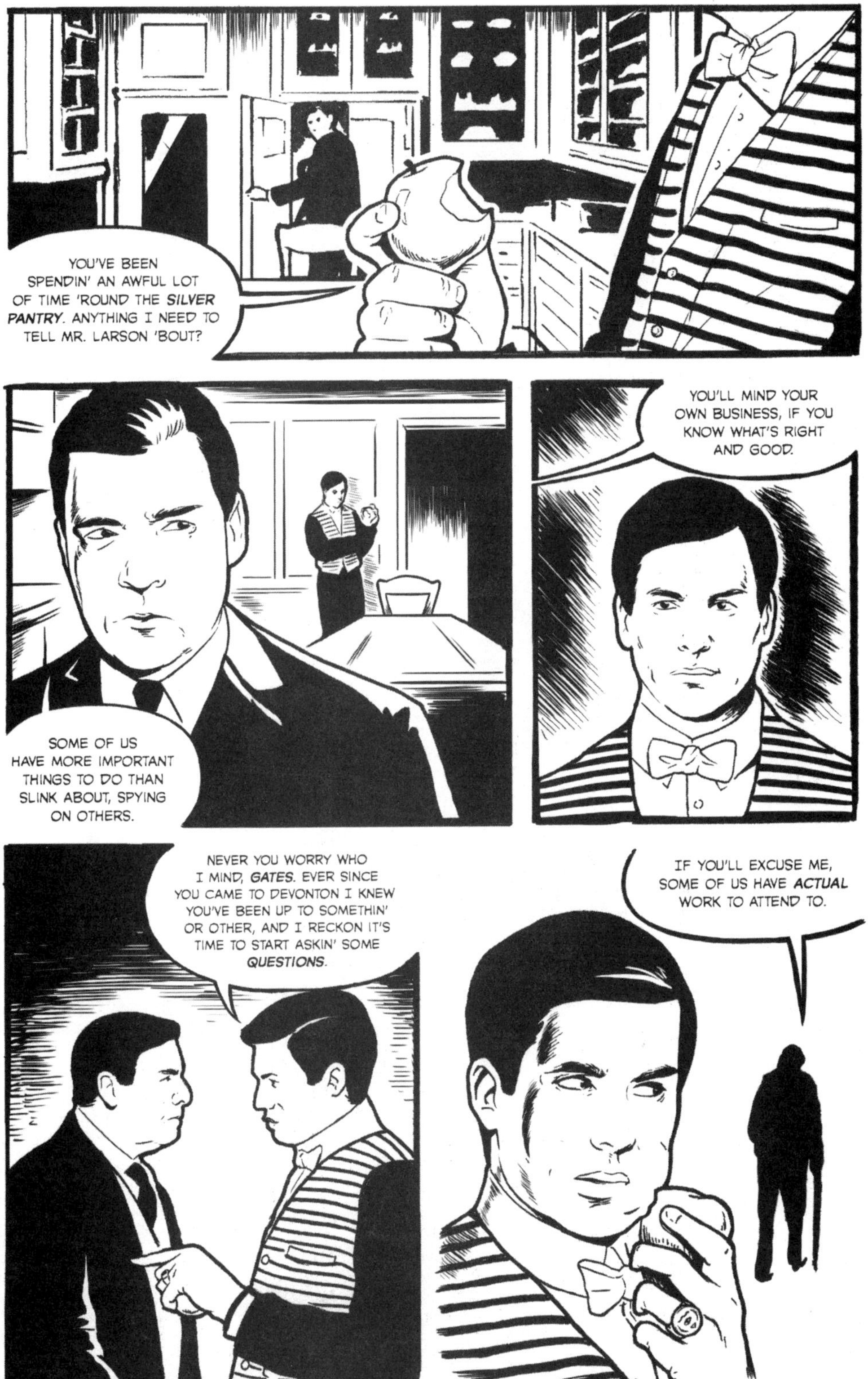
YOU'VE BEEN SPENDIN' AN AWFUL LOT OF TIME 'ROUND THE SILVER PANTRY. ANYTHING I NEED TO TELL MR. LARSON 'BOUT?
SOME OF US HAVE MORE IMPORTANT THINGS TO DO THAN SLINK ABOUT, SPYING ON OTHERS.
YOU'LL MIND YOUR OWN BUSINESS, IF YOU KNOW WHAT'S RIGHT AND GOOD.
NEVER YOU WORRY WHO I MIND, GATES. EVER SINCE YOU CAME TO DEVONTON I KNEW YOU'VE BEEN UP TO SOMETHIN' OR OTHER, AND I RECKON IT'S TIME TO START ASKIN' SOME QUESTIONS.
IF YOU'LL EXCUSE ME, SOME OF US HAVE ACTUAL WORK TO ATTEND TO.

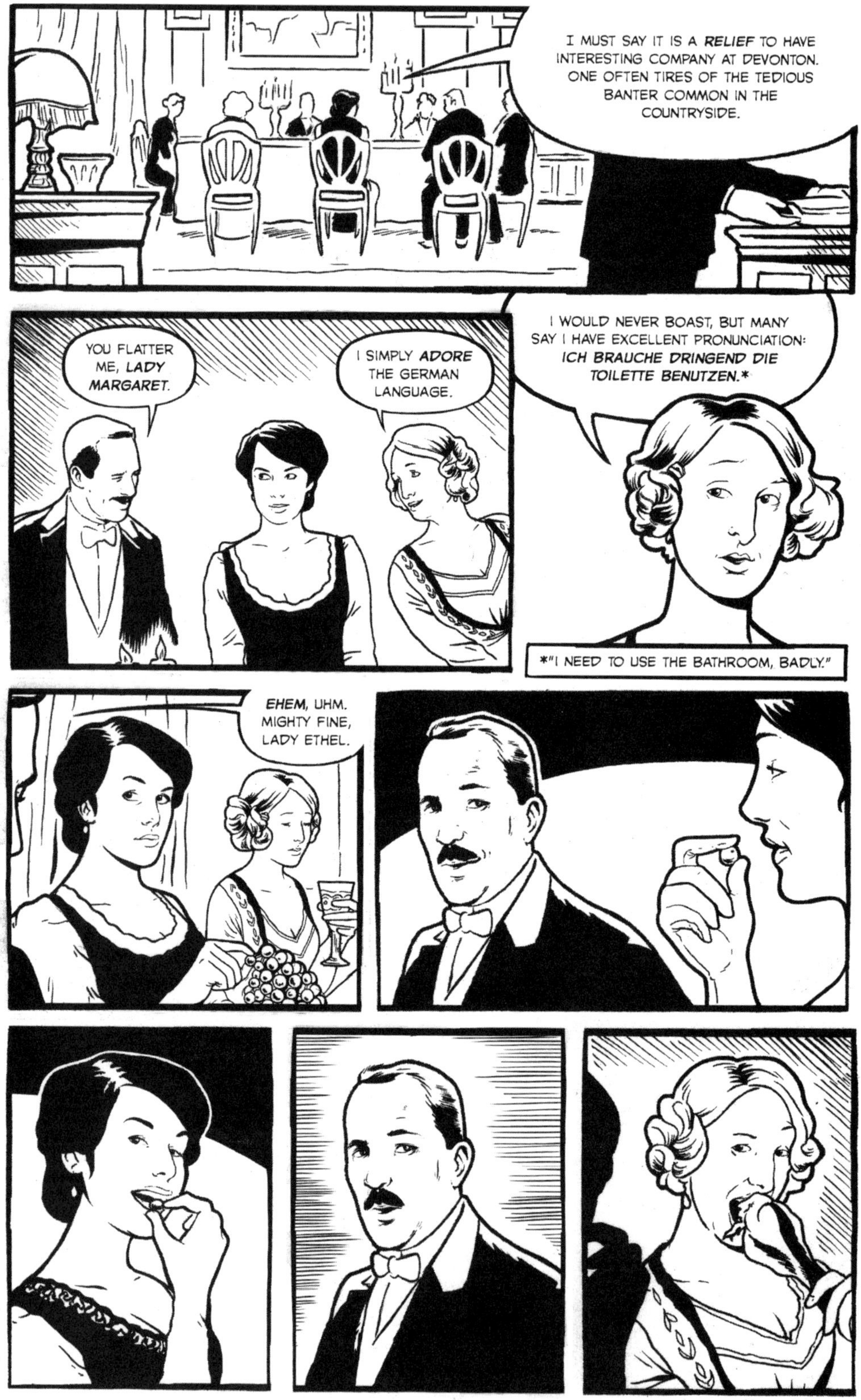
I MUST SAY IT IS A *RELIEF* TO HAVE INTERESTING COMPANY AT DEVONTON. ONE OFTEN TIRES OF THE TEDIOUS BANTER COMMON IN THE COUNTRYSIDE.
YOU FLATTER ME, *LADY MARGARET*.
I SIMPLY *ADORE* THE GERMAN LANGUAGE.
I WOULD NEVER BOAST, BUT MANY SAY I HAVE EXCELLENT PRONUNCIATION: *ICH BRAUCHE DRINGEND DIE TOILETTE BENUTZEN.**
*"I NEED TO USE THE BATHROOM, BADLY."
EHEM, UHM. MIGHTY FINE, LADY ETHEL.

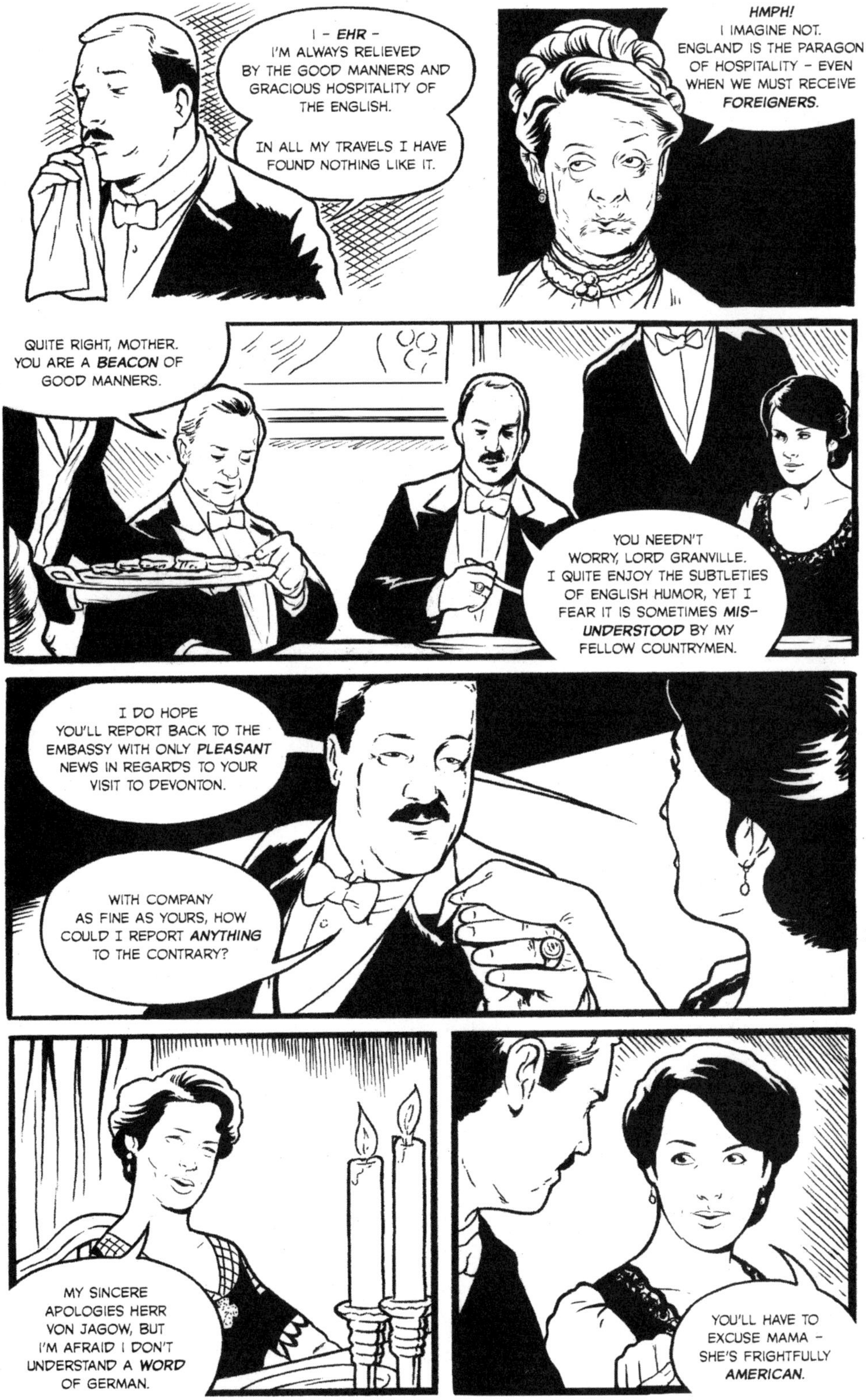
I - EHR -
I'M ALWAYS RELIEVED BY THE GOOD MANNERS AND GRACIOUS HOSPITALITY OF THE ENGLISH.
IN ALL MY TRAVELS I HAVE FOUND NOTHING LIKE IT.
HMPH!
I IMAGINE NOT. ENGLAND IS THE PARAGON OF HOSPITALITY - EVEN WHEN WE MUST RECEIVE FOREIGNERS.
QUITE RIGHT, MOTHER. YOU ARE A BEACON OF GOOD MANNERS.
YOU NEEDN'T WORRY, LORD GRANVILLE. I QUITE ENJOY THE SUBTLETIES OF ENGLISH HUMOR, YET I FEAR IT IS SOMETIMES MIS-UNDERSTOOD BY MY FELLOW COUNTRYMEN.
I DO HOPE YOU'LL REPORT BACK TO THE EMBASSY WITH ONLY PLEASANT NEWS IN REGARDS TO YOUR VISIT TO DEVONTON.
WITH COMPANY AS FINE AS YOURS, HOW COULD I REPORT ANYTHING TO THE CONTRARY?
MY SINCERE APOLOGIES HERR VON JAGOW, BUT I'M AFRAID I DON'T UNDERSTAND A WORD OF GERMAN.
YOU'LL HAVE TO EXCUSE MAMA - SHE'S FRIGHTFULLY AMERICAN.

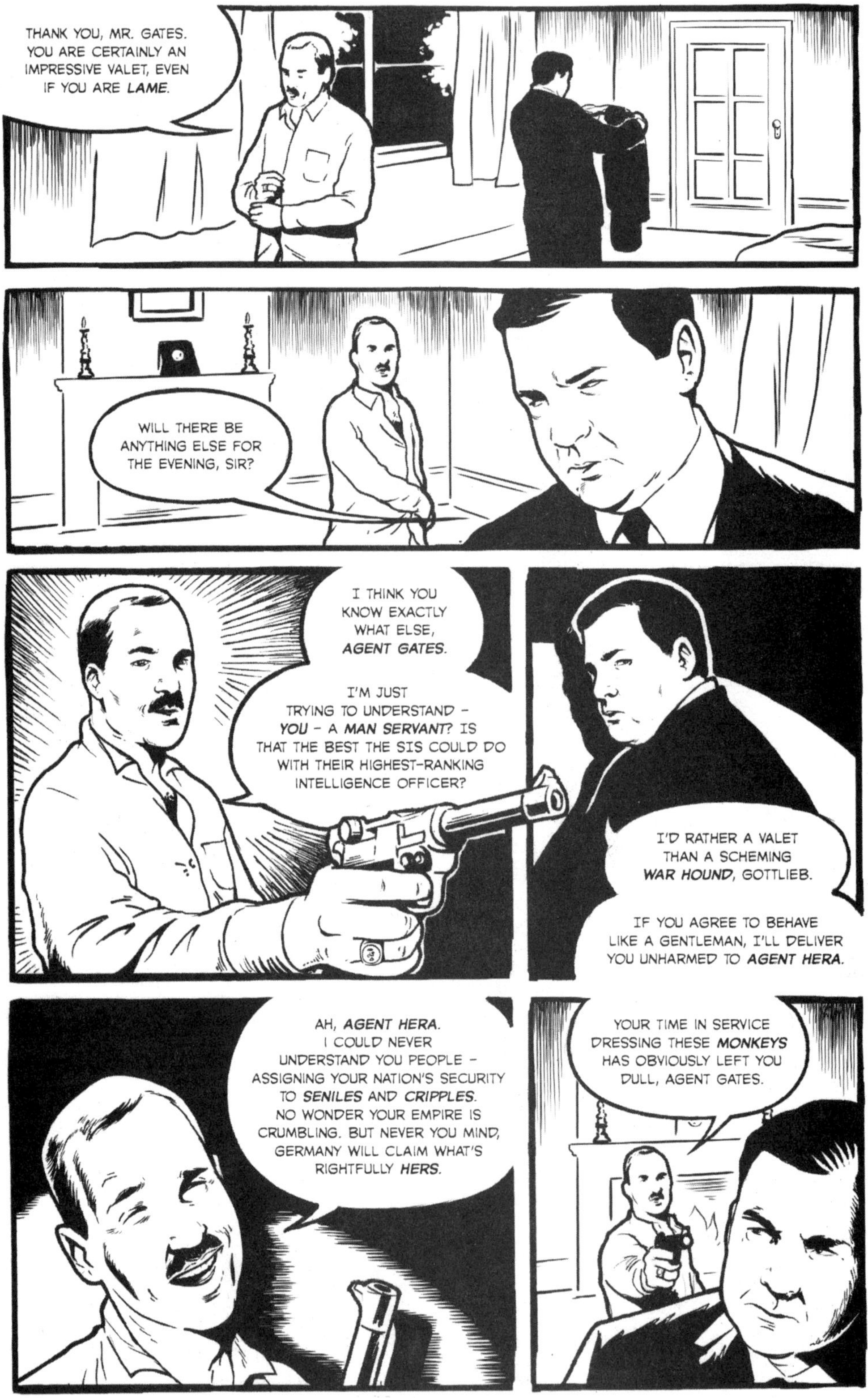
THANK YOU, MR. GATES. YOU ARE CERTAINLY AN IMPRESSIVE VALET, EVEN IF YOU ARE *LAME*.
WILL THERE BE ANYTHING ELSE FOR THE EVENING, SIR?
I THINK YOU KNOW EXACTLY WHAT ELSE, *AGENT GATES*.
I'M JUST TRYING TO UNDERSTAND - *YOU* - A *MAN SERVANT*? IS THAT THE BEST THE SIS COULD DO WITH THEIR HIGHEST-RANKING INTELLIGENCE OFFICER?
I'D RATHER A VALET THAN A SCHEMING *WAR HOUND*, GOTTLIEB.
IF YOU AGREE TO BEHAVE LIKE A GENTLEMAN, I'LL DELIVER YOU UNHARMED TO *AGENT HERA*.
AH, *AGENT HERA*. I COULD NEVER UNDERSTAND YOU PEOPLE - ASSIGNING YOUR NATION'S SECURITY TO *SENILES* AND *CRIPPLES*. NO WONDER YOUR EMPIRE IS CRUMBLING. BUT NEVER YOU MIND, GERMANY WILL CLAIM WHAT'S RIGHTFULLY *HERS*.
YOUR TIME IN SERVICE DRESSING THESE *MONKEYS* HAS OBVIOUSLY LEFT YOU DULL, AGENT GATES.

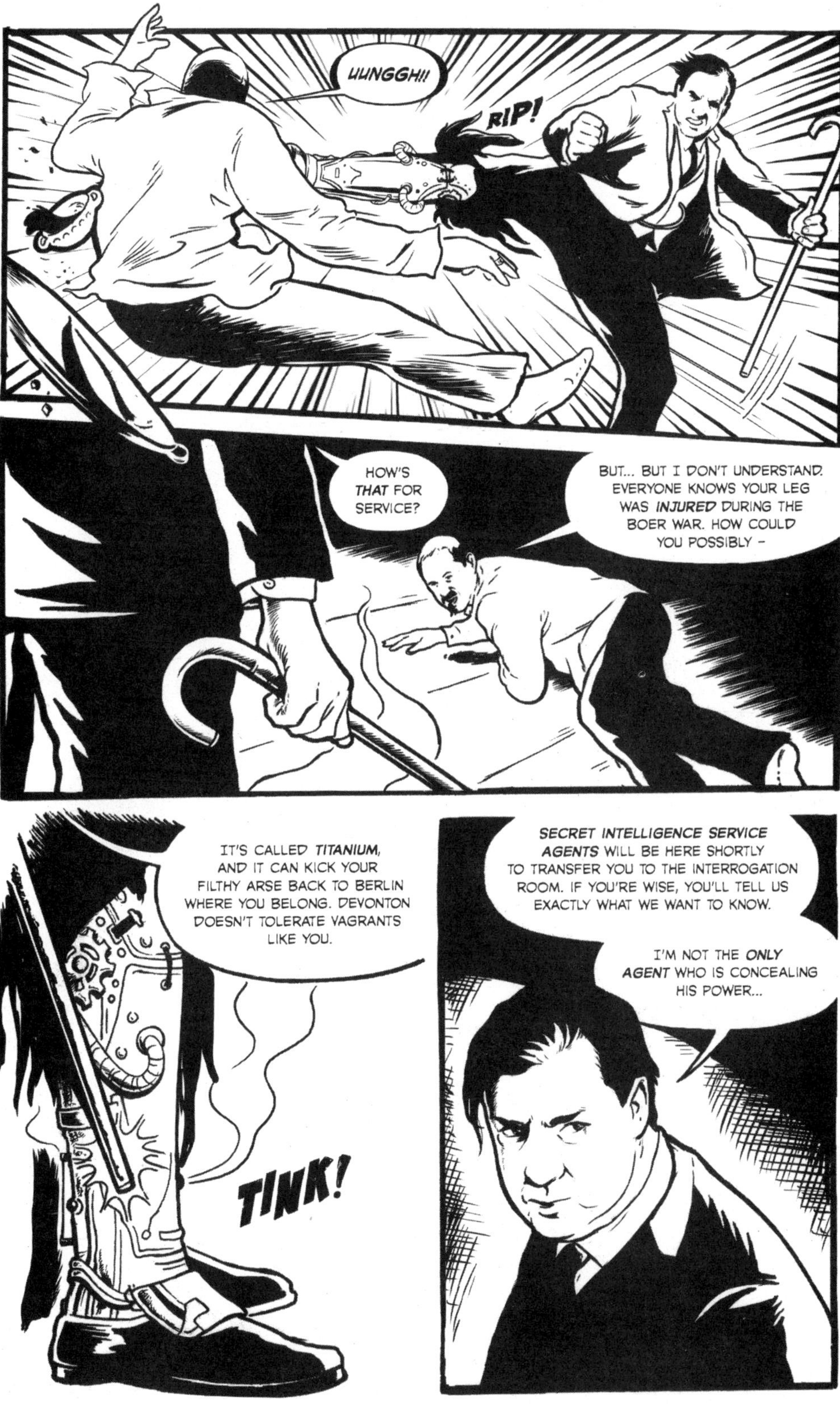
UUNGGH!!
RIP!
HOW'S THAT FOR SERVICE?
BUT... BUT I DON'T UNDERSTAND. EVERYONE KNOWS YOUR LEG WAS INJURED DURING THE BOER WAR. HOW COULD YOU POSSIBLY –
IT'S CALLED TITANIUM, AND IT CAN KICK YOUR FILTHY ARSE BACK TO BERLIN WHERE YOU BELONG. DEVONTON DOESN'T TOLERATE VAGRANTS LIKE YOU.
TINK!
SECRET INTELLIGENCE SERVICE AGENTS WILL BE HERE SHORTLY TO TRANSFER YOU TO THE INTERROGATION ROOM. IF YOU'RE WISE, YOU'LL TELL US EXACTLY WHAT WE WANT TO KNOW.
I'M NOT THE ONLY AGENT WHO IS CONCEALING HIS POWER...

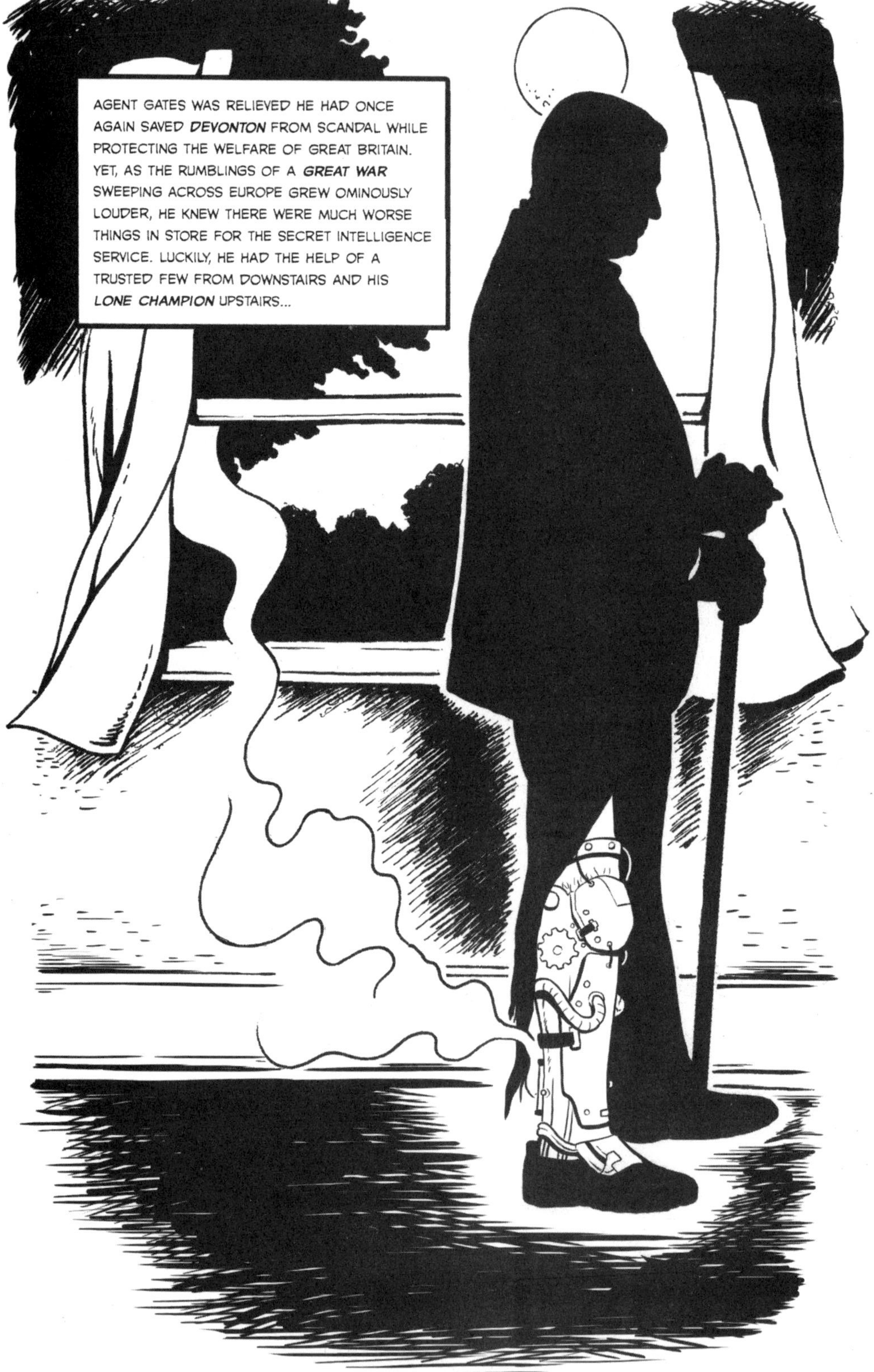
AGENT GATES WAS RELIEVED HE HAD ONCE AGAIN SAVED ***DEVONTON*** FROM SCANDAL WHILE PROTECTING THE WELFARE OF GREAT BRITAIN. YET, AS THE RUMBLINGS OF A ***GREAT WAR*** SWEEPING ACROSS EUROPE GREW OMINOUSLY LOUDER, HE KNEW THERE WERE MUCH WORSE THINGS IN STORE FOR THE SECRET INTELLIGENCE SERVICE. LUCKILY, HE HAD THE HELP OF A TRUSTED FEW FROM DOWNSTAIRS AND HIS ***LONE CHAMPION*** UPSTAIRS...

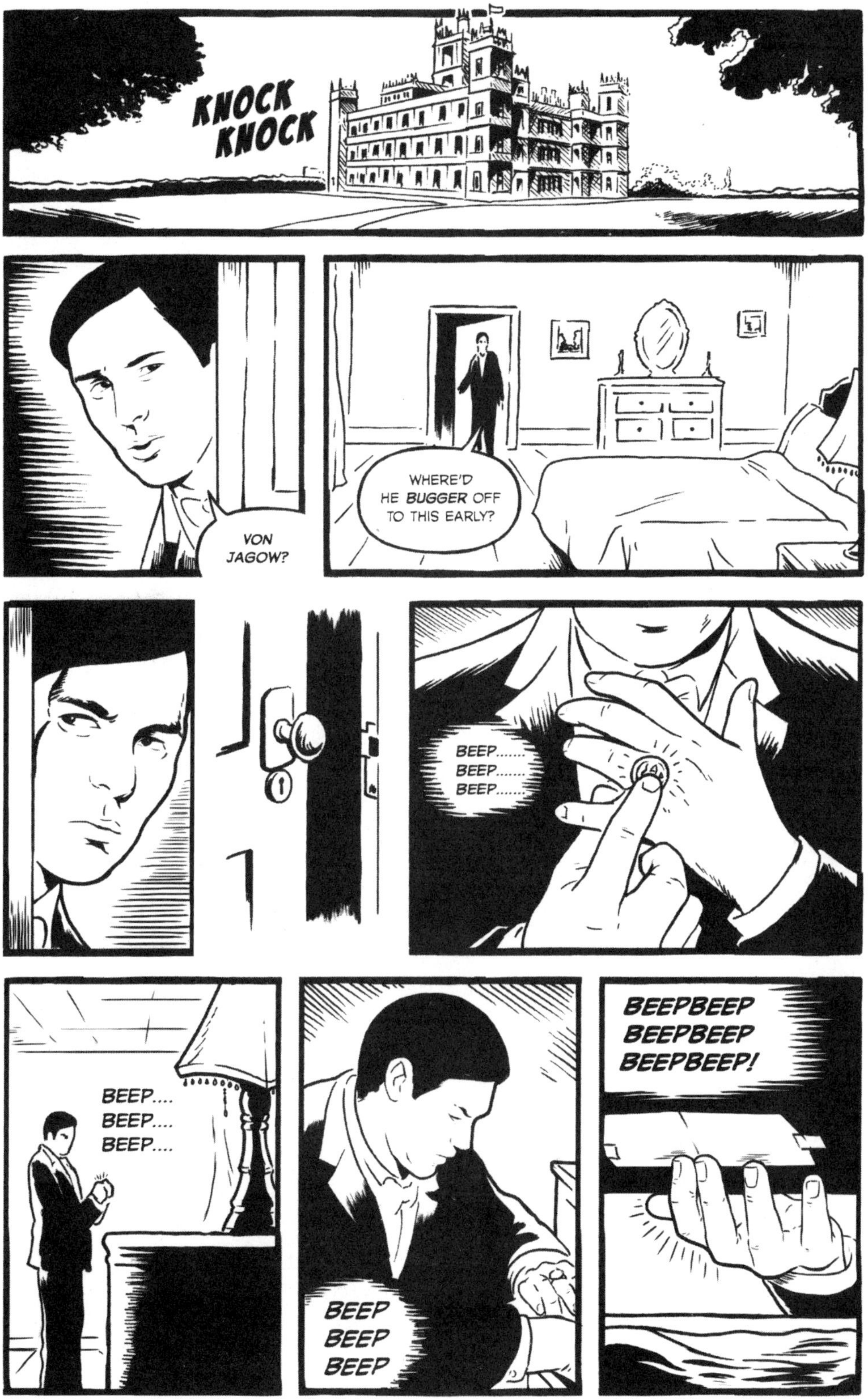
KNOCK KNOCK
VON JAGOW?
WHERE'D HE **BUGGER** OFF TO THIS EARLY?
BEEP...... BEEP...... BEEP......
BEEP.... BEEP.... BEEP....
BEEP BEEP BEEP
BEEPBEEP BEEPBEEP BEEPBEEP!

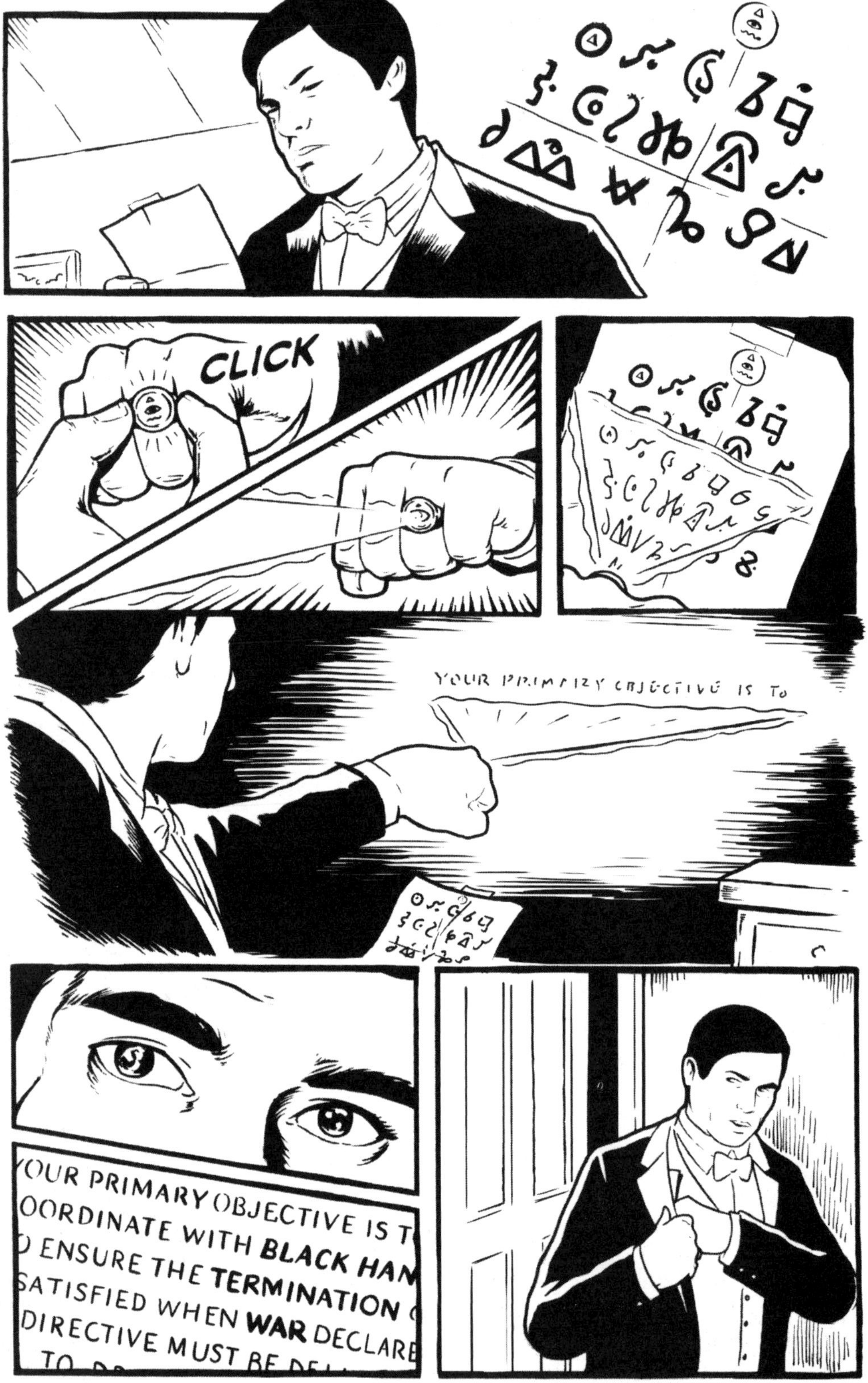
CLICK
YOUR PRIMARY OBJECTIVE IS TO
YOUR PRIMARY OBJECTIVE IS T
OORDINATE WITH BLACK HAN
ENSURE THE TERMINATION
SATISFIED WHEN WAR DECLARE
DIRECTIVE MUST BE DE

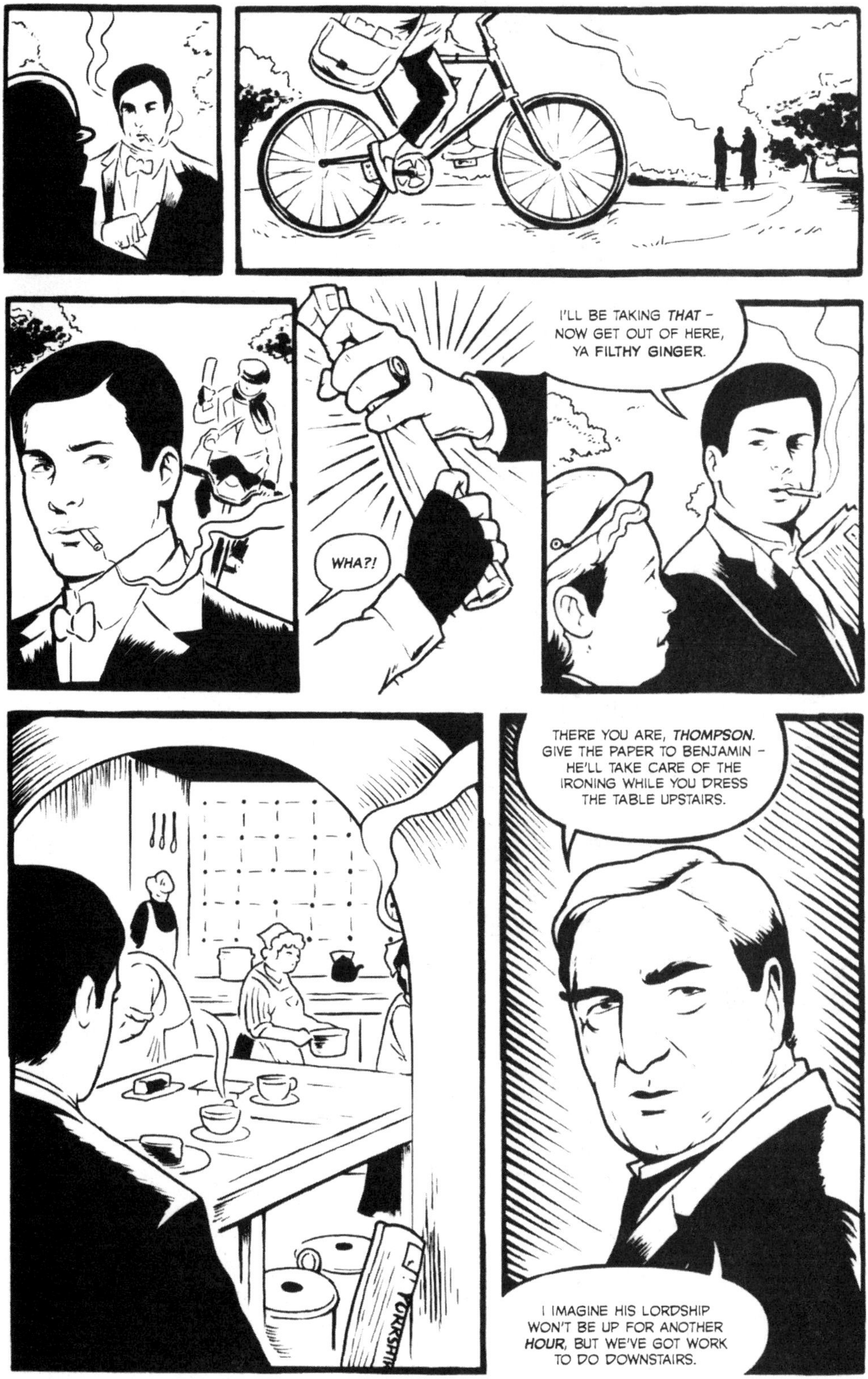
WHA?!
I'LL BE TAKING THAT – NOW GET OUT OF HERE, YA FILTHY GINGER.
THERE YOU ARE, THOMPSON. GIVE THE PAPER TO BENJAMIN – HE'LL TAKE CARE OF THE IRONING WHILE YOU DRESS THE TABLE UPSTAIRS.
I IMAGINE HIS LORDSHIP WON'T BE UP FOR ANOTHER HOUR, BUT WE'VE GOT WORK TO DO DOWNSTAIRS.

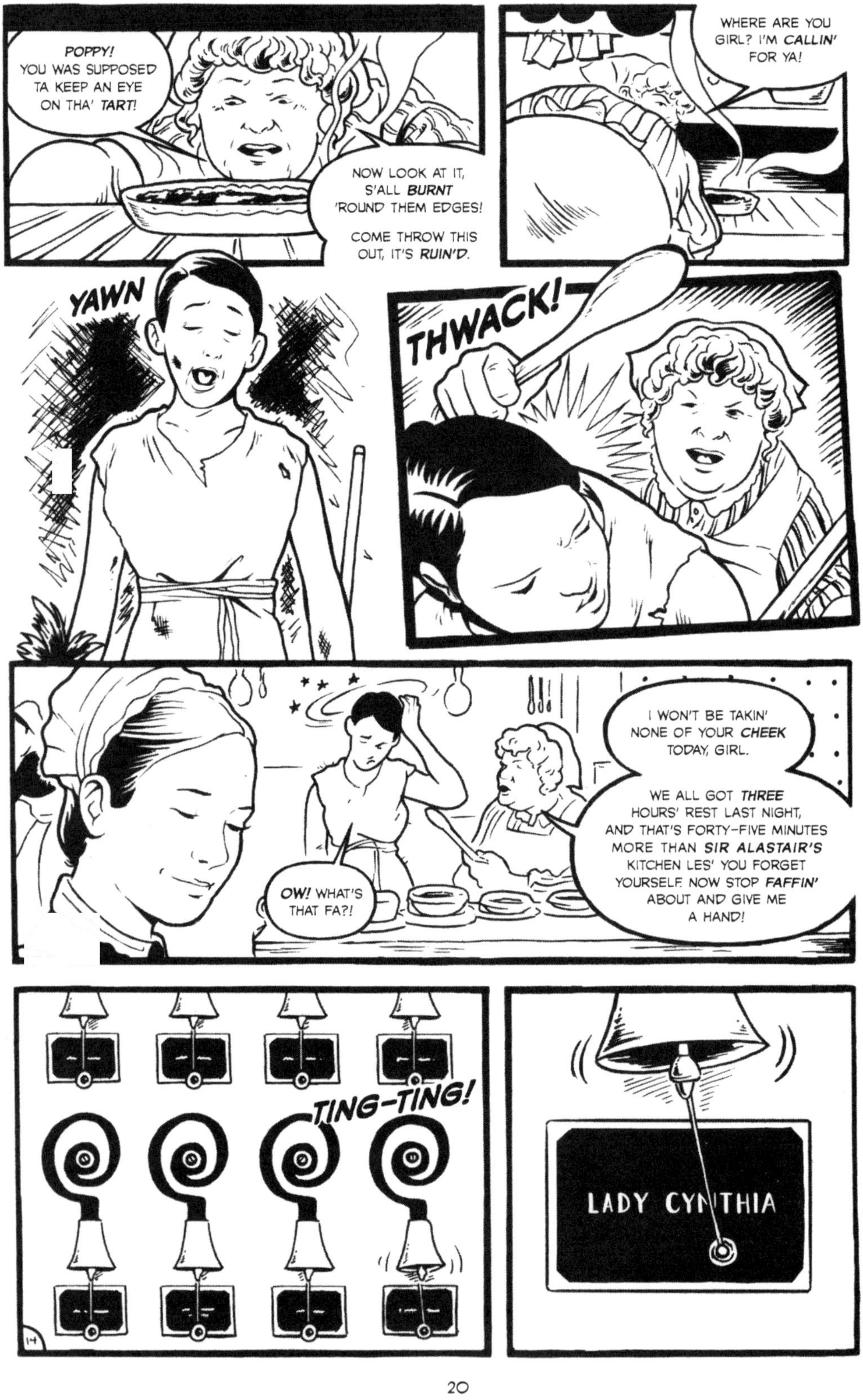
POPPY! YOU WAS SUPPOSED TA KEEP AN EYE ON THA' TART!
NOW LOOK AT IT, S'ALL BURNT 'ROUND THEM EDGES!
COME THROW THIS OUT, IT'S RUIN'D.
WHERE ARE YOU GIRL? I'M CALLIN' FOR YA!
YAWN
THWACK!
OW! WHAT'S THAT FA?!
I WON'T BE TAKIN' NONE OF YOUR CHEEK TODAY, GIRL.
WE ALL GOT THREE HOURS' REST LAST NIGHT, AND THAT'S FORTY-FIVE MINUTES MORE THAN SIR ALASTAIR'S KITCHEN LES' YOU FORGET YOURSELF. NOW STOP FAFFIN' ABOUT AND GIVE ME A HAND!
TING-TING!
LADY CYNTHIA

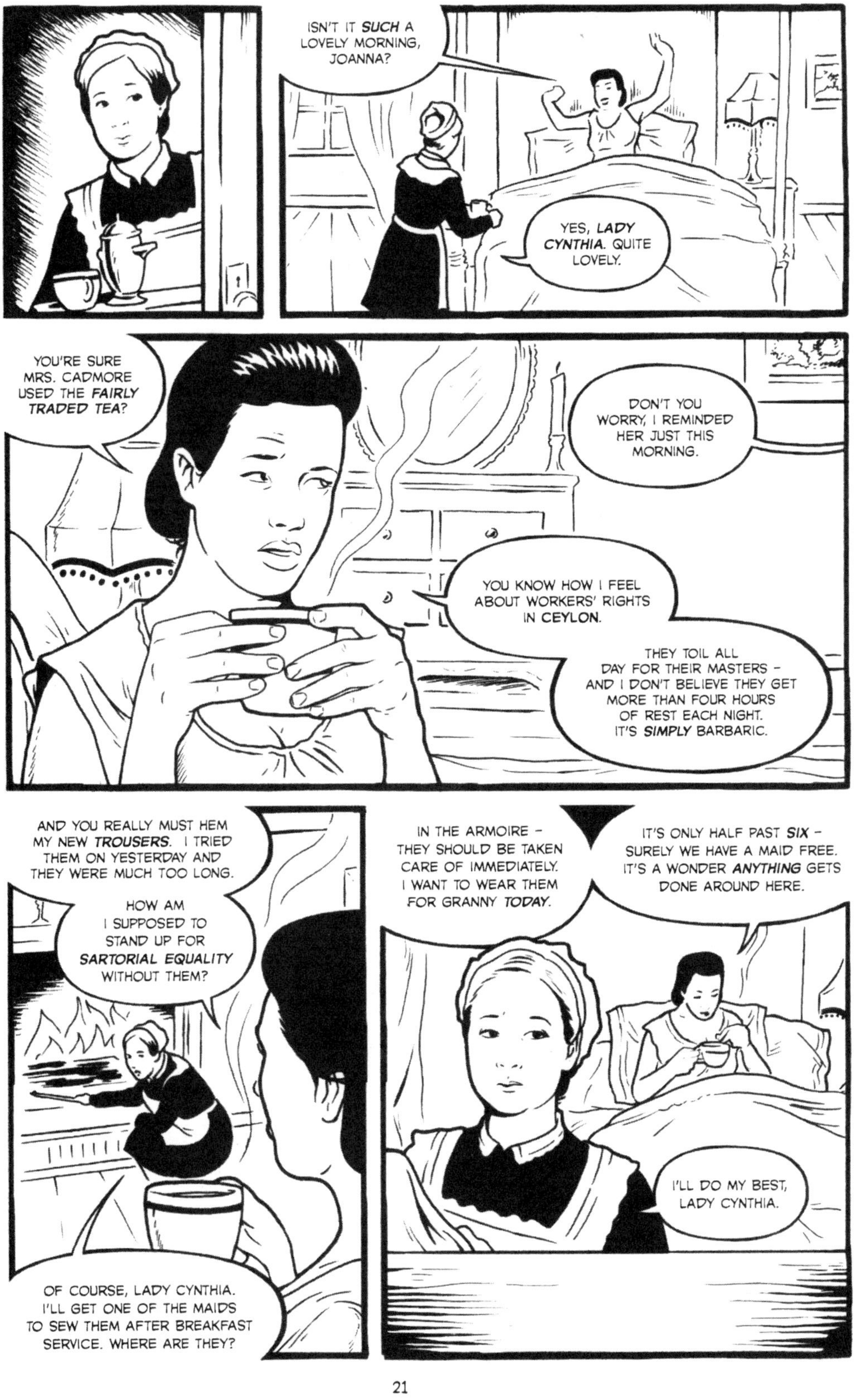
ISN'T IT SUCH A LOVELY MORNING, JOANNA?
YES, LADY CYNTHIA. QUITE LOVELY.
YOU'RE SURE MRS. CADMORE USED THE FAIRLY TRADED TEA?
DON'T YOU WORRY, I REMINDED HER JUST THIS MORNING.
YOU KNOW HOW I FEEL ABOUT WORKERS' RIGHTS IN CEYLON.
THEY TOIL ALL DAY FOR THEIR MASTERS - AND I DON'T BELIEVE THEY GET MORE THAN FOUR HOURS OF REST EACH NIGHT. IT'S SIMPLY BARBARIC.
AND YOU REALLY MUST HEM MY NEW TROUSERS. I TRIED THEM ON YESTERDAY AND THEY WERE MUCH TOO LONG.
HOW AM I SUPPOSED TO STAND UP FOR SARTORIAL EQUALITY WITHOUT THEM?
OF COURSE, LADY CYNTHIA. I'LL GET ONE OF THE MAIDS TO SEW THEM AFTER BREAKFAST SERVICE. WHERE ARE THEY?
IN THE ARMOIRE - THEY SHOULD BE TAKEN CARE OF IMMEDIATELY. I WANT TO WEAR THEM FOR GRANNY TODAY.
IT'S ONLY HALF PAST SIX - SURELY WE HAVE A MAID FREE. IT'S A WONDER ANYTHING GETS DONE AROUND HERE.
I'LL DO MY BEST, LADY CYNTHIA.

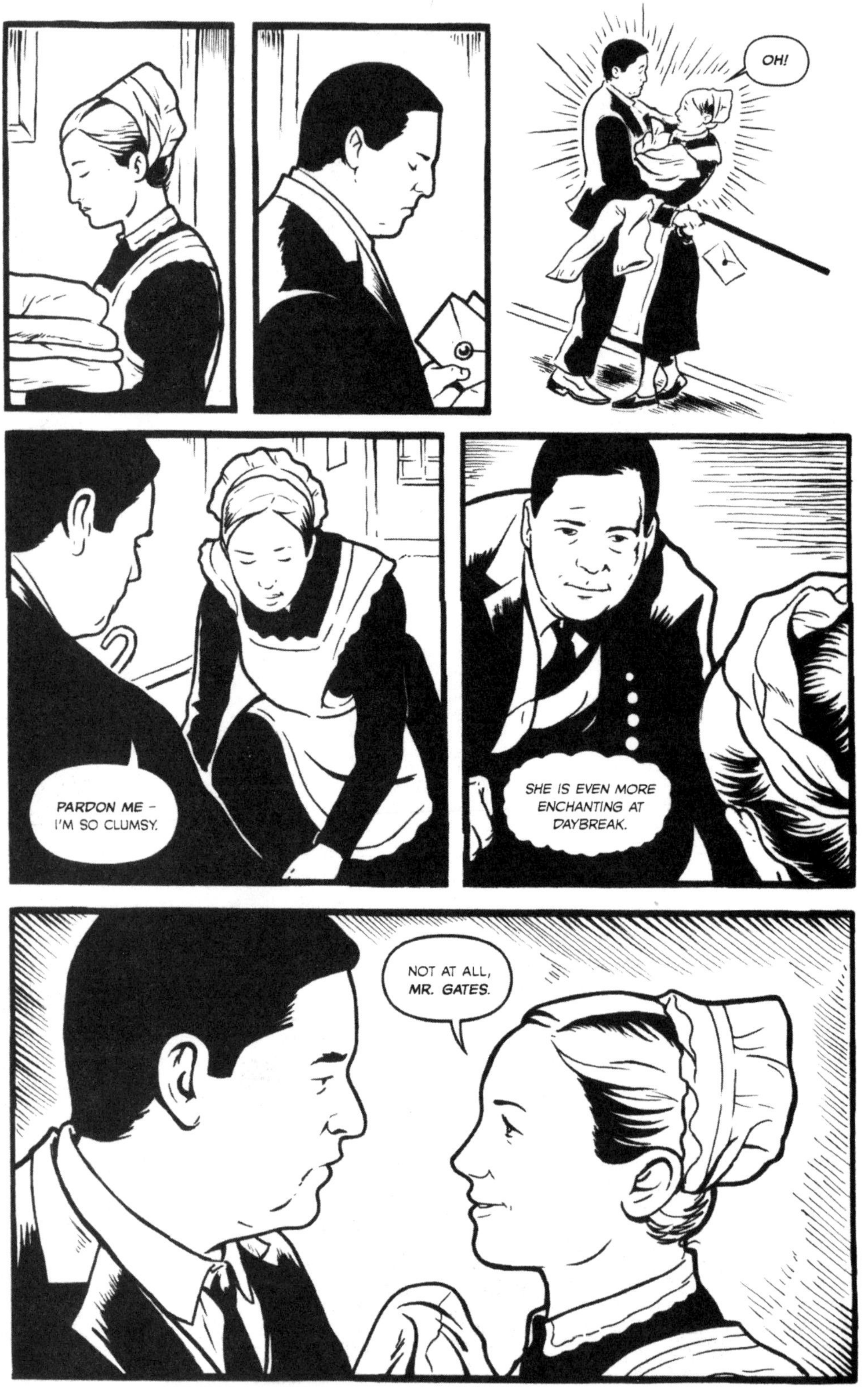
OH!
PARDON ME – I'M SO CLUMSY.
SHE IS EVEN MORE ENCHANTING AT DAYBREAK.
NOT AT ALL, MR. GATES.

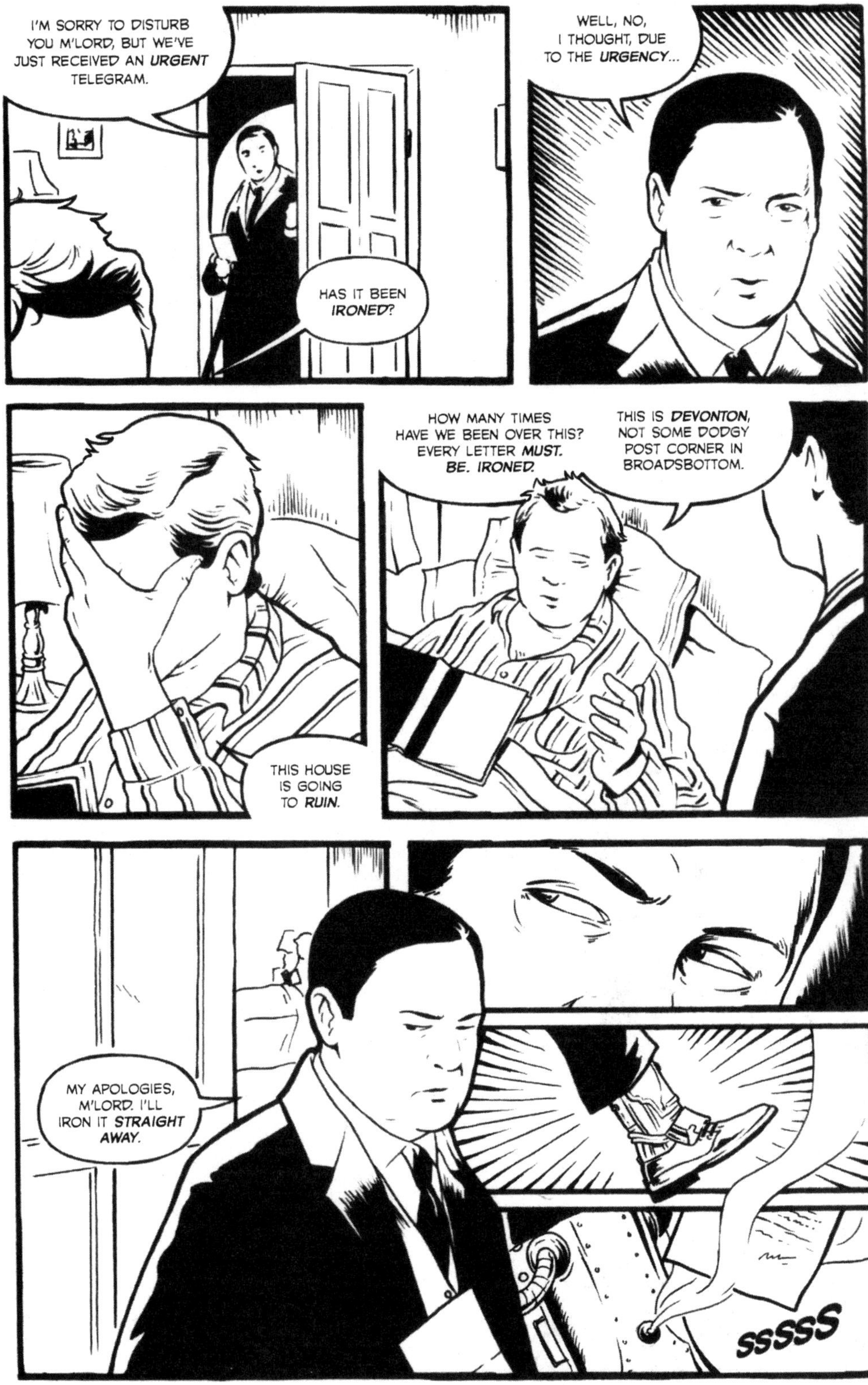
I'M SORRY TO DISTURB YOU M'LORD, BUT WE'VE JUST RECEIVED AN URGENT TELEGRAM.
HAS IT BEEN IRONED?
WELL, NO, I THOUGHT, DUE TO THE URGENCY...
THIS HOUSE IS GOING TO RUIN.
HOW MANY TIMES HAVE WE BEEN OVER THIS? EVERY LETTER MUST. BE. IRONED.
THIS IS DEVONTON, NOT SOME DODGY POST CORNER IN BROADSBOTTOM.
MY APOLOGIES, M'LORD. I'LL IRON IT STRAIGHT AWAY.
SSSSS

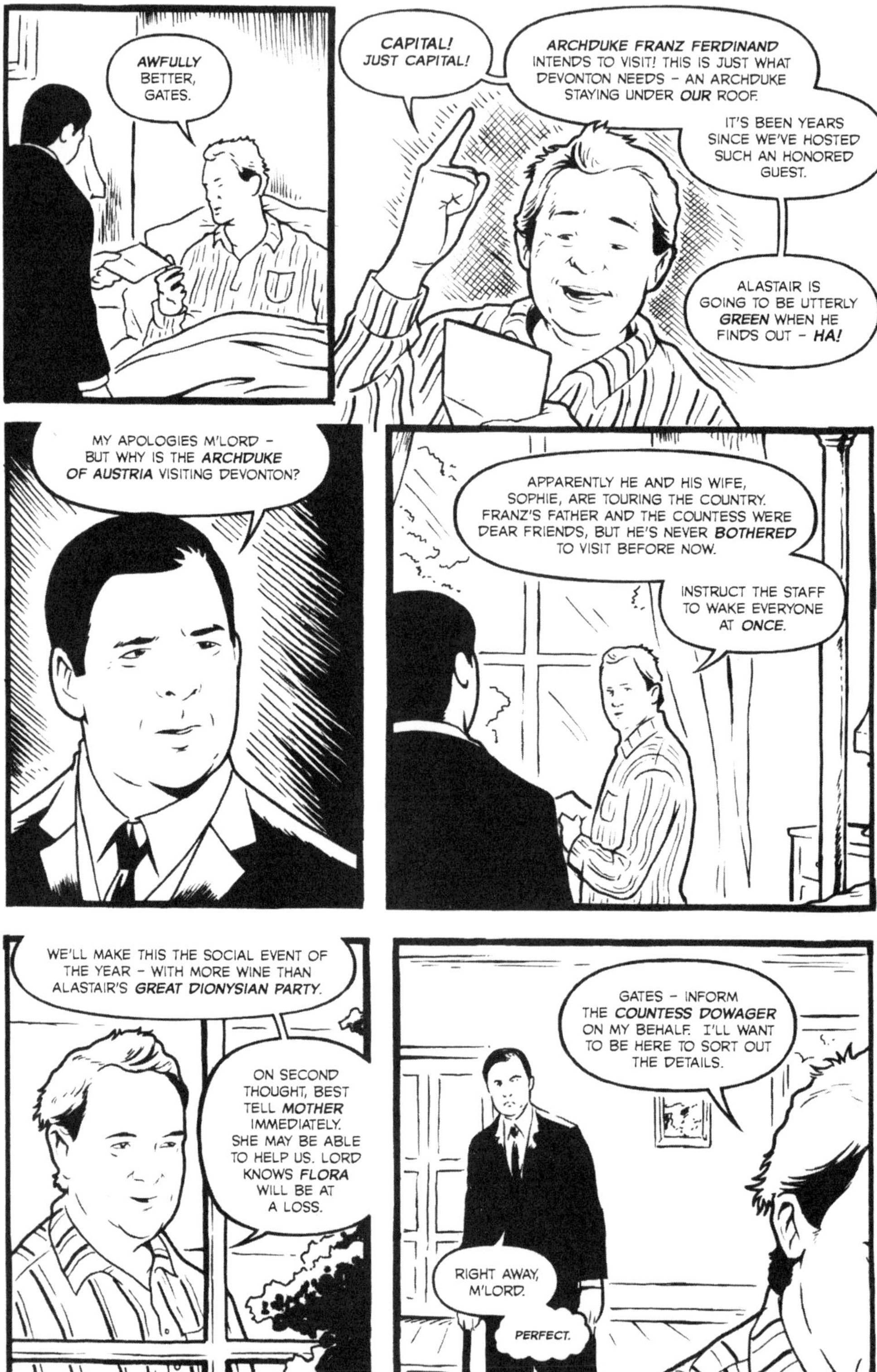
AWFULLY BETTER, GATES.
CAPITAL! JUST CAPITAL!
ARCHDUKE FRANZ FERDINAND INTENDS TO VISIT! THIS IS JUST WHAT DEVONTON NEEDS - AN ARCHDUKE STAYING UNDER OUR ROOF.
IT'S BEEN YEARS SINCE WE'VE HOSTED SUCH AN HONORED GUEST.
ALASTAIR IS GOING TO BE UTTERLY GREEN WHEN HE FINDS OUT - HA!
MY APOLOGIES M'LORD - BUT WHY IS THE ARCHDUKE OF AUSTRIA VISITING DEVONTON?
APPARENTLY HE AND HIS WIFE, SOPHIE, ARE TOURING THE COUNTRY. FRANZ'S FATHER AND THE COUNTESS WERE DEAR FRIENDS, BUT HE'S NEVER BOTHERED TO VISIT BEFORE NOW.
INSTRUCT THE STAFF TO WAKE EVERYONE AT ONCE.
WE'LL MAKE THIS THE SOCIAL EVENT OF THE YEAR - WITH MORE WINE THAN ALASTAIR'S GREAT DIONYSIAN PARTY.
ON SECOND THOUGHT, BEST TELL MOTHER IMMEDIATELY. SHE MAY BE ABLE TO HELP US. LORD KNOWS FLORA WILL BE AT A LOSS.
GATES - INFORM THE COUNTESS DOWAGER ON MY BEHALF. I'LL WANT TO BE HERE TO SORT OUT THE DETAILS.
RIGHT AWAY, M'LORD.
PERFECT.

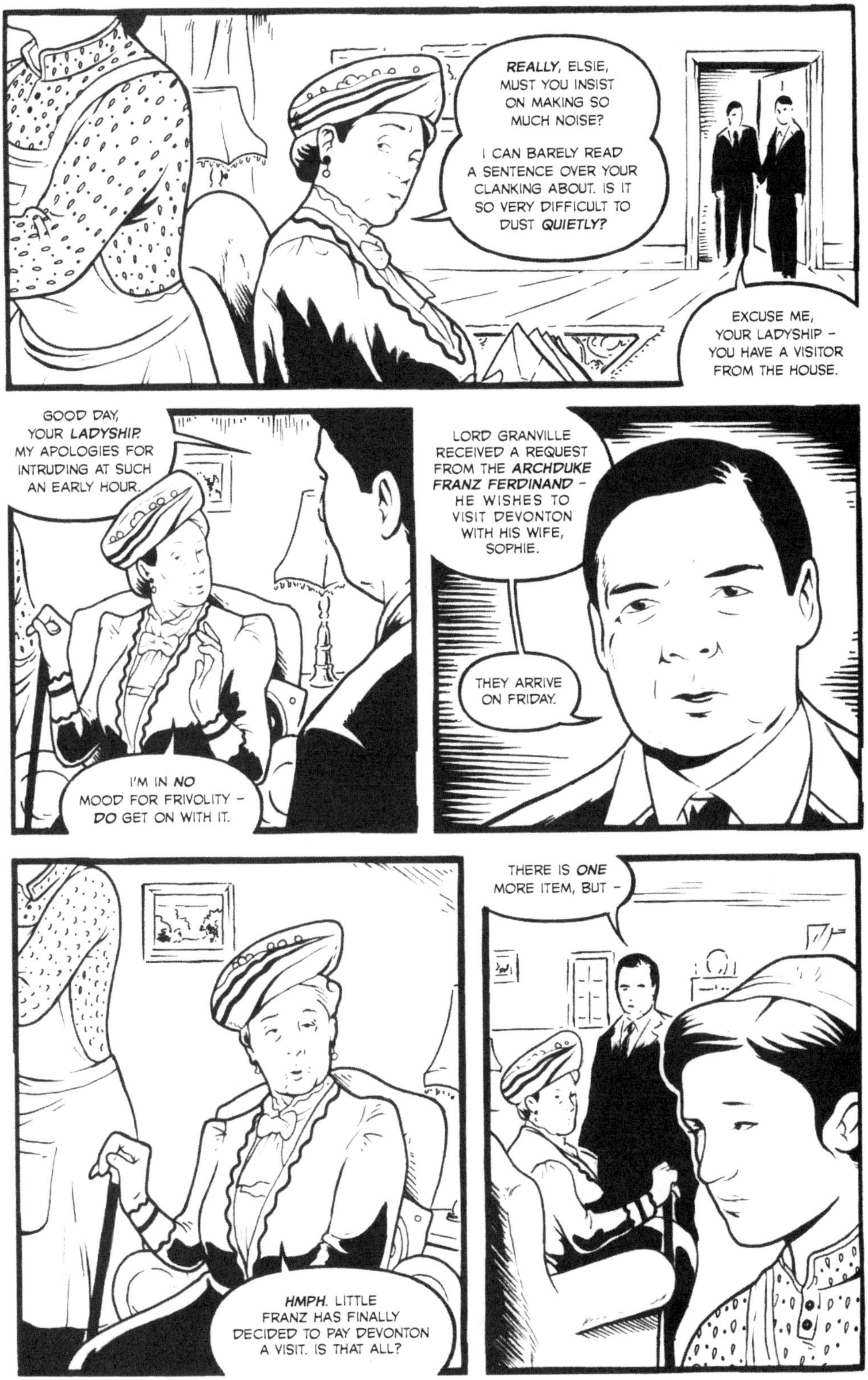
REALLY, ELSIE, MUST YOU INSIST ON MAKING SO MUCH NOISE?
I CAN BARELY READ A SENTENCE OVER YOUR CLANKING ABOUT. IS IT SO VERY DIFFICULT TO DUST QUIETLY?
EXCUSE ME, YOUR LADYSHIP - YOU HAVE A VISITOR FROM THE HOUSE.
GOOD DAY, YOUR LADYSHIP. MY APOLOGIES FOR INTRUDING AT SUCH AN EARLY HOUR.
I'M IN NO MOOD FOR FRIVOLITY - DO GET ON WITH IT.
LORD GRANVILLE RECEIVED A REQUEST FROM THE ARCHDUKE FRANZ FERDINAND - HE WISHES TO VISIT DEVONTON WITH HIS WIFE, SOPHIE.
THEY ARRIVE ON FRIDAY.
HMPH. LITTLE FRANZ HAS FINALLY DECIDED TO PAY DEVONTON A VISIT. IS THAT ALL?
THERE IS ONE MORE ITEM, BUT -

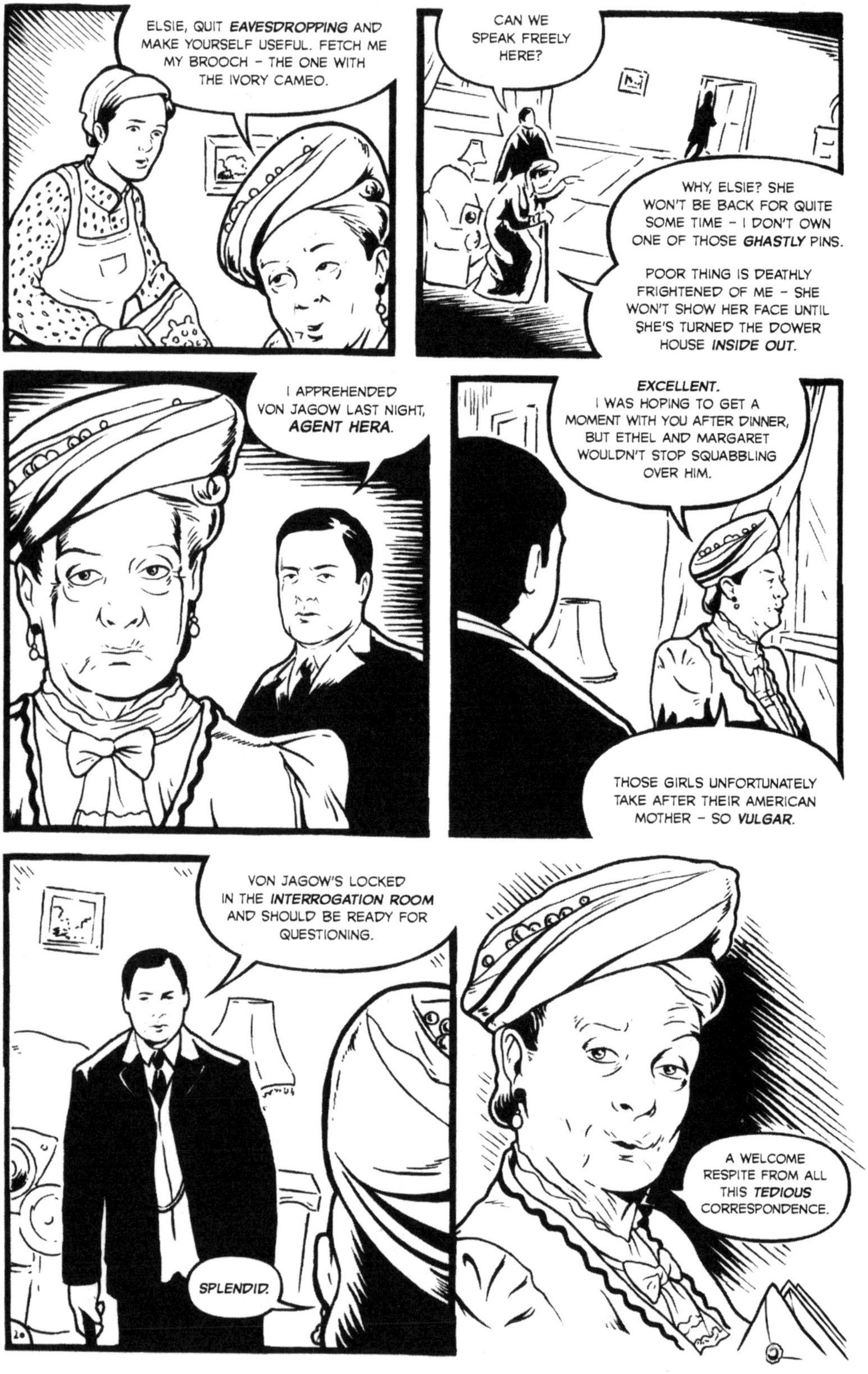

ELSIE, QUIT EAVESDROPPING AND MAKE YOURSELF USEFUL. FETCH ME MY BROOCH - THE ONE WITH THE IVORY CAMEO.
CAN WE SPEAK FREELY HERE?
WHY, ELSIE? SHE WON'T BE BACK FOR QUITE SOME TIME - I DON'T OWN ONE OF THOSE GHASTLY PINS.
POOR THING IS DEATHLY FRIGHTENED OF ME - SHE WON'T SHOW HER FACE UNTIL SHE'S TURNED THE DOWER HOUSE INSIDE OUT.
I APPREHENDED VON JAGOW LAST NIGHT, AGENT HERA.
EXCELLENT. I WAS HOPING TO GET A MOMENT WITH YOU AFTER DINNER, BUT ETHEL AND MARGARET WOULDN'T STOP SQUABBLING OVER HIM.
THOSE GIRLS UNFORTUNATELY TAKE AFTER THEIR AMERICAN MOTHER - SO VULGAR.
VON JAGOW'S LOCKED IN THE INTERROGATION ROOM AND SHOULD BE READY FOR QUESTIONING.
SPLENDID.
A WELCOME RESPITE FROM ALL THIS TEDIOUS CORRESPONDENCE.

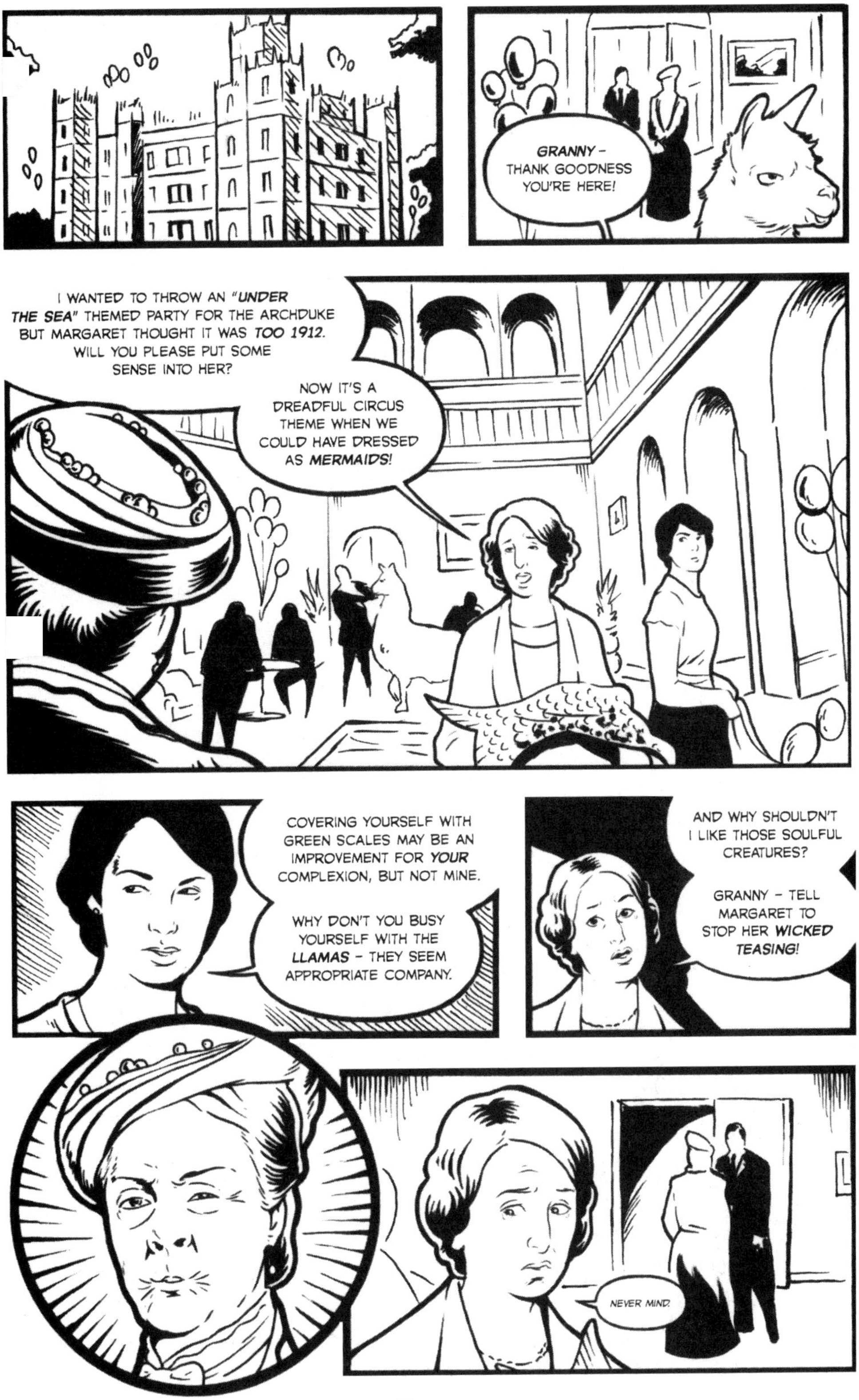
GRANNY – THANK GOODNESS YOU'RE HERE!
I WANTED TO THROW AN "UNDER THE SEA" THEMED PARTY FOR THE ARCHDUKE BUT MARGARET THOUGHT IT WAS TOO 1912. WILL YOU PLEASE PUT SOME SENSE INTO HER?
NOW IT'S A DREADFUL CIRCUS THEME WHEN WE COULD HAVE DRESSED AS MERMAIDS!
COVERING YOURSELF WITH GREEN SCALES MAY BE AN IMPROVEMENT FOR YOUR COMPLEXION, BUT NOT MINE.
WHY DON'T YOU BUSY YOURSELF WITH THE LLAMAS – THEY SEEM APPROPRIATE COMPANY.
AND WHY SHOULDN'T I LIKE THOSE SOULFUL CREATURES?
GRANNY – TELL MARGARET TO STOP HER WICKED TEASING!
NEVER MIND.

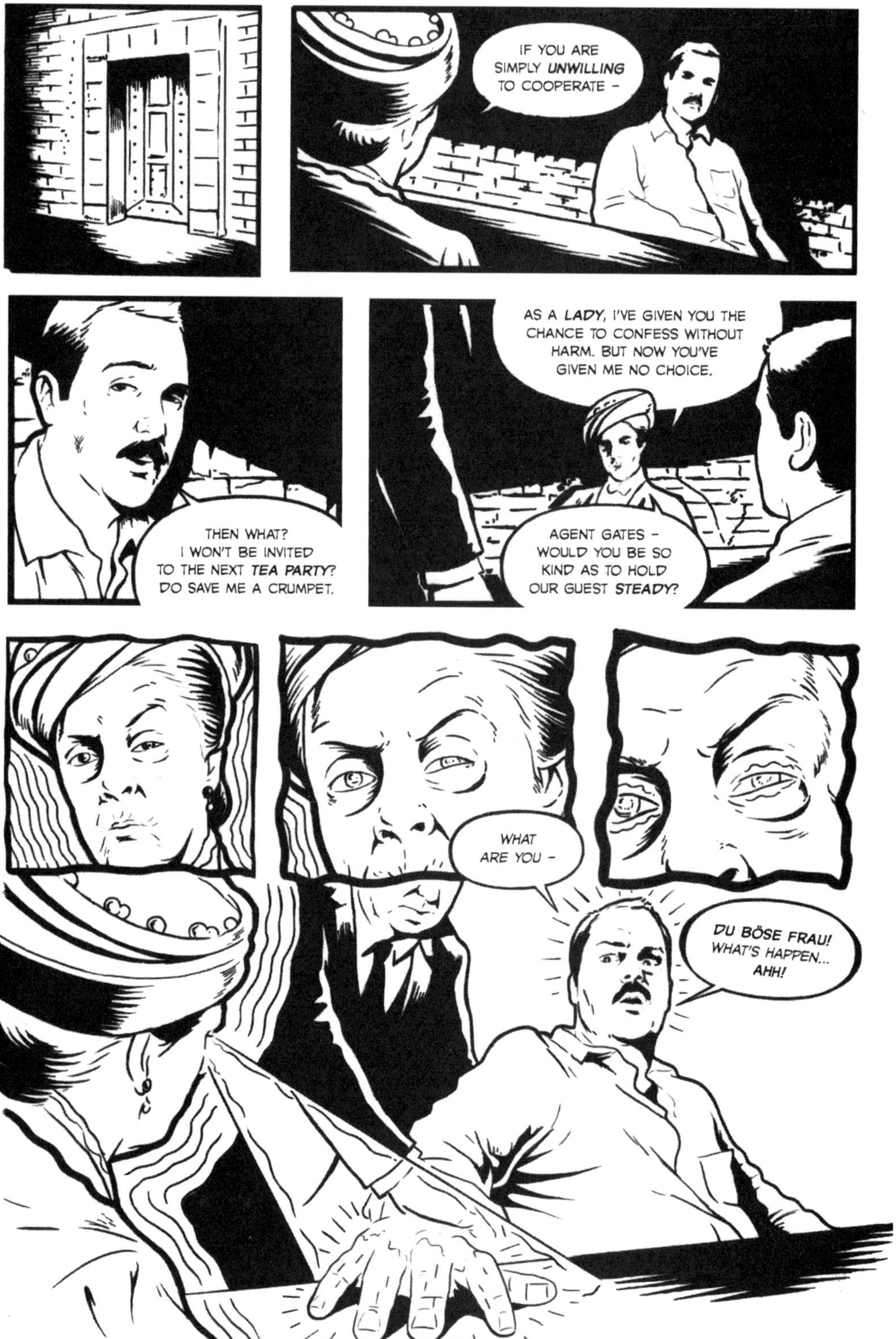
IF YOU ARE SIMPLY UNWILLING TO COOPERATE -
THEN WHAT? I WON'T BE INVITED TO THE NEXT TEA PARTY? DO SAVE ME A CRUMPET.
AS A LADY, I'VE GIVEN YOU THE CHANCE TO CONFESS WITHOUT HARM. BUT NOW YOU'VE GIVEN ME NO CHOICE.
AGENT GATES - WOULD YOU BE SO KIND AS TO HOLD OUR GUEST STEADY?
WHAT ARE YOU -
DU BÖSE FRAU! WHAT'S HAPPEN... AHH!

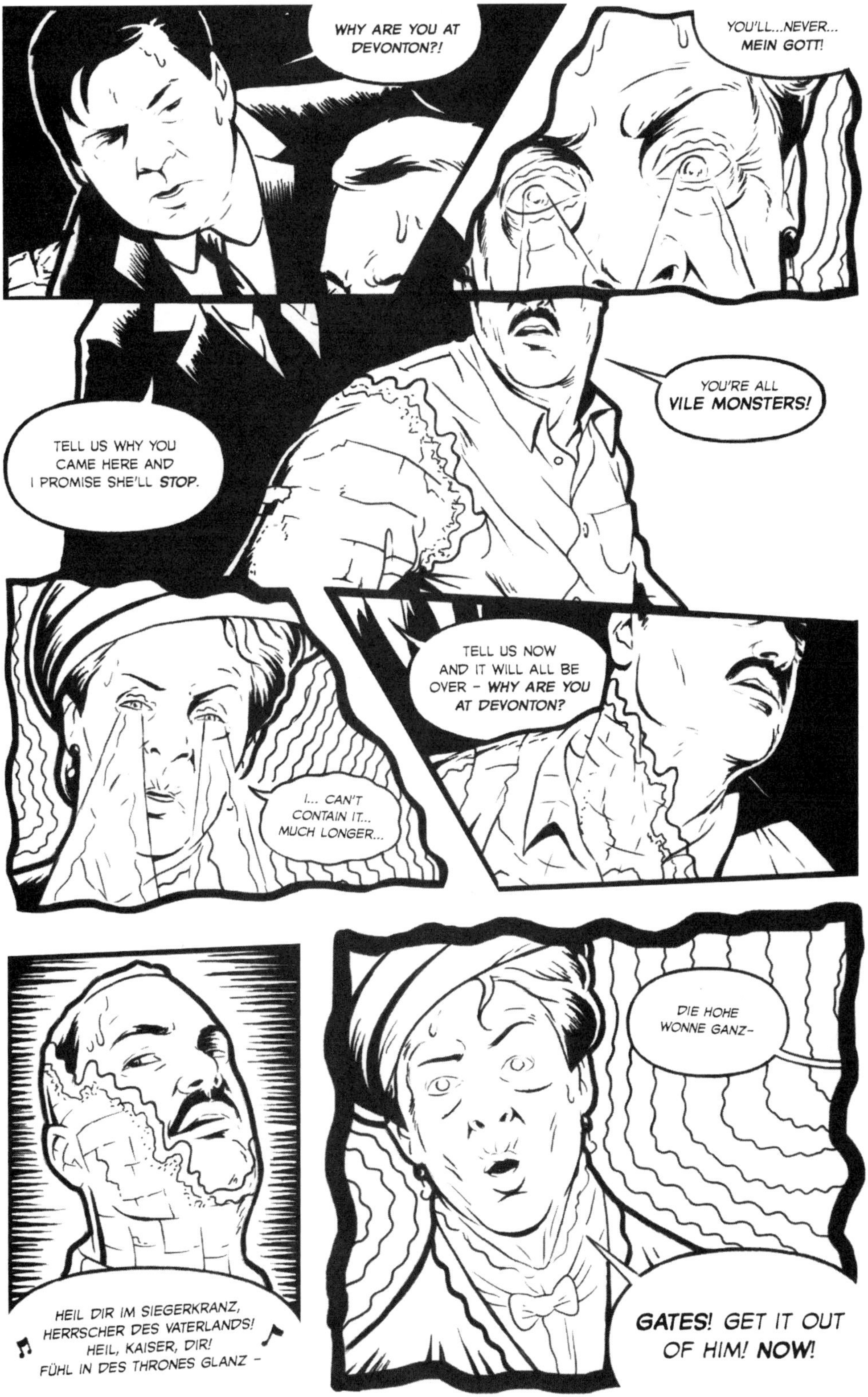
WHY ARE YOU AT DEVONTON?!
YOU'LL...NEVER... MEIN GOTT!
YOU'RE ALL VILE MONSTERS!
TELL US WHY YOU CAME HERE AND I PROMISE SHE'LL STOP.
I... CAN'T CONTAIN IT... MUCH LONGER...
TELL US NOW AND IT WILL ALL BE OVER - WHY ARE YOU AT DEVONTON?
HEIL DIR IM SIEGERKRANZ, HERRSCHER DES VATERLANDS! HEIL, KAISER, DIR! FÜHL IN DES THRONES GLANZ -
DIE HOHE WONNE GANZ-
GATES! GET IT OUT OF HIM! NOW!

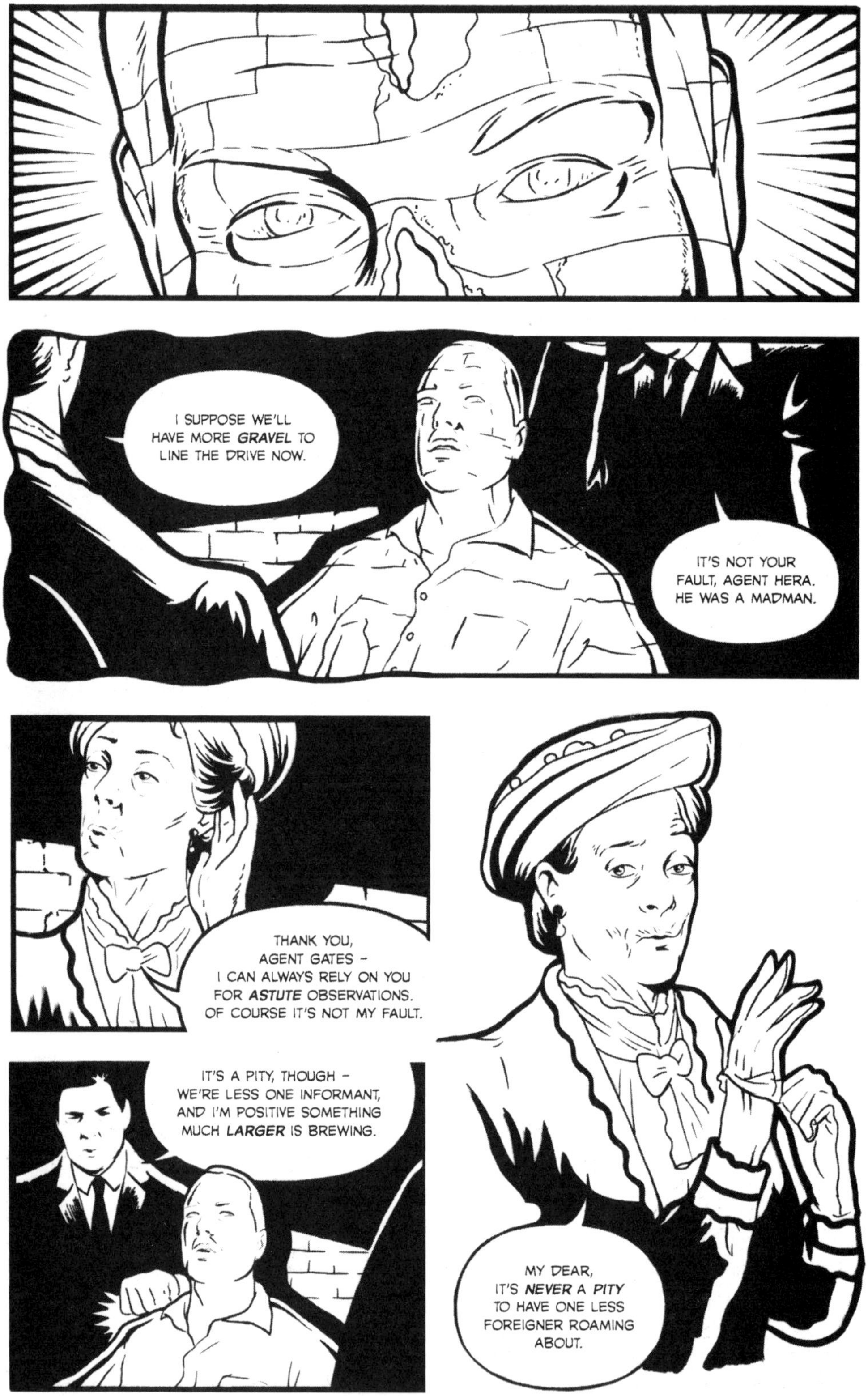

I SUPPOSE WE'LL HAVE MORE **GRAVEL** TO LINE THE DRIVE NOW.
IT'S NOT YOUR FAULT, AGENT HERA. HE WAS A MADMAN.
THANK YOU, AGENT GATES - I CAN ALWAYS RELY ON YOU FOR **ASTUTE** OBSERVATIONS. OF COURSE IT'S NOT MY FAULT.
IT'S A PITY, THOUGH - WE'RE LESS ONE INFORMANT, AND I'M POSITIVE SOMETHING MUCH **LARGER** IS BREWING.
MY DEAR, IT'S **NEVER** A **PITY** TO HAVE ONE LESS FOREIGNER ROAMING ABOUT.

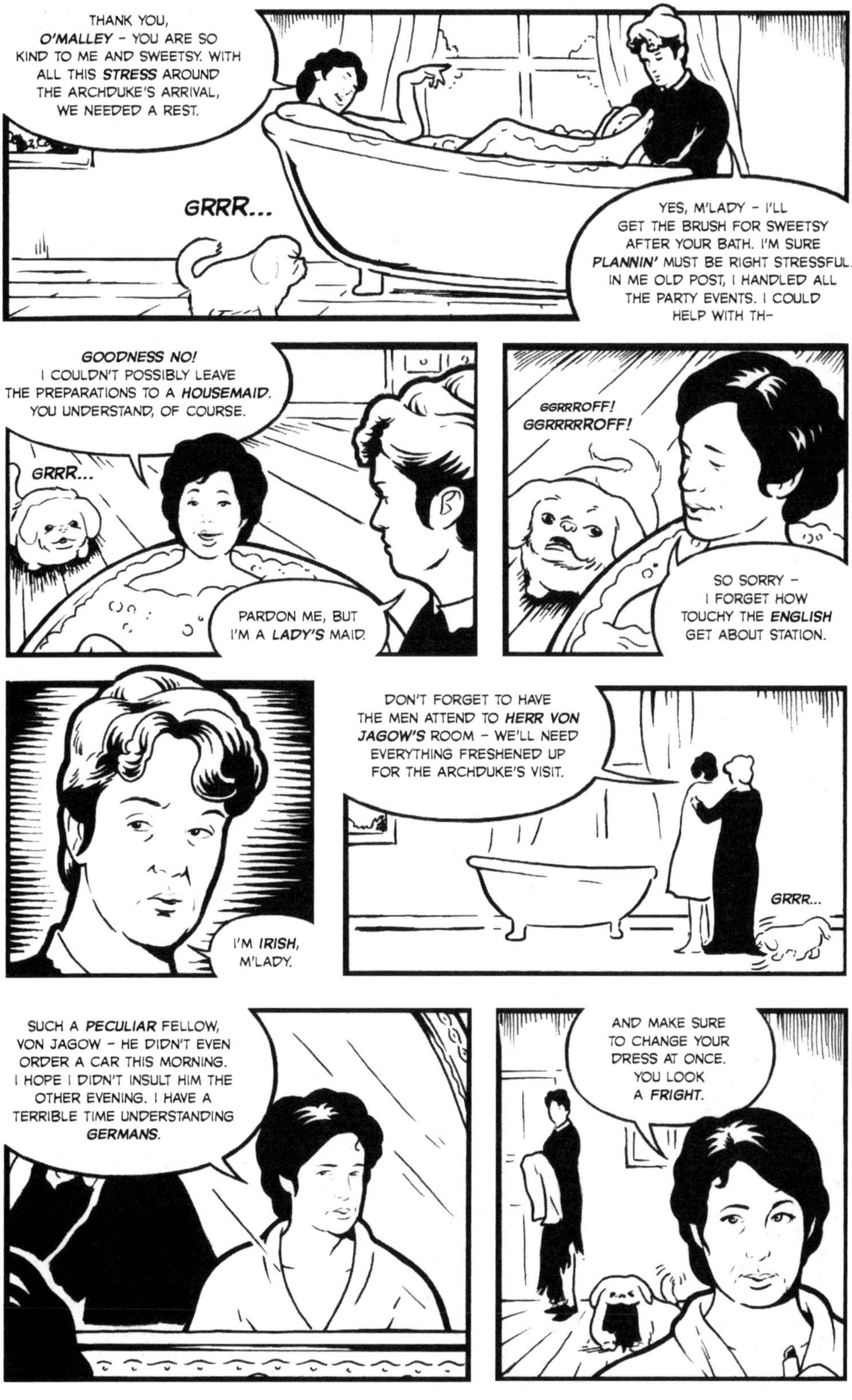
THANK YOU, O'MALLEY - YOU ARE SO KIND TO ME AND SWEETSY. WITH ALL THIS STRESS AROUND THE ARCHDUKE'S ARRIVAL, WE NEEDED A REST.
GRRR...
YES, M'LADY - I'LL GET THE BRUSH FOR SWEETSY AFTER YOUR BATH. I'M SURE PLANNIN' MUST BE RIGHT STRESSFUL. IN ME OLD POST, I HANDLED ALL THE PARTY EVENTS. I COULD HELP WITH TH-
GOODNESS NO! I COULDN'T POSSIBLY LEAVE THE PREPARATIONS TO A HOUSEMAID. YOU UNDERSTAND, OF COURSE.
GRRR...
PARDON ME, BUT I'M A LADY'S MAID.
GGRRROFF! GGRRRRROFF!
SO SORRY - I FORGET HOW TOUCHY THE ENGLISH GET ABOUT STATION.
I'M IRISH, M'LADY.
DON'T FORGET TO HAVE THE MEN ATTEND TO HERR VON JAGOW'S ROOM - WE'LL NEED EVERYTHING FRESHENED UP FOR THE ARCHDUKE'S VISIT.
GRRR...
SUCH A PECULIAR FELLOW, VON JAGOW - HE DIDN'T EVEN ORDER A CAR THIS MORNING. I HOPE I DIDN'T INSULT HIM THE OTHER EVENING. I HAVE A TERRIBLE TIME UNDERSTANDING GERMANS.
AND MAKE SURE TO CHANGE YOUR DRESS AT ONCE. YOU LOOK A FRIGHT.

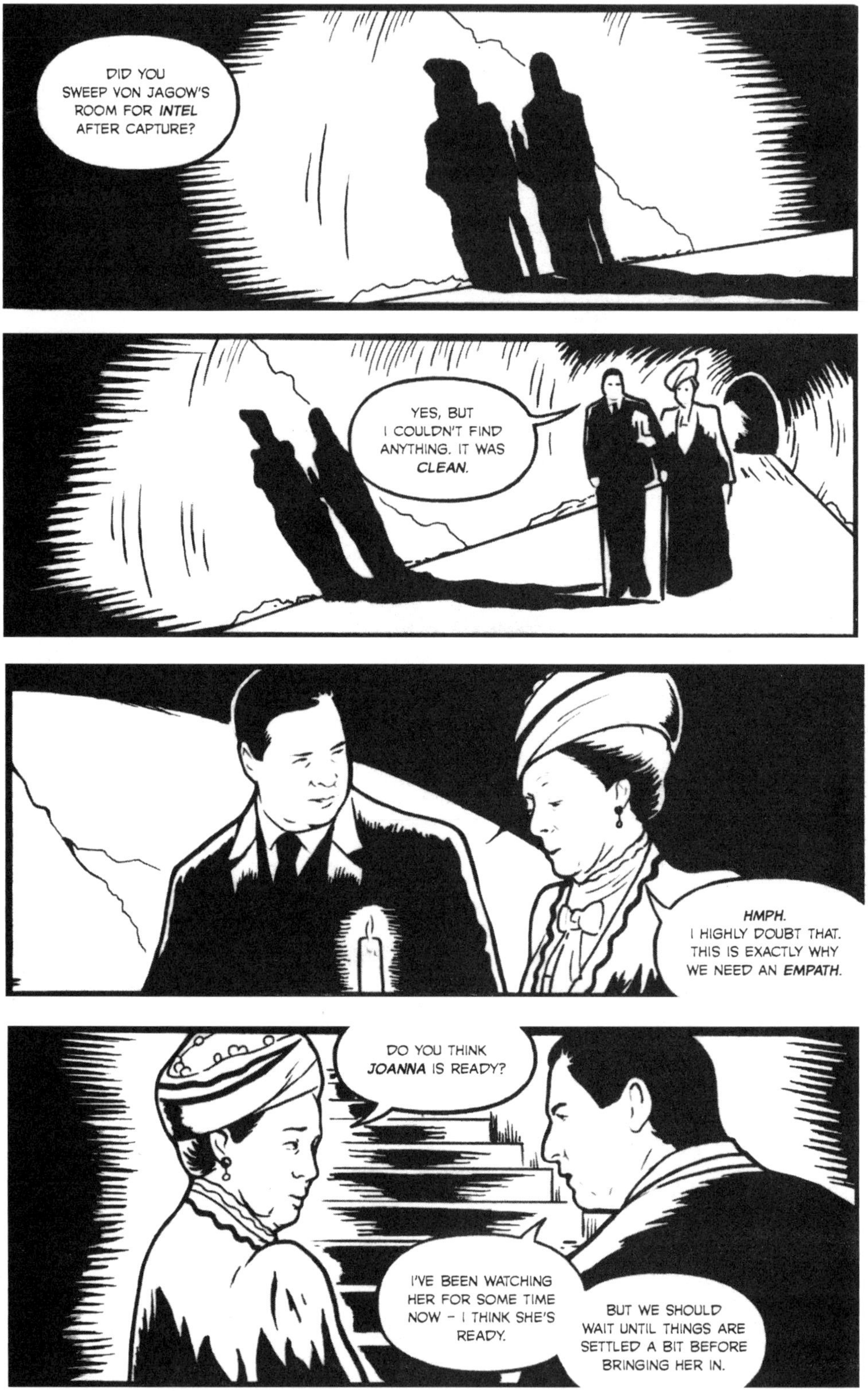
DID YOU SWEEP VON JAGOW'S ROOM FOR INTEL AFTER CAPTURE?
YES, BUT I COULDN'T FIND ANYTHING. IT WAS CLEAN.
HMPH. I HIGHLY DOUBT THAT. THIS IS EXACTLY WHY WE NEED AN EMPATH.
DO YOU THINK JOANNA IS READY?
I'VE BEEN WATCHING HER FOR SOME TIME NOW - I THINK SHE'S READY.
BUT WE SHOULD WAIT UNTIL THINGS ARE SETTLED A BIT BEFORE BRINGING HER IN.

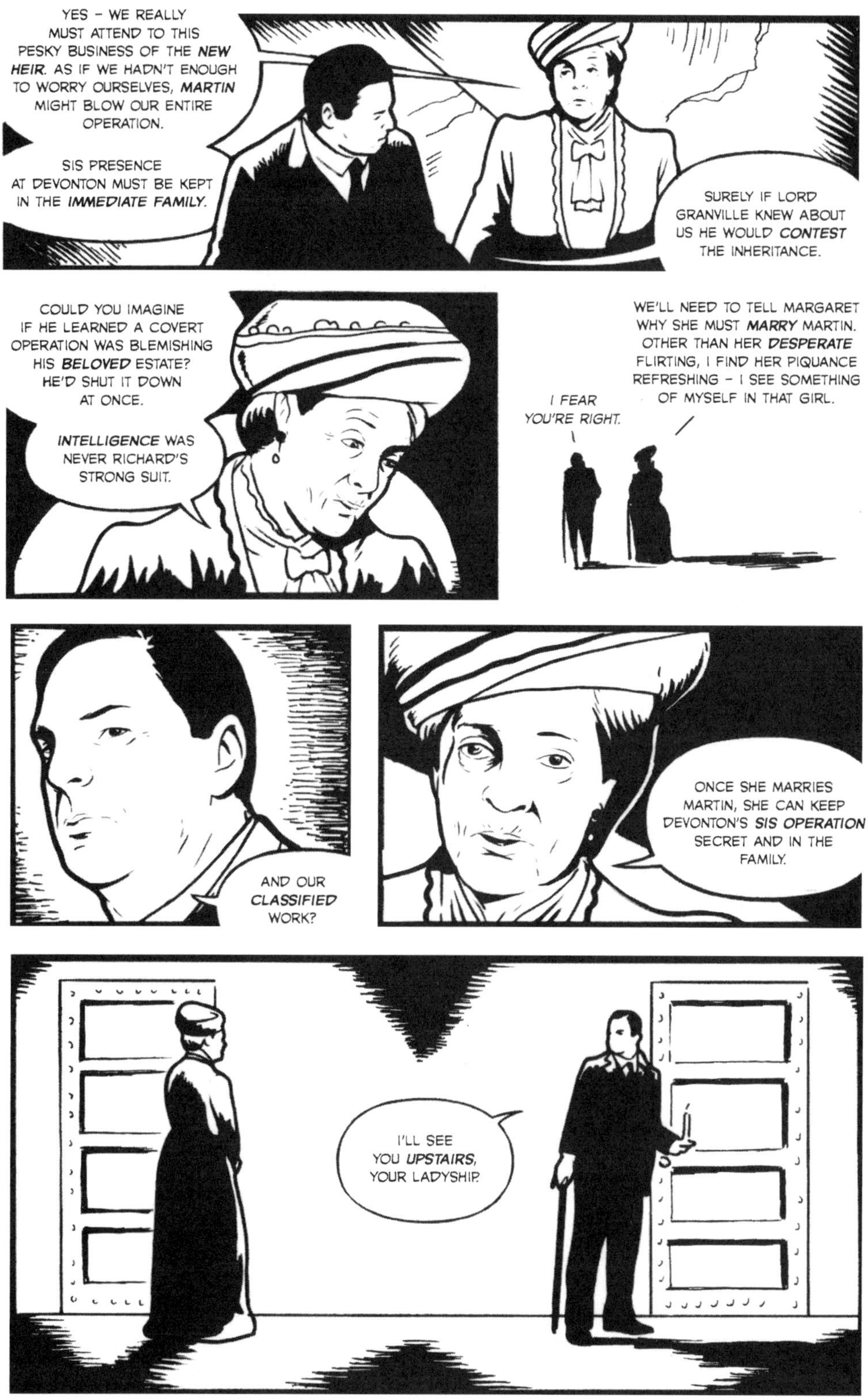
YES - WE REALLY MUST ATTEND TO THIS PESKY BUSINESS OF THE NEW HEIR. AS IF WE HADN'T ENOUGH TO WORRY OURSELVES, MARTIN MIGHT BLOW OUR ENTIRE OPERATION.
SIS PRESENCE AT DEVONTON MUST BE KEPT IN THE IMMEDIATE FAMILY.
SURELY IF LORD GRANVILLE KNEW ABOUT US HE WOULD CONTEST THE INHERITANCE.
COULD YOU IMAGINE IF HE LEARNED A COVERT OPERATION WAS BLEMISHING HIS BELOVED ESTATE? HE'D SHUT IT DOWN AT ONCE.
INTELLIGENCE WAS NEVER RICHARD'S STRONG SUIT.
I FEAR YOU'RE RIGHT.
WE'LL NEED TO TELL MARGARET WHY SHE MUST MARRY MARTIN. OTHER THAN HER DESPERATE FLIRTING, I FIND HER PIQUANCE REFRESHING - I SEE SOMETHING OF MYSELF IN THAT GIRL.
AND OUR CLASSIFIED WORK?
ONCE SHE MARRIES MARTIN, SHE CAN KEEP DEVONTON'S SIS OPERATION SECRET AND IN THE FAMILY.
I'LL SEE YOU UPSTAIRS, YOUR LADYSHIP.

CHAP

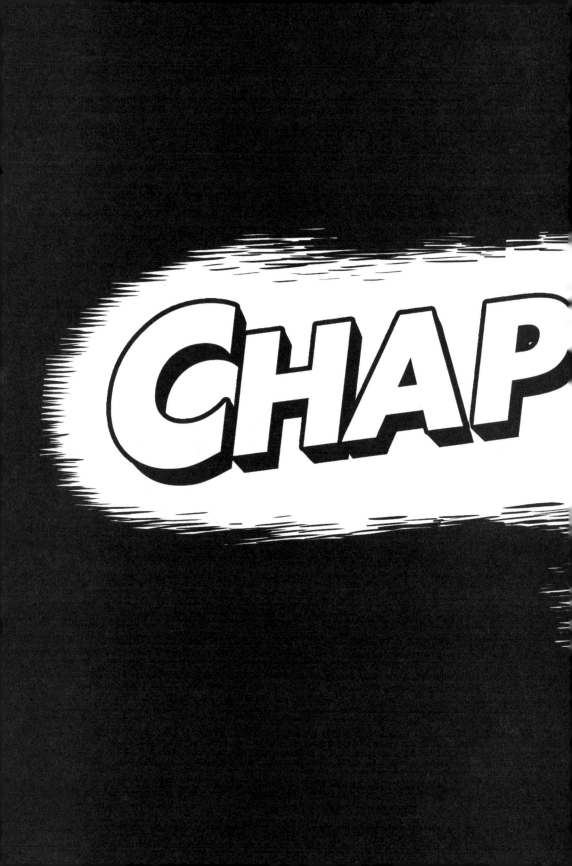

TER TWO

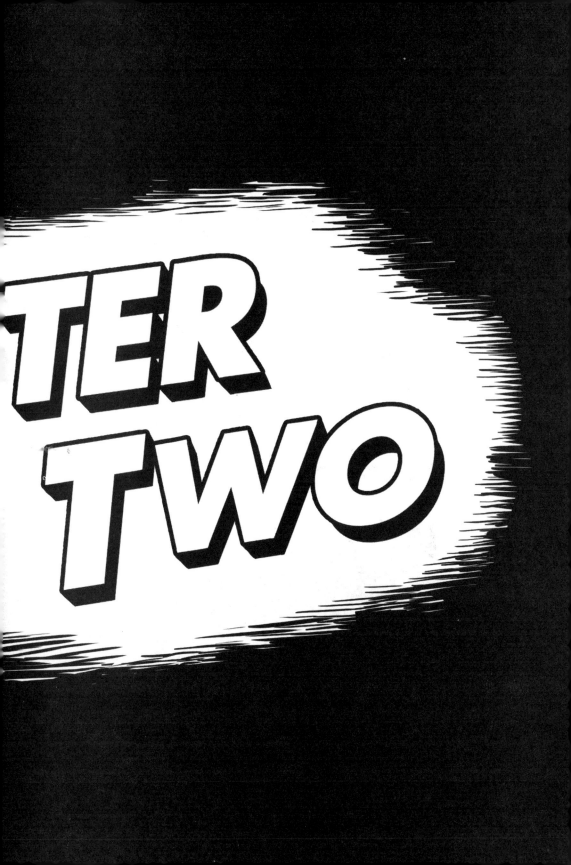

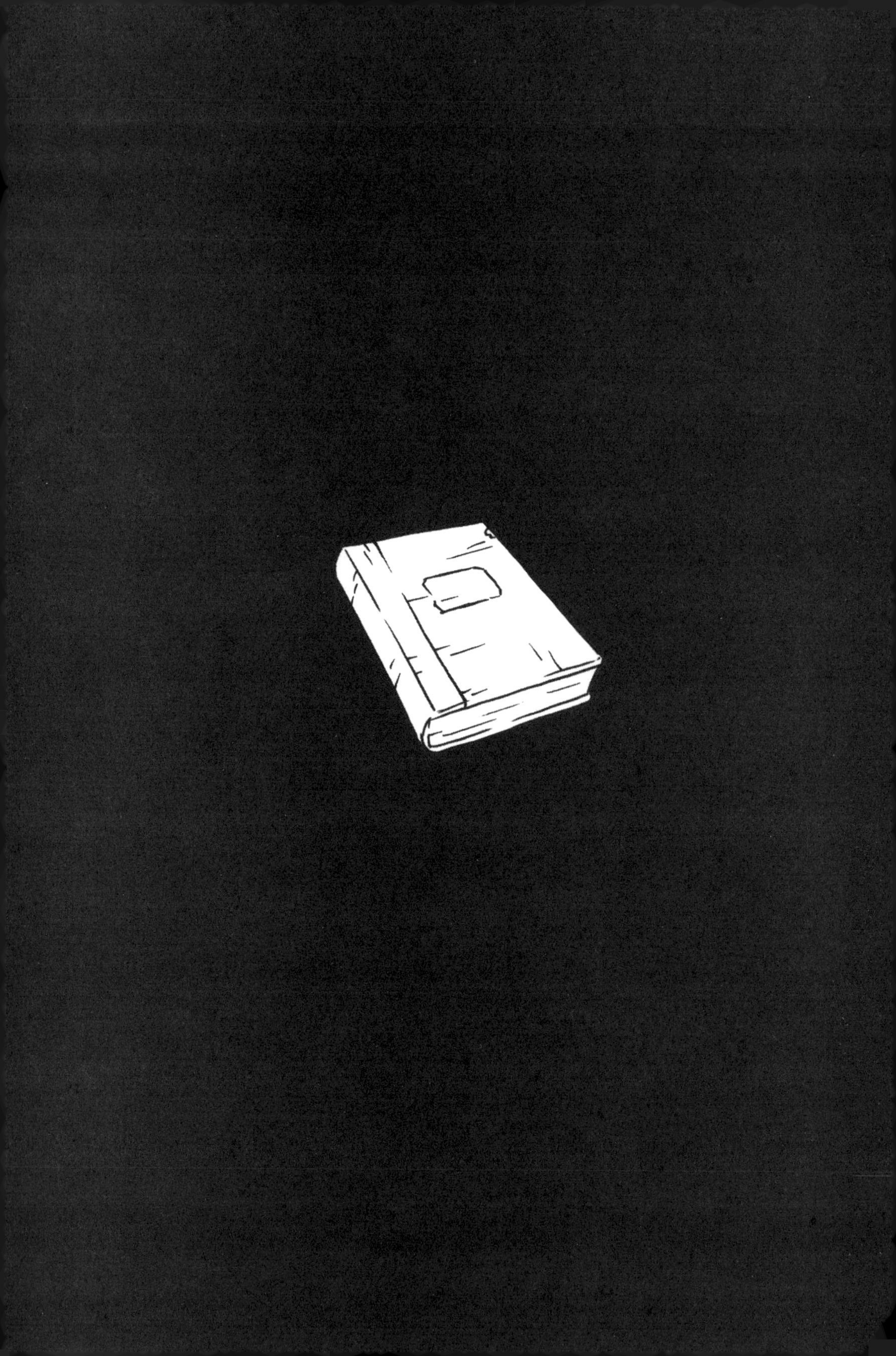

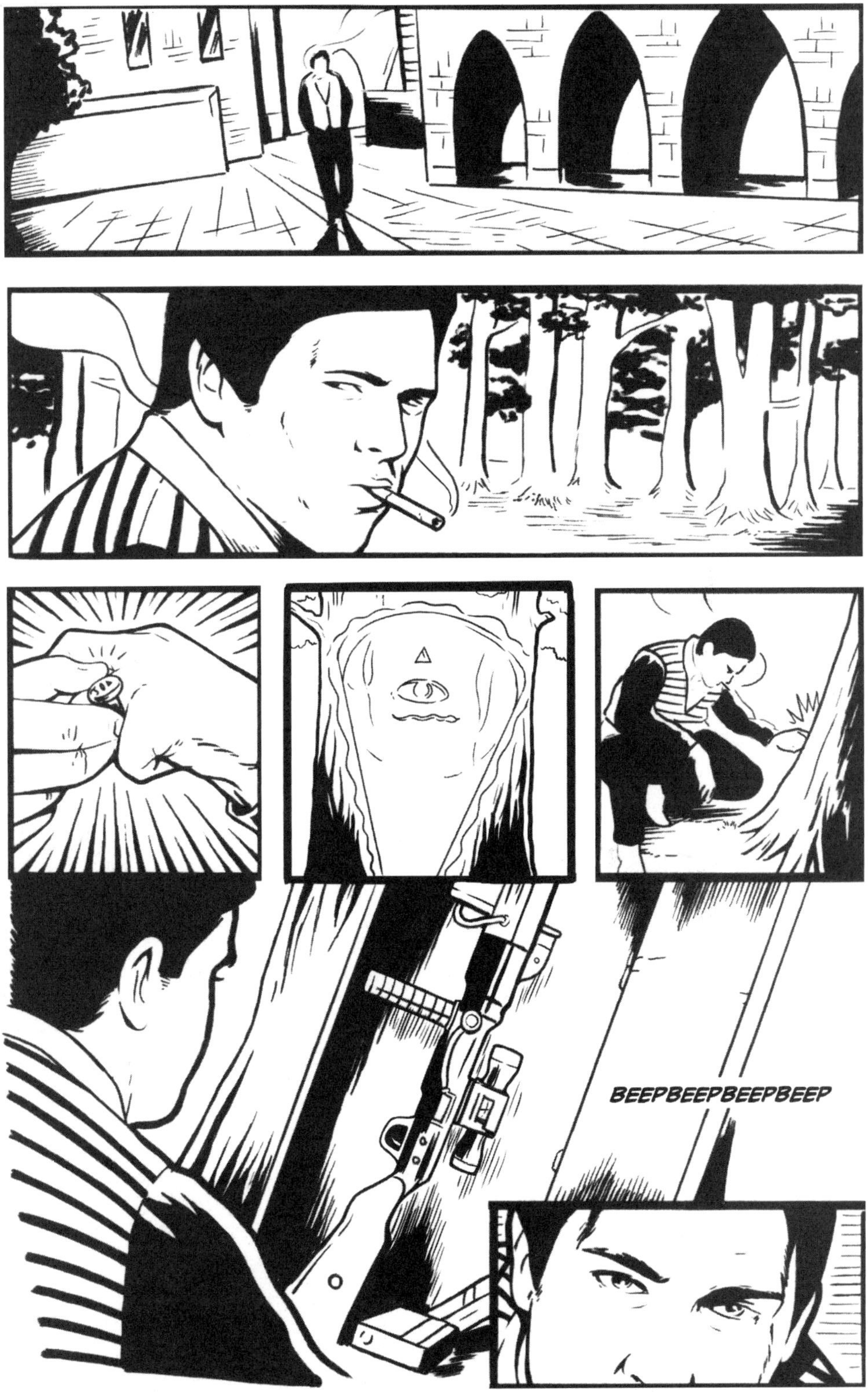
BEEPBEEPBEEPBEEP

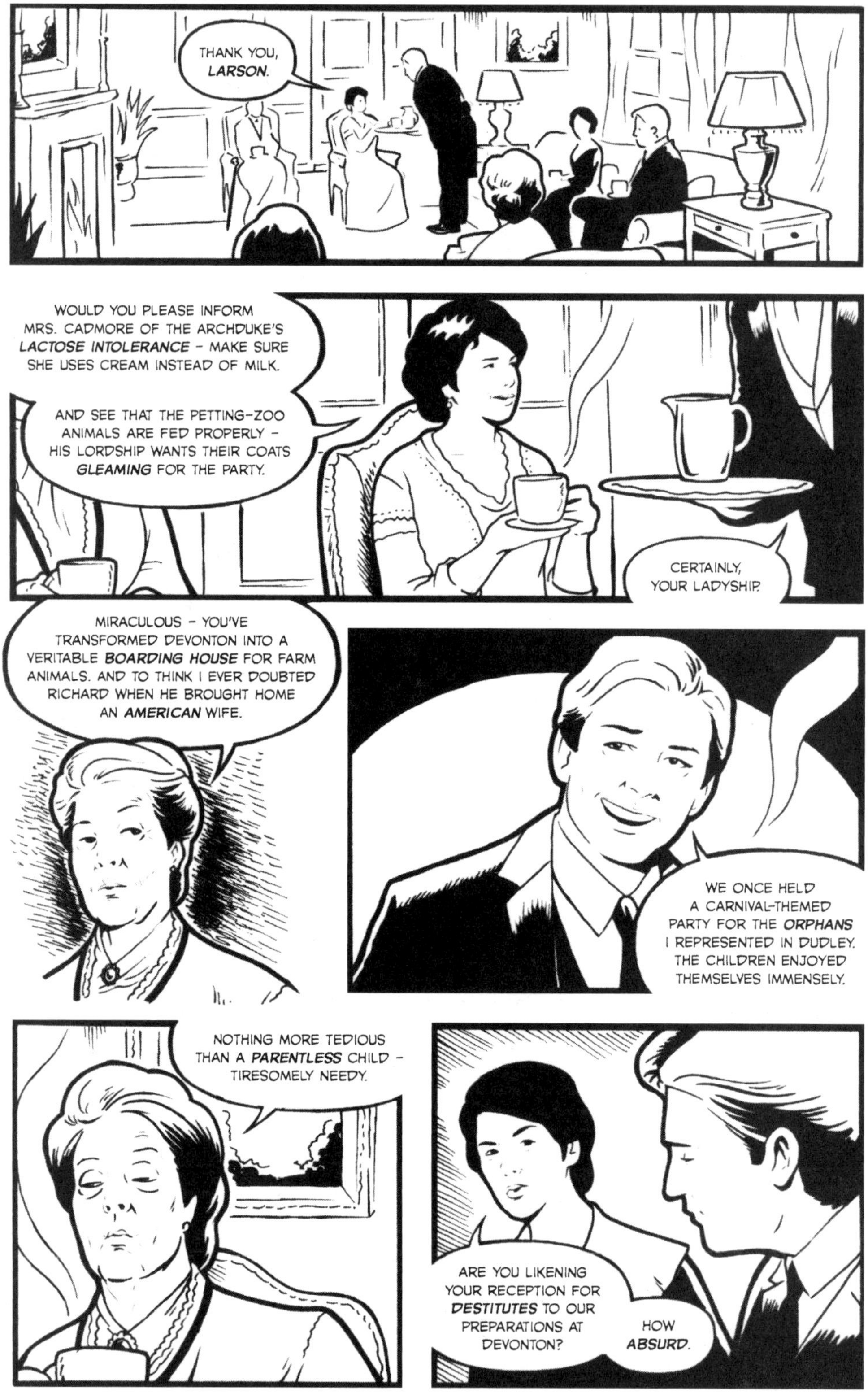
THANK YOU, LARSON.
WOULD YOU PLEASE INFORM MRS. CADMORE OF THE ARCHDUKE'S LACTOSE INTOLERANCE - MAKE SURE SHE USES CREAM INSTEAD OF MILK.
AND SEE THAT THE PETTING-ZOO ANIMALS ARE FED PROPERLY - HIS LORDSHIP WANTS THEIR COATS GLEAMING FOR THE PARTY.
CERTAINLY, YOUR LADYSHIP.
MIRACULOUS - YOU'VE TRANSFORMED DEVONTON INTO A VERITABLE BOARDING HOUSE FOR FARM ANIMALS. AND TO THINK I EVER DOUBTED RICHARD WHEN HE BROUGHT HOME AN AMERICAN WIFE.
WE ONCE HELD A CARNIVAL-THEMED PARTY FOR THE ORPHANS I REPRESENTED IN DUDLEY. THE CHILDREN ENJOYED THEMSELVES IMMENSELY.
NOTHING MORE TEDIOUS THAN A PARENTLESS CHILD - TIRESOMELY NEEDY.
ARE YOU LIKENING YOUR RECEPTION FOR DESTITUTES TO OUR PREPARATIONS AT DEVONTON?
HOW ABSURD.

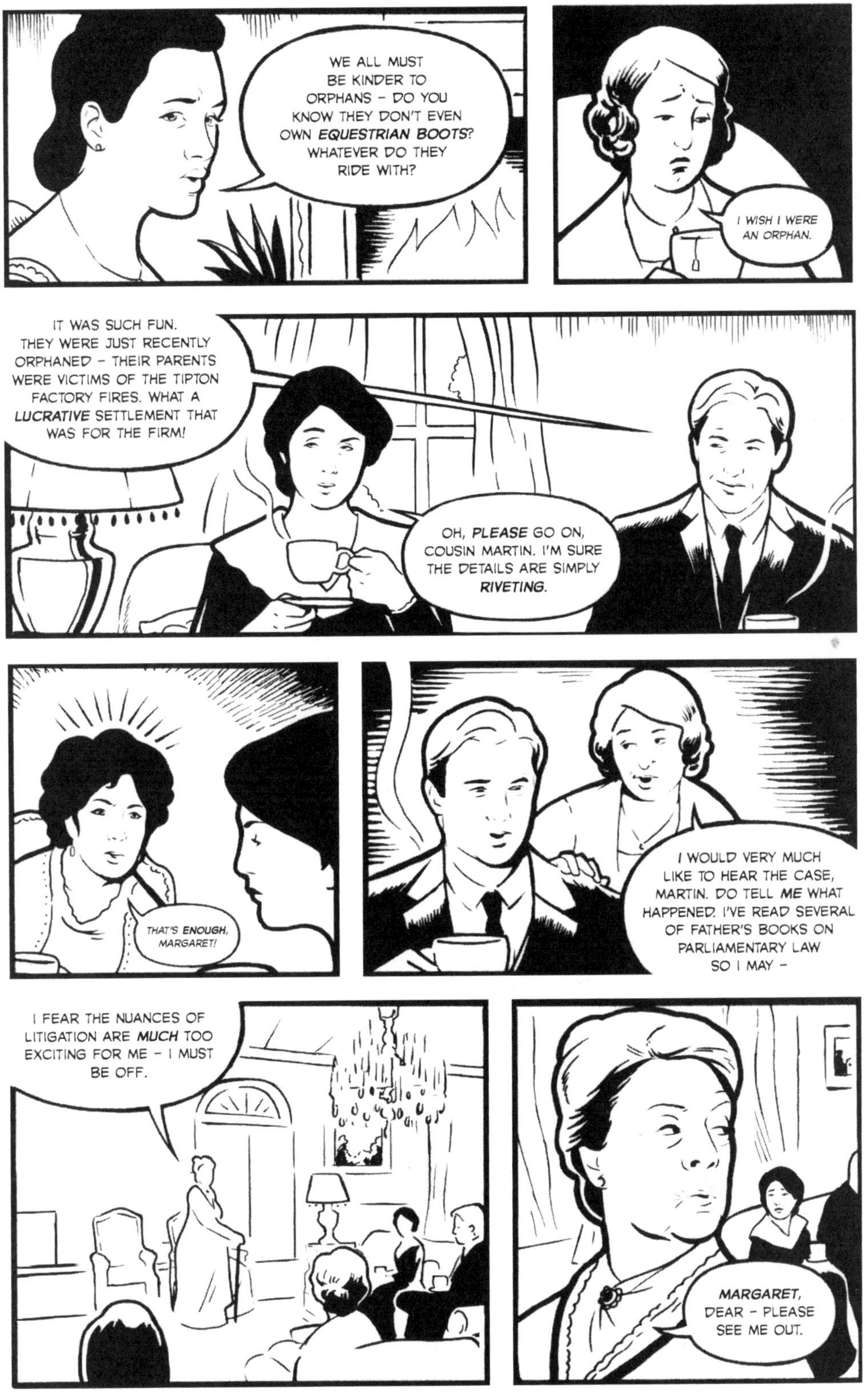
WE ALL MUST BE KINDER TO ORPHANS - DO YOU KNOW THEY DON'T EVEN OWN EQUESTRIAN BOOTS? WHATEVER DO THEY RIDE WITH?
I WISH I WERE AN ORPHAN.
IT WAS SUCH FUN. THEY WERE JUST RECENTLY ORPHANED - THEIR PARENTS WERE VICTIMS OF THE TIPTON FACTORY FIRES. WHAT A LUCRATIVE SETTLEMENT THAT WAS FOR THE FIRM!
OH, PLEASE GO ON, COUSIN MARTIN. I'M SURE THE DETAILS ARE SIMPLY RIVETING.
THAT'S ENOUGH, MARGARET!
I WOULD VERY MUCH LIKE TO HEAR THE CASE, MARTIN. DO TELL ME WHAT HAPPENED. I'VE READ SEVERAL OF FATHER'S BOOKS ON PARLIAMENTARY LAW SO I MAY -
I FEAR THE NUANCES OF LITIGATION ARE MUCH TOO EXCITING FOR ME - I MUST BE OFF.
MARGARET, DEAR - PLEASE SEE ME OUT.

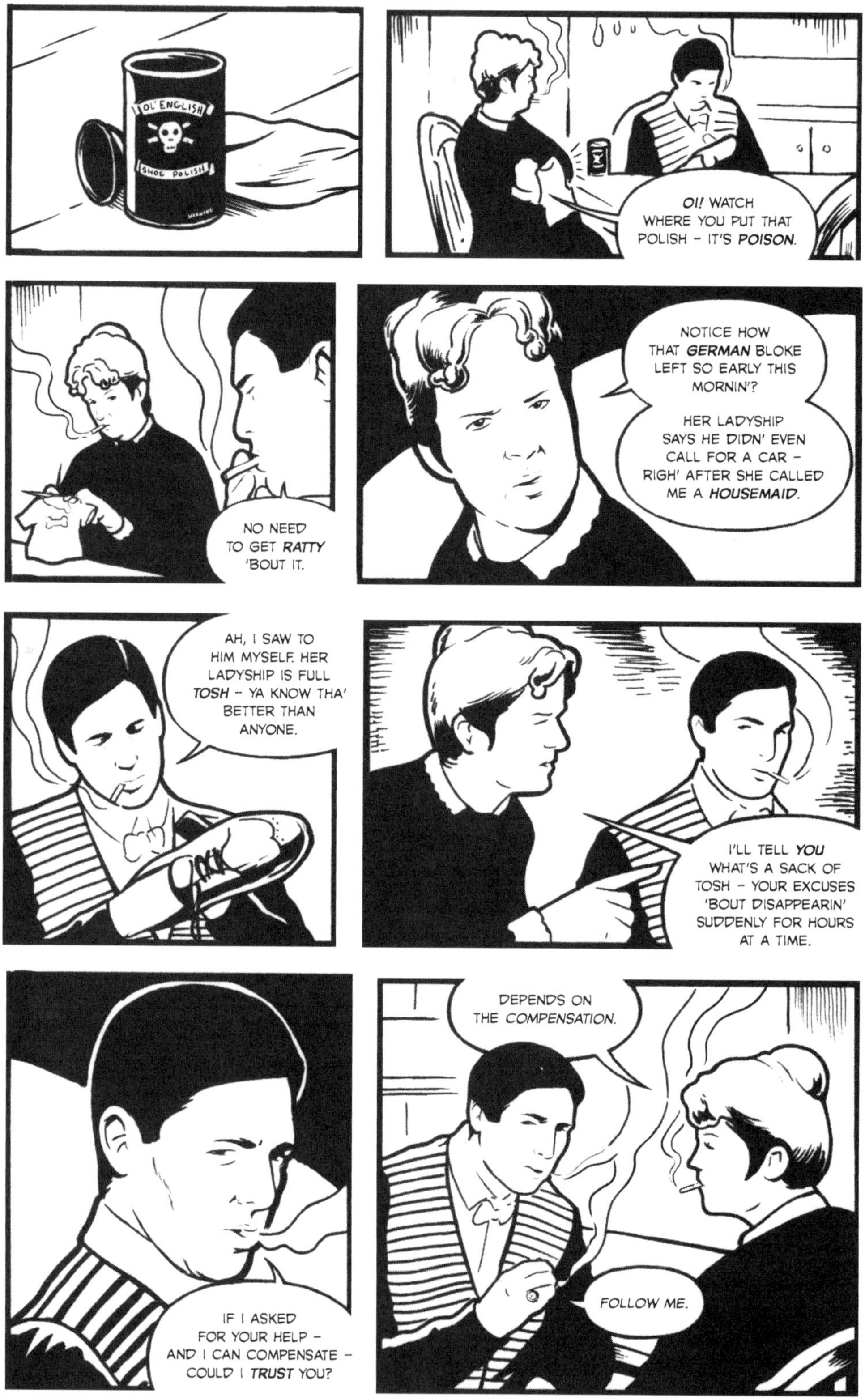
OL' ENGLISH
SHOE POLISH
OI! WATCH WHERE YOU PUT THAT POLISH – IT'S POISON.
NO NEED TO GET RATTY 'BOUT IT.
NOTICE HOW THAT GERMAN BLOKE LEFT SO EARLY THIS MORNIN'?
HER LADYSHIP SAYS HE DIDN' EVEN CALL FOR A CAR – RIGH' AFTER SHE CALLED ME A HOUSEMAID.
AH, I SAW TO HIM MYSELF. HER LADYSHIP IS FULL TOSH – YA KNOW THA' BETTER THAN ANYONE.
I'LL TELL YOU WHAT'S A SACK OF TOSH – YOUR EXCUSES 'BOUT DISAPPEARIN' SUDDENLY FOR HOURS AT A TIME.
IF I ASKED FOR YOUR HELP – AND I CAN COMPENSATE – COULD I TRUST YOU?
DEPENDS ON THE COMPENSATION.
FOLLOW ME.

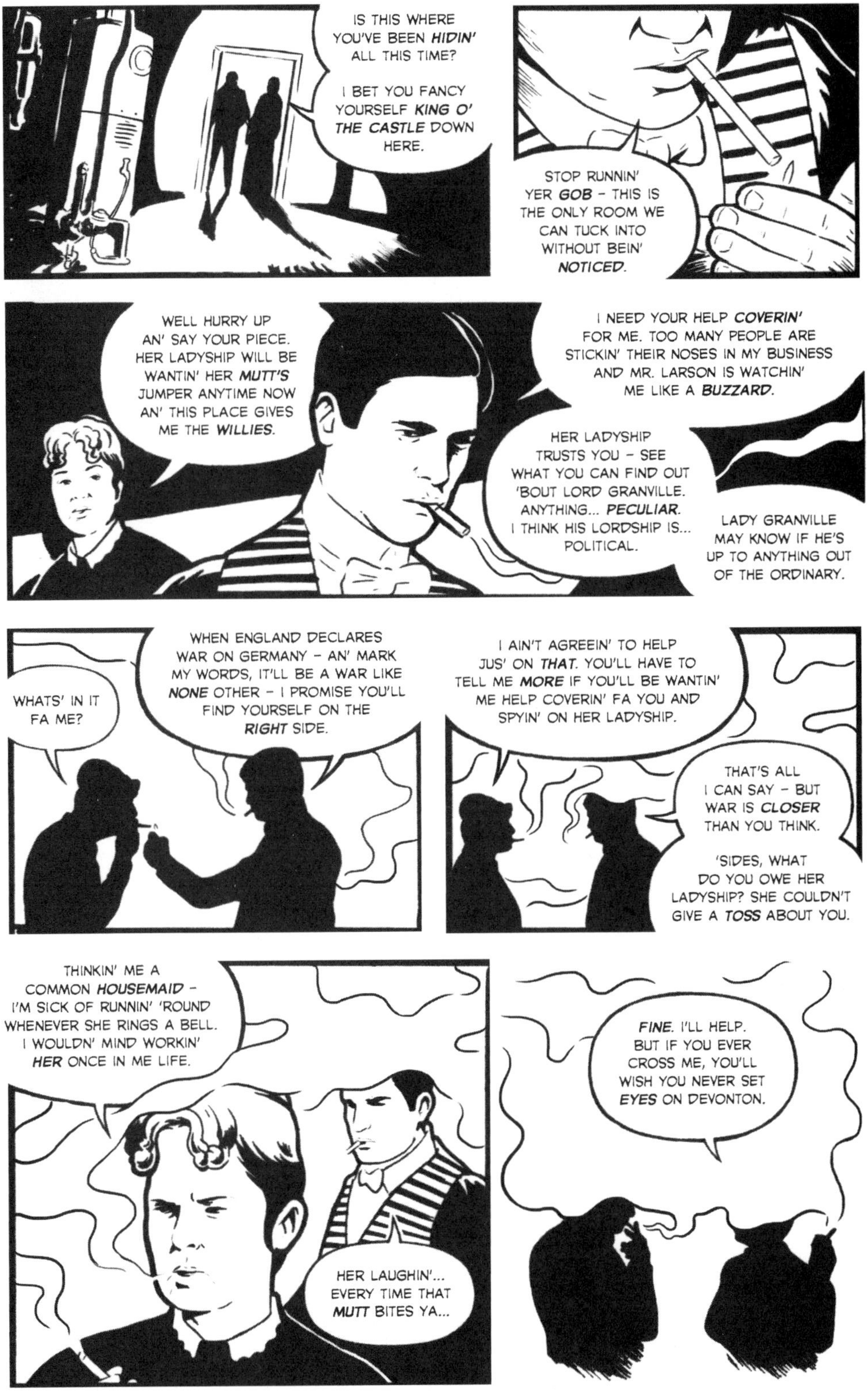
IS THIS WHERE YOU'VE BEEN HIDIN' ALL THIS TIME?
I BET YOU FANCY YOURSELF KING O' THE CASTLE DOWN HERE.
STOP RUNNIN' YER GOB - THIS IS THE ONLY ROOM WE CAN TUCK INTO WITHOUT BEIN' NOTICED.
WELL HURRY UP AN' SAY YOUR PIECE. HER LADYSHIP WILL BE WANTIN' HER MUTT'S JUMPER ANYTIME NOW AN' THIS PLACE GIVES ME THE WILLIES.
I NEED YOUR HELP COVERIN' FOR ME. TOO MANY PEOPLE ARE STICKIN' THEIR NOSES IN MY BUSINESS AND MR. LARSON IS WATCHIN' ME LIKE A BUZZARD.
HER LADYSHIP TRUSTS YOU - SEE WHAT YOU CAN FIND OUT 'BOUT LORD GRANVILLE. ANYTHING... PECULIAR. I THINK HIS LORDSHIP IS... POLITICAL.
LADY GRANVILLE MAY KNOW IF HE'S UP TO ANYTHING OUT OF THE ORDINARY.
WHATS' IN IT FA ME?
WHEN ENGLAND DECLARES WAR ON GERMANY - AN' MARK MY WORDS, IT'LL BE A WAR LIKE NONE OTHER - I PROMISE YOU'LL FIND YOURSELF ON THE RIGHT SIDE.
I AIN'T AGREEIN' TO HELP JUS' ON THAT. YOU'LL HAVE TO TELL ME MORE IF YOU'LL BE WANTIN' ME HELP COVERIN' FA YOU AND SPYIN' ON HER LADYSHIP.
THAT'S ALL I CAN SAY - BUT WAR IS CLOSER THAN YOU THINK.
'SIDES, WHAT DO YOU OWE HER LADYSHIP? SHE COULDN'T GIVE A TOSS ABOUT YOU.
THINKIN' ME A COMMON HOUSEMAID - I'M SICK OF RUNNIN' 'ROUND WHENEVER SHE RINGS A BELL. I WOULDN' MIND WORKIN' HER ONCE IN ME LIFE.
HER LAUGHIN'... EVERY TIME THAT MUTT BITES YA...
FINE. I'LL HELP. BUT IF YOU EVER CROSS ME, YOU'LL WISH YOU NEVER SET EYES ON DEVONTON.

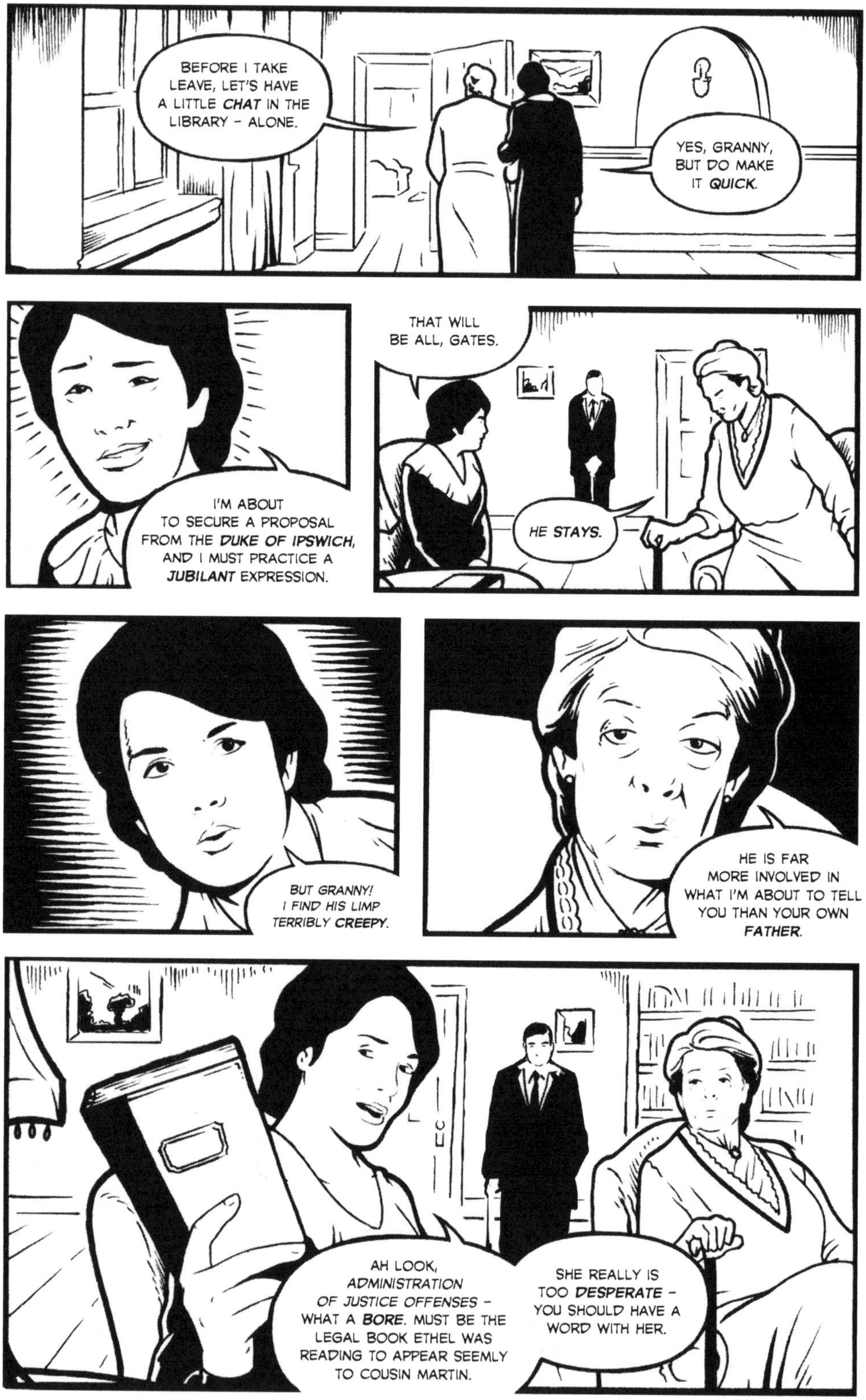
BEFORE I TAKE LEAVE, LET'S HAVE A LITTLE CHAT IN THE LIBRARY - ALONE.
YES, GRANNY, BUT DO MAKE IT QUICK.
I'M ABOUT TO SECURE A PROPOSAL FROM THE DUKE OF IPSWICH, AND I MUST PRACTICE A JUBILANT EXPRESSION.
THAT WILL BE ALL, GATES.
HE STAYS.
BUT GRANNY! I FIND HIS LIMP TERRIBLY CREEPY.
HE IS FAR MORE INVOLVED IN WHAT I'M ABOUT TO TELL YOU THAN YOUR OWN FATHER.
AH LOOK, ADMINISTRATION OF JUSTICE OFFENSES - WHAT A BORE. MUST BE THE LEGAL BOOK ETHEL WAS READING TO APPEAR SEEMLY TO COUSIN MARTIN.
SHE REALLY IS TOO DESPERATE - YOU SHOULD HAVE A WORD WITH HER.

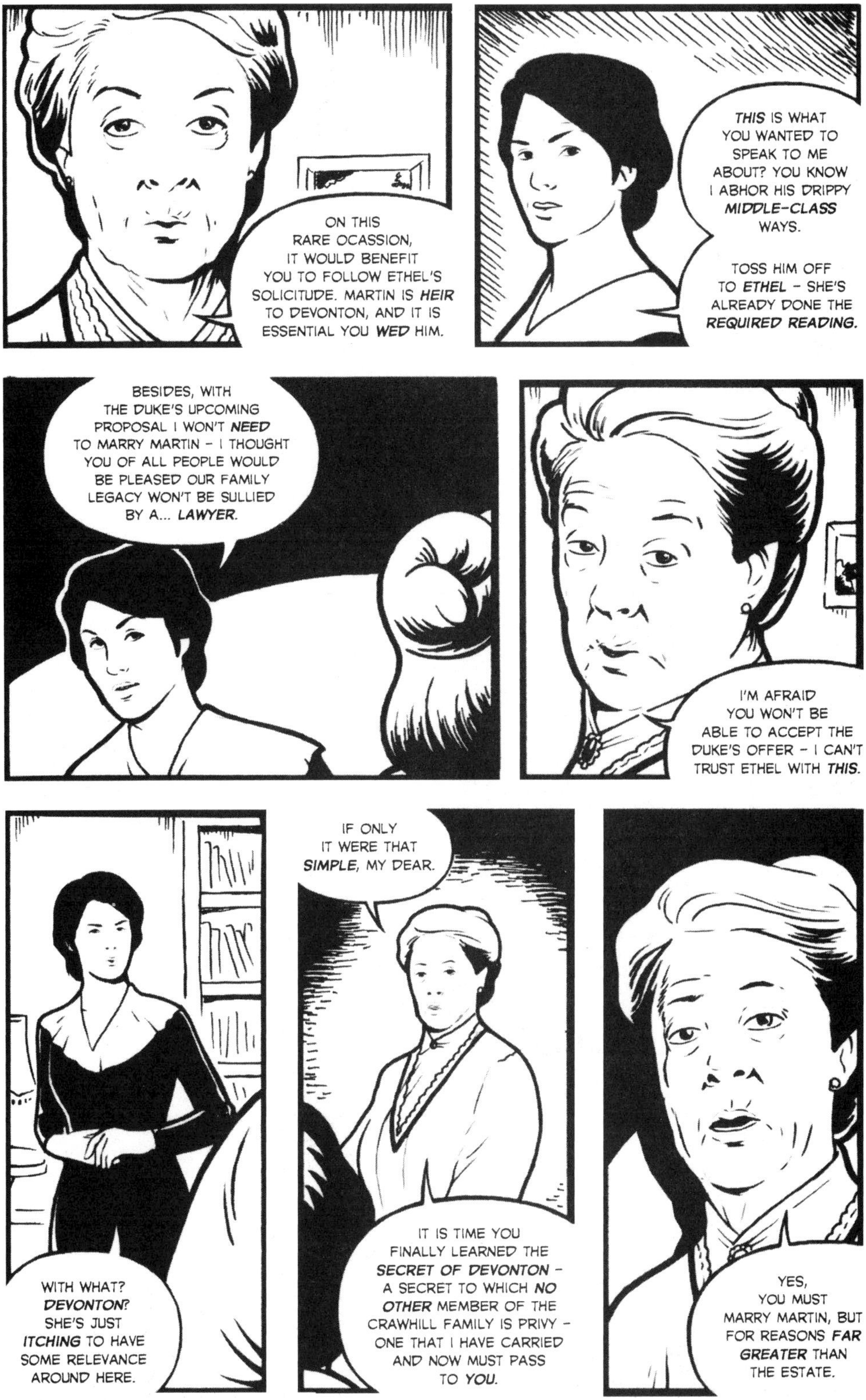
ON THIS RARE OCASSION, IT WOULD BENEFIT YOU TO FOLLOW ETHEL'S SOLICITUDE. MARTIN IS HEIR TO DEVONTON, AND IT IS ESSENTIAL YOU WED HIM.
THIS IS WHAT YOU WANTED TO SPEAK TO ME ABOUT? YOU KNOW I ABHOR HIS DRIPPY MIDDLE-CLASS WAYS.
TOSS HIM OFF TO ETHEL - SHE'S ALREADY DONE THE REQUIRED READING.
BESIDES, WITH THE DUKE'S UPCOMING PROPOSAL I WON'T NEED TO MARRY MARTIN - I THOUGHT YOU OF ALL PEOPLE WOULD BE PLEASED OUR FAMILY LEGACY WON'T BE SULLIED BY A... LAWYER.
I'M AFRAID YOU WON'T BE ABLE TO ACCEPT THE DUKE'S OFFER - I CAN'T TRUST ETHEL WITH THIS.
WITH WHAT? DEVONTON? SHE'S JUST ITCHING TO HAVE SOME RELEVANCE AROUND HERE.
IF ONLY IT WERE THAT SIMPLE, MY DEAR.
IT IS TIME YOU FINALLY LEARNED THE SECRET OF DEVONTON - A SECRET TO WHICH NO OTHER MEMBER OF THE CRAWHILL FAMILY IS PRIVY - ONE THAT I HAVE CARRIED AND NOW MUST PASS TO YOU.
YES, YOU MUST MARRY MARTIN, BUT FOR REASONS FAR GREATER THAN THE ESTATE.

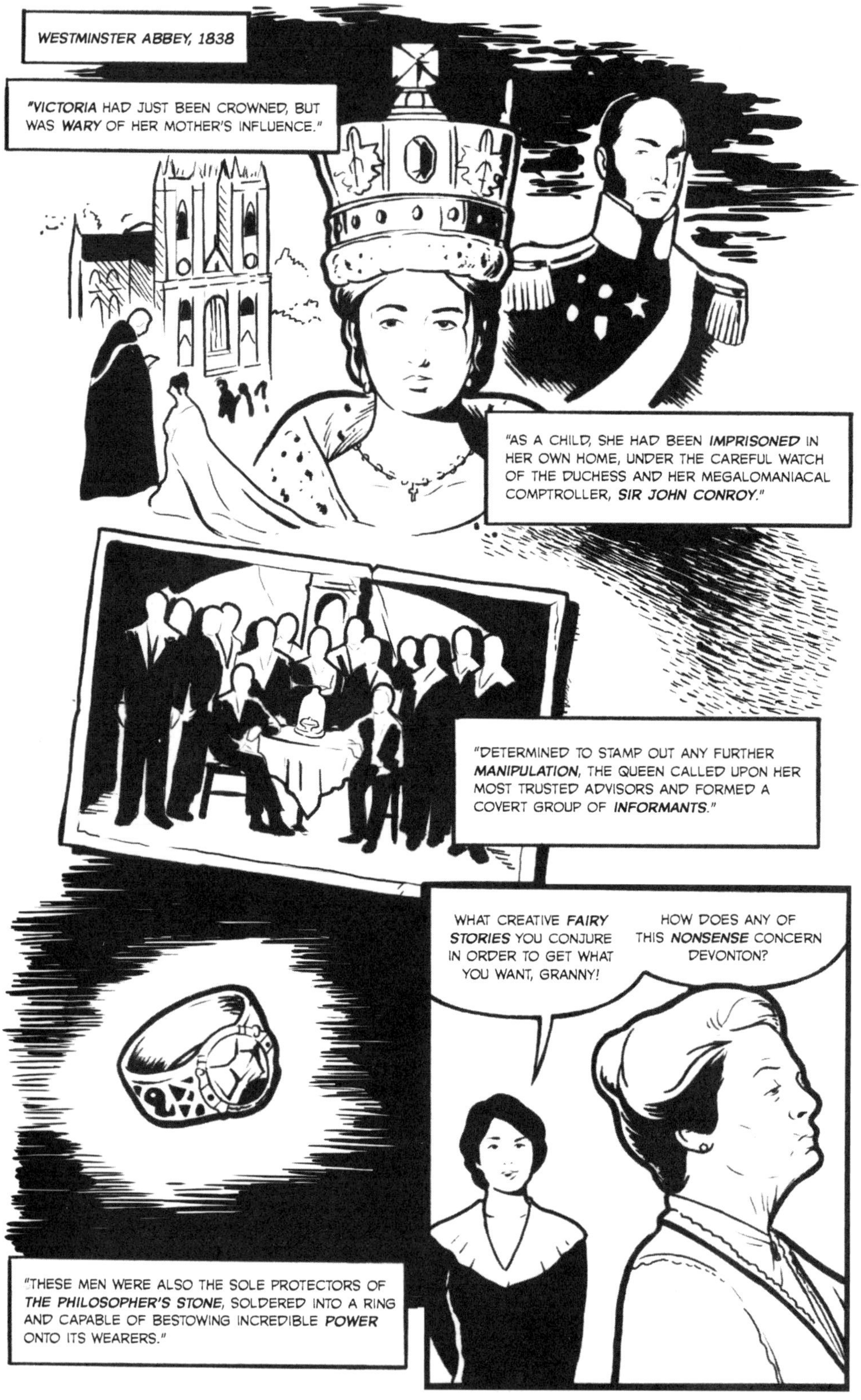
WESTMINSTER ABBEY, 1838
"VICTORIA HAD JUST BEEN CROWNED, BUT WAS WARY OF HER MOTHER'S INFLUENCE."
"AS A CHILD, SHE HAD BEEN IMPRISONED IN HER OWN HOME, UNDER THE CAREFUL WATCH OF THE DUCHESS AND HER MEGALOMANIACAL COMPTROLLER, SIR JOHN CONROY."
"DETERMINED TO STAMP OUT ANY FURTHER MANIPULATION, THE QUEEN CALLED UPON HER MOST TRUSTED ADVISORS AND FORMED A COVERT GROUP OF INFORMANTS."
"THESE MEN WERE ALSO THE SOLE PROTECTORS OF THE PHILOSOPHER'S STONE, SOLDERED INTO A RING AND CAPABLE OF BESTOWING INCREDIBLE POWER ONTO ITS WEARERS."
WHAT CREATIVE FAIRY STORIES YOU CONJURE IN ORDER TO GET WHAT YOU WANT, GRANNY!
HOW DOES ANY OF THIS NONSENSE CONCERN DEVONTON?

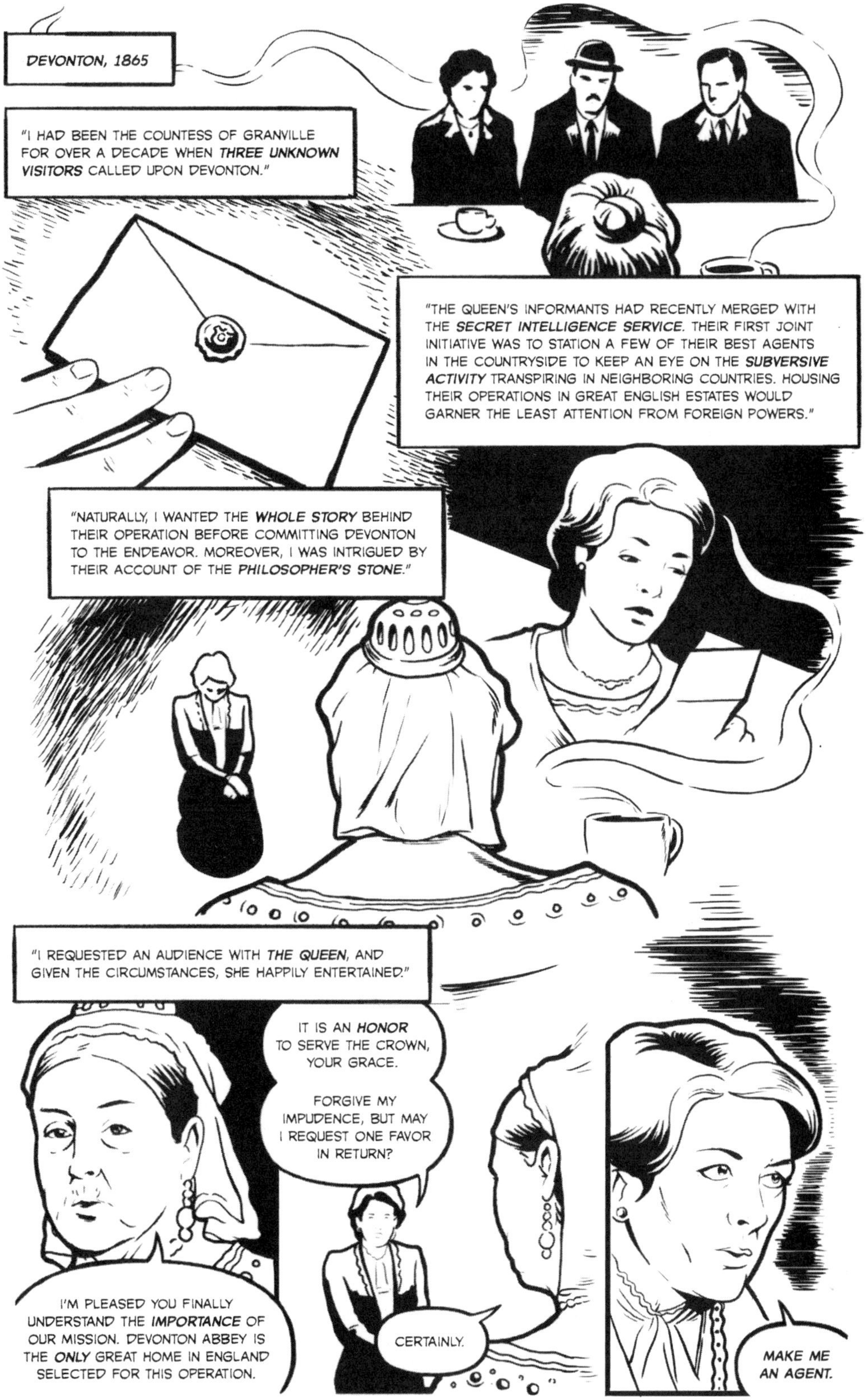
DEVONTON, 1865
"I HAD BEEN THE COUNTESS OF GRANVILLE FOR OVER A DECADE WHEN THREE UNKNOWN VISITORS CALLED UPON DEVONTON."
"THE QUEEN'S INFORMANTS HAD RECENTLY MERGED WITH THE SECRET INTELLIGENCE SERVICE. THEIR FIRST JOINT INITIATIVE WAS TO STATION A FEW OF THEIR BEST AGENTS IN THE COUNTRYSIDE TO KEEP AN EYE ON THE SUBVERSIVE ACTIVITY TRANSPIRING IN NEIGHBORING COUNTRIES. HOUSING THEIR OPERATIONS IN GREAT ENGLISH ESTATES WOULD GARNER THE LEAST ATTENTION FROM FOREIGN POWERS."
"NATURALLY, I WANTED THE WHOLE STORY BEHIND THEIR OPERATION BEFORE COMMITTING DEVONTON TO THE ENDEAVOR. MOREOVER, I WAS INTRIGUED BY THEIR ACCOUNT OF THE PHILOSOPHER'S STONE."
"I REQUESTED AN AUDIENCE WITH THE QUEEN, AND GIVEN THE CIRCUMSTANCES, SHE HAPPILY ENTERTAINED."
I'M PLEASED YOU FINALLY UNDERSTAND THE IMPORTANCE OF OUR MISSION. DEVONTON ABBEY IS THE ONLY GREAT HOME IN ENGLAND SELECTED FOR THIS OPERATION.
IT IS AN HONOR TO SERVE THE CROWN, YOUR GRACE.
FORGIVE MY IMPUDENCE, BUT MAY I REQUEST ONE FAVOR IN RETURN?
CERTAINLY.
MAKE ME AN AGENT.

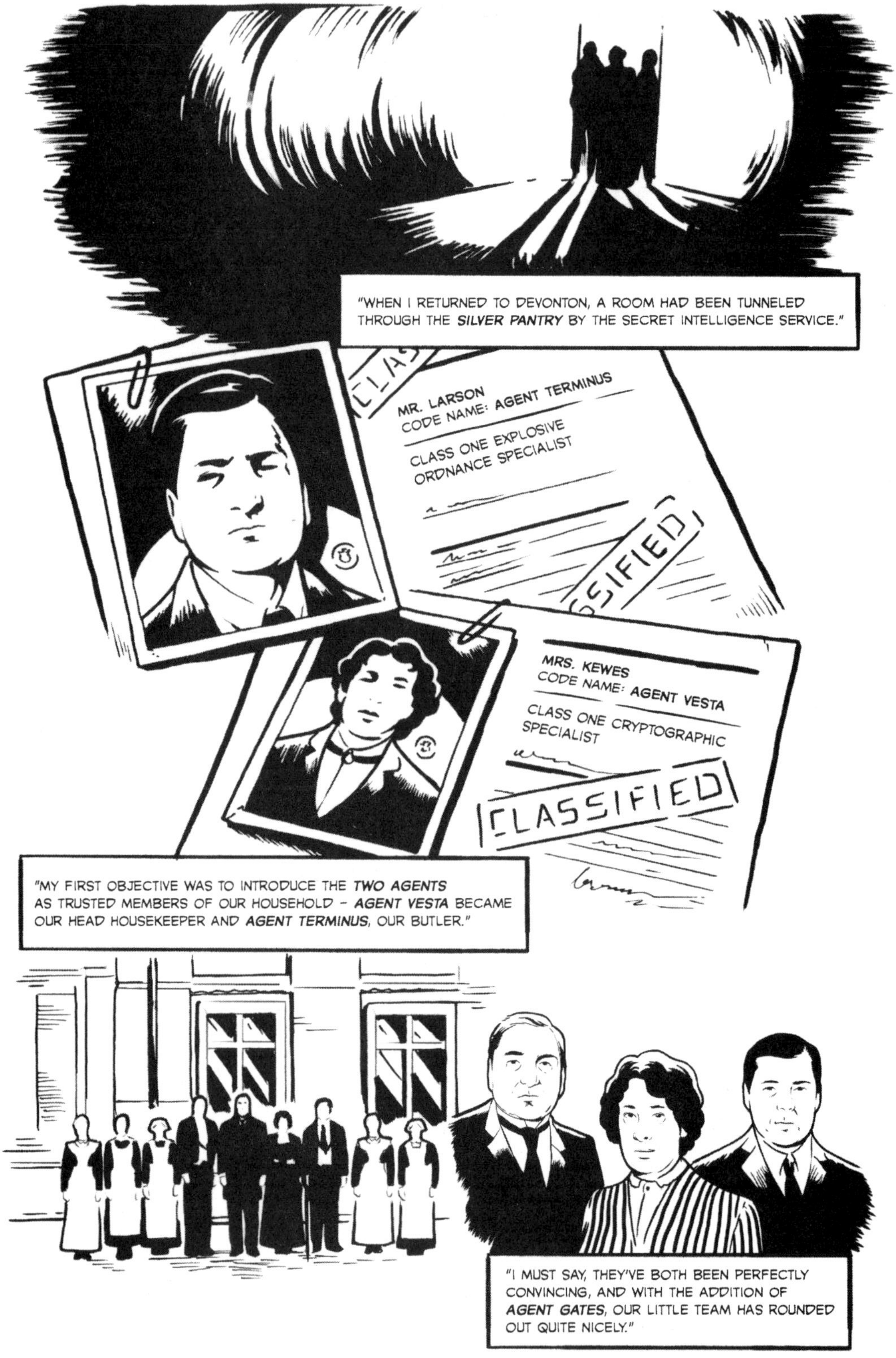
"WHEN I RETURNED TO DEVONTON, A ROOM HAD BEEN TUNNELED THROUGH THE SILVER PANTRY BY THE SECRET INTELLIGENCE SERVICE."
MR. LARSON
CODE NAME: AGENT TERMINUS
CLASS ONE EXPLOSIVE ORDNANCE SPECIALIST
MRS. KEWES
CODE NAME: AGENT VESTA
CLASS ONE CRYPTOGRAPHIC SPECIALIST
CLASSIFIED
"MY FIRST OBJECTIVE WAS TO INTRODUCE THE TWO AGENTS AS TRUSTED MEMBERS OF OUR HOUSEHOLD - AGENT VESTA BECAME OUR HEAD HOUSEKEEPER AND AGENT TERMINUS, OUR BUTLER."
"I MUST SAY, THEY'VE BOTH BEEN PERFECTLY CONVINCING, AND WITH THE ADDITION OF AGENT GATES, OUR LITTLE TEAM HAS ROUNDED OUT QUITE NICELY."

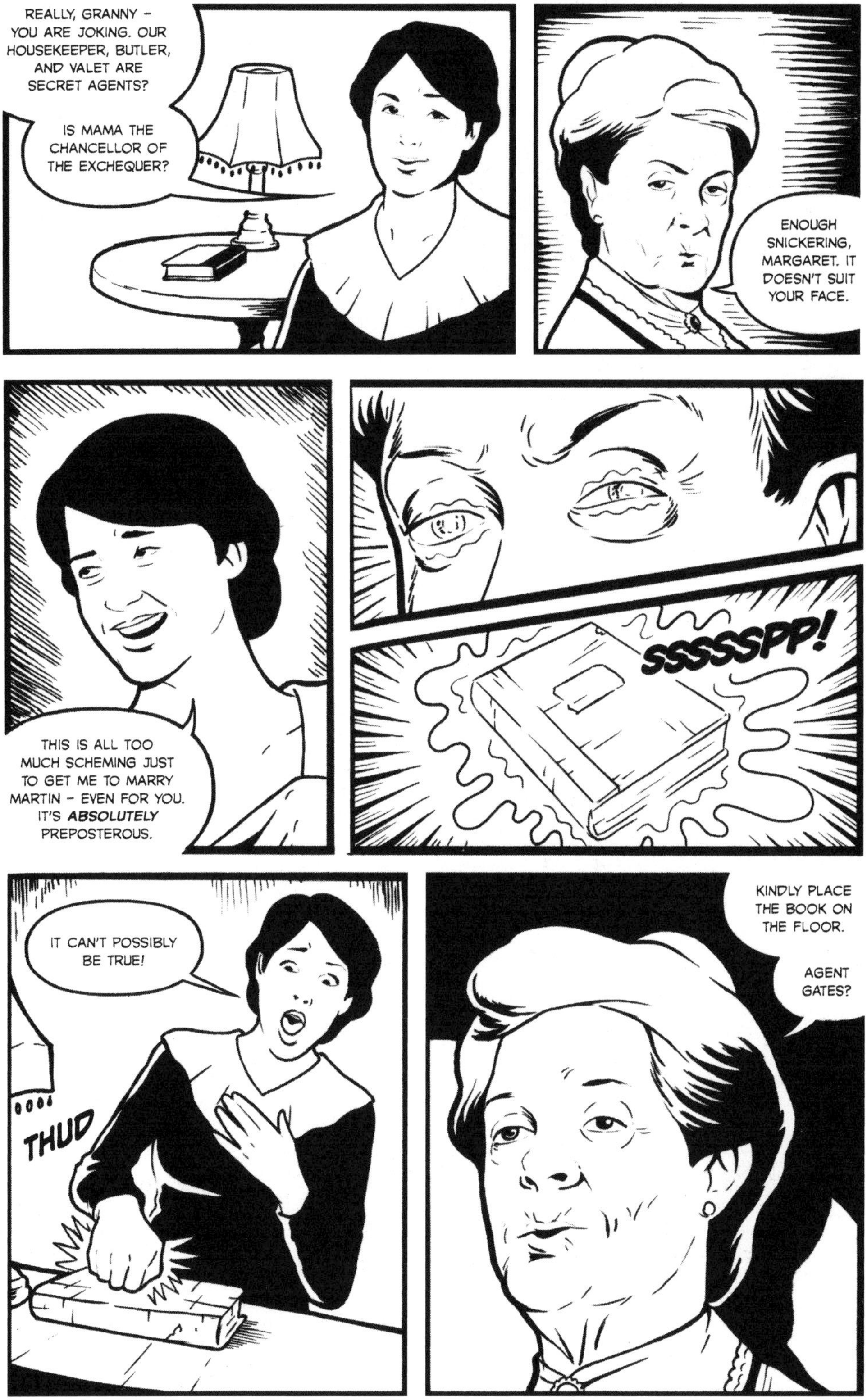
REALLY, GRANNY - YOU ARE JOKING. OUR HOUSEKEEPER, BUTLER, AND VALET ARE SECRET AGENTS?
IS MAMA THE CHANCELLOR OF THE EXCHEQUER?
ENOUGH SNICKERING, MARGARET. IT DOESN'T SUIT YOUR FACE.
THIS IS ALL TOO MUCH SCHEMING JUST TO GET ME TO MARRY MARTIN - EVEN FOR YOU. IT'S ***ABSOLUTELY*** PREPOSTEROUS.
SSSSSPP!
IT CAN'T POSSIBLY BE TRUE!
THUD
KINDLY PLACE THE BOOK ON THE FLOOR.
AGENT GATES?

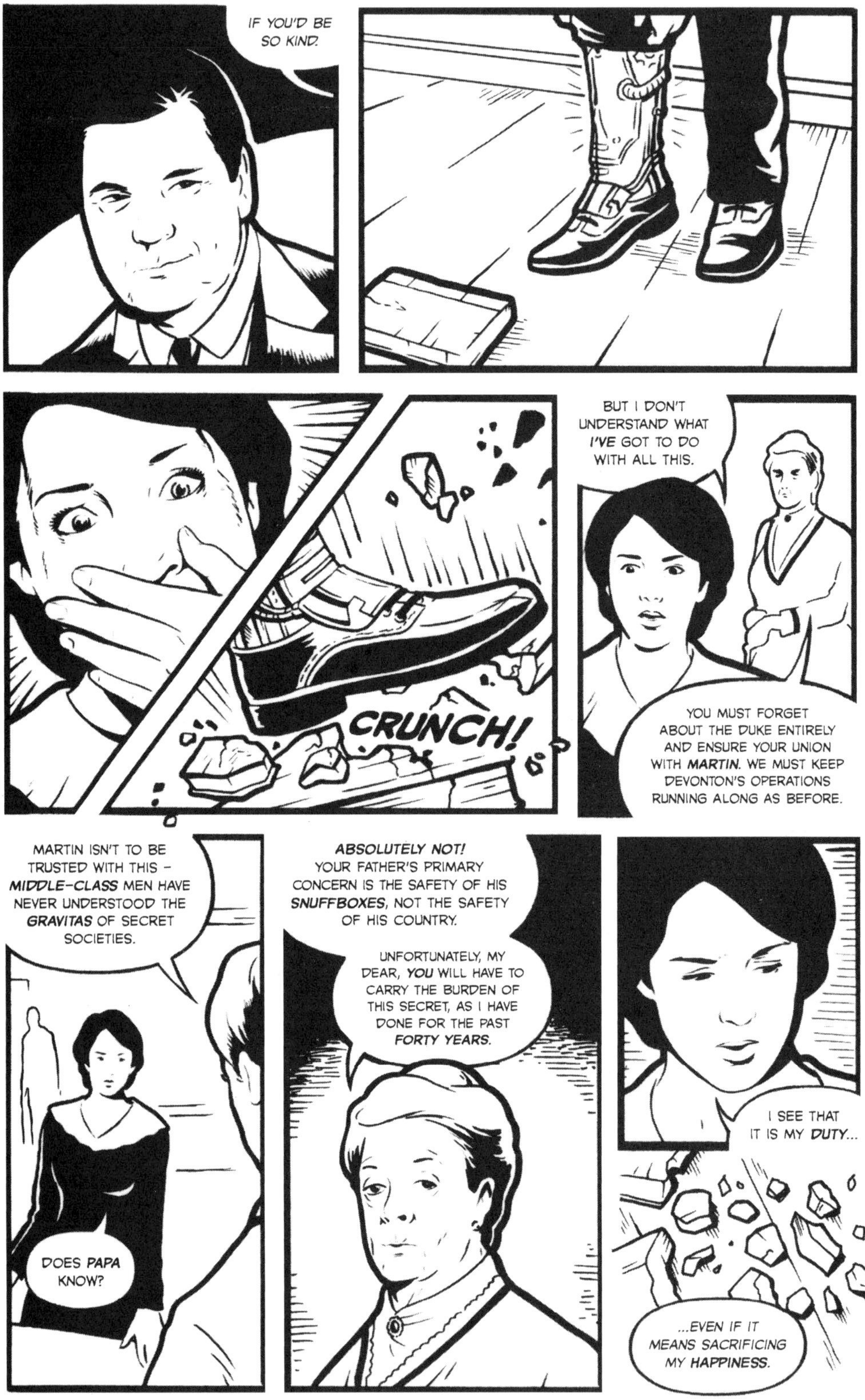
IF YOU'D BE SO KIND.
CRUNCH!
BUT I DON'T UNDERSTAND WHAT I'VE GOT TO DO WITH ALL THIS.
YOU MUST FORGET ABOUT THE DUKE ENTIRELY AND ENSURE YOUR UNION WITH MARTIN. WE MUST KEEP DEVONTON'S OPERATIONS RUNNING ALONG AS BEFORE.
MARTIN ISN'T TO BE TRUSTED WITH THIS – MIDDLE-CLASS MEN HAVE NEVER UNDERSTOOD THE GRAVITAS OF SECRET SOCIETIES.
DOES PAPA KNOW?
ABSOLUTELY NOT! YOUR FATHER'S PRIMARY CONCERN IS THE SAFETY OF HIS SNUFFBOXES, NOT THE SAFETY OF HIS COUNTRY.
UNFORTUNATELY, MY DEAR, YOU WILL HAVE TO CARRY THE BURDEN OF THIS SECRET, AS I HAVE DONE FOR THE PAST FORTY YEARS.
I SEE THAT IT IS MY DUTY...
...EVEN IF IT MEANS SACRIFICING MY HAPPINESS.

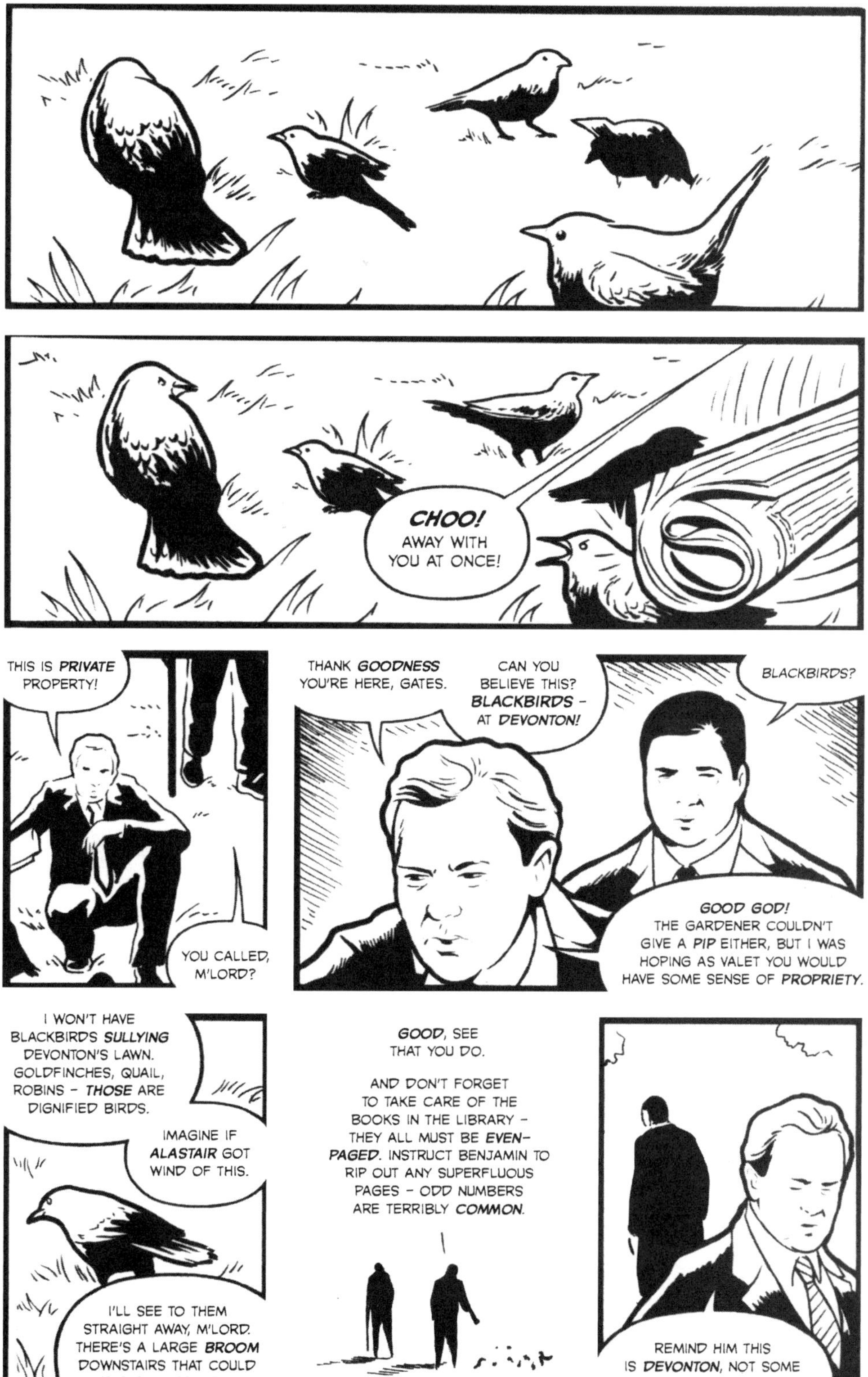
CHOO!
AWAY WITH YOU AT ONCE!
THIS IS PRIVATE PROPERTY!
YOU CALLED, M'LORD?
THANK GOODNESS YOU'RE HERE, GATES.
CAN YOU BELIEVE THIS? BLACKBIRDS - AT DEVONTON!
BLACKBIRDS?
GOOD GOD! THE GARDENER COULDN'T GIVE A PIP EITHER, BUT I WAS HOPING AS VALET YOU WOULD HAVE SOME SENSE OF PROPRIETY.
I WON'T HAVE BLACKBIRDS SULLYING DEVONTON'S LAWN. GOLDFINCHES, QUAIL, ROBINS - THOSE ARE DIGNIFIED BIRDS.
IMAGINE IF ALASTAIR GOT WIND OF THIS.
I'LL SEE TO THEM STRAIGHT AWAY, M'LORD. THERE'S A LARGE BROOM DOWNSTAIRS THAT COULD HELP SCATTER THEM.
GOOD, SEE THAT YOU DO.
AND DON'T FORGET TO TAKE CARE OF THE BOOKS IN THE LIBRARY - THEY ALL MUST BE EVEN-PAGED. INSTRUCT BENJAMIN TO RIP OUT ANY SUPERFLUOUS PAGES - ODD NUMBERS ARE TERRIBLY COMMON.
REMIND HIM THIS IS DEVONTON, NOT SOME RUDDY CARREL IN WEEFORD.

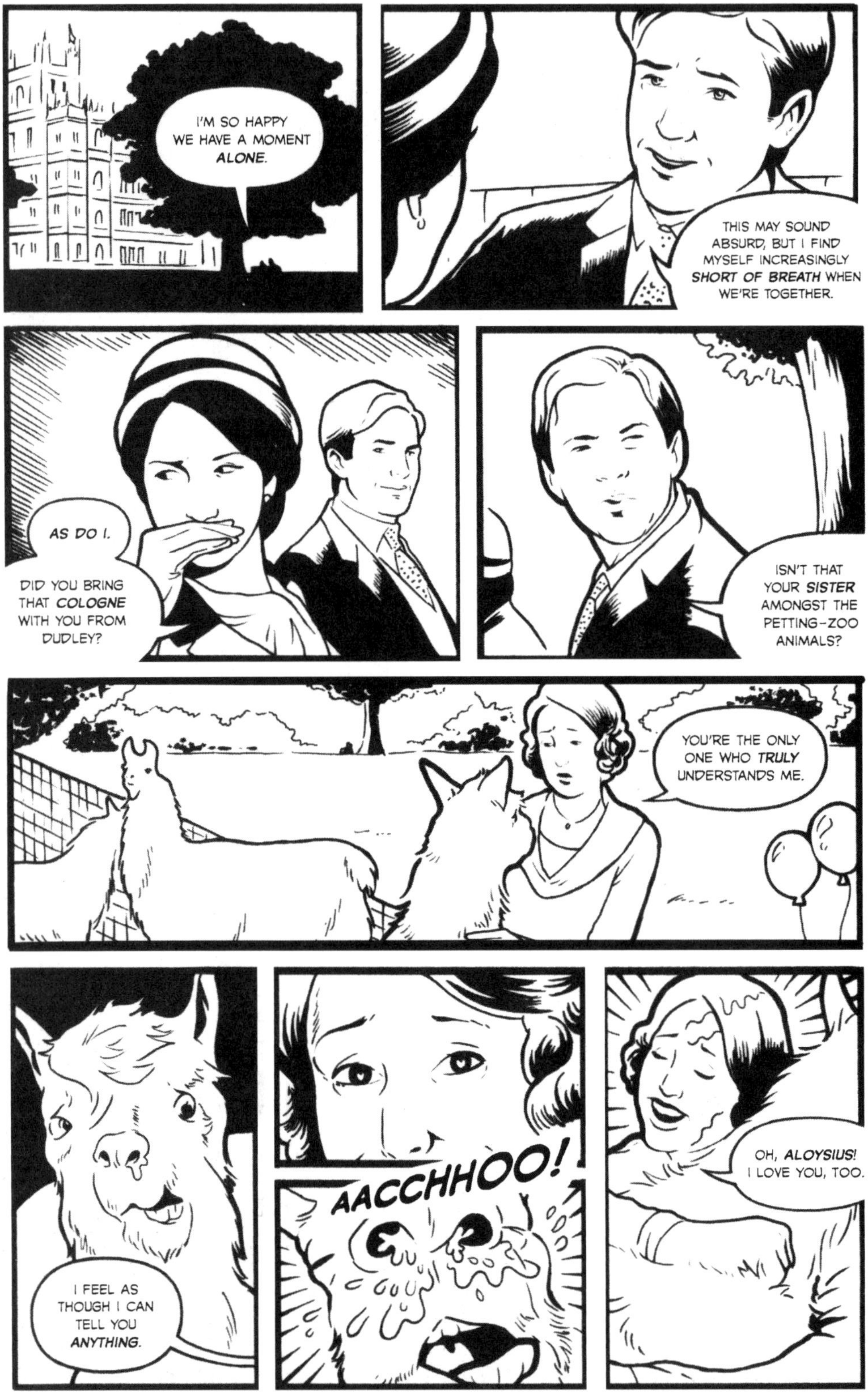
I'M SO HAPPY WE HAVE A MOMENT ALONE.
THIS MAY SOUND ABSURD, BUT I FIND MYSELF INCREASINGLY SHORT OF BREATH WHEN WE'RE TOGETHER.
AS DO I.
DID YOU BRING THAT COLOGNE WITH YOU FROM DUDLEY?
ISN'T THAT YOUR SISTER AMONGST THE PETTING-ZOO ANIMALS?
YOU'RE THE ONLY ONE WHO TRULY UNDERSTANDS ME.
I FEEL AS THOUGH I CAN TELL YOU ANYTHING.
AACCHHOO!
OH, ALOYSIUS! I LOVE YOU, TOO.

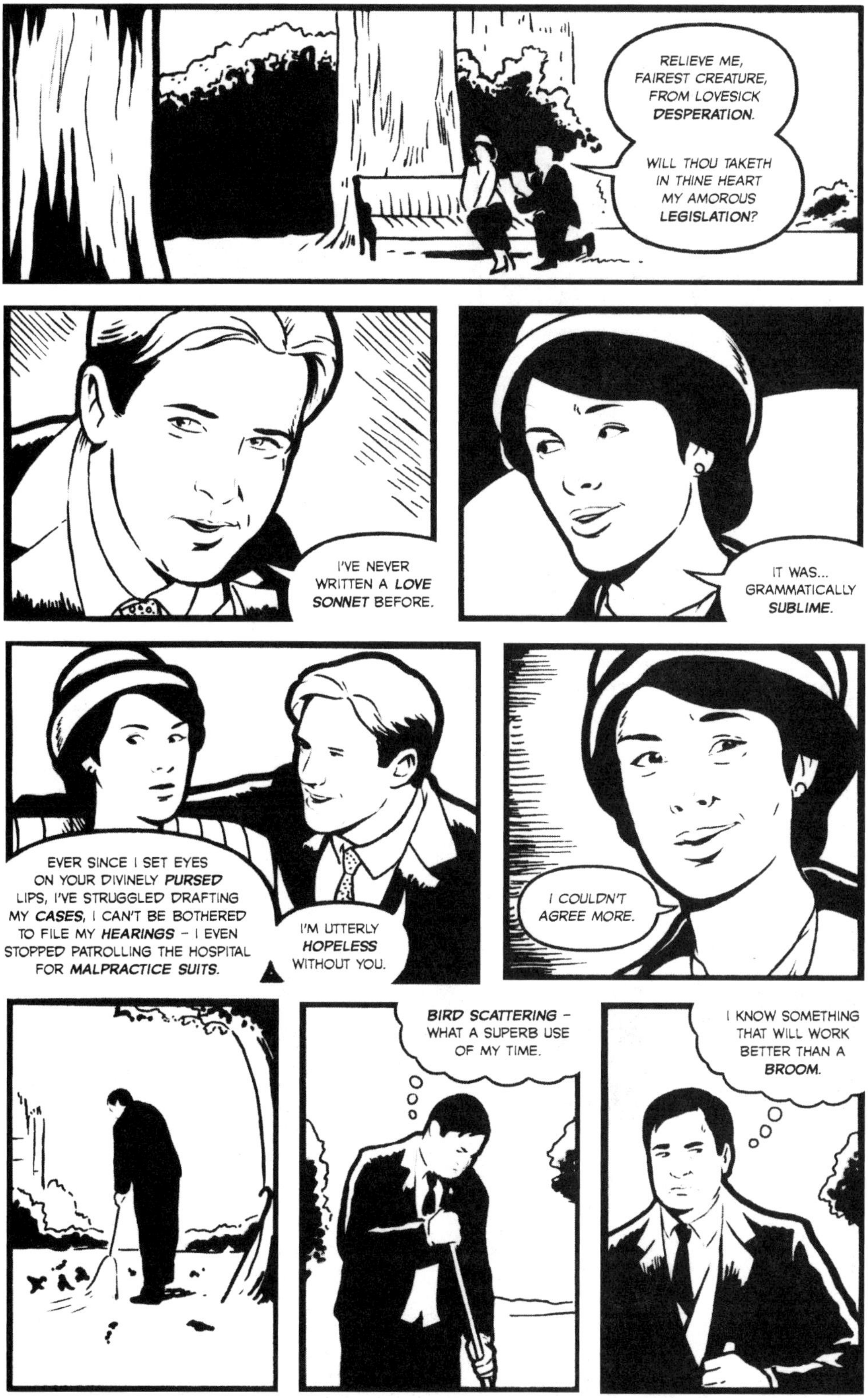
RELIEVE ME, FAIREST CREATURE, FROM LOVESICK DESPERATION.
WILL THOU TAKETH IN THINE HEART MY AMOROUS LEGISLATION?
I'VE NEVER WRITTEN A LOVE SONNET BEFORE.
IT WAS... GRAMMATICALLY SUBLIME.
EVER SINCE I SET EYES ON YOUR DIVINELY PURSED LIPS, I'VE STRUGGLED DRAFTING MY CASES, I CAN'T BE BOTHERED TO FILE MY HEARINGS – I EVEN STOPPED PATROLLING THE HOSPITAL FOR MALPRACTICE SUITS.
I'M UTTERLY HOPELESS WITHOUT YOU.
I COULDN'T AGREE MORE.
BIRD SCATTERING – WHAT A SUPERB USE OF MY TIME.
I KNOW SOMETHING THAT WILL WORK BETTER THAN A BROOM.

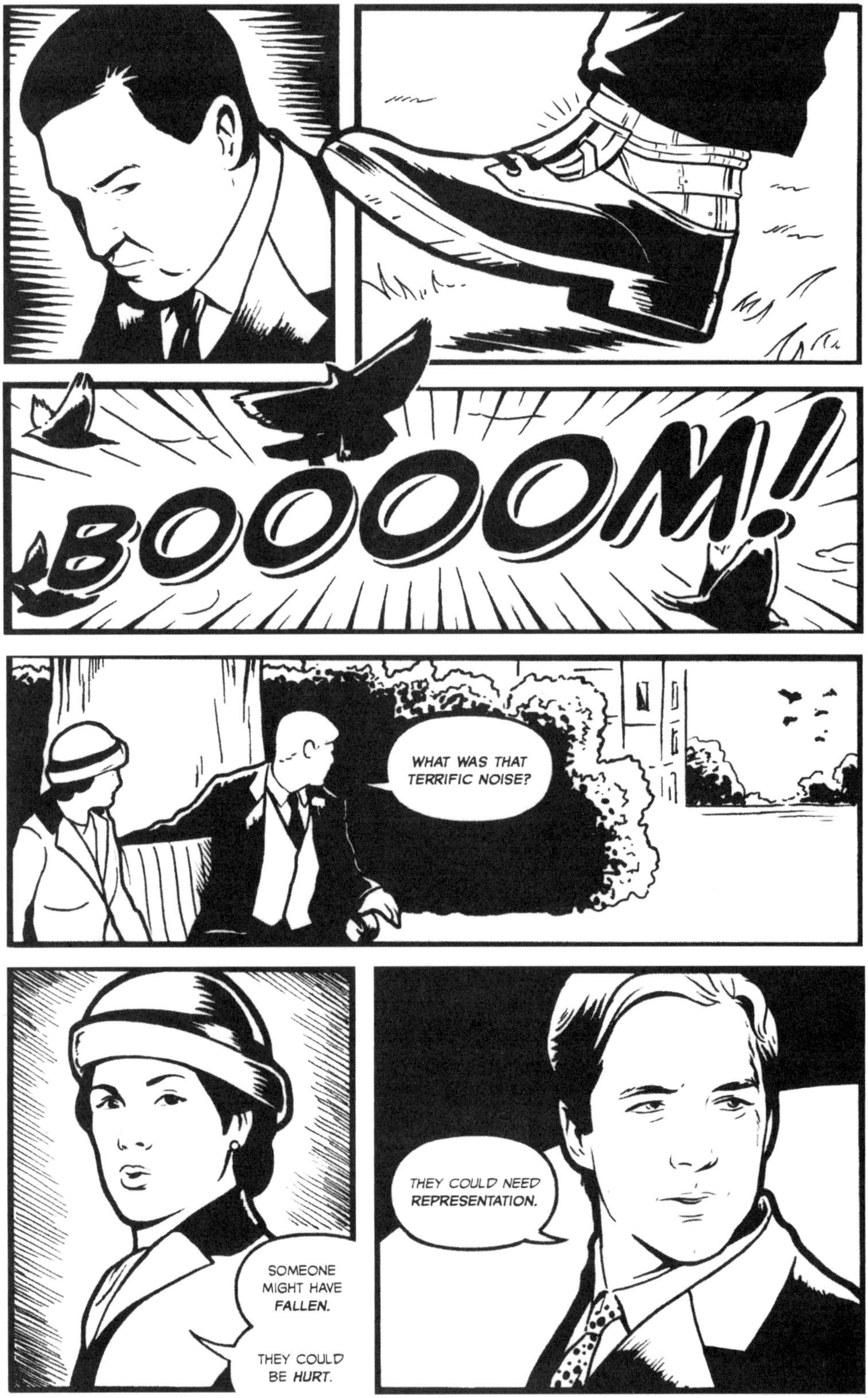
BOOOOOM!
WHAT WAS THAT TERRIFIC NOISE?
SOMEONE MIGHT HAVE FALLEN.
THEY COULD BE HURT.
THEY COULD NEED REPRESENTATION.

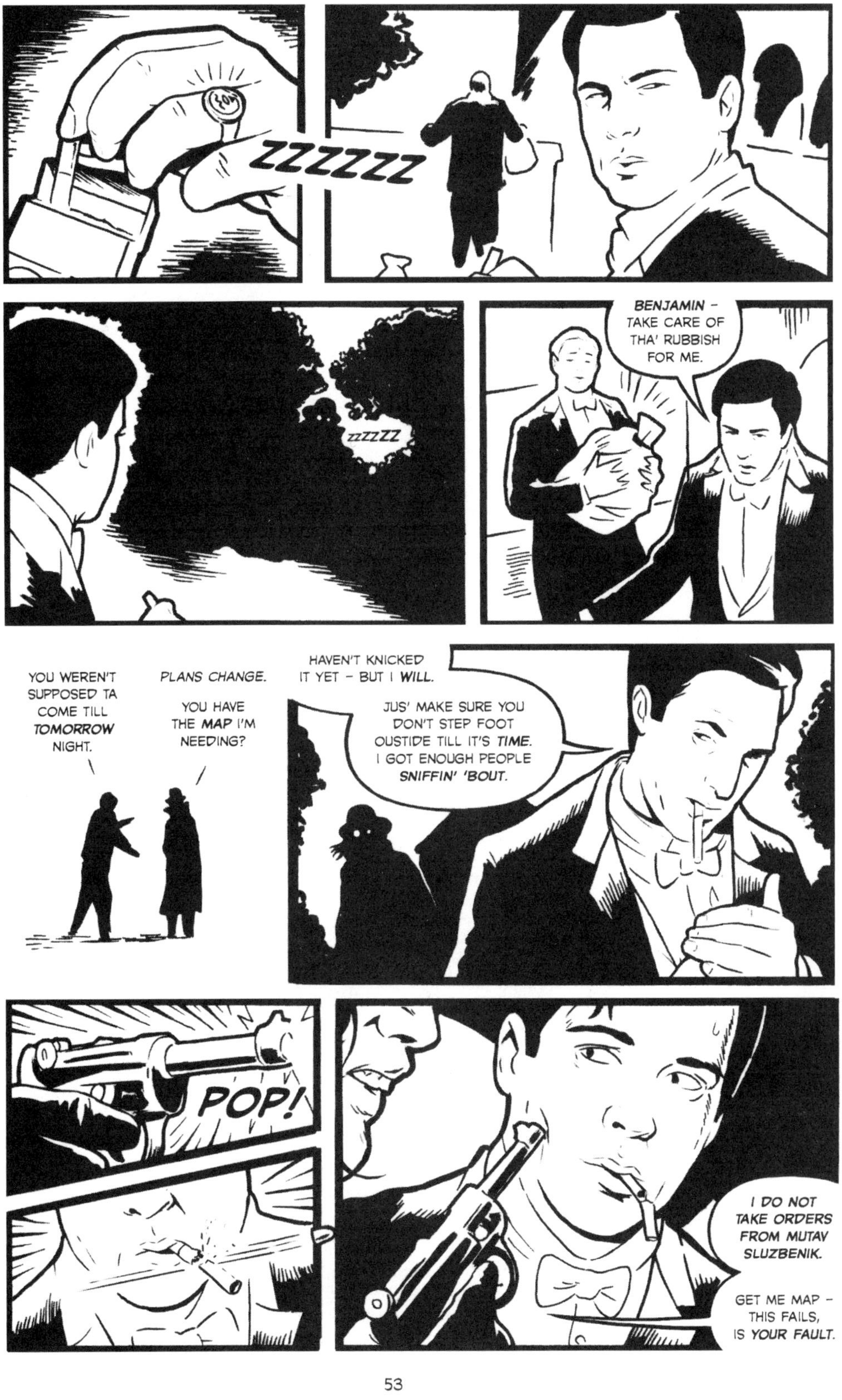
ZZZZZZZ
ZZZZZ
BENJAMIN - TAKE CARE OF THA' RUBBISH FOR ME.
YOU WEREN'T SUPPOSED TA COME TILL TOMORROW NIGHT.
PLANS CHANGE.
YOU HAVE THE MAP I'M NEEDING?
HAVEN'T KNICKED IT YET - BUT I WILL.
JUS' MAKE SURE YOU DON'T STEP FOOT OUSTIDE TILL IT'S TIME. I GOT ENOUGH PEOPLE SNIFFIN' 'BOUT.
POP!
I DO NOT TAKE ORDERS FROM MUTAV SLUZBENIK.
GET ME MAP - THIS FAILS, IS YOUR FAULT.

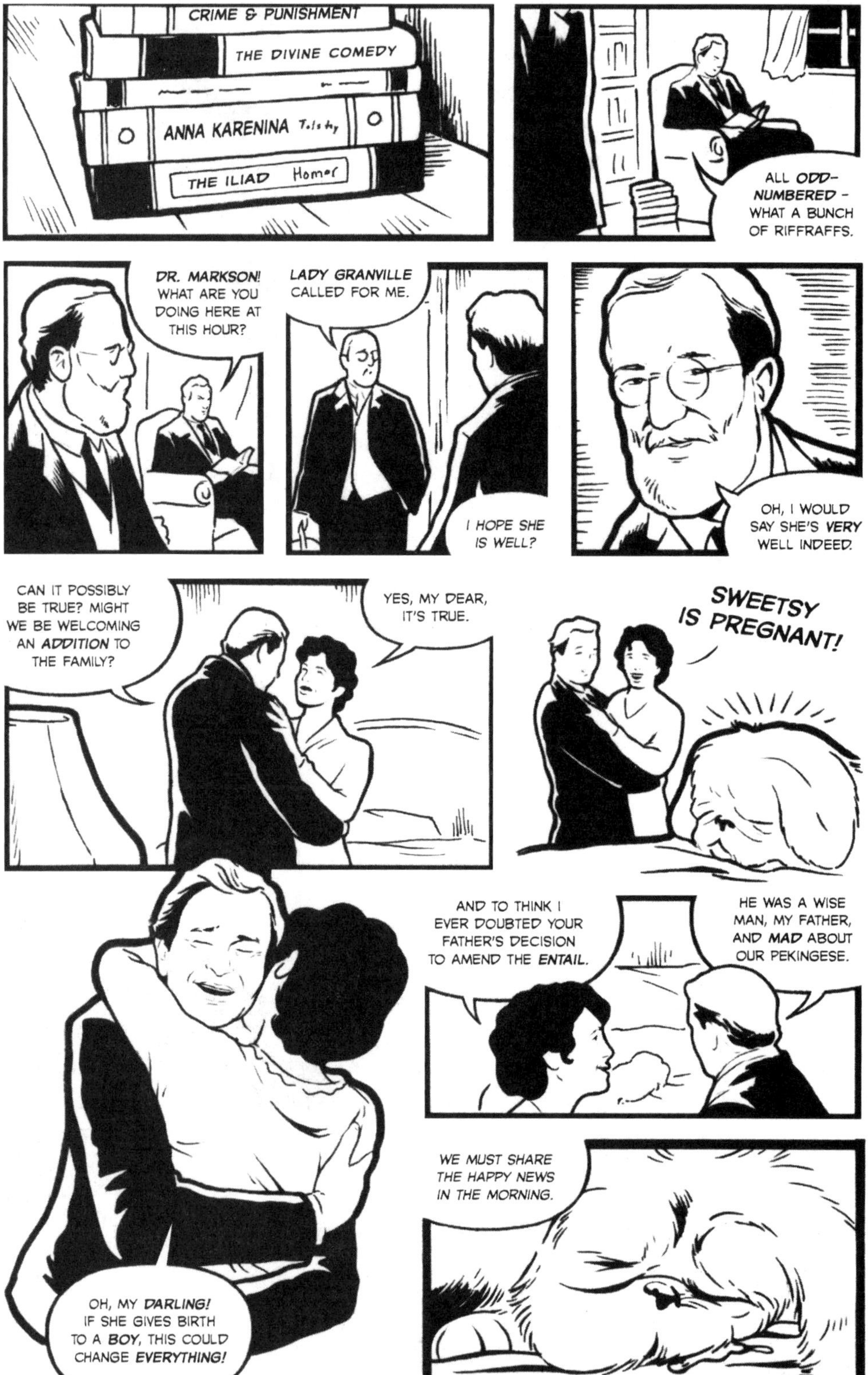
CRIME & PUNISHMENT
THE DIVINE COMEDY
ANNA KARENINA Tolstoy
THE ILIAD Homer
ALL ODD-NUMBERED - WHAT A BUNCH OF RIFFRAFFS.
DR. MARKSON! WHAT ARE YOU DOING HERE AT THIS HOUR?
LADY GRANVILLE CALLED FOR ME.
I HOPE SHE IS WELL?
OH, I WOULD SAY SHE'S VERY WELL INDEED.
CAN IT POSSIBLY BE TRUE? MIGHT WE BE WELCOMING AN ADDITION TO THE FAMILY?
YES, MY DEAR, IT'S TRUE.
SWEETSY IS PREGNANT!
AND TO THINK I EVER DOUBTED YOUR FATHER'S DECISION TO AMEND THE ENTAIL.
HE WAS A WISE MAN, MY FATHER, AND MAD ABOUT OUR PEKINGESE.
WE MUST SHARE THE HAPPY NEWS IN THE MORNING.
OH, MY DARLING! IF SHE GIVES BIRTH TO A BOY, THIS COULD CHANGE EVERYTHING!

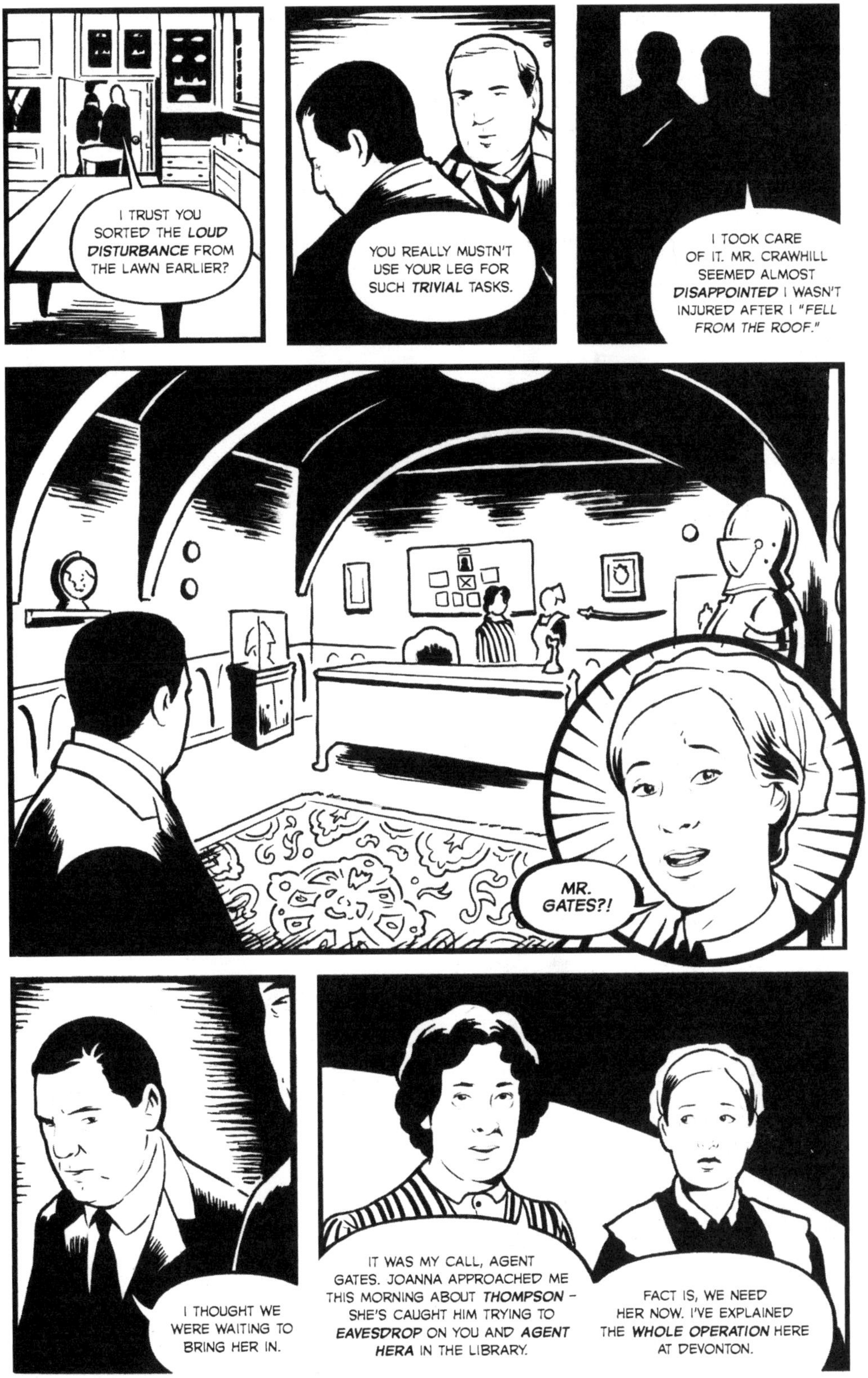
I TRUST YOU SORTED THE LOUD DISTURBANCE FROM THE LAWN EARLIER?
YOU REALLY MUSTN'T USE YOUR LEG FOR SUCH TRIVIAL TASKS.
I TOOK CARE OF IT. MR. CRAWHILL SEEMED ALMOST DISAPPOINTED I WASN'T INJURED AFTER I "FELL FROM THE ROOF."
MR. GATES?!
I THOUGHT WE WERE WAITING TO BRING HER IN.
IT WAS MY CALL, AGENT GATES. JOANNA APPROACHED ME THIS MORNING ABOUT THOMPSON – SHE'S CAUGHT HIM TRYING TO EAVESDROP ON YOU AND AGENT HERA IN THE LIBRARY.
FACT IS, WE NEED HER NOW. I'VE EXPLAINED THE WHOLE OPERATION HERE AT DEVONTON.

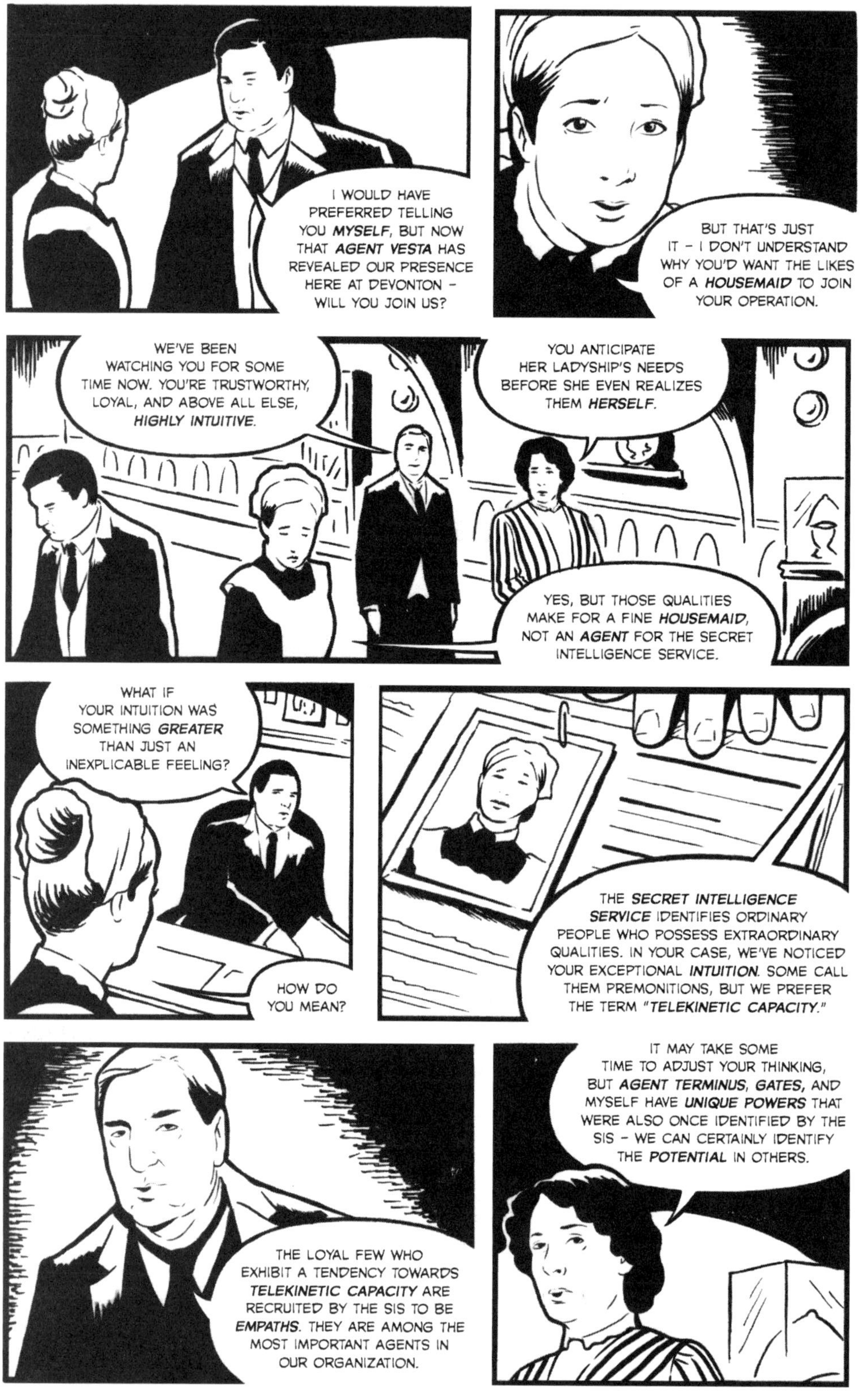
I WOULD HAVE PREFERRED TELLING YOU MYSELF, BUT NOW THAT AGENT VESTA HAS REVEALED OUR PRESENCE HERE AT DEVONTON - WILL YOU JOIN US?
BUT THAT'S JUST IT - I DON'T UNDERSTAND WHY YOU'D WANT THE LIKES OF A HOUSEMAID TO JOIN YOUR OPERATION.
WE'VE BEEN WATCHING YOU FOR SOME TIME NOW. YOU'RE TRUSTWORTHY, LOYAL, AND ABOVE ALL ELSE, HIGHLY INTUITIVE.
YOU ANTICIPATE HER LADYSHIP'S NEEDS BEFORE SHE EVEN REALIZES THEM HERSELF.
YES, BUT THOSE QUALITIES MAKE FOR A FINE HOUSEMAID, NOT AN AGENT FOR THE SECRET INTELLIGENCE SERVICE.
WHAT IF YOUR INTUITION WAS SOMETHING GREATER THAN JUST AN INEXPLICABLE FEELING?
HOW DO YOU MEAN?
THE SECRET INTELLIGENCE SERVICE IDENTIFIES ORDINARY PEOPLE WHO POSSESS EXTRAORDINARY QUALITIES. IN YOUR CASE, WE'VE NOTICED YOUR EXCEPTIONAL INTUITION. SOME CALL THEM PREMONITIONS, BUT WE PREFER THE TERM "TELEKINETIC CAPACITY."
THE LOYAL FEW WHO EXHIBIT A TENDENCY TOWARDS TELEKINETIC CAPACITY ARE RECRUITED BY THE SIS TO BE EMPATHS. THEY ARE AMONG THE MOST IMPORTANT AGENTS IN OUR ORGANIZATION.
IT MAY TAKE SOME TIME TO ADJUST YOUR THINKING, BUT AGENT TERMINUS, GATES, AND MYSELF HAVE UNIQUE POWERS THAT WERE ALSO ONCE IDENTIFIED BY THE SIS - WE CAN CERTAINLY IDENTIFY THE POTENTIAL IN OTHERS.

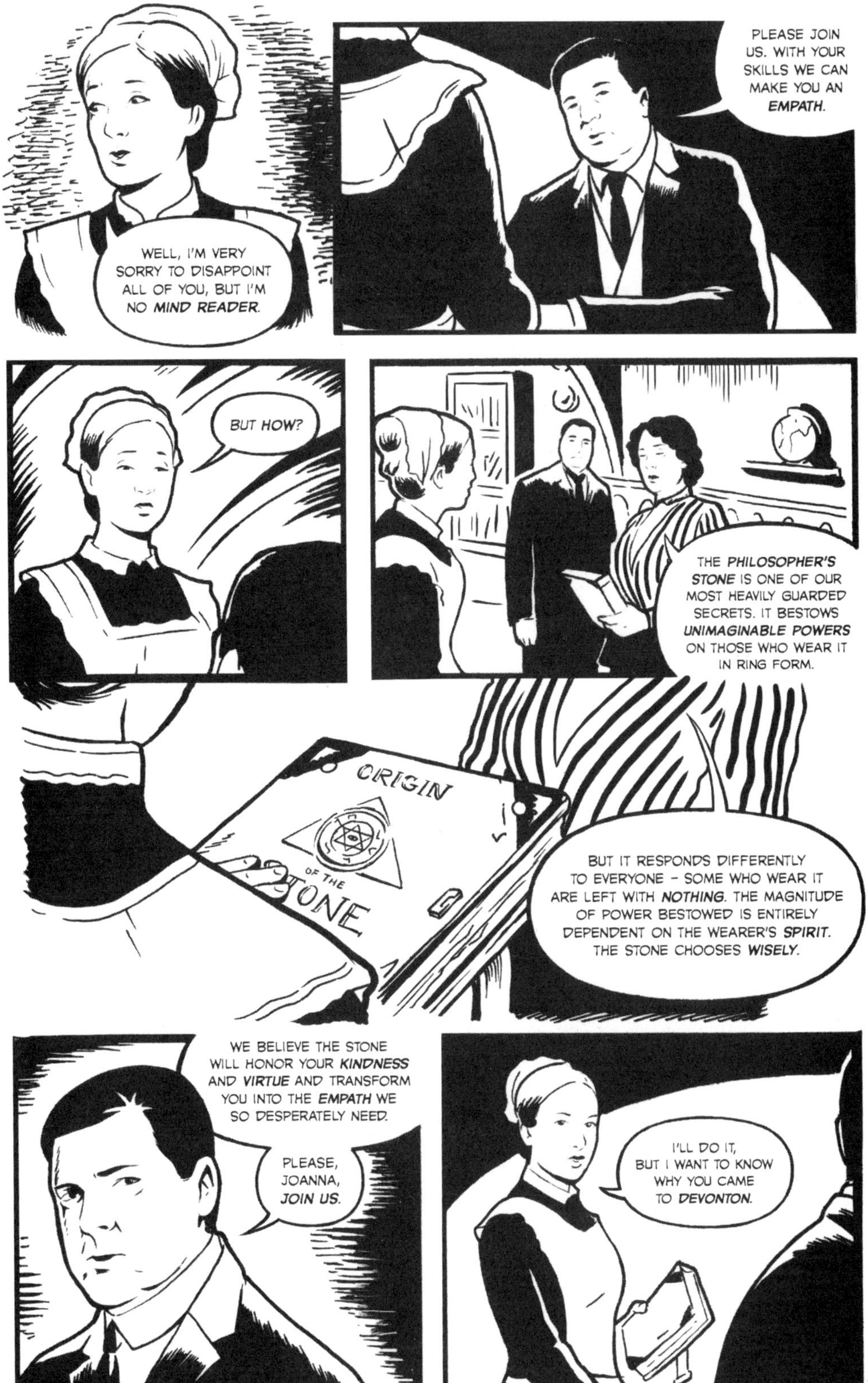
WELL, I'M VERY SORRY TO DISAPPOINT ALL OF YOU, BUT I'M NO MIND READER.
PLEASE JOIN US. WITH YOUR SKILLS WE CAN MAKE YOU AN EMPATH.
BUT HOW?
THE PHILOSOPHER'S STONE IS ONE OF OUR MOST HEAVILY GUARDED SECRETS. IT BESTOWS UNIMAGINABLE POWERS ON THOSE WHO WEAR IT IN RING FORM.
ORIGIN OF THE STONE
BUT IT RESPONDS DIFFERENTLY TO EVERYONE - SOME WHO WEAR IT ARE LEFT WITH NOTHING. THE MAGNITUDE OF POWER BESTOWED IS ENTIRELY DEPENDENT ON THE WEARER'S SPIRIT. THE STONE CHOOSES WISELY.
WE BELIEVE THE STONE WILL HONOR YOUR KINDNESS AND VIRTUE AND TRANSFORM YOU INTO THE EMPATH WE SO DESPERATELY NEED.
PLEASE, JOANNA, JOIN US.
I'LL DO IT, BUT I WANT TO KNOW WHY YOU CAME TO DEVONTON.

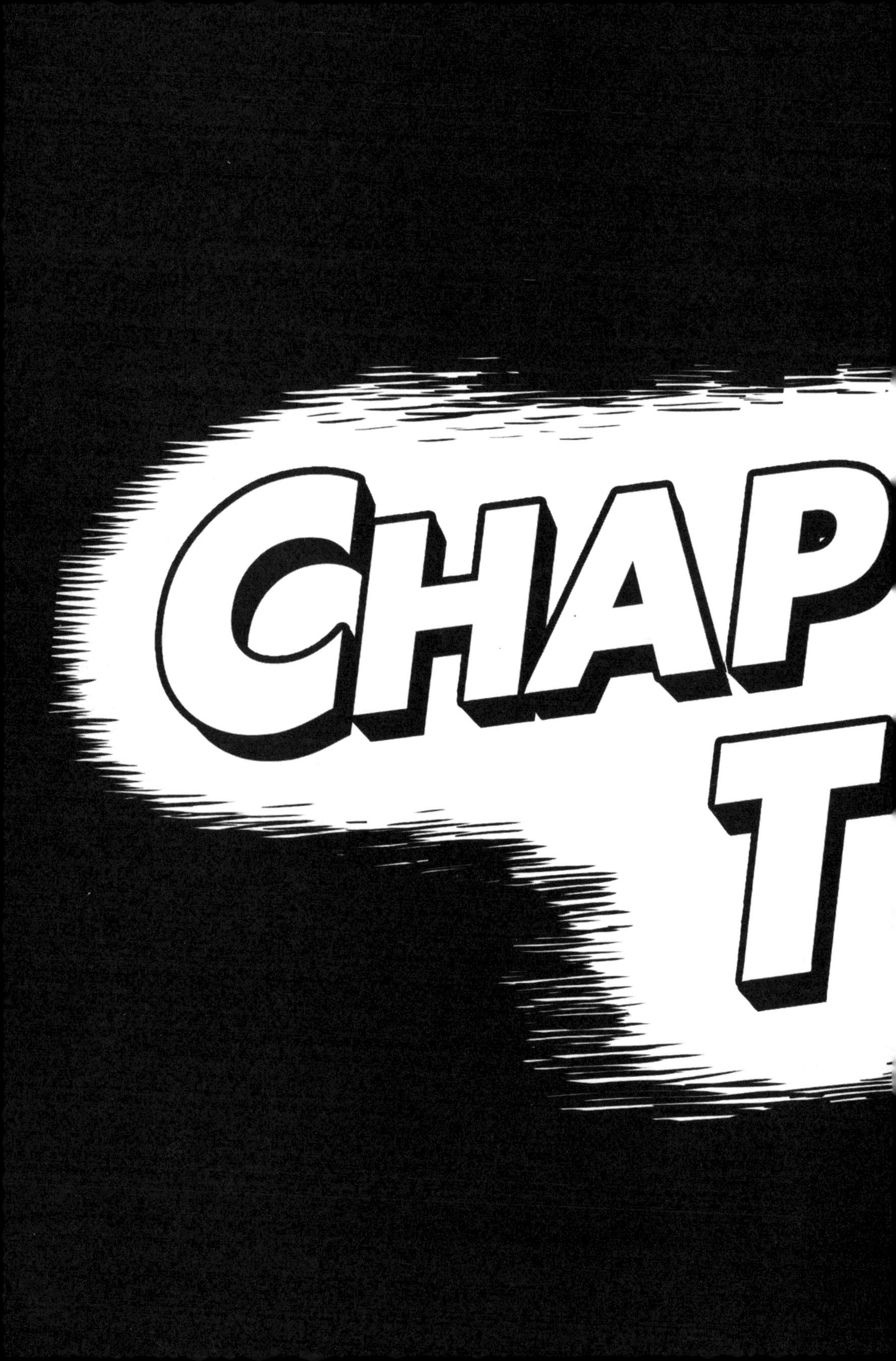
CHAP
T

TER
HREE

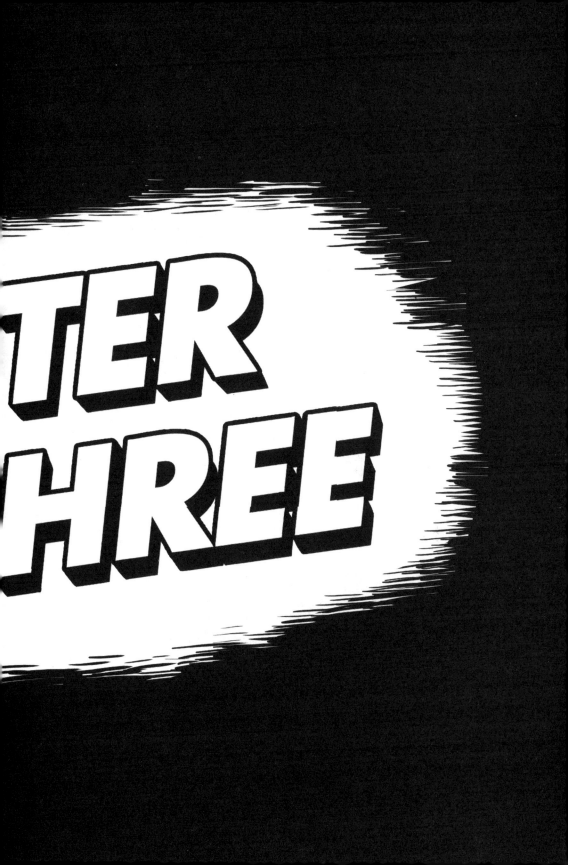

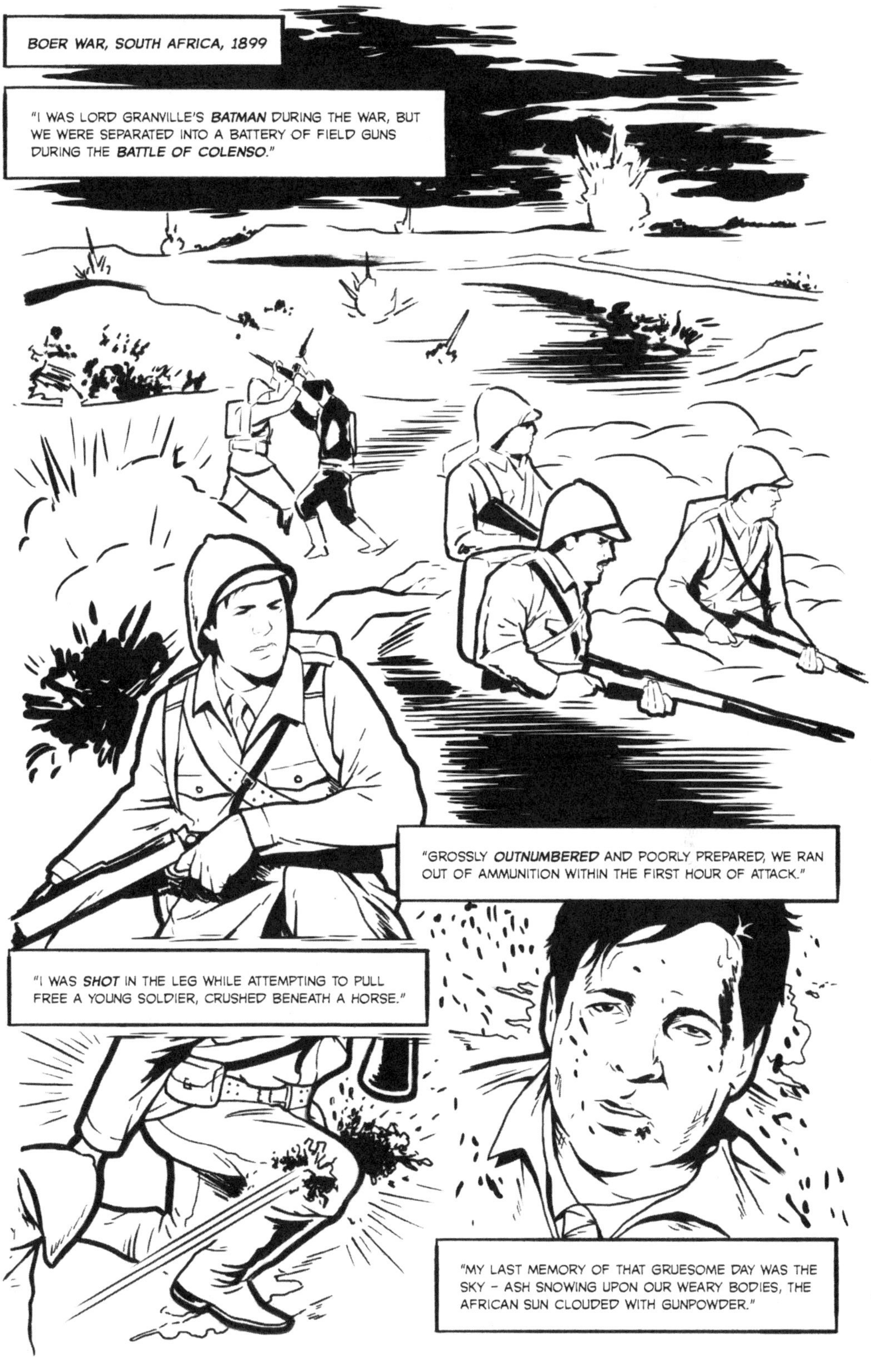
BOER WAR, SOUTH AFRICA, 1899
"I WAS LORD GRANVILLE'S BATMAN DURING THE WAR, BUT WE WERE SEPARATED INTO A BATTERY OF FIELD GUNS DURING THE BATTLE OF COLENSO."
"GROSSLY OUTNUMBERED AND POORLY PREPARED, WE RAN OUT OF AMMUNITION WITHIN THE FIRST HOUR OF ATTACK."
"I WAS SHOT IN THE LEG WHILE ATTEMPTING TO PULL FREE A YOUNG SOLDIER, CRUSHED BENEATH A HORSE."
"MY LAST MEMORY OF THAT GRUESOME DAY WAS THE SKY - ASH SNOWING UPON OUR WEARY BODIES, THE AFRICAN SUN CLOUDED WITH GUNPOWDER."

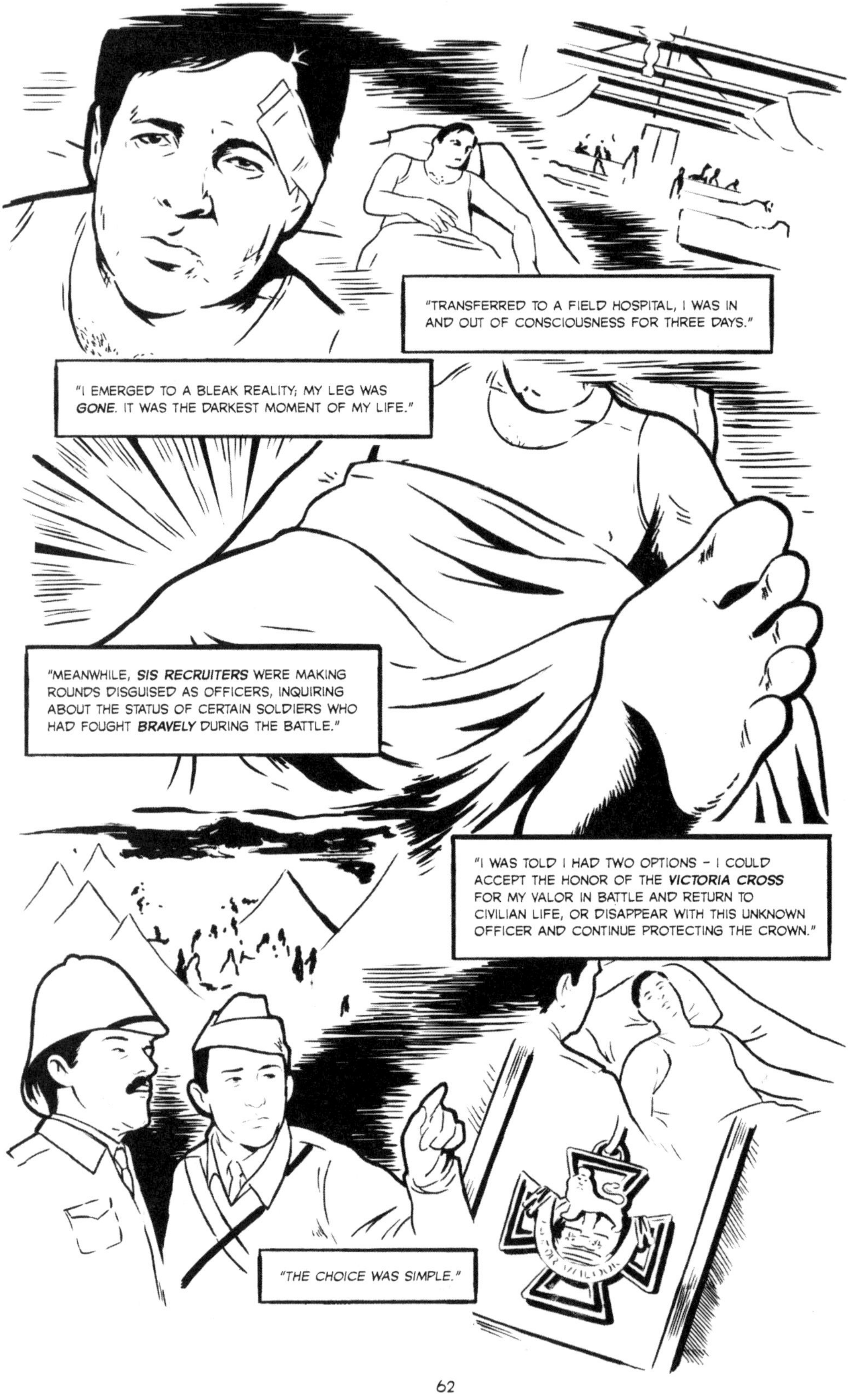
"TRANSFERRED TO A FIELD HOSPITAL, I WAS IN AND OUT OF CONSCIOUSNESS FOR THREE DAYS."
"I EMERGED TO A BLEAK REALITY; MY LEG WAS *GONE*. IT WAS THE DARKEST MOMENT OF MY LIFE."
"MEANWHILE, ***SIS RECRUITERS*** WERE MAKING ROUNDS DISGUISED AS OFFICERS, INQUIRING ABOUT THE STATUS OF CERTAIN SOLDIERS WHO HAD FOUGHT ***BRAVELY*** DURING THE BATTLE."
"I WAS TOLD I HAD TWO OPTIONS – I COULD ACCEPT THE HONOR OF THE ***VICTORIA CROSS*** FOR MY VALOR IN BATTLE AND RETURN TO CIVILIAN LIFE, OR DISAPPEAR WITH THIS UNKNOWN OFFICER AND CONTINUE PROTECTING THE CROWN."
"THE CHOICE WAS SIMPLE."

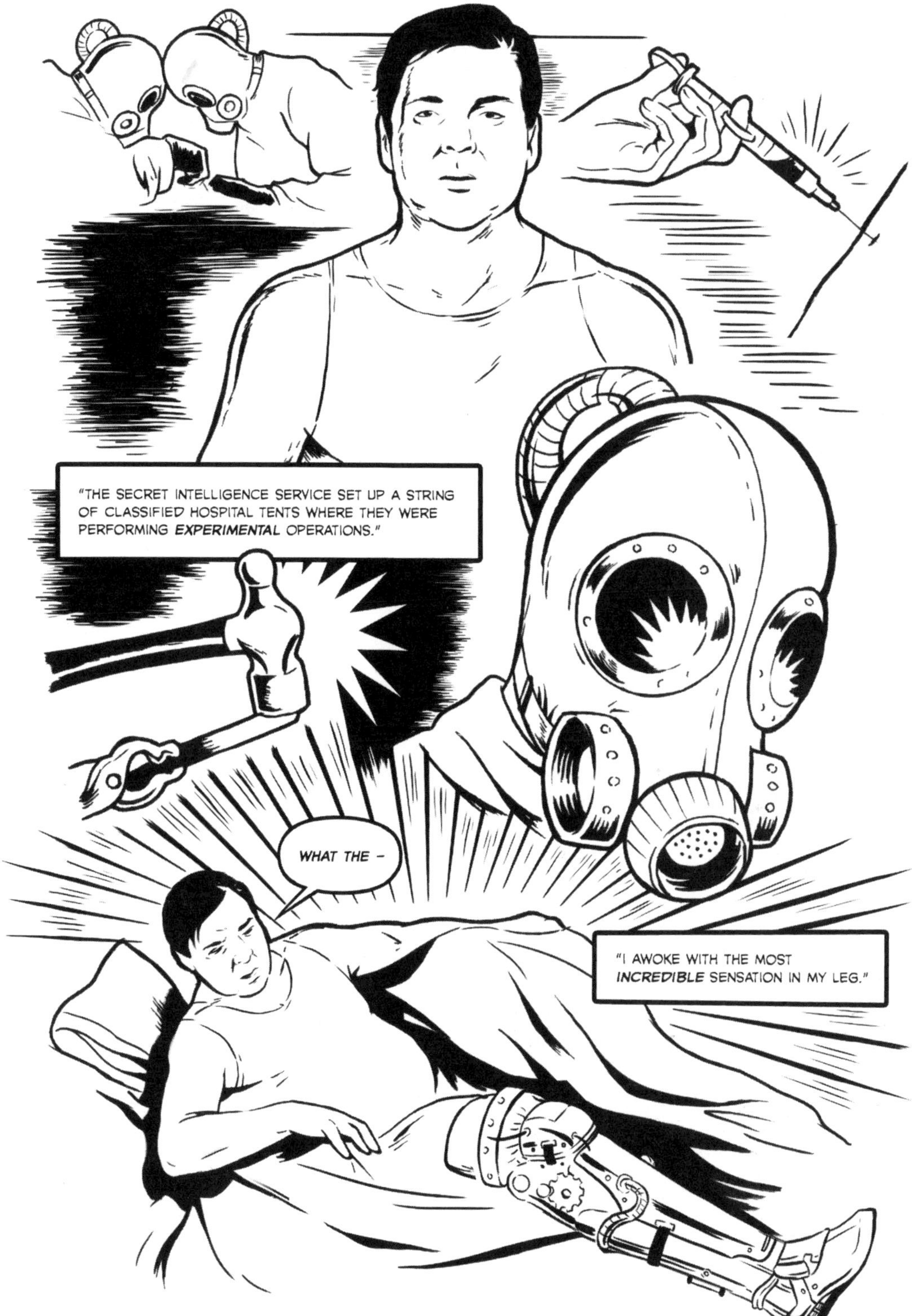
"THE SECRET INTELLIGENCE SERVICE SET UP A STRING OF CLASSIFIED HOSPITAL TENTS WHERE THEY WERE PERFORMING EXPERIMENTAL OPERATIONS."
WHAT THE –
"I AWOKE WITH THE MOST INCREDIBLE SENSATION IN MY LEG."

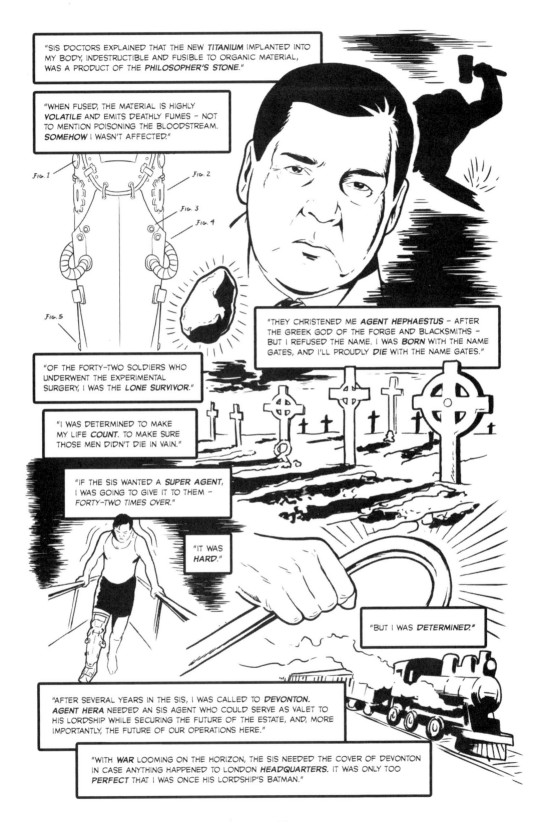

"SIS DOCTORS EXPLAINED THAT THE NEW *TITANIUM* IMPLANTED INTO MY BODY, INDESTRUCTIBLE AND FUSIBLE TO ORGANIC MATERIAL, WAS A PRODUCT OF THE *PHILOSOPHER'S STONE.*"

"WHEN FUSED, THE MATERIAL IS HIGHLY *VOLATILE* AND EMITS DEATHLY FUMES – NOT TO MENTION POISONING THE BLOODSTREAM. *SOMEHOW* I WASN'T AFFECTED."

"THEY CHRISTENED ME *AGENT HEPHAESTUS* – AFTER THE GREEK GOD OF THE FORGE AND BLACKSMITHS – BUT I REFUSED THE NAME. I WAS *BORN* WITH THE NAME GATES, AND I'LL PROUDLY *DIE* WITH THE NAME GATES."

"OF THE FORTY-TWO SOLDIERS WHO UNDERWENT THE EXPERIMENTAL SURGERY, I WAS THE *LONE SURVIVOR.*"

"I WAS DETERMINED TO MAKE MY LIFE *COUNT.* TO MAKE SURE THOSE MEN DIDN'T DIE IN VAIN."

"IF THE SIS WANTED A *SUPER AGENT,* I WAS GOING TO GIVE IT TO THEM – FORTY-TWO TIMES OVER."

"IT WAS *HARD.*"

"BUT I WAS *DETERMINED.*"

"AFTER SEVERAL YEARS IN THE SIS, I WAS CALLED TO *DEVONTON.* *AGENT HERA* NEEDED AN SIS AGENT WHO COULD SERVE AS VALET TO HIS LORDSHIP WHILE SECURING THE FUTURE OF THE ESTATE, AND, MORE IMPORTANTLY, THE FUTURE OF OUR OPERATIONS HERE."

"WITH *WAR* LOOMING ON THE HORIZON, THE SIS NEEDED THE COVER OF DEVONTON IN CASE ANYTHING HAPPENED TO LONDON *HEADQUARTERS.* IT WAS ONLY TOO *PERFECT* THAT I WAS ONCE HIS LORDSHIP'S BATMAN."

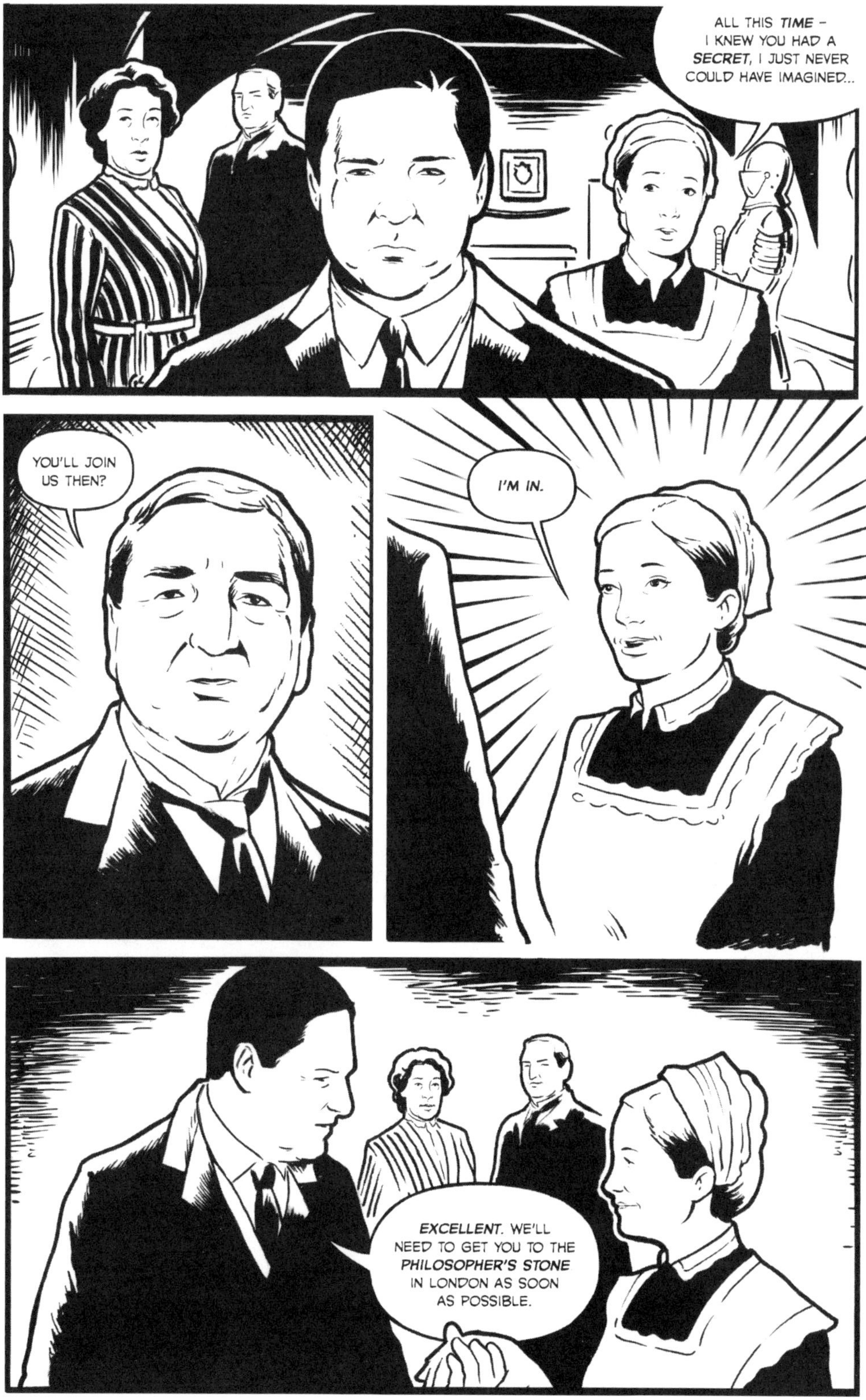
ALL THIS *TIME* – I KNEW YOU HAD A *SECRET*, I JUST NEVER COULD HAVE IMAGINED...
YOU'LL JOIN US THEN?
I'M IN.
EXCELLENT. WE'LL NEED TO GET YOU TO THE *PHILOSOPHER'S STONE* IN LONDON AS SOON AS POSSIBLE.

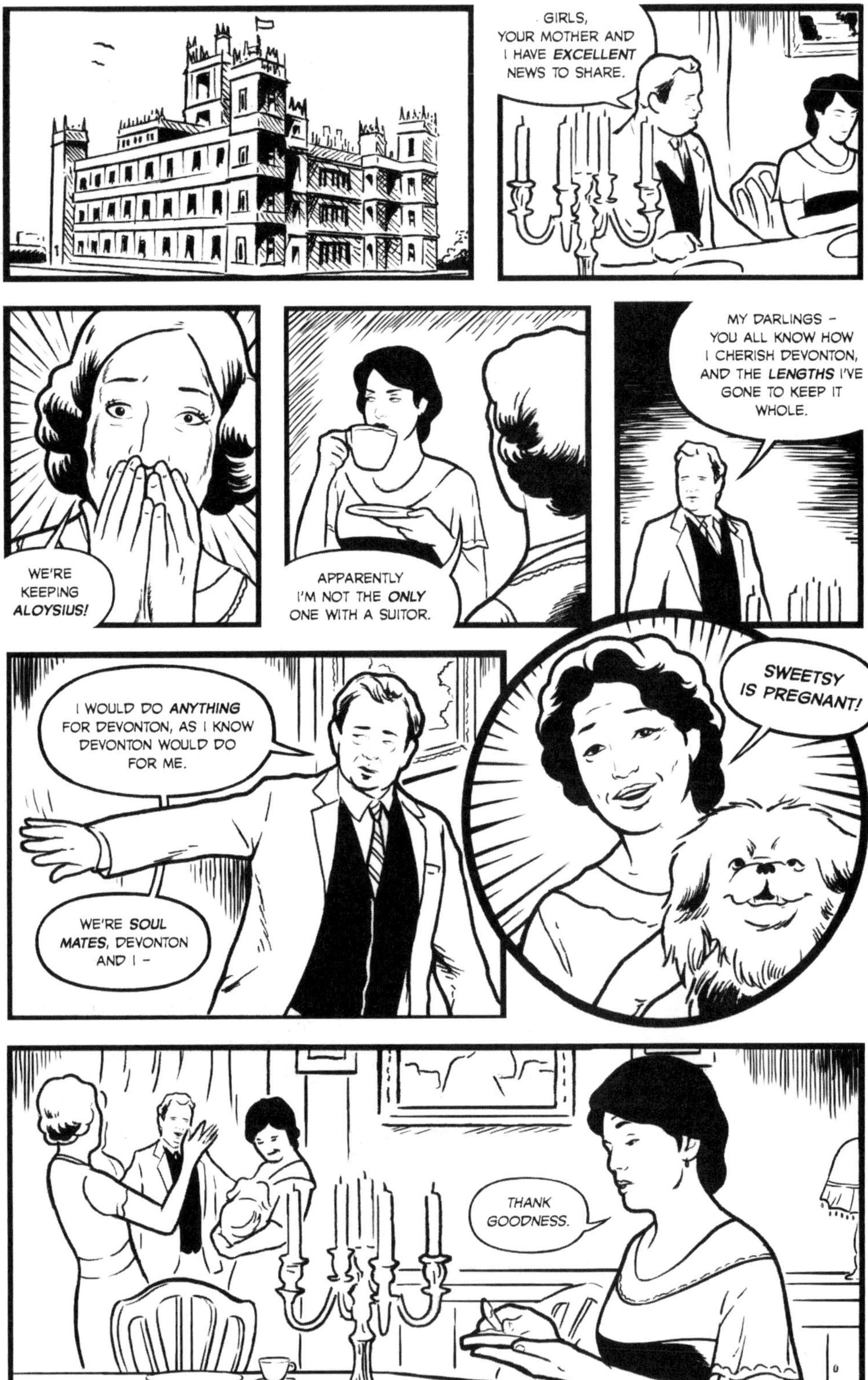
GIRLS,
YOUR MOTHER AND I HAVE EXCELLENT NEWS TO SHARE.
WE'RE KEEPING ALOYSIUS!
APPARENTLY I'M NOT THE ONLY ONE WITH A SUITOR.
MY DARLINGS - YOU ALL KNOW HOW I CHERISH DEVONTON, AND THE LENGTHS I'VE GONE TO KEEP IT WHOLE.
I WOULD DO ANYTHING FOR DEVONTON, AS I KNOW DEVONTON WOULD DO FOR ME.
WE'RE SOUL MATES, DEVONTON AND I -
SWEETSY IS PREGNANT!
THANK GOODNESS.

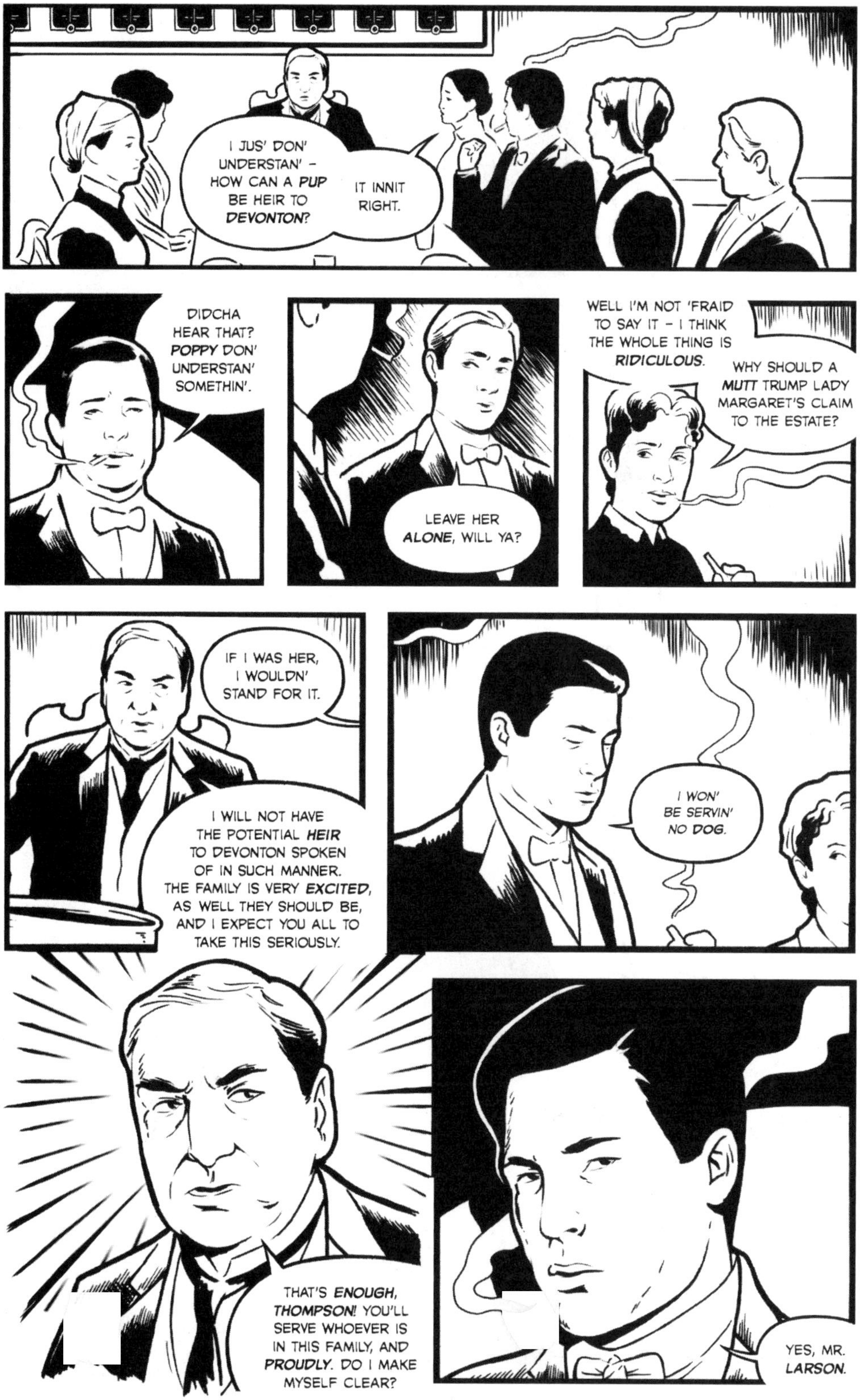

I JUS' DON' UNDERSTAN' – HOW CAN A PUP BE HEIR TO DEVONTON?
IT INNIT RIGHT.
DIDCHA HEAR THAT? POPPY DON' UNDERSTAN' SOMETHIN'.
LEAVE HER ALONE, WILL YA?
WELL I'M NOT 'FRAID TO SAY IT – I THINK THE WHOLE THING IS RIDICULOUS.
WHY SHOULD A MUTT TRUMP LADY MARGARET'S CLAIM TO THE ESTATE?
IF I WAS HER, I WOULDN' STAND FOR IT.
I WILL NOT HAVE THE POTENTIAL HEIR TO DEVONTON SPOKEN OF IN SUCH MANNER. THE FAMILY IS VERY EXCITED, AS WELL THEY SHOULD BE, AND I EXPECT YOU ALL TO TAKE THIS SERIOUSLY.
I WON' BE SERVIN' NO DOG.
THAT'S ENOUGH, THOMPSON! YOU'LL SERVE WHOEVER IS IN THIS FAMILY, AND PROUDLY. DO I MAKE MYSELF CLEAR?
YES, MR. LARSON.

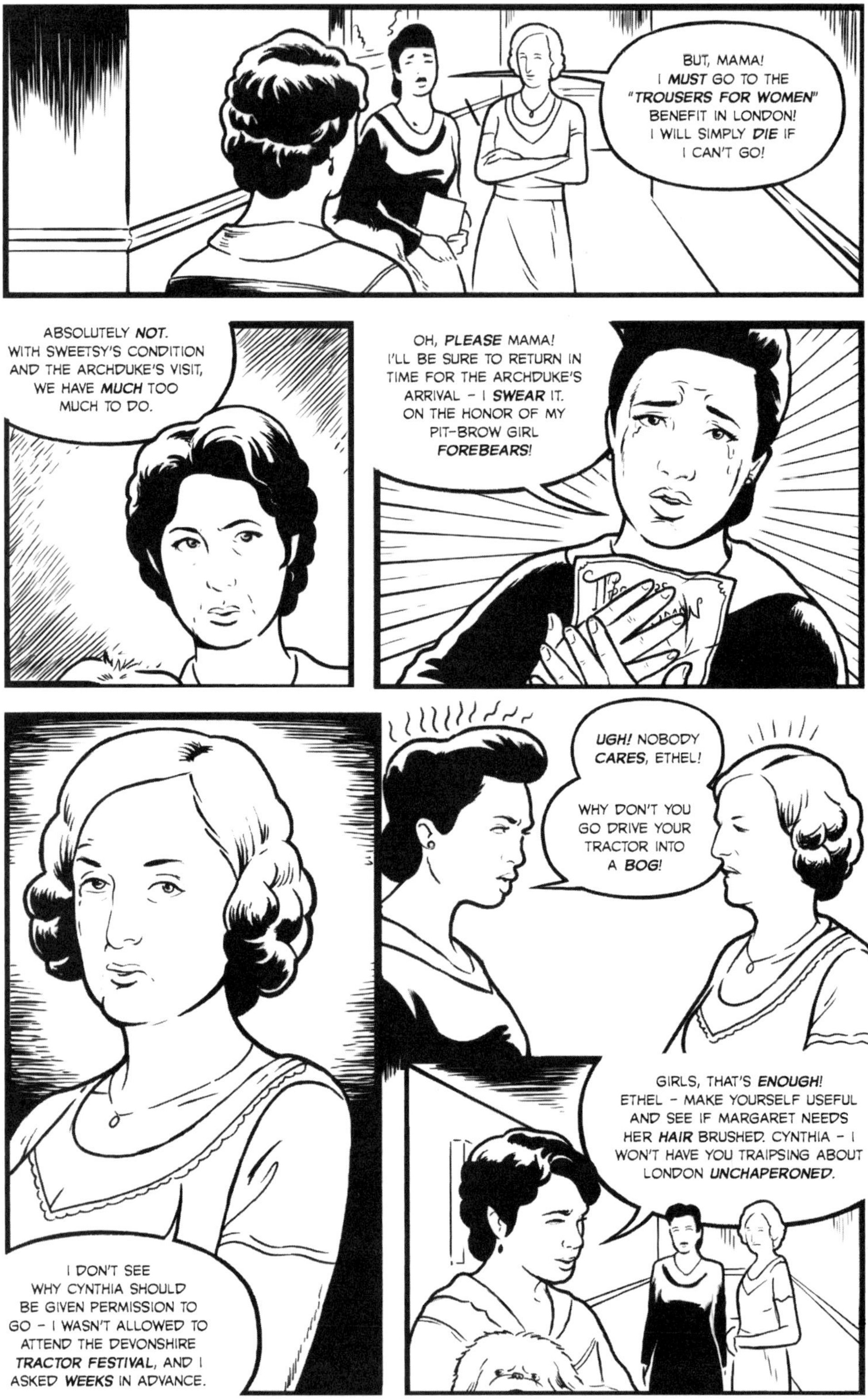
BUT, MAMA! I MUST GO TO THE "TROUSERS FOR WOMEN" BENEFIT IN LONDON! I WILL SIMPLY DIE IF I CAN'T GO!
ABSOLUTELY NOT. WITH SWEETSY'S CONDITION AND THE ARCHDUKE'S VISIT, WE HAVE MUCH TOO MUCH TO DO.
OH, PLEASE MAMA! I'LL BE SURE TO RETURN IN TIME FOR THE ARCHDUKE'S ARRIVAL - I SWEAR IT. ON THE HONOR OF MY PIT-BROW GIRL FOREBEARS!
I DON'T SEE WHY CYNTHIA SHOULD BE GIVEN PERMISSION TO GO - I WASN'T ALLOWED TO ATTEND THE DEVONSHIRE TRACTOR FESTIVAL, AND I ASKED WEEKS IN ADVANCE.
UGH! NOBODY CARES, ETHEL!
WHY DON'T YOU GO DRIVE YOUR TRACTOR INTO A BOG!
GIRLS, THAT'S ENOUGH! ETHEL - MAKE YOURSELF USEFUL AND SEE IF MARGARET NEEDS HER HAIR BRUSHED. CYNTHIA - I WON'T HAVE YOU TRAIPSING ABOUT LONDON UNCHAPERONED.

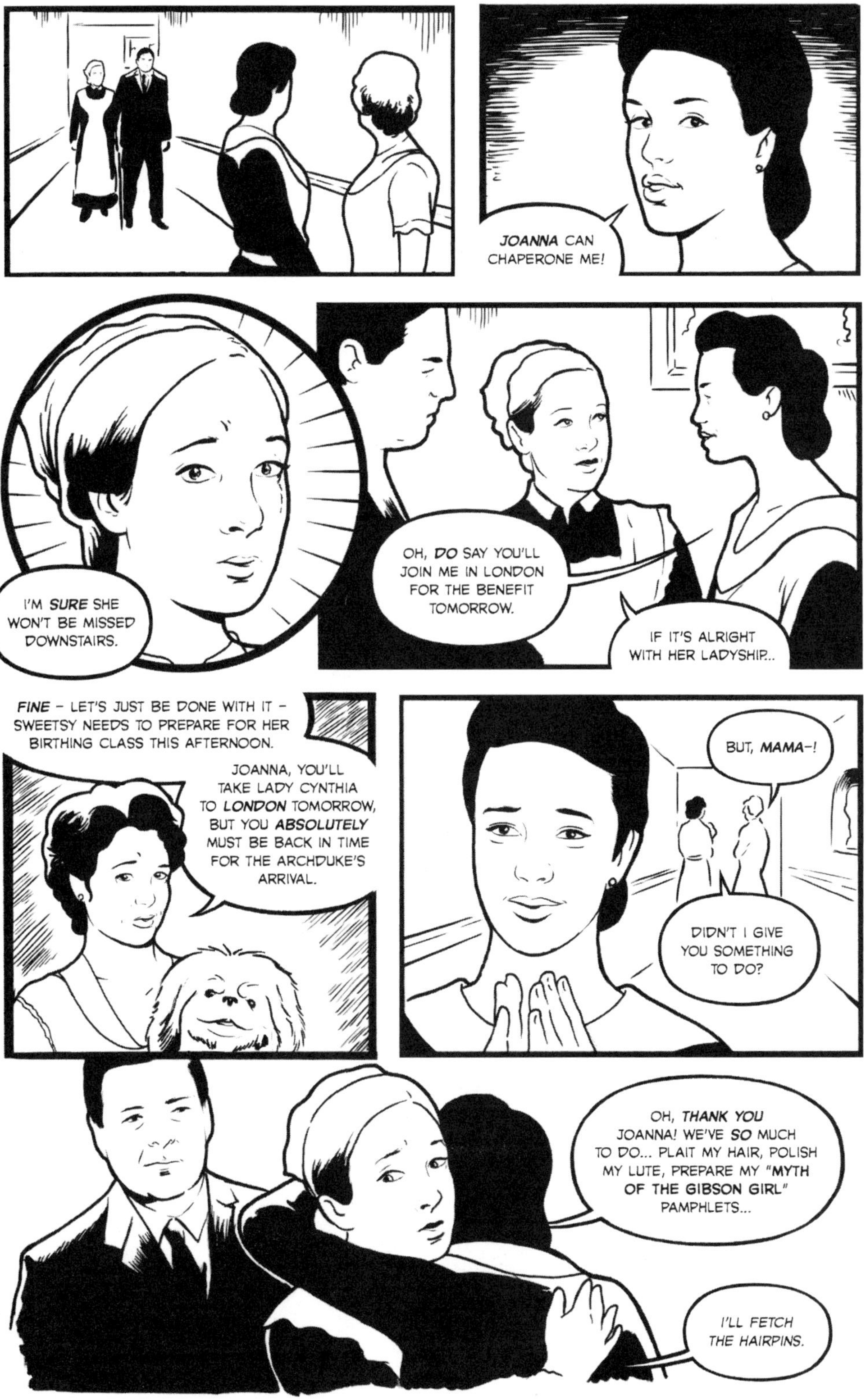
JOANNA CAN CHAPERONE ME!
OH, DO SAY YOU'LL JOIN ME IN LONDON FOR THE BENEFIT TOMORROW.
I'M SURE SHE WON'T BE MISSED DOWNSTAIRS.
IF IT'S ALRIGHT WITH HER LADYSHIP...
FINE - LET'S JUST BE DONE WITH IT - SWEETSY NEEDS TO PREPARE FOR HER BIRTHING CLASS THIS AFTERNOON.
JOANNA, YOU'LL TAKE LADY CYNTHIA TO LONDON TOMORROW, BUT YOU ABSOLUTELY MUST BE BACK IN TIME FOR THE ARCHDUKE'S ARRIVAL.
BUT, MAMA-!
DIDN'T I GIVE YOU SOMETHING TO DO?
OH, THANK YOU JOANNA! WE'VE SO MUCH TO DO... PLAIT MY HAIR, POLISH MY LUTE, PREPARE MY "MYTH OF THE GIBSON GIRL" PAMPHLETS...
I'LL FETCH THE HAIRPINS.

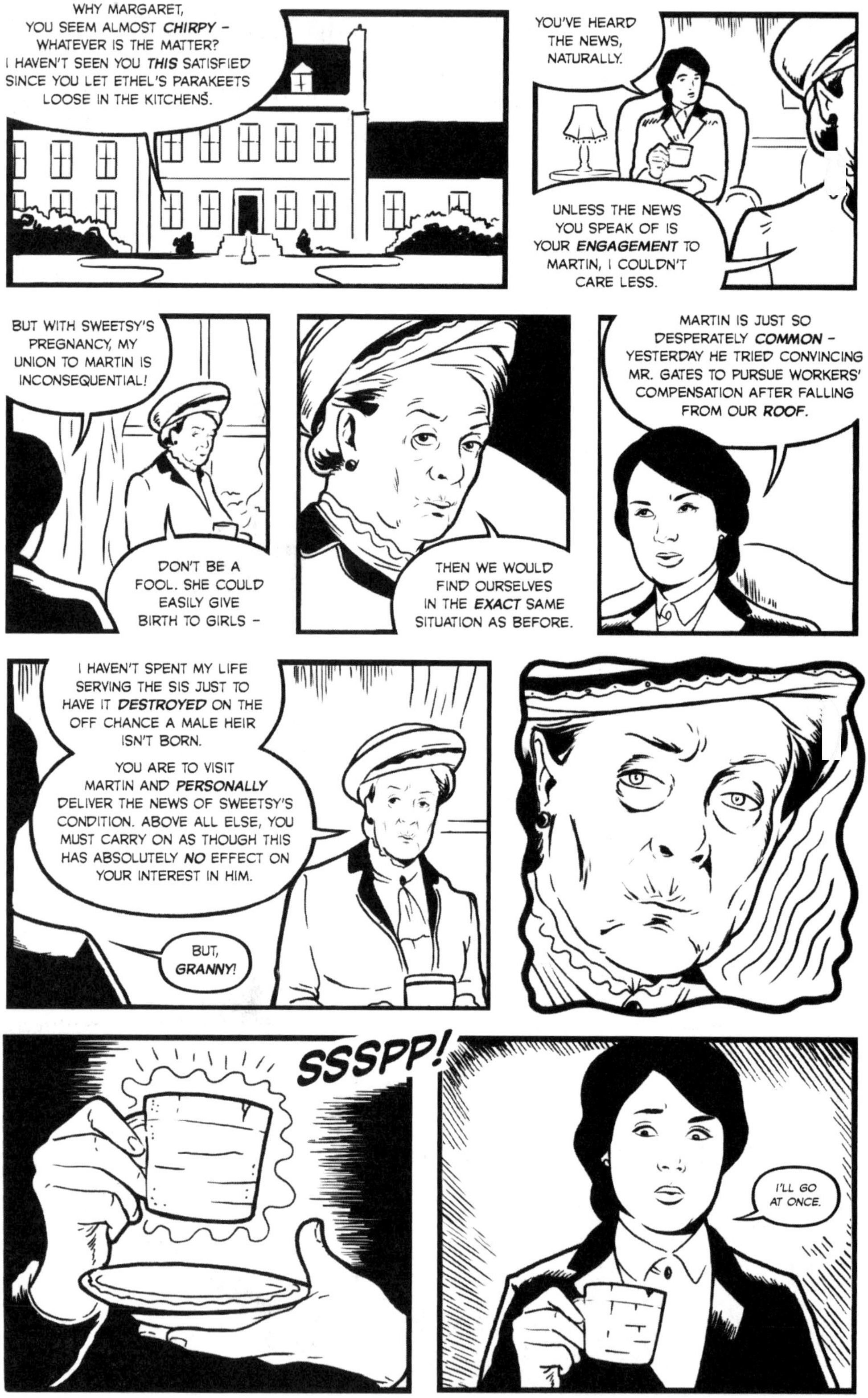
WHY MARGARET, YOU SEEM ALMOST CHIRPY – WHATEVER IS THE MATTER? I HAVEN'T SEEN YOU THIS SATISFIED SINCE YOU LET ETHEL'S PARAKEETS LOOSE IN THE KITCHENS.
YOU'VE HEARD THE NEWS, NATURALLY.
UNLESS THE NEWS YOU SPEAK OF IS YOUR ENGAGEMENT TO MARTIN, I COULDN'T CARE LESS.
BUT WITH SWEETSY'S PREGNANCY, MY UNION TO MARTIN IS INCONSEQUENTIAL!
DON'T BE A FOOL. SHE COULD EASILY GIVE BIRTH TO GIRLS –
THEN WE WOULD FIND OURSELVES IN THE EXACT SAME SITUATION AS BEFORE.
MARTIN IS JUST SO DESPERATELY COMMON – YESTERDAY HE TRIED CONVINCING MR. GATES TO PURSUE WORKERS' COMPENSATION AFTER FALLING FROM OUR ROOF.
I HAVEN'T SPENT MY LIFE SERVING THE SIS JUST TO HAVE IT DESTROYED ON THE OFF CHANCE A MALE HEIR ISN'T BORN.
YOU ARE TO VISIT MARTIN AND PERSONALLY DELIVER THE NEWS OF SWEETSY'S CONDITION. ABOVE ALL ELSE, YOU MUST CARRY ON AS THOUGH THIS HAS ABSOLUTELY NO EFFECT ON YOUR INTEREST IN HIM.
BUT, GRANNY!
SSSPP!
I'LL GO AT ONCE.

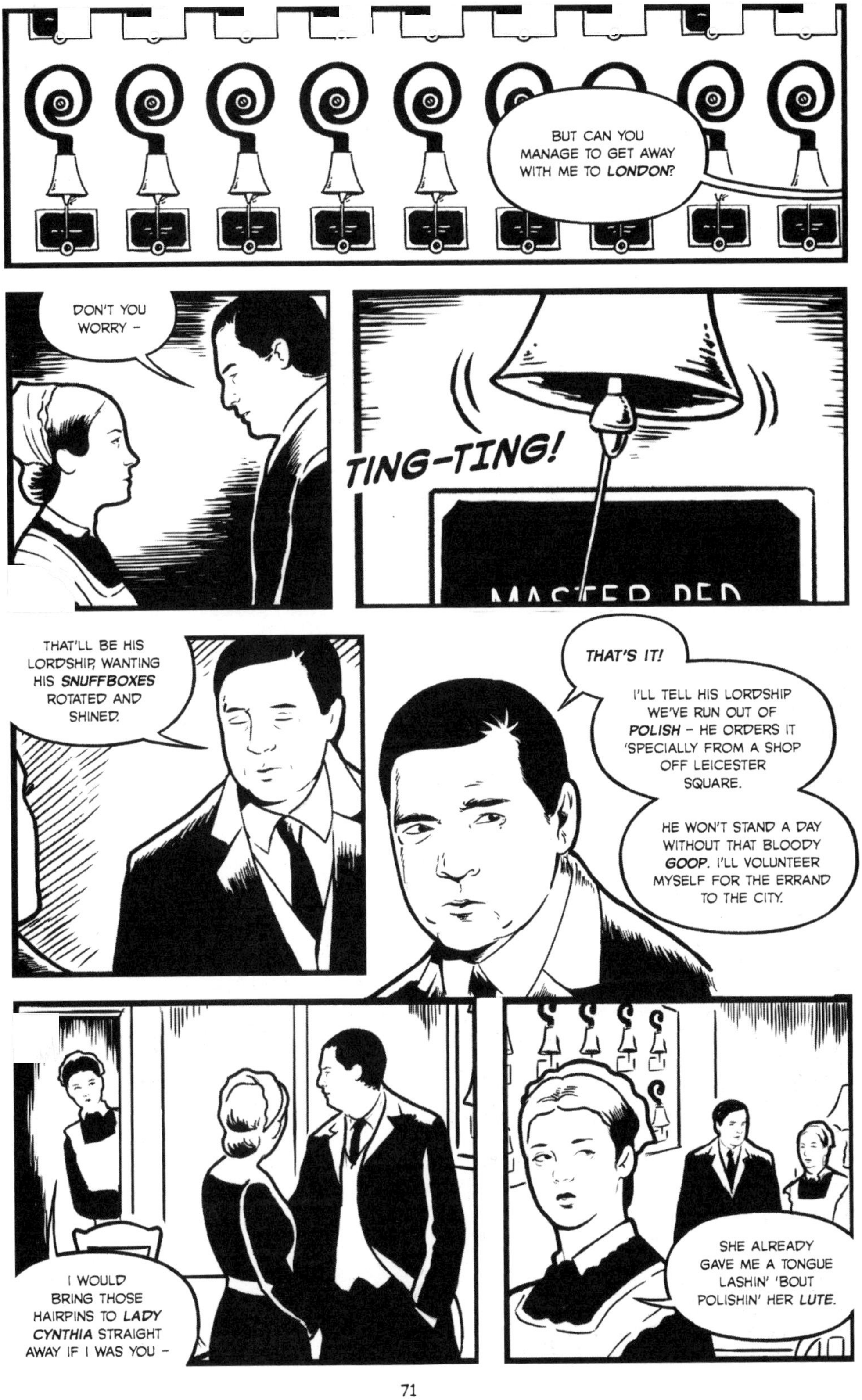
BUT CAN YOU MANAGE TO GET AWAY WITH ME TO LONDON?
DON'T YOU WORRY -
TING-TING!
THAT'LL BE HIS LORDSHIP, WANTING HIS SNUFFBOXES ROTATED AND SHINED.
THAT'S IT!
I'LL TELL HIS LORDSHIP WE'VE RUN OUT OF POLISH - HE ORDERS IT 'SPECIALLY FROM A SHOP OFF LEICESTER SQUARE.
HE WON'T STAND A DAY WITHOUT THAT BLOODY GOOP. I'LL VOLUNTEER MYSELF FOR THE ERRAND TO THE CITY.
I WOULD BRING THOSE HAIRPINS TO LADY CYNTHIA STRAIGHT AWAY IF I WAS YOU -
SHE ALREADY GAVE ME A TONGUE LASHIN' 'BOUT POLISHIN' HER LUTE.

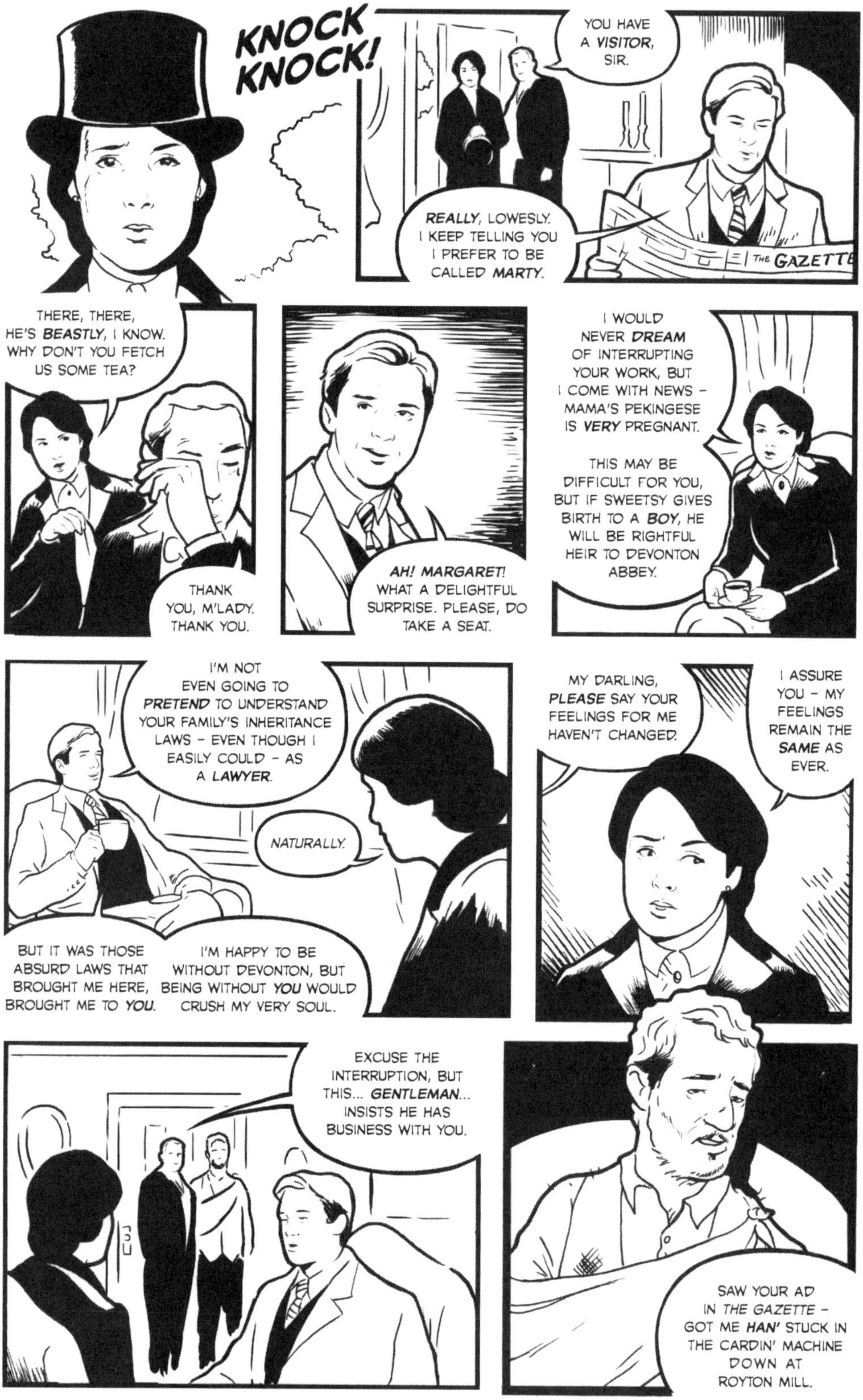
KNOCK KNOCK!
YOU HAVE A *VISITOR*, SIR.
REALLY, LOWESLY. I KEEP TELLING YOU I PREFER TO BE CALLED *MARTY*.
THE GAZETTE
THERE, THERE, HE'S *BEASTLY*, I KNOW. WHY DON'T YOU FETCH US SOME TEA?
THANK YOU, M'LADY. THANK YOU.
AH! MARGARET! WHAT A DELIGHTFUL SURPRISE. PLEASE, DO TAKE A SEAT.
I WOULD NEVER *DREAM* OF INTERRUPTING YOUR WORK, BUT I COME WITH NEWS - MAMA'S PEKINGESE IS *VERY* PREGNANT.
THIS MAY BE DIFFICULT FOR YOU, BUT IF SWEETSY GIVES BIRTH TO A *BOY*, HE WILL BE RIGHTFUL HEIR TO DEVONTON ABBEY.
I'M NOT EVEN GOING TO *PRETEND* TO UNDERSTAND YOUR FAMILY'S INHERITANCE LAWS - EVEN THOUGH I EASILY COULD - AS A *LAWYER*.
NATURALLY.
BUT IT WAS THOSE ABSURD LAWS THAT BROUGHT ME HERE, BROUGHT ME TO *YOU*.
I'M HAPPY TO BE WITHOUT DEVONTON, BUT BEING WITHOUT *YOU* WOULD CRUSH MY VERY SOUL.
MY DARLING, *PLEASE* SAY YOUR FEELINGS FOR ME HAVEN'T CHANGED.
I ASSURE YOU - MY FEELINGS REMAIN THE *SAME* AS EVER.
EXCUSE THE INTERRUPTION, BUT THIS... *GENTLEMAN*... INSISTS HE HAS BUSINESS WITH YOU.
SAW YOUR AD IN *THE GAZETTE* - GOT ME *HAN'* STUCK IN THE CARDIN' MACHINE DOWN AT ROYTON MILL.

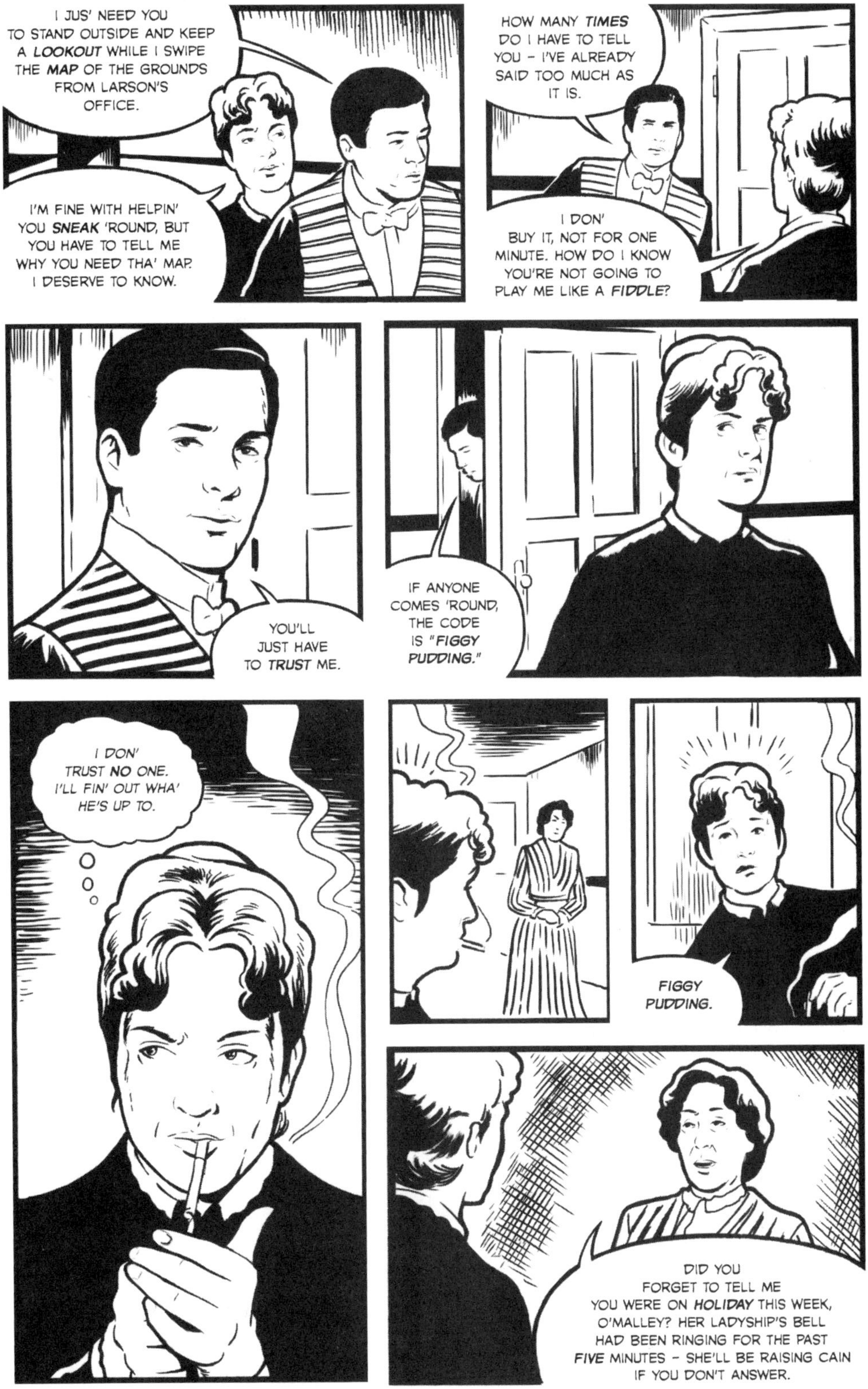
I JUS' NEED YOU TO STAND OUTSIDE AND KEEP A LOOKOUT WHILE I SWIPE THE MAP OF THE GROUNDS FROM LARSON'S OFFICE.
I'M FINE WITH HELPIN' YOU SNEAK 'ROUND, BUT YOU HAVE TO TELL ME WHY YOU NEED THA' MAP. I DESERVE TO KNOW.
HOW MANY TIMES DO I HAVE TO TELL YOU - I'VE ALREADY SAID TOO MUCH AS IT IS.
I DON' BUY IT, NOT FOR ONE MINUTE. HOW DO I KNOW YOU'RE NOT GOING TO PLAY ME LIKE A FIDDLE?
YOU'LL JUST HAVE TO TRUST ME.
IF ANYONE COMES 'ROUND, THE CODE IS "FIGGY PUDDING."
I DON' TRUST NO ONE. I'LL FIN' OUT WHA' HE'S UP TO.
FIGGY PUDDING.
DID YOU FORGET TO TELL ME YOU WERE ON HOLIDAY THIS WEEK, O'MALLEY? HER LADYSHIP'S BELL HAD BEEN RINGING FOR THE PAST FIVE MINUTES - SHE'LL BE RAISING CAIN IF YOU DON'T ANSWER.

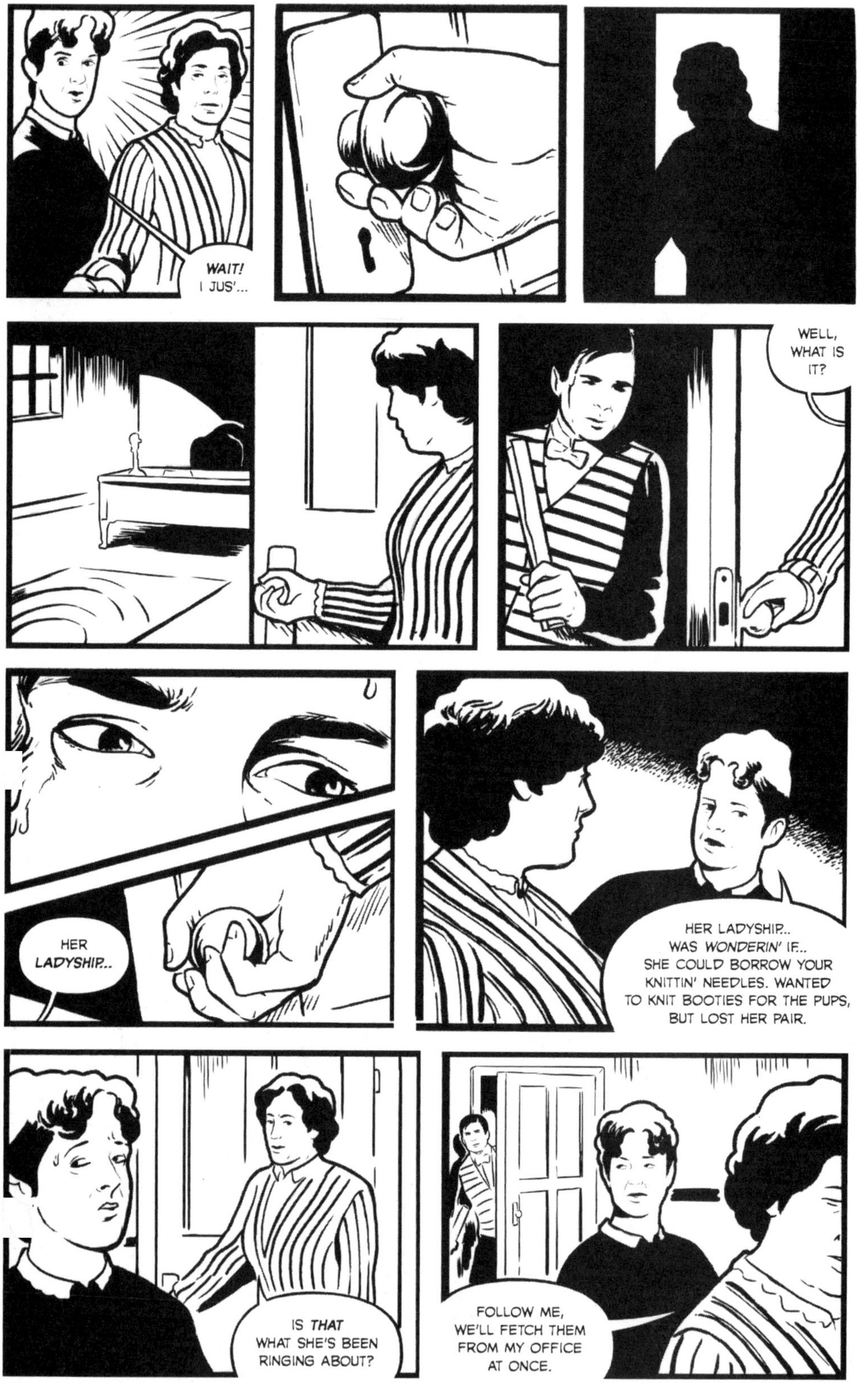
WAIT!
I JUS'...
WELL, WHAT IS IT?
HER LADYSHIP...
HER LADYSHIP.. WAS WONDERIN' IF... SHE COULD BORROW YOUR KNITTIN' NEEDLES. WANTED TO KNIT BOOTIES FOR THE PUPS, BUT LOST HER PAIR.
IS THAT WHAT SHE'S BEEN RINGING ABOUT?
FOLLOW ME, WE'LL FETCH THEM FROM MY OFFICE AT ONCE.

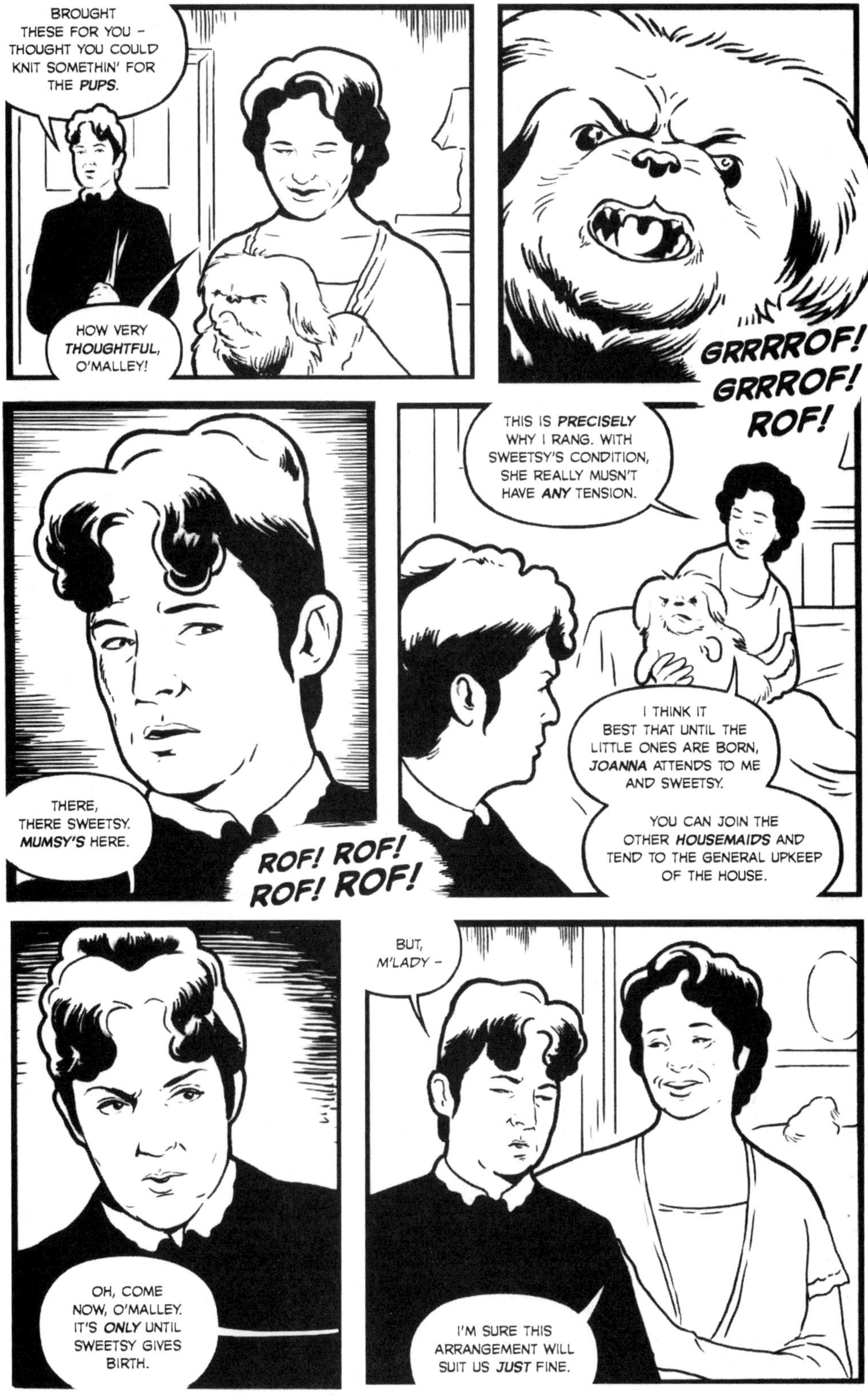
BROUGHT THESE FOR YOU - THOUGHT YOU COULD KNIT SOMETHIN' FOR THE *PUPS*.
HOW VERY *THOUGHTFUL*, O'MALLEY!
GRRRROF! GRRROF! ROF!
THERE, THERE SWEETSY. *MUMSY'S* HERE.
ROF! ROF! ROF! ROF!
THIS IS *PRECISELY* WHY I RANG. WITH SWEETSY'S CONDITION, SHE REALLY MUSN'T HAVE *ANY* TENSION.
I THINK IT BEST THAT UNTIL THE LITTLE ONES ARE BORN, *JOANNA* ATTENDS TO ME AND SWEETSY.
YOU CAN JOIN THE OTHER *HOUSEMAIDS* AND TEND TO THE GENERAL UPKEEP OF THE HOUSE.
OH, COME NOW, O'MALLEY. IT'S *ONLY* UNTIL SWEETSY GIVES BIRTH.
BUT, M'LADY -
I'M SURE THIS ARRANGEMENT WILL SUIT US *JUST* FINE.

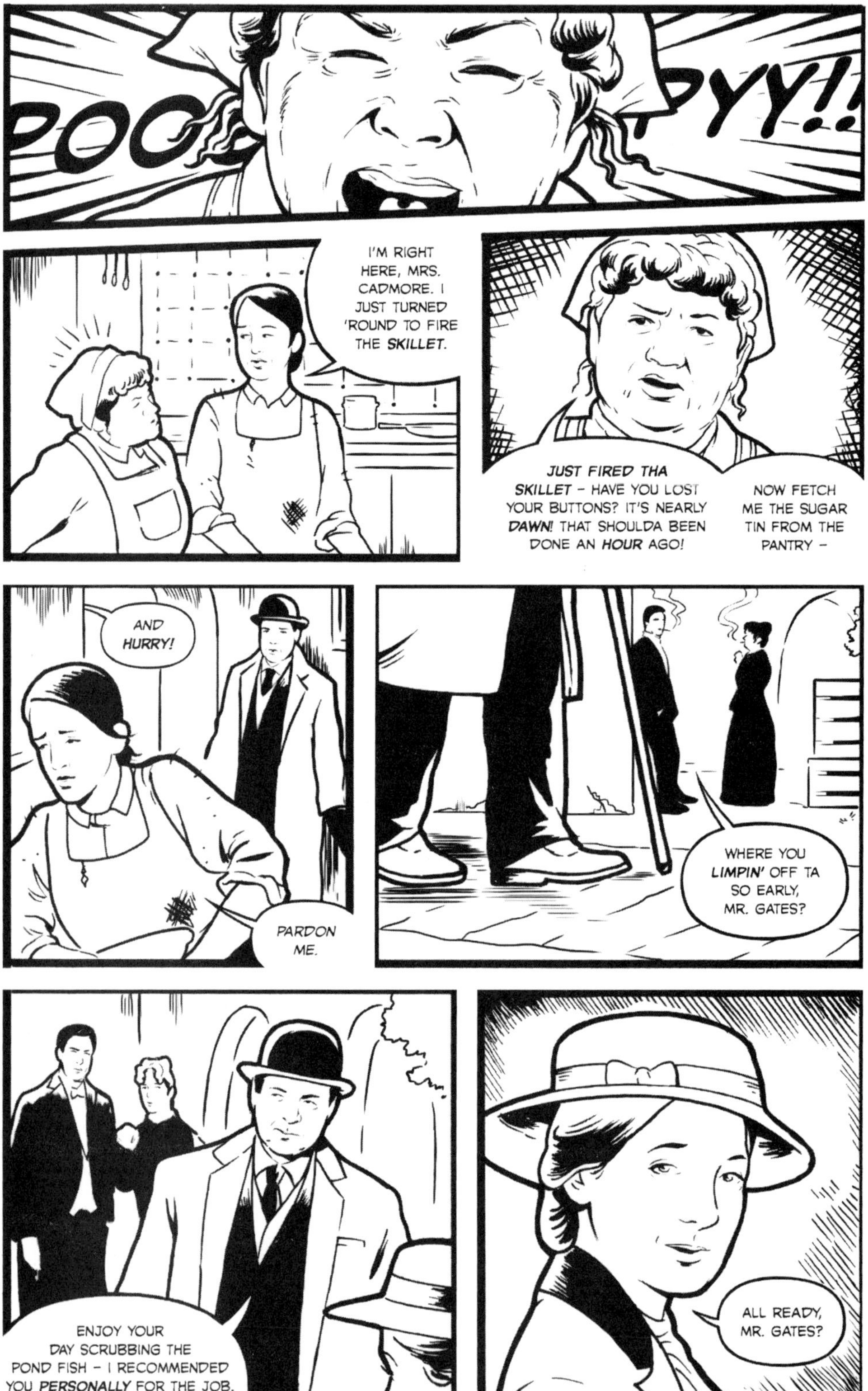
POO
OYY!!
I'M RIGHT HERE, MRS. CADMORE. I JUST TURNED 'ROUND TO FIRE THE SKILLET.
JUST FIRED THA SKILLET – HAVE YOU LOST YOUR BUTTONS? IT'S NEARLY DAWN! THAT SHOULDA BEEN DONE AN HOUR AGO!
NOW FETCH ME THE SUGAR TIN FROM THE PANTRY –
AND HURRY!
PARDON ME.
WHERE YOU LIMPIN' OFF TA SO EARLY, MR. GATES?
ENJOY YOUR DAY SCRUBBING THE POND FISH – I RECOMMENDED YOU PERSONALLY FOR THE JOB.
ALL READY, MR. GATES?

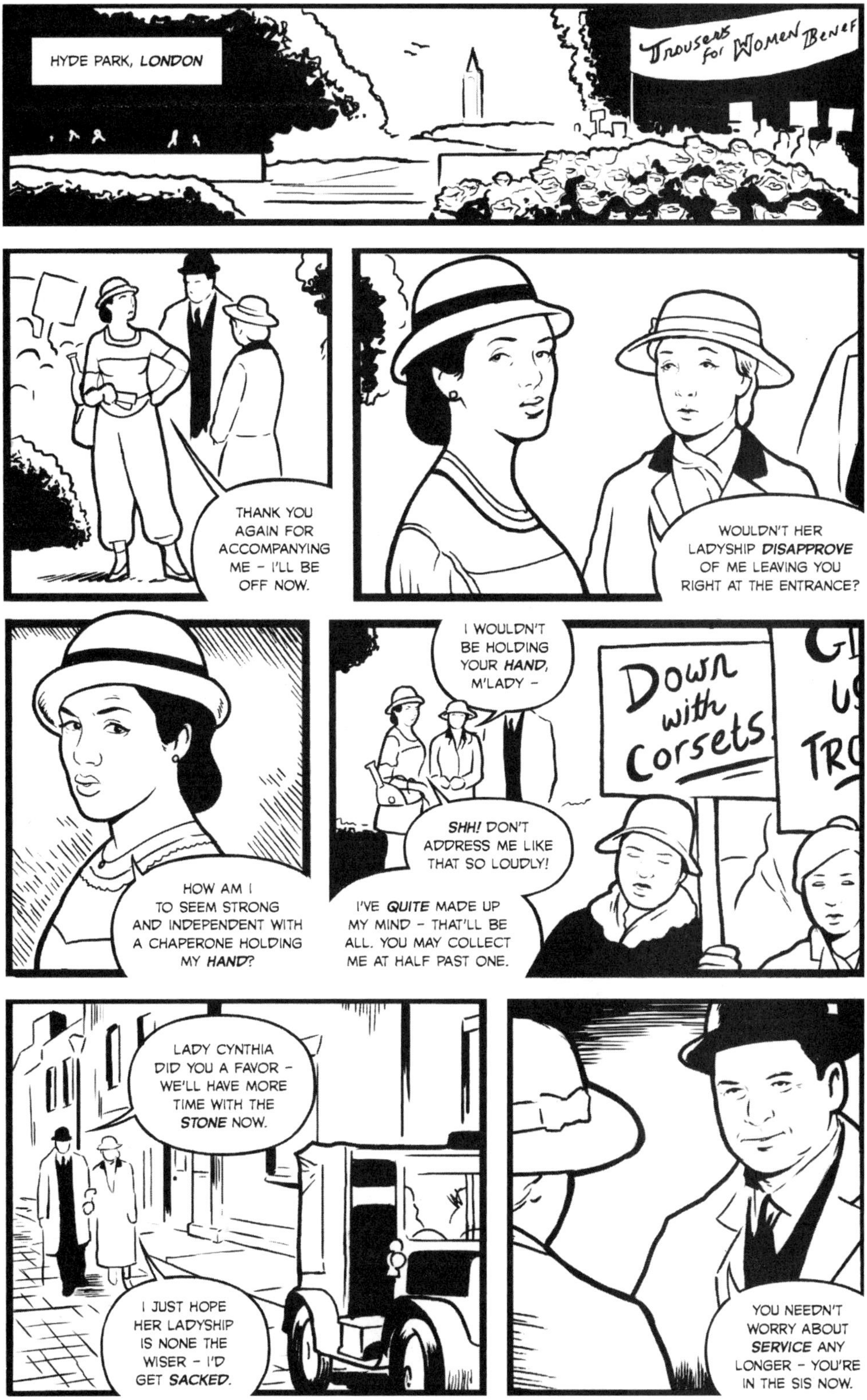
HYDE PARK, LONDON
Trousers for Women Benef
THANK YOU AGAIN FOR ACCOMPANYING ME – I'LL BE OFF NOW.
WOULDN'T HER LADYSHIP **DISAPPROVE** OF ME LEAVING YOU RIGHT AT THE ENTRANCE?
HOW AM I TO SEEM STRONG AND INDEPENDENT WITH A CHAPERONE HOLDING MY **HAND**?
I WOULDN'T BE HOLDING YOUR **HAND**, M'LADY –
Down with Corsets
SHH! DON'T ADDRESS ME LIKE THAT SO LOUDLY!
I'VE **QUITE** MADE UP MY MIND – THAT'LL BE ALL. YOU MAY COLLECT ME AT HALF PAST ONE.
LADY CYNTHIA DID YOU A FAVOR – WE'LL HAVE MORE TIME WITH THE **STONE** NOW.
I JUST HOPE HER LADYSHIP IS NONE THE WISER – I'D GET **SACKED**.
YOU NEEDN'T WORRY ABOUT **SERVICE** ANY LONGER – YOU'RE IN THE SIS NOW.

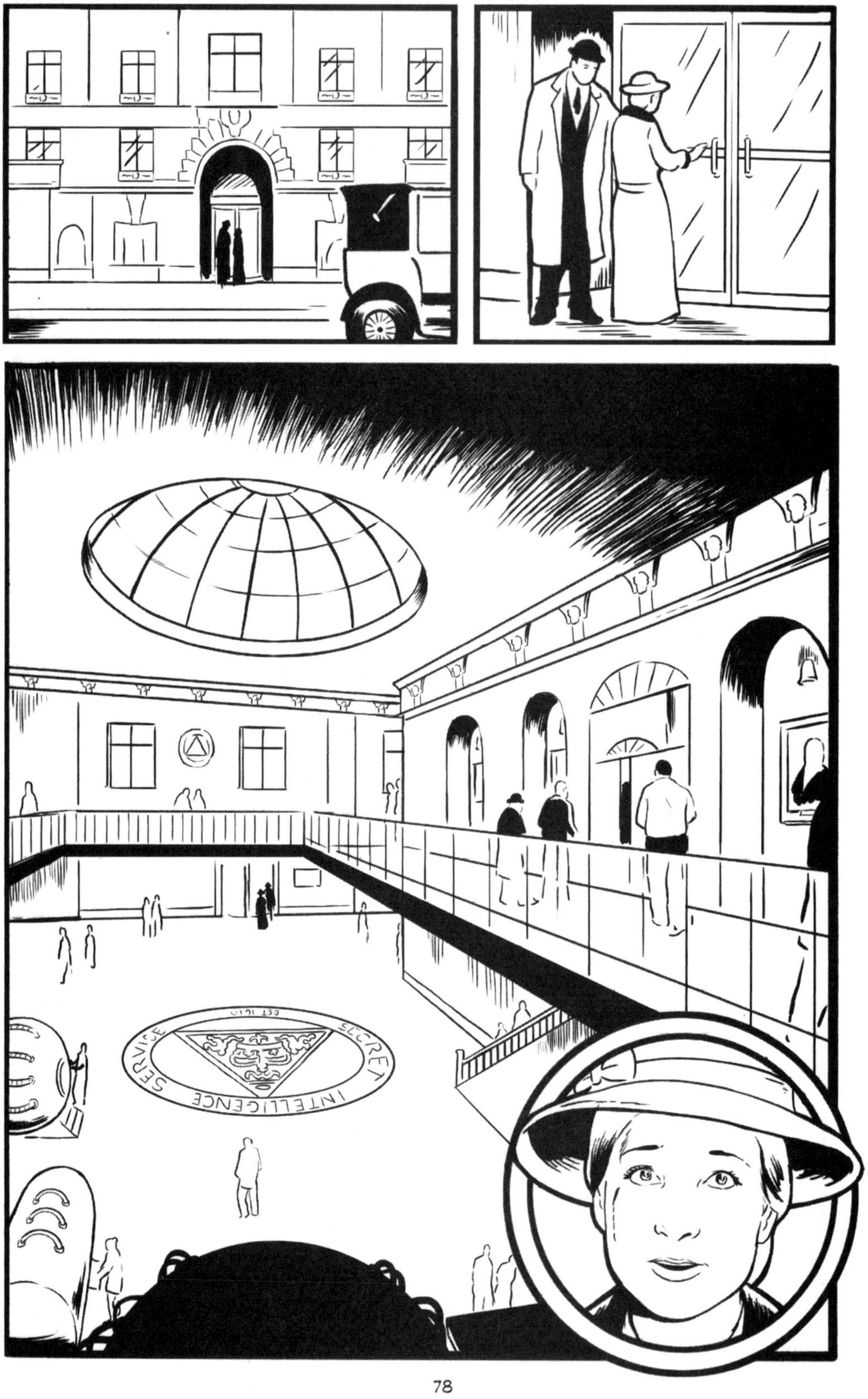
SECRET INTELLIGENCE SERVICE
EST 1910

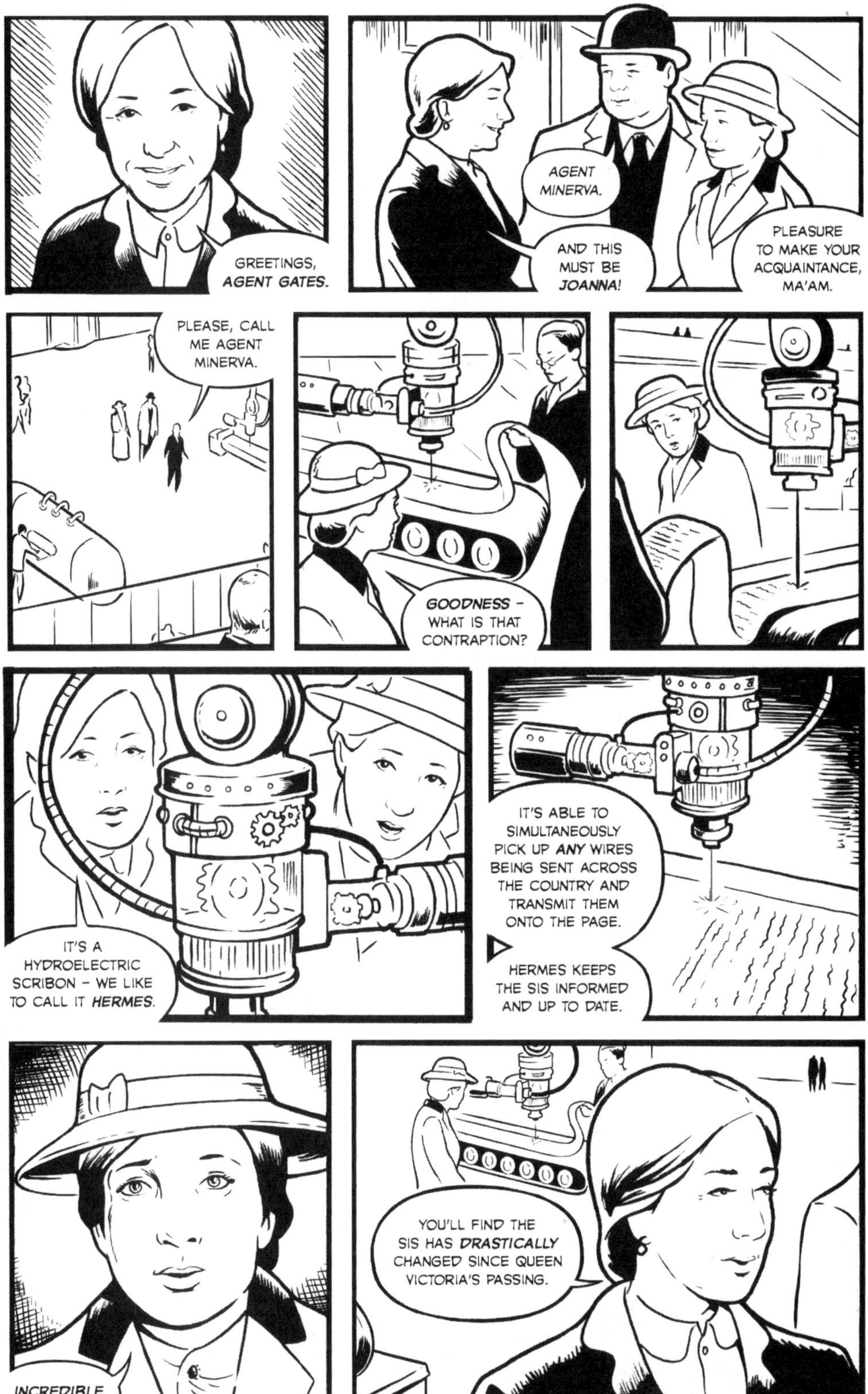
GREETINGS, AGENT GATES.
AGENT MINERVA.
AND THIS MUST BE JOANNA!
PLEASURE TO MAKE YOUR ACQUAINTANCE, MA'AM.
PLEASE, CALL ME AGENT MINERVA.
GOODNESS - WHAT IS THAT CONTRAPTION?
IT'S A HYDROELECTRIC SCRIBON - WE LIKE TO CALL IT HERMES.
IT'S ABLE TO SIMULTANEOUSLY PICK UP ANY WIRES BEING SENT ACROSS THE COUNTRY AND TRANSMIT THEM ONTO THE PAGE.
HERMES KEEPS THE SIS INFORMED AND UP TO DATE.
INCREDIBLE.
YOU'LL FIND THE SIS HAS DRASTICALLY CHANGED SINCE QUEEN VICTORIA'S PASSING.

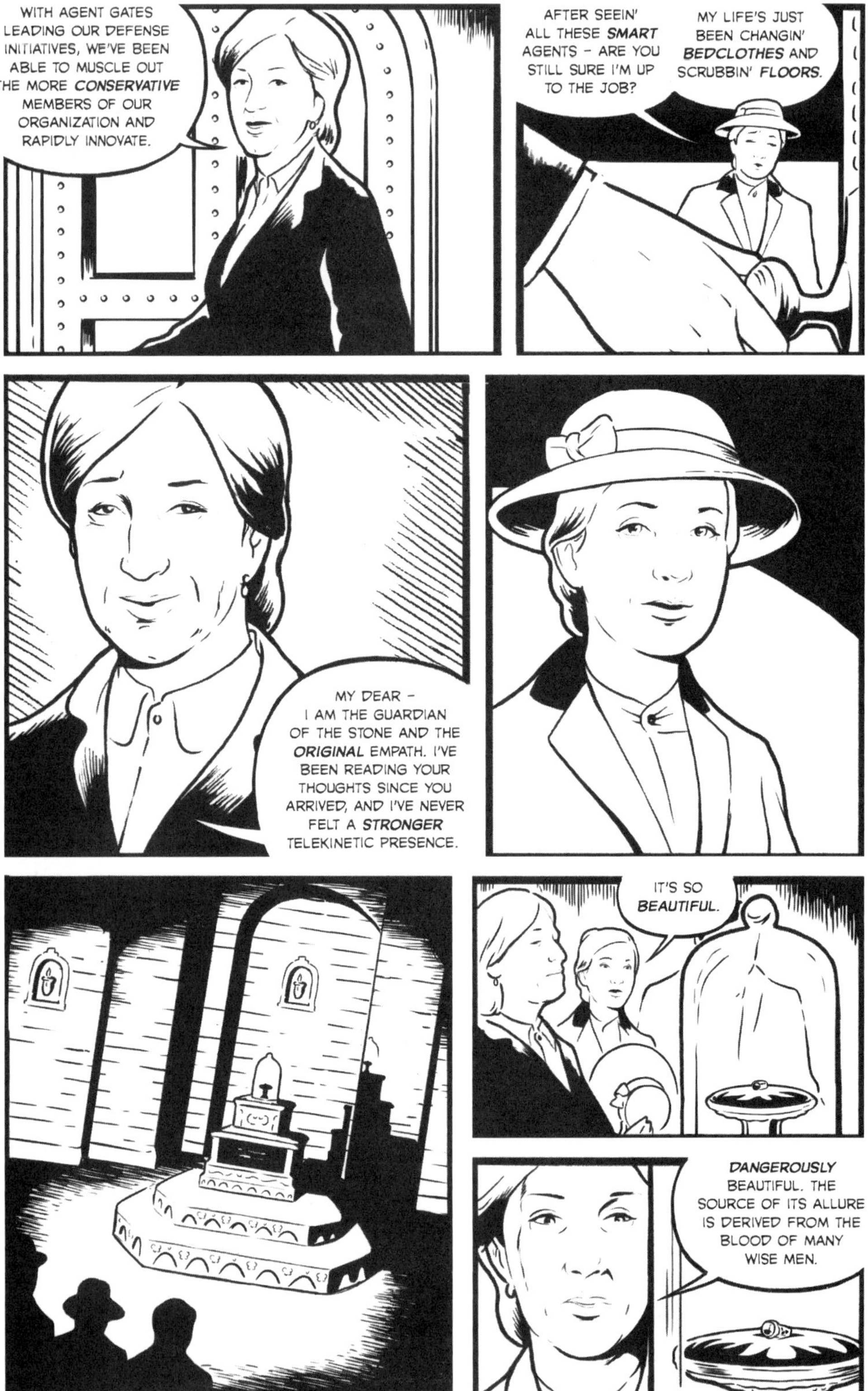
WITH AGENT GATES LEADING OUR DEFENSE INITIATIVES, WE'VE BEEN ABLE TO MUSCLE OUT THE MORE CONSERVATIVE MEMBERS OF OUR ORGANIZATION AND RAPIDLY INNOVATE.
AFTER SEEIN' ALL THESE SMART AGENTS - ARE YOU STILL SURE I'M UP TO THE JOB?
MY LIFE'S JUST BEEN CHANGIN' BEDCLOTHES AND SCRUBBIN' FLOORS.
MY DEAR - I AM THE GUARDIAN OF THE STONE AND THE ORIGINAL EMPATH. I'VE BEEN READING YOUR THOUGHTS SINCE YOU ARRIVED, AND I'VE NEVER FELT A STRONGER TELEKINETIC PRESENCE.
IT'S SO BEAUTIFUL.
DANGEROUSLY BEAUTIFUL. THE SOURCE OF ITS ALLURE IS DERIVED FROM THE BLOOD OF MANY WISE MEN.

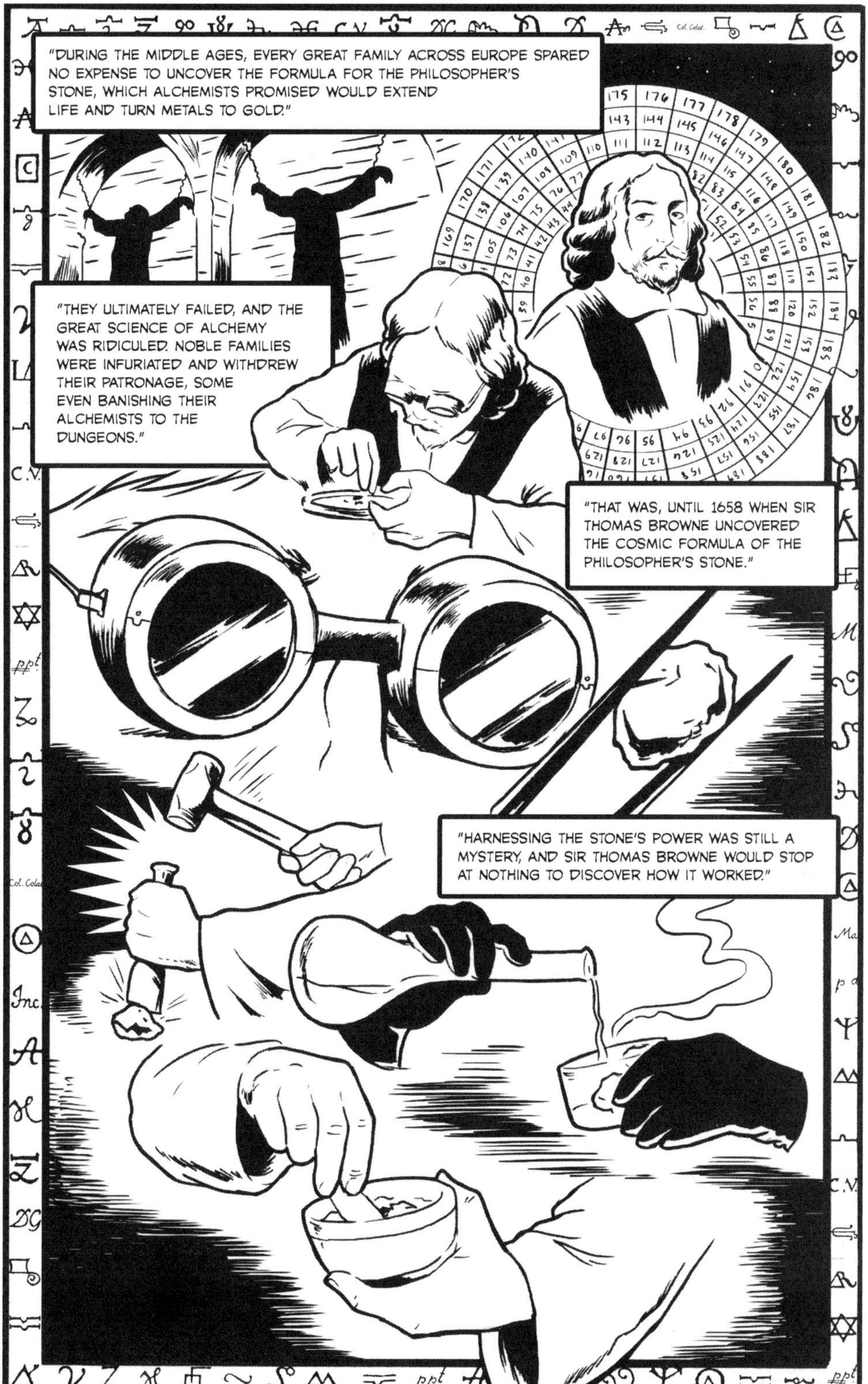
"DURING THE MIDDLE AGES, EVERY GREAT FAMILY ACROSS EUROPE SPARED NO EXPENSE TO UNCOVER THE FORMULA FOR THE PHILOSOPHER'S STONE, WHICH ALCHEMISTS PROMISED WOULD EXTEND LIFE AND TURN METALS TO GOLD."
"THEY ULTIMATELY FAILED, AND THE GREAT SCIENCE OF ALCHEMY WAS RIDICULED. NOBLE FAMILIES WERE INFURIATED AND WITHDREW THEIR PATRONAGE, SOME EVEN BANISHING THEIR ALCHEMISTS TO THE DUNGEONS."
"THAT WAS, UNTIL 1658 WHEN SIR THOMAS BROWNE UNCOVERED THE COSMIC FORMULA OF THE PHILOSOPHER'S STONE."
"HARNESSING THE STONE'S POWER WAS STILL A MYSTERY, AND SIR THOMAS BROWNE WOULD STOP AT NOTHING TO DISCOVER HOW IT WORKED."

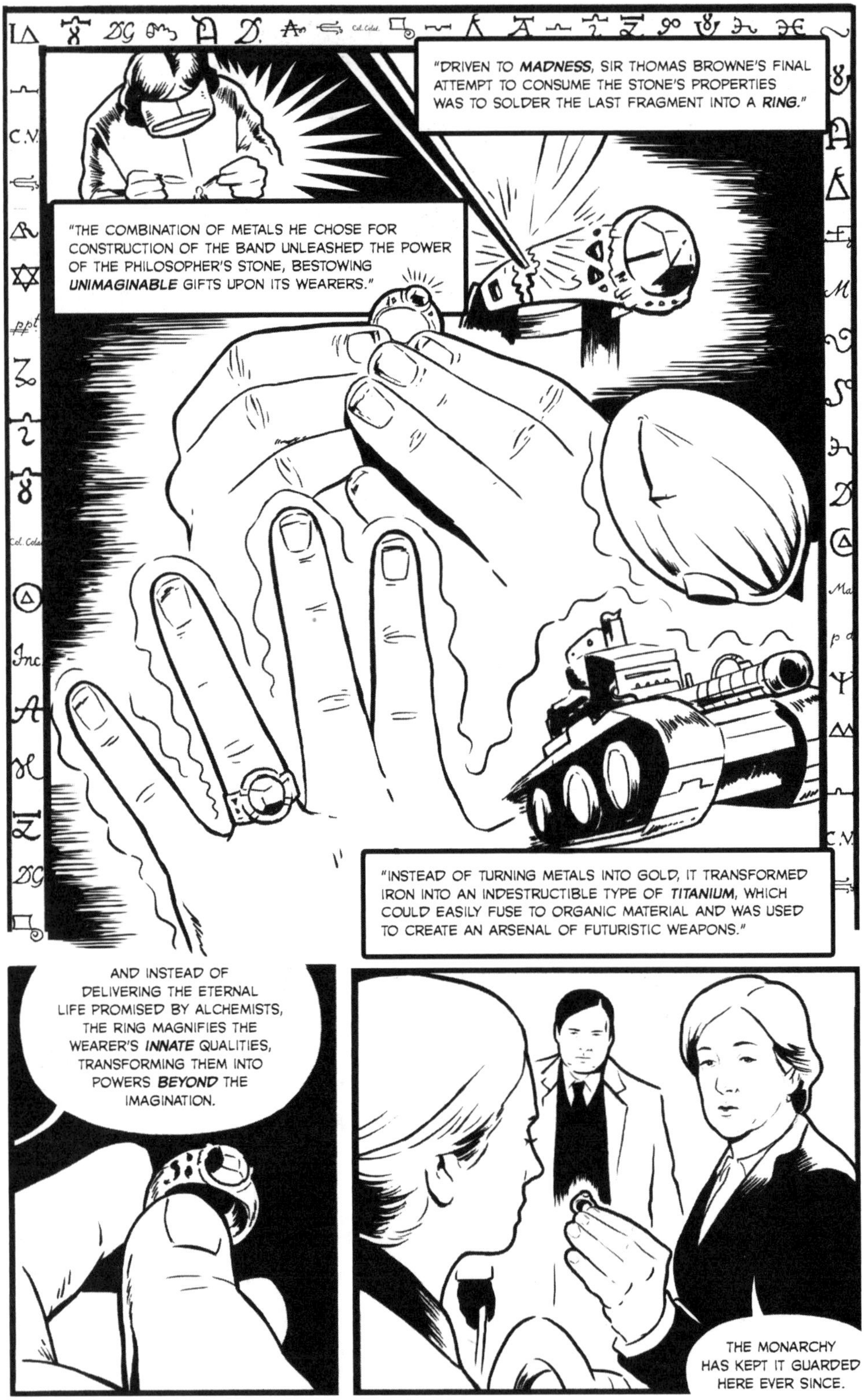
"DRIVEN TO MADNESS, SIR THOMAS BROWNE'S FINAL ATTEMPT TO CONSUME THE STONE'S PROPERTIES WAS TO SOLDER THE LAST FRAGMENT INTO A RING."
"THE COMBINATION OF METALS HE CHOSE FOR CONSTRUCTION OF THE BAND UNLEASHED THE POWER OF THE PHILOSOPHER'S STONE, BESTOWING UNIMAGINABLE GIFTS UPON ITS WEARERS."
"INSTEAD OF TURNING METALS INTO GOLD, IT TRANSFORMED IRON INTO AN INDESTRUCTIBLE TYPE OF TITANIUM, WHICH COULD EASILY FUSE TO ORGANIC MATERIAL AND WAS USED TO CREATE AN ARSENAL OF FUTURISTIC WEAPONS."
AND INSTEAD OF DELIVERING THE ETERNAL LIFE PROMISED BY ALCHEMISTS, THE RING MAGNIFIES THE WEARER'S INNATE QUALITIES, TRANSFORMING THEM INTO POWERS BEYOND THE IMAGINATION.
THE MONARCHY HAS KEPT IT GUARDED HERE EVER SINCE.

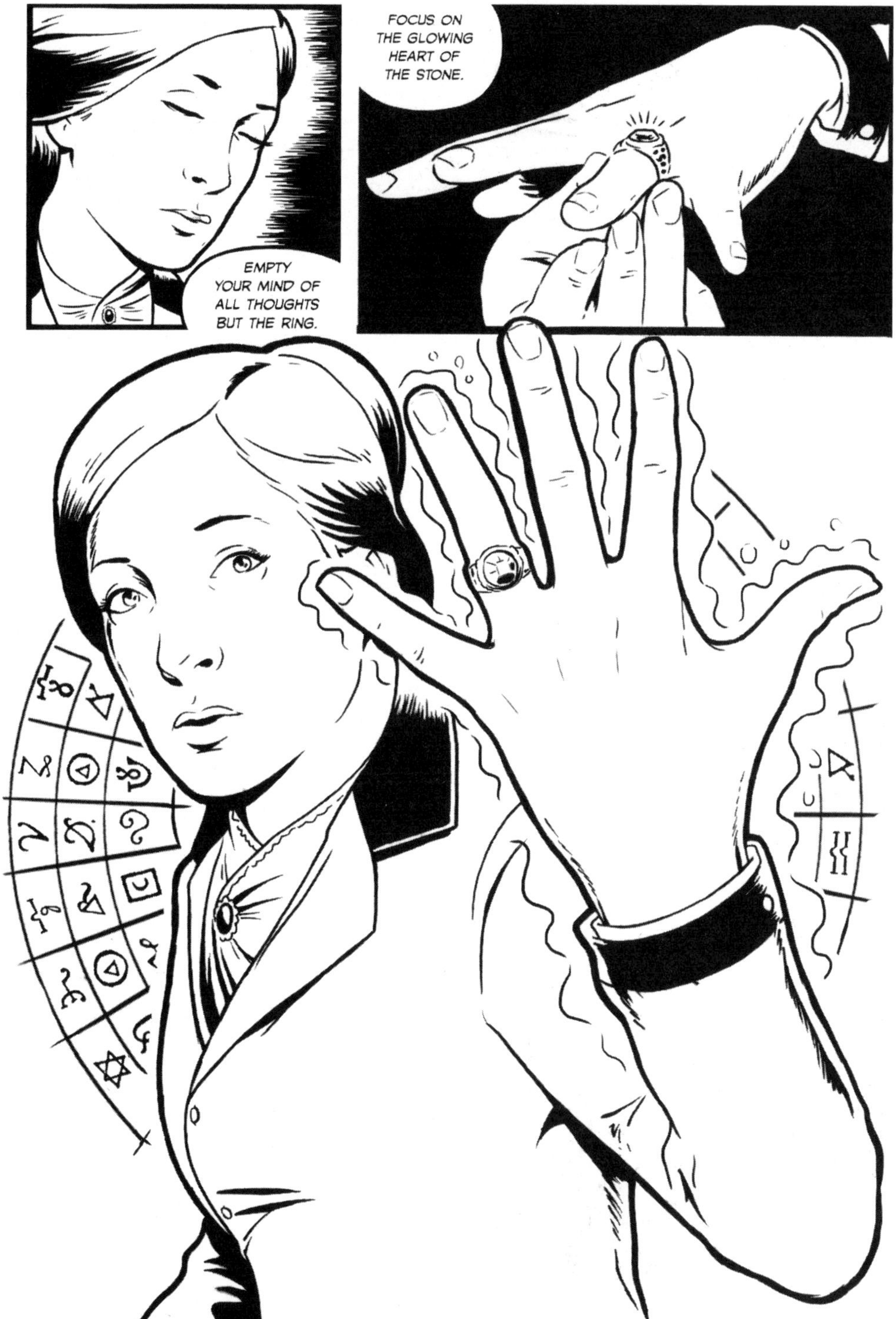
EMPTY YOUR MIND OF ALL THOUGHTS BUT THE RING.
FOCUS ON THE GLOWING HEART OF THE STONE.

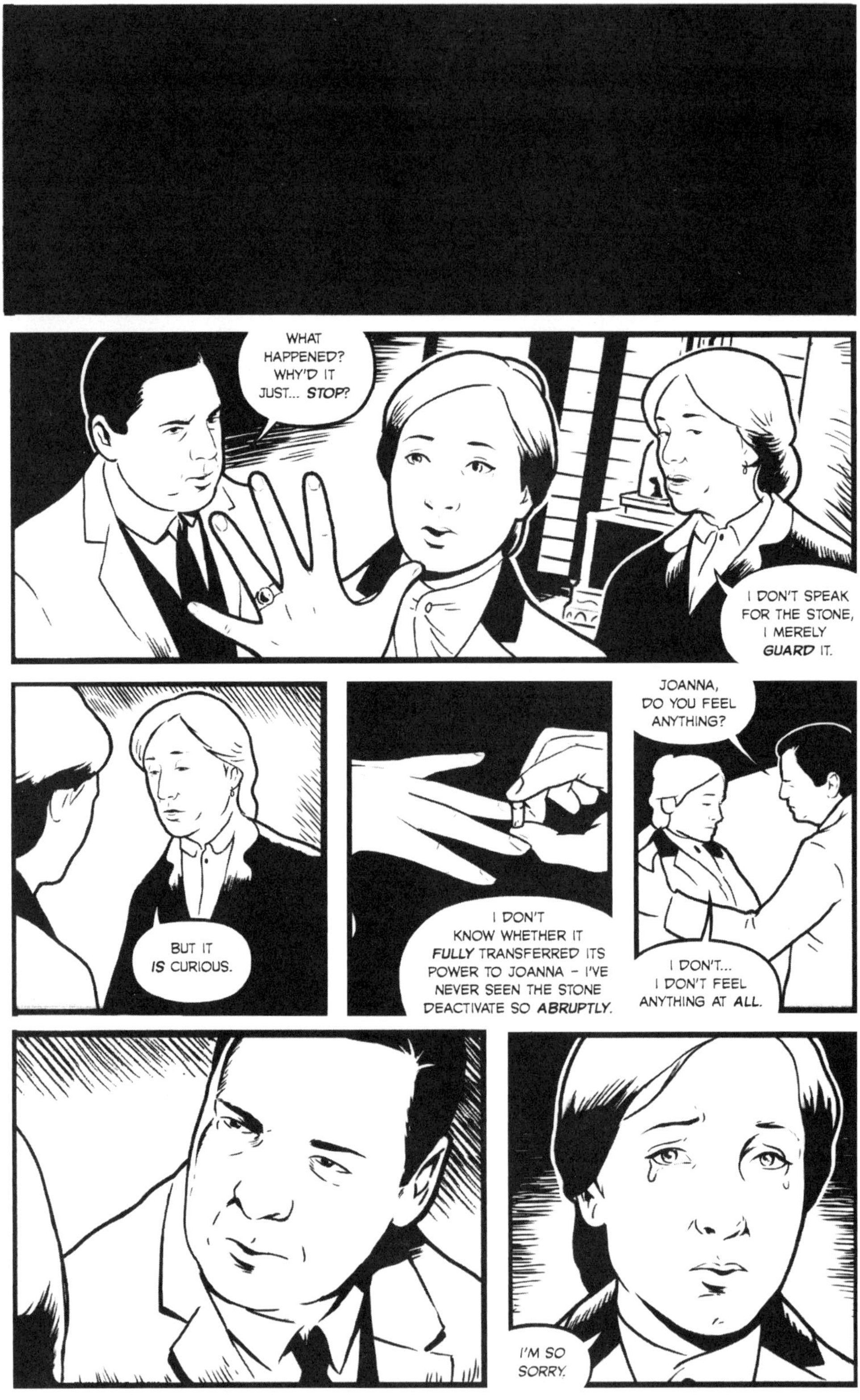
WHAT HAPPENED? WHY'D IT JUST... STOP?
I DON'T SPEAK FOR THE STONE, I MERELY GUARD IT.
BUT IT IS CURIOUS.
I DON'T KNOW WHETHER IT FULLY TRANSFERRED ITS POWER TO JOANNA - I'VE NEVER SEEN THE STONE DEACTIVATE SO ABRUPTLY.
JOANNA, DO YOU FEEL ANYTHING?
I DON'T... I DON'T FEEL ANYTHING AT ALL.
I'M SO SORRY.

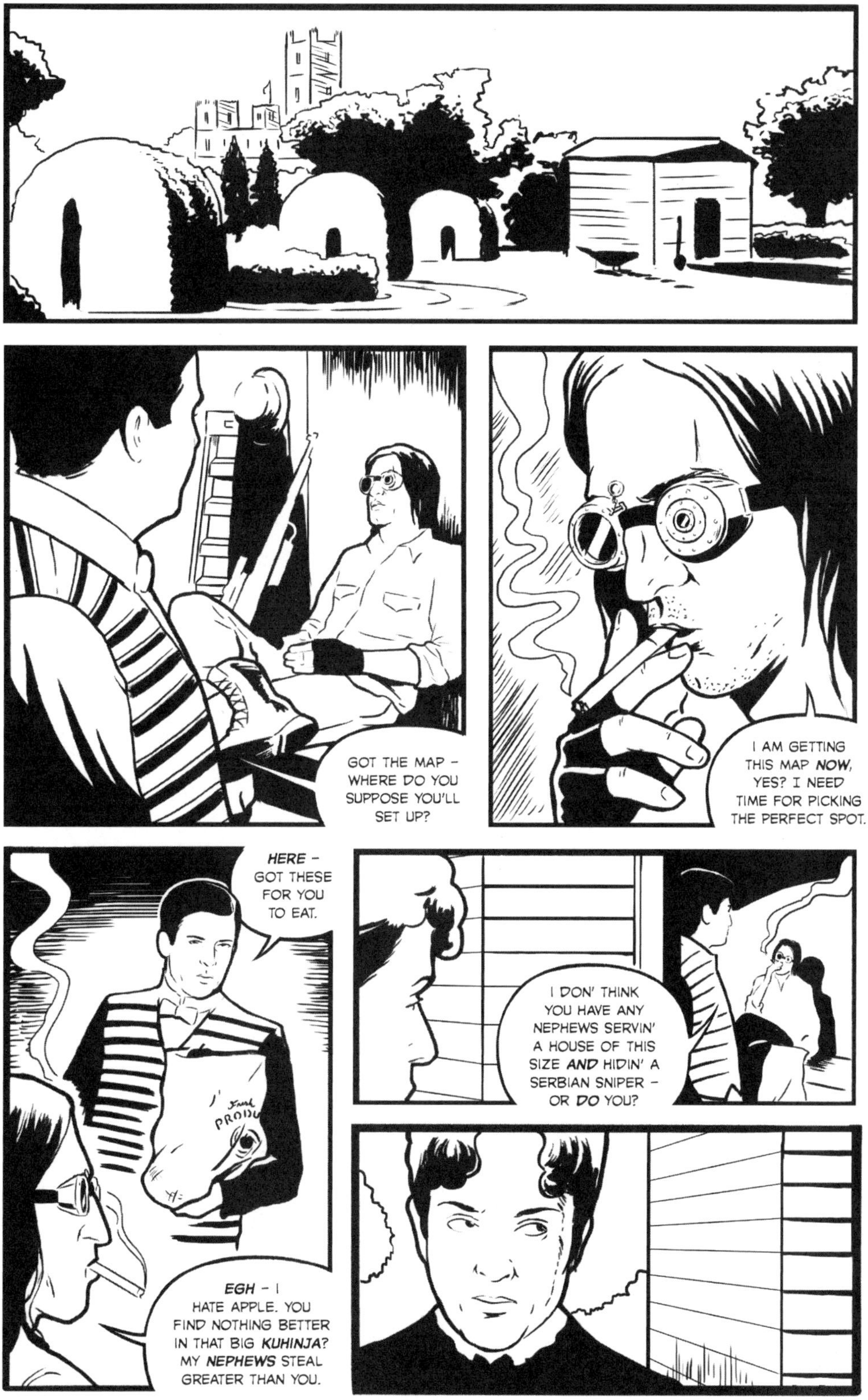
GOT THE MAP - WHERE DO YOU SUPPOSE YOU'LL SET UP?
I AM GETTING THIS MAP NOW, YES? I NEED TIME FOR PICKING THE PERFECT SPOT.
HERE - GOT THESE FOR YOU TO EAT.
Fresh PRODU
EGH - I HATE APPLE. YOU FIND NOTHING BETTER IN THAT BIG KUHINJA? MY NEPHEWS STEAL GREATER THAN YOU.
I DON' THINK YOU HAVE ANY NEPHEWS SERVIN' A HOUSE OF THIS SIZE AND HIDIN' A SERBIAN SNIPER - OR DO YOU?

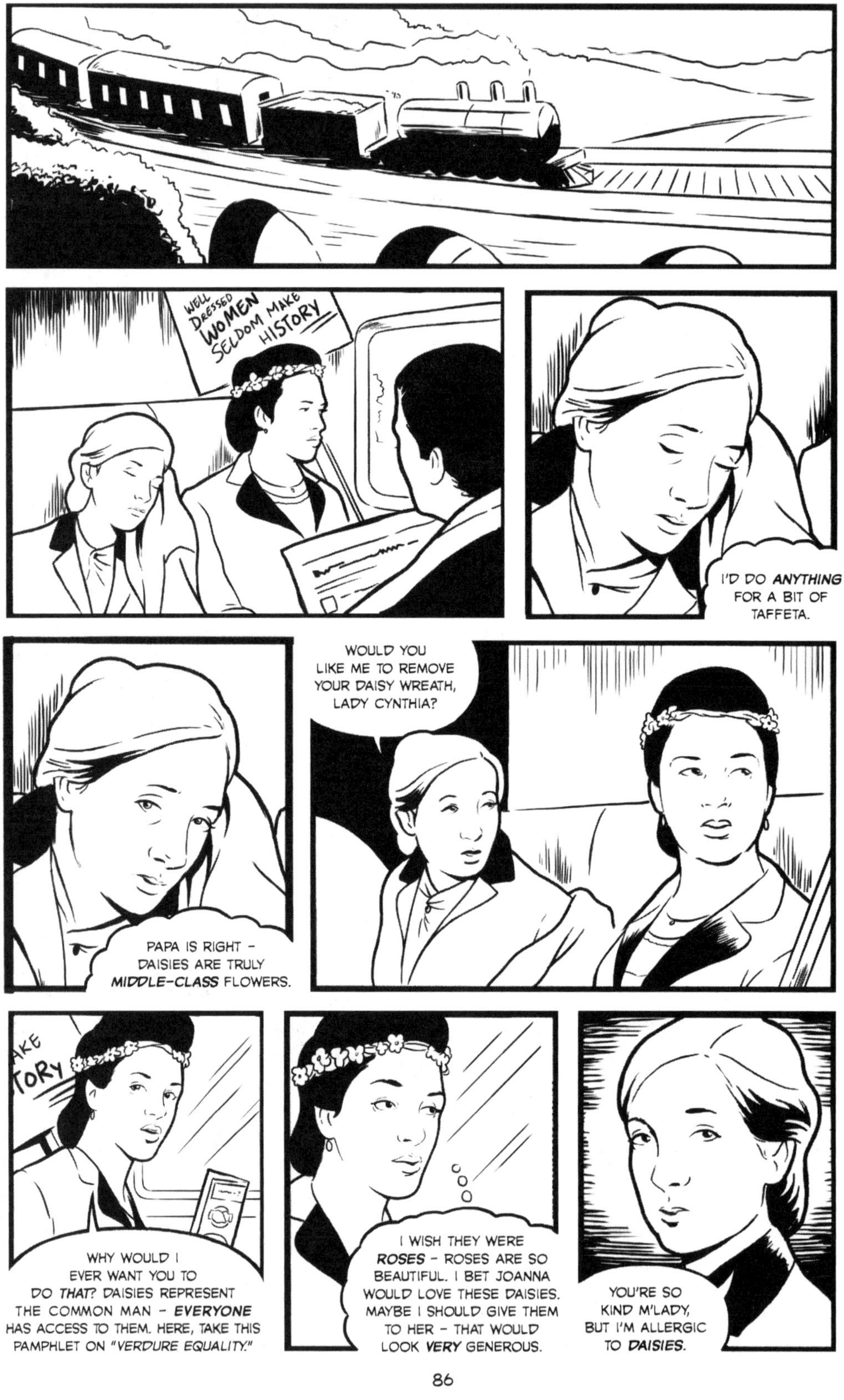
WELL DRESSED WOMEN SELDOM MAKE HISTORY
I'D DO ANYTHING FOR A BIT OF TAFFETA.
PAPA IS RIGHT - DAISIES ARE TRULY MIDDLE-CLASS FLOWERS.
WOULD YOU LIKE ME TO REMOVE YOUR DAISY WREATH, LADY CYNTHIA?
WHY WOULD I EVER WANT YOU TO DO THAT? DAISIES REPRESENT THE COMMON MAN - EVERYONE HAS ACCESS TO THEM. HERE, TAKE THIS PAMPHLET ON "VERDURE EQUALITY."
I WISH THEY WERE ROSES - ROSES ARE SO BEAUTIFUL. I BET JOANNA WOULD LOVE THESE DAISIES. MAYBE I SHOULD GIVE THEM TO HER - THAT WOULD LOOK VERY GENEROUS.
YOU'RE SO KIND M'LADY, BUT I'M ALLERGIC TO DAISIES.

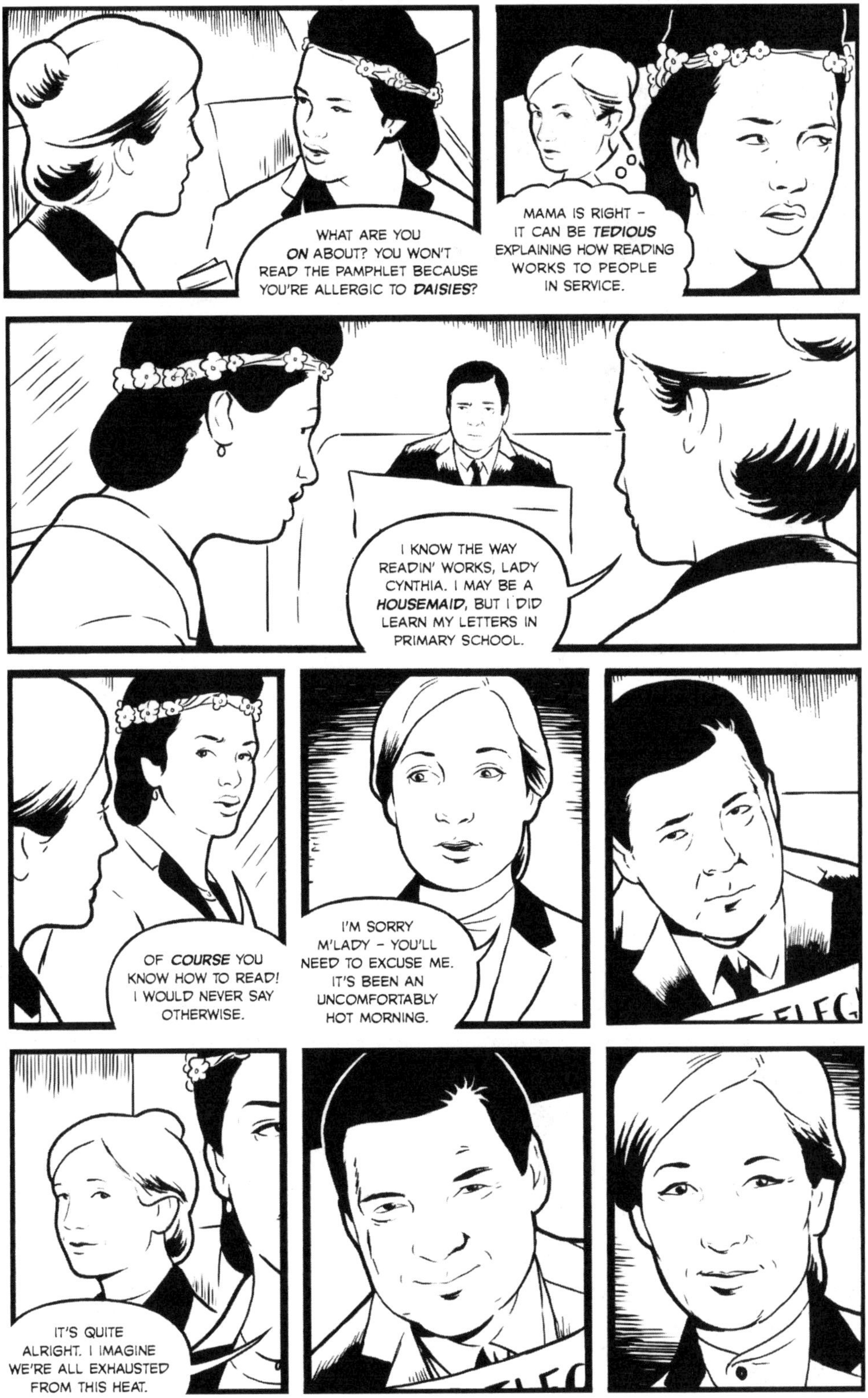
WHAT ARE YOU ON ABOUT? YOU WON'T READ THE PAMPHLET BECAUSE YOU'RE ALLERGIC TO DAISIES?
MAMA IS RIGHT - IT CAN BE TEDIOUS EXPLAINING HOW READING WORKS TO PEOPLE IN SERVICE.
I KNOW THE WAY READIN' WORKS, LADY CYNTHIA. I MAY BE A HOUSEMAID, BUT I DID LEARN MY LETTERS IN PRIMARY SCHOOL.
OF COURSE YOU KNOW HOW TO READ! I WOULD NEVER SAY OTHERWISE.
I'M SORRY M'LADY - YOU'LL NEED TO EXCUSE ME. IT'S BEEN AN UNCOMFORTABLY HOT MORNING.
IT'S QUITE ALRIGHT. I IMAGINE WE'RE ALL EXHAUSTED FROM THIS HEAT.

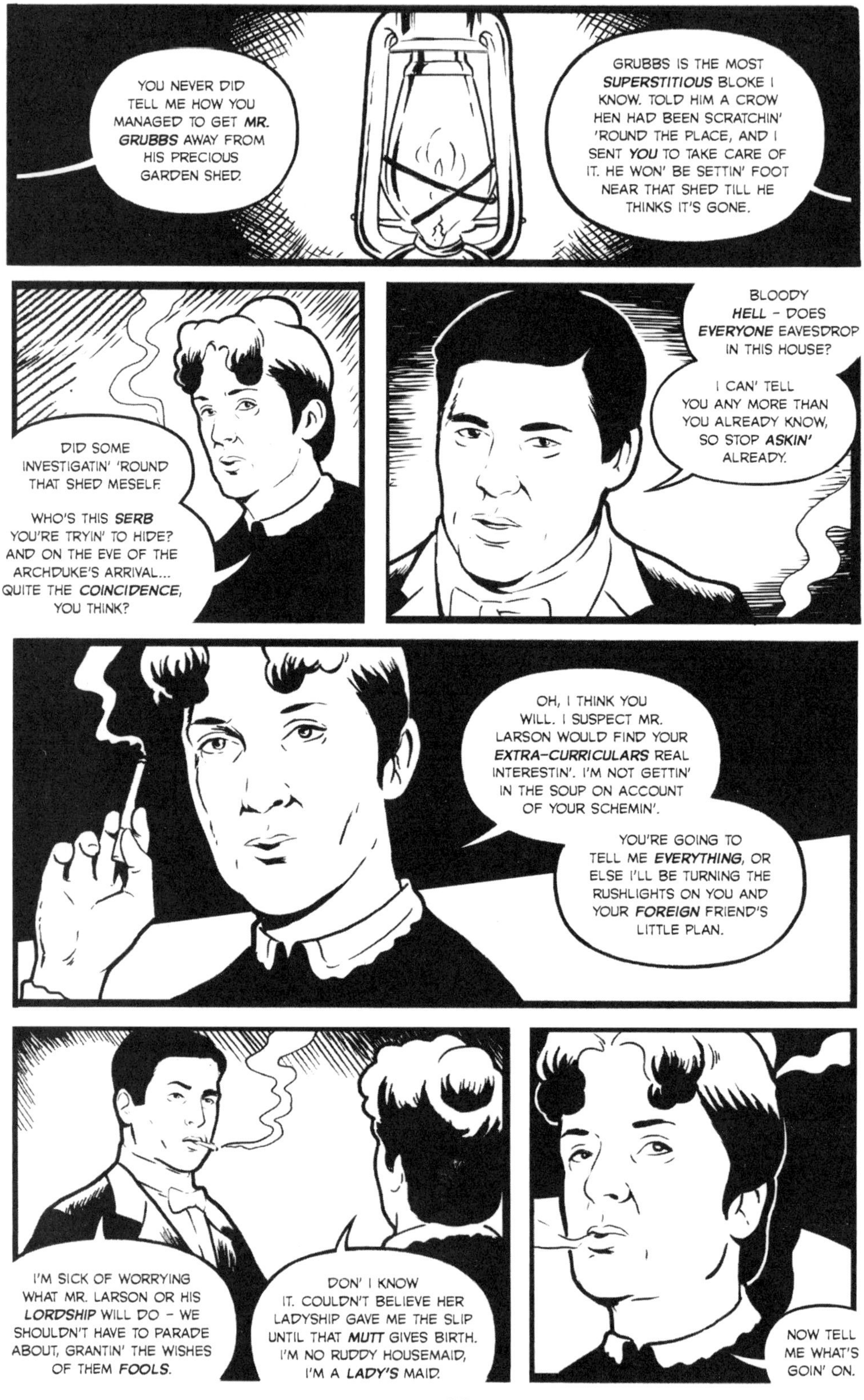
YOU NEVER DID TELL ME HOW YOU MANAGED TO GET MR. GRUBBS AWAY FROM HIS PRECIOUS GARDEN SHED.
GRUBBS IS THE MOST SUPERSTITIOUS BLOKE I KNOW. TOLD HIM A CROW HEN HAD BEEN SCRATCHIN' 'ROUND THE PLACE, AND I SENT YOU TO TAKE CARE OF IT. HE WON' BE SETTIN' FOOT NEAR THAT SHED TILL HE THINKS IT'S GONE.
DID SOME INVESTIGATIN' 'ROUND THAT SHED MESELF.
WHO'S THIS SERB YOU'RE TRYIN' TO HIDE? AND ON THE EVE OF THE ARCHDUKE'S ARRIVAL... QUITE THE COINCIDENCE, YOU THINK?
BLOODY HELL - DOES EVERYONE EAVESDROP IN THIS HOUSE?
I CAN' TELL YOU ANY MORE THAN YOU ALREADY KNOW, SO STOP ASKIN' ALREADY.
OH, I THINK YOU WILL. I SUSPECT MR. LARSON WOULD FIND YOUR EXTRA-CURRICULARS REAL INTERESTIN'. I'M NOT GETTIN' IN THE SOUP ON ACCOUNT OF YOUR SCHEMIN'.
YOU'RE GOING TO TELL ME EVERYTHING, OR ELSE I'LL BE TURNING THE RUSHLIGHTS ON YOU AND YOUR FOREIGN FRIEND'S LITTLE PLAN.
I'M SICK OF WORRYING WHAT MR. LARSON OR HIS LORDSHIP WILL DO - WE SHOULDN'T HAVE TO PARADE ABOUT, GRANTIN' THE WISHES OF THEM FOOLS.
DON' I KNOW IT. COULDN'T BELIEVE HER LADYSHIP GAVE ME THE SLIP UNTIL THAT MUTT GIVES BIRTH. I'M NO RUDDY HOUSEMAID, I'M A LADY'S MAID.
NOW TELL ME WHAT'S GOIN' ON.

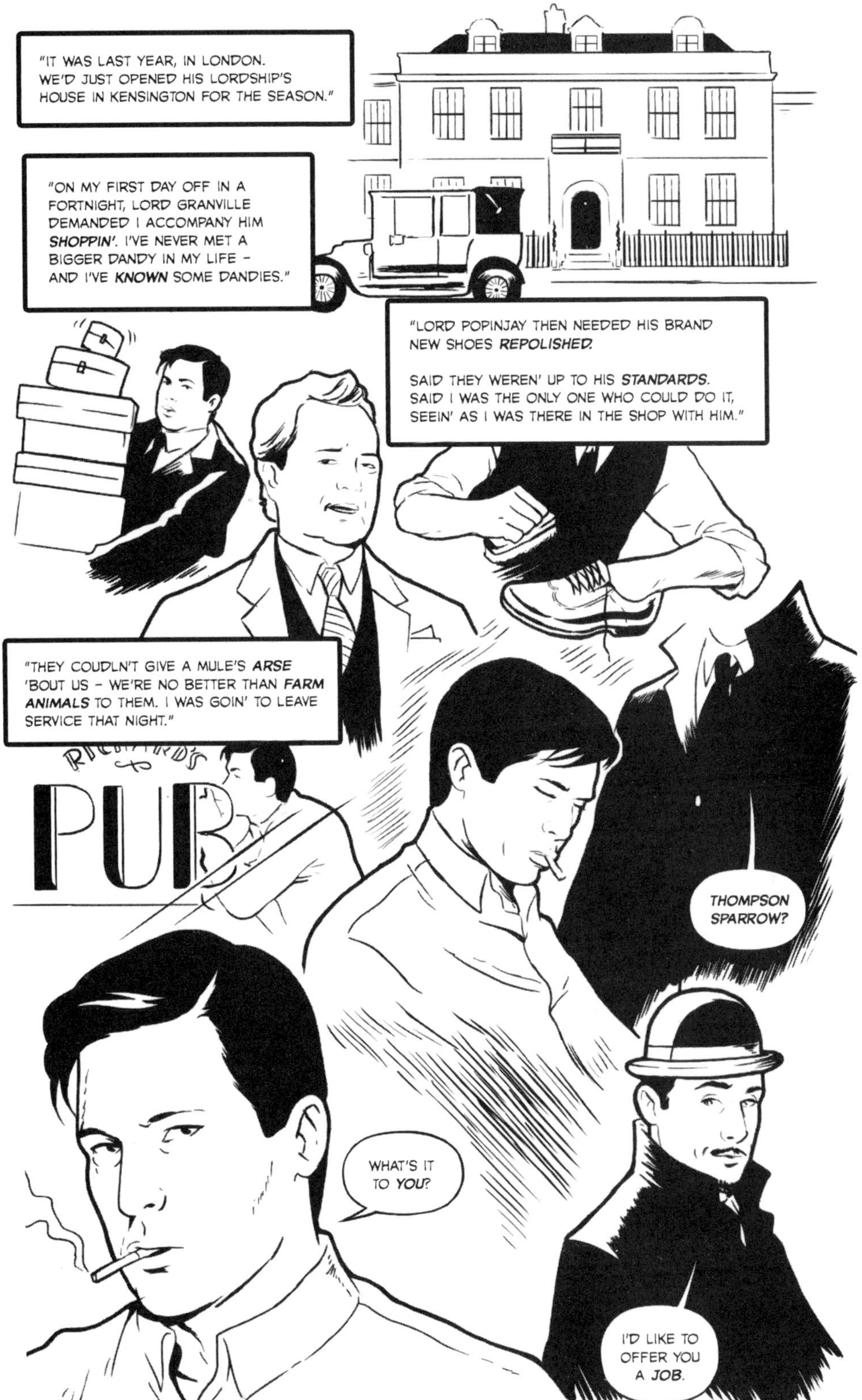
"IT WAS LAST YEAR, IN LONDON. WE'D JUST OPENED HIS LORDSHIP'S HOUSE IN KENSINGTON FOR THE SEASON."
"ON MY FIRST DAY OFF IN A FORTNIGHT, LORD GRANVILLE DEMANDED I ACCOMPANY HIM *SHOPPIN'*. I'VE NEVER MET A BIGGER DANDY IN MY LIFE – AND I'VE *KNOWN* SOME DANDIES."
"LORD POPINJAY THEN NEEDED HIS BRAND NEW SHOES *REPOLISHED*.
SAID THEY WEREN' UP TO HIS *STANDARDS*. SAID I WAS THE ONLY ONE WHO COULD DO IT, SEEIN' AS I WAS THERE IN THE SHOP WITH HIM."
"THEY COUDLN'T GIVE A MULE'S *ARSE* 'BOUT US – WE'RE NO BETTER THAN *FARM ANIMALS* TO THEM. I WAS GOIN' TO LEAVE SERVICE THAT NIGHT."
PUB
THOMPSON SPARROW?
WHAT'S IT TO *YOU*?
I'D LIKE TO OFFER YOU A *JOB*.

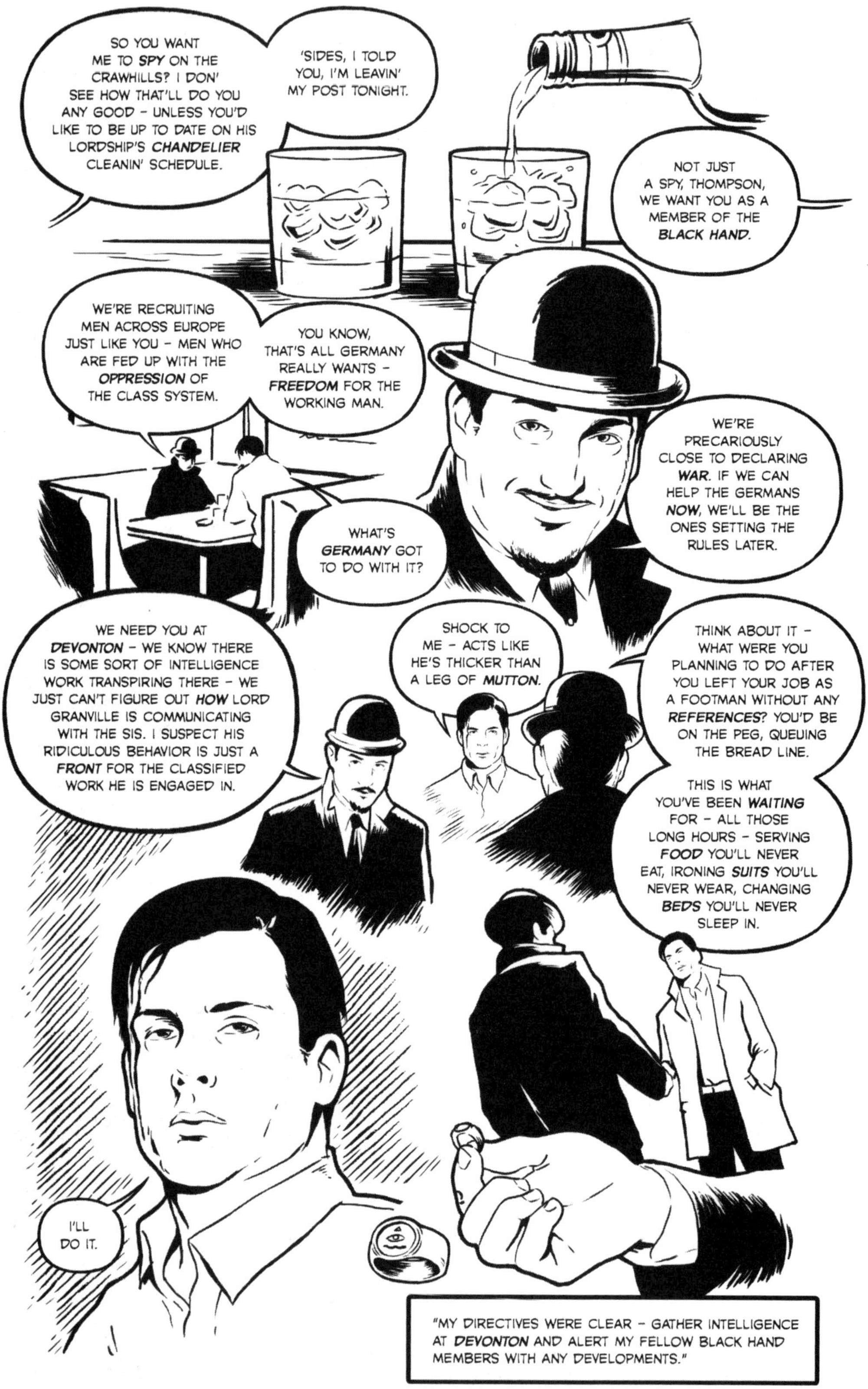
SO YOU WANT ME TO SPY ON THE CRAWHILLS? I DON' SEE HOW THAT'LL DO YOU ANY GOOD - UNLESS YOU'D LIKE TO BE UP TO DATE ON HIS LORDSHIP'S CHANDELIER CLEANIN' SCHEDULE.
'SIDES, I TOLD YOU, I'M LEAVIN' MY POST TONIGHT.
NOT JUST A SPY, THOMPSON, WE WANT YOU AS A MEMBER OF THE BLACK HAND.
WE'RE RECRUITING MEN ACROSS EUROPE JUST LIKE YOU - MEN WHO ARE FED UP WITH THE OPPRESSION OF THE CLASS SYSTEM.
YOU KNOW, THAT'S ALL GERMANY REALLY WANTS - FREEDOM FOR THE WORKING MAN.
WHAT'S GERMANY GOT TO DO WITH IT?
WE'RE PRECARIOUSLY CLOSE TO DECLARING WAR. IF WE CAN HELP THE GERMANS NOW, WE'LL BE THE ONES SETTING THE RULES LATER.
WE NEED YOU AT DEVONTON - WE KNOW THERE IS SOME SORT OF INTELLIGENCE WORK TRANSPIRING THERE - WE JUST CAN'T FIGURE OUT HOW LORD GRANVILLE IS COMMUNICATING WITH THE SIS. I SUSPECT HIS RIDICULOUS BEHAVIOR IS JUST A FRONT FOR THE CLASSIFIED WORK HE IS ENGAGED IN.
SHOCK TO ME - ACTS LIKE HE'S THICKER THAN A LEG OF MUTTON.
THINK ABOUT IT - WHAT WERE YOU PLANNING TO DO AFTER YOU LEFT YOUR JOB AS A FOOTMAN WITHOUT ANY REFERENCES? YOU'D BE ON THE PEG, QUEUING THE BREAD LINE.
THIS IS WHAT YOU'VE BEEN WAITING FOR - ALL THOSE LONG HOURS - SERVING FOOD YOU'LL NEVER EAT, IRONING SUITS YOU'LL NEVER WEAR, CHANGING BEDS YOU'LL NEVER SLEEP IN.
I'LL DO IT.
"MY DIRECTIVES WERE CLEAR - GATHER INTELLIGENCE AT DEVONTON AND ALERT MY FELLOW BLACK HAND MEMBERS WITH ANY DEVELOPMENTS."

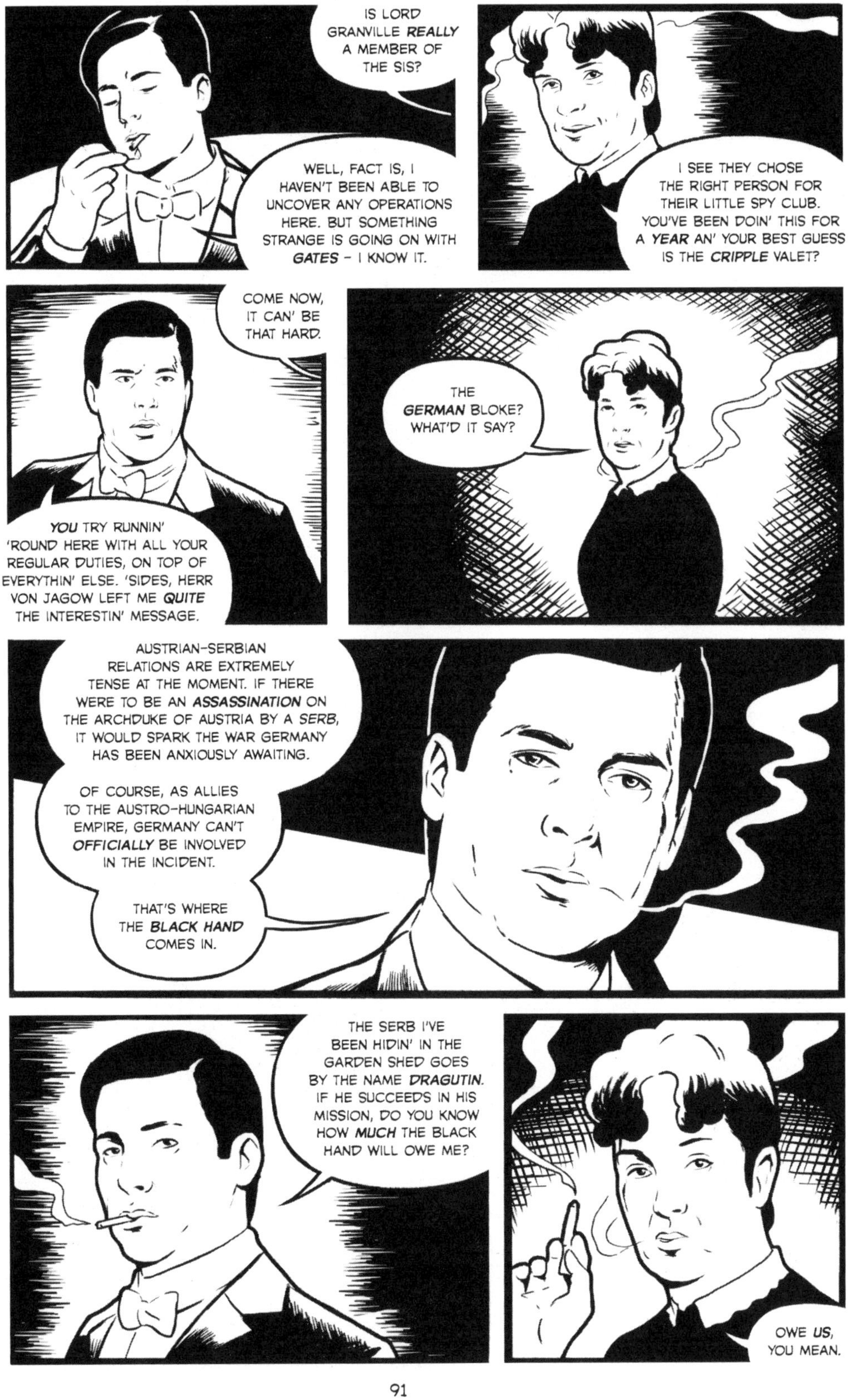
IS LORD GRANVILLE REALLY A MEMBER OF THE SIS?
WELL, FACT IS, I HAVEN'T BEEN ABLE TO UNCOVER ANY OPERATIONS HERE. BUT SOMETHING STRANGE IS GOING ON WITH GATES - I KNOW IT.
I SEE THEY CHOSE THE RIGHT PERSON FOR THEIR LITTLE SPY CLUB. YOU'VE BEEN DOIN' THIS FOR A YEAR AN' YOUR BEST GUESS IS THE CRIPPLE VALET?
COME NOW, IT CAN' BE THAT HARD.
YOU TRY RUNNIN' 'ROUND HERE WITH ALL YOUR REGULAR DUTIES, ON TOP OF EVERYTHIN' ELSE. 'SIDES, HERR VON JAGOW LEFT ME QUITE THE INTERESTIN' MESSAGE.
THE GERMAN BLOKE? WHAT'D IT SAY?
AUSTRIAN-SERBIAN RELATIONS ARE EXTREMELY TENSE AT THE MOMENT. IF THERE WERE TO BE AN ASSASSINATION ON THE ARCHDUKE OF AUSTRIA BY A SERB, IT WOULD SPARK THE WAR GERMANY HAS BEEN ANXIOUSLY AWAITING.
OF COURSE, AS ALLIES TO THE AUSTRO-HUNGARIAN EMPIRE, GERMANY CAN'T OFFICIALLY BE INVOLVED IN THE INCIDENT.
THAT'S WHERE THE BLACK HAND COMES IN.
THE SERB I'VE BEEN HIDIN' IN THE GARDEN SHED GOES BY THE NAME DRAGUTIN. IF HE SUCCEEDS IN HIS MISSION, DO YOU KNOW HOW MUCH THE BLACK HAND WILL OWE ME?
OWE US, YOU MEAN.

CHAP

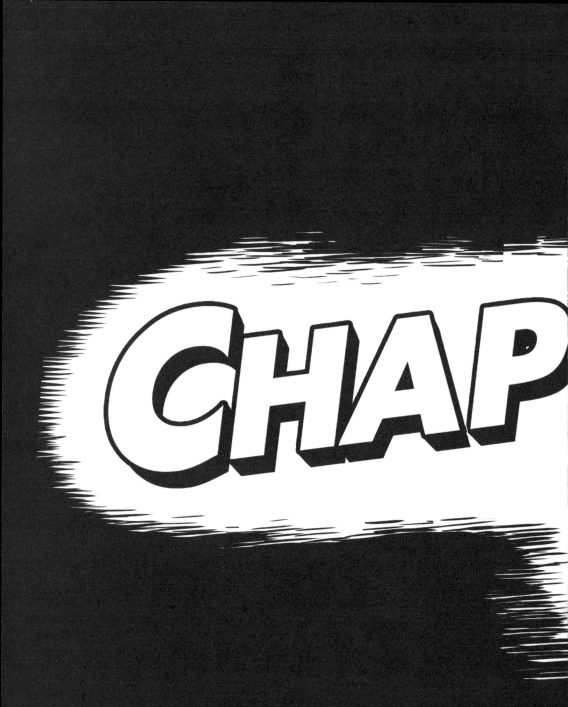

TER
FOUR

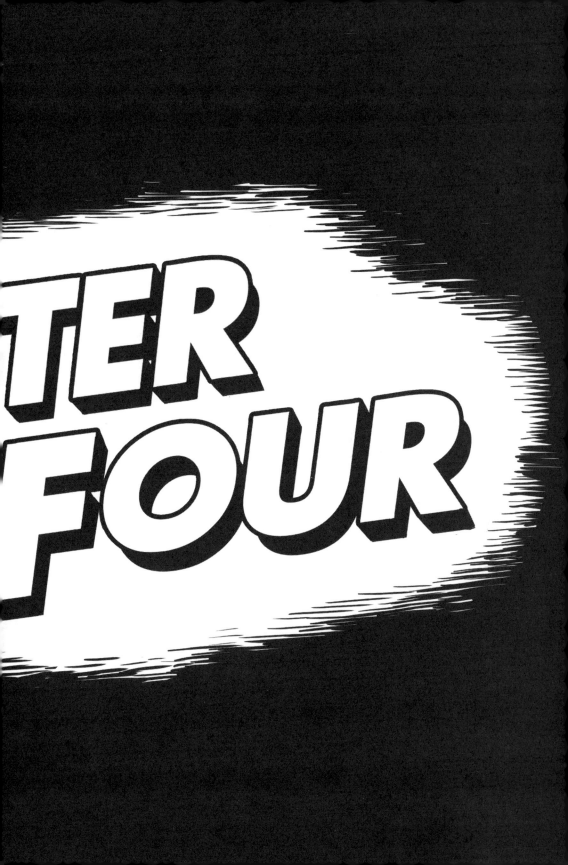

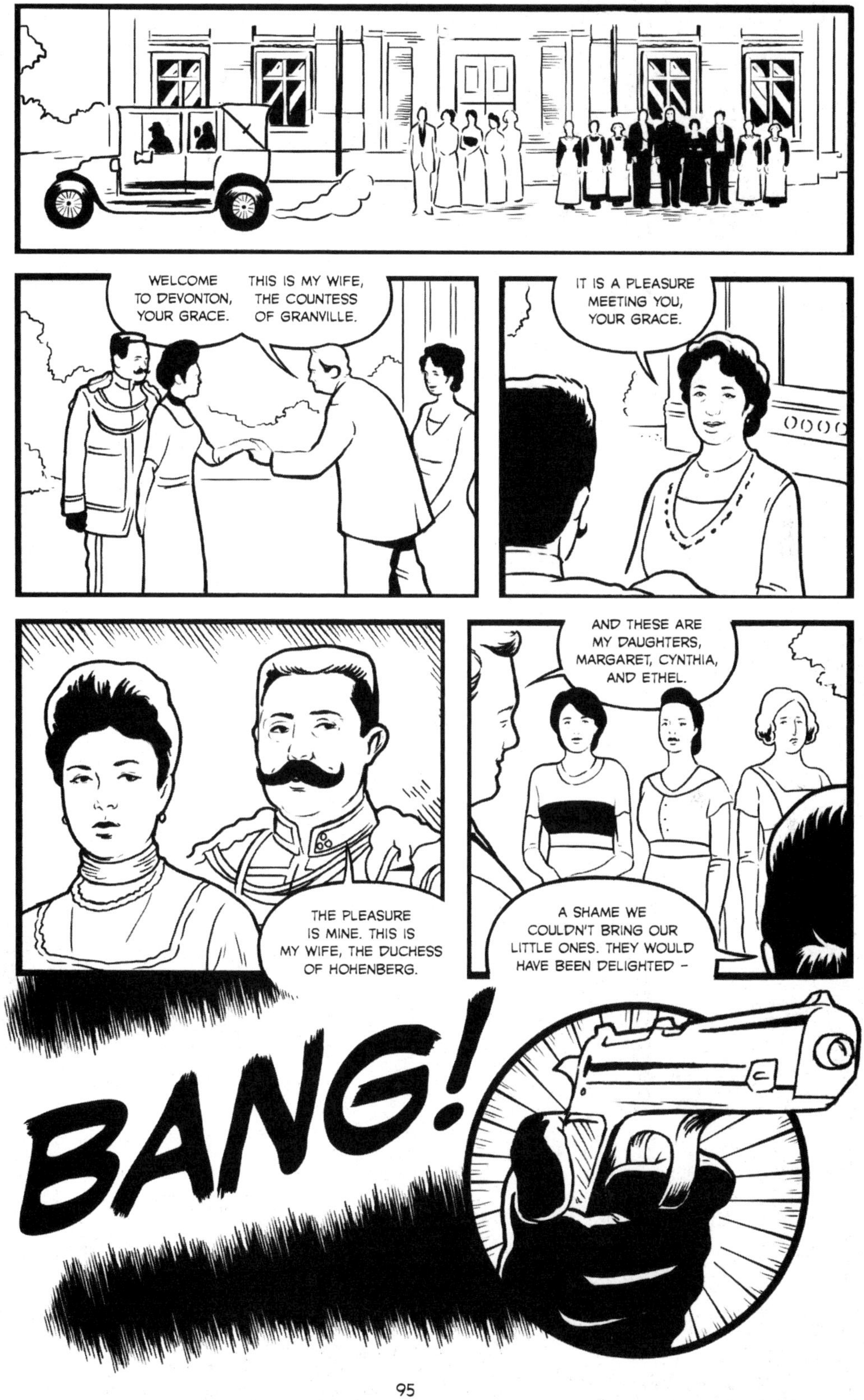
WELCOME TO DEVONTON, YOUR GRACE.
THIS IS MY WIFE, THE COUNTESS OF GRANVILLE.
IT IS A PLEASURE MEETING YOU, YOUR GRACE.
THE PLEASURE IS MINE. THIS IS MY WIFE, THE DUCHESS OF HOHENBERG.
AND THESE ARE MY DAUGHTERS, MARGARET, CYNTHIA, AND ETHEL.
A SHAME WE COULDN'T BRING OUR LITTLE ONES. THEY WOULD HAVE BEEN DELIGHTED –
BANG!

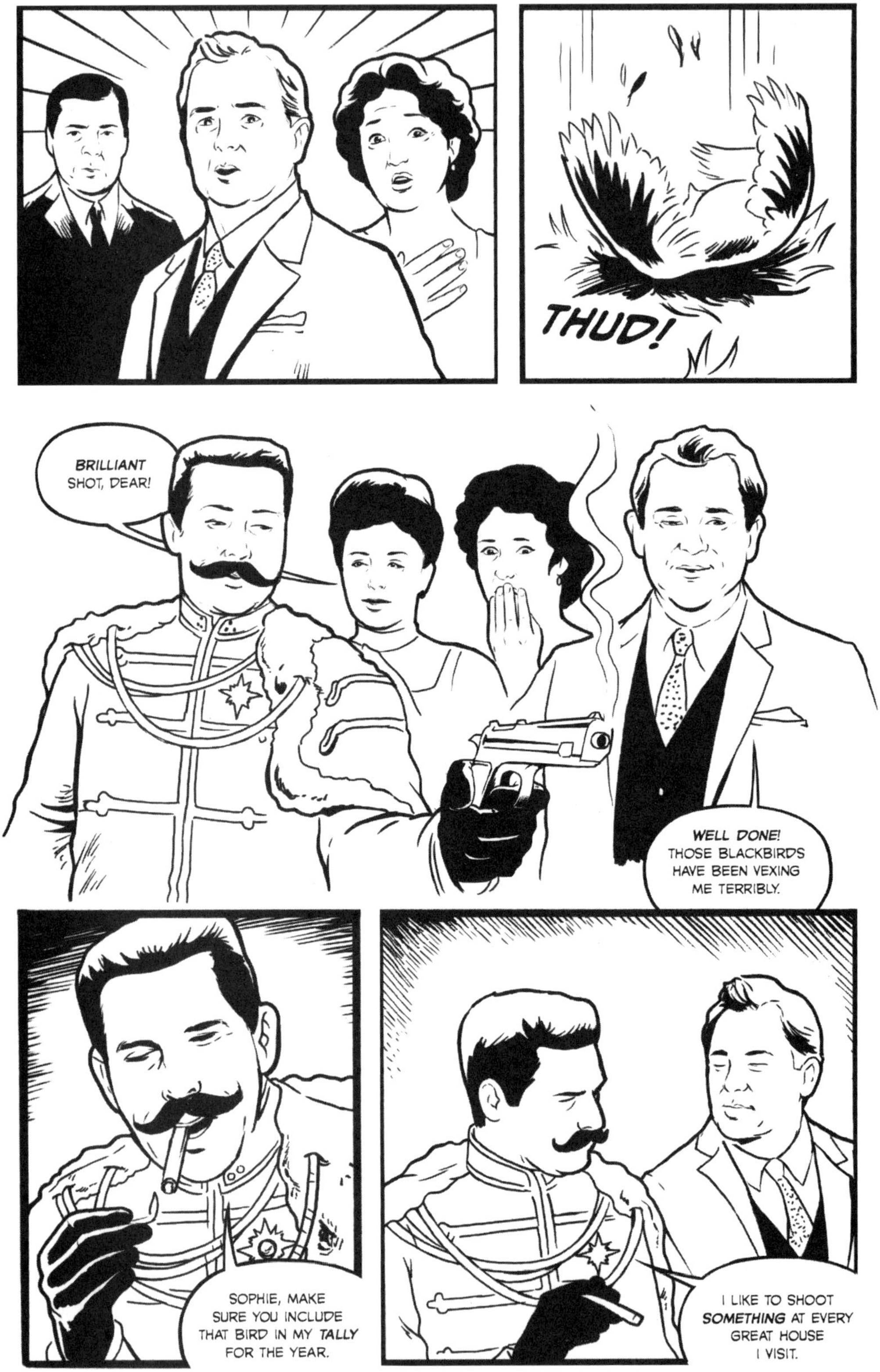
THUD!
BRILLIANT SHOT, DEAR!
WELL DONE! THOSE BLACKBIRDS HAVE BEEN VEXING ME TERRIBLY.
SOPHIE, MAKE SURE YOU INCLUDE THAT BIRD IN MY TALLY FOR THE YEAR.
I LIKE TO SHOOT SOMETHING AT EVERY GREAT HOUSE I VISIT.

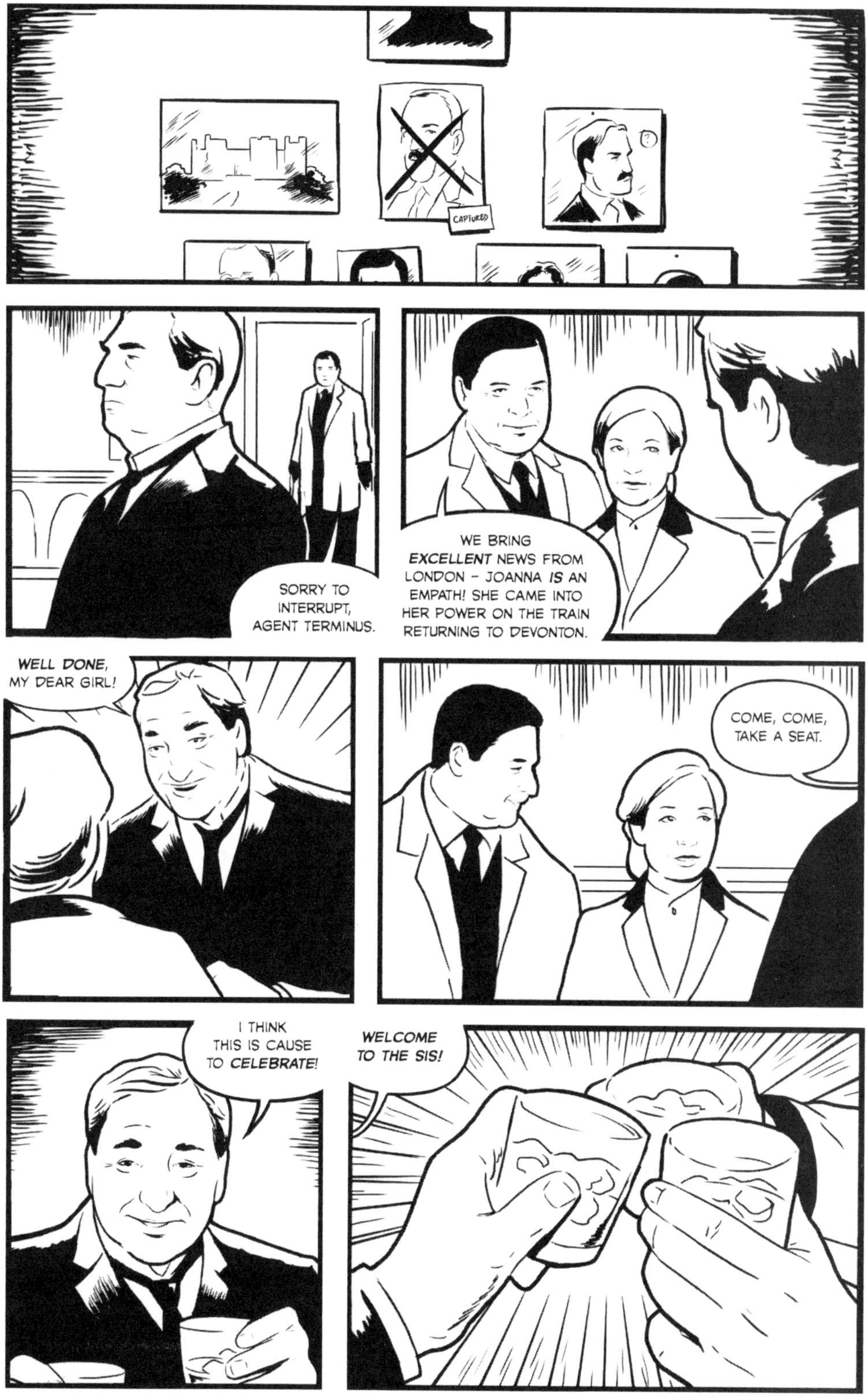
CAPTURED
SORRY TO INTERRUPT, AGENT TERMINUS.
WE BRING *EXCELLENT* NEWS FROM LONDON - JOANNA *IS* AN EMPATH! SHE CAME INTO HER POWER ON THE TRAIN RETURNING TO DEVONTON.
WELL DONE, MY DEAR GIRL!
COME, COME, TAKE A SEAT.
I THINK THIS IS CAUSE TO *CELEBRATE!*
WELCOME TO THE SIS!

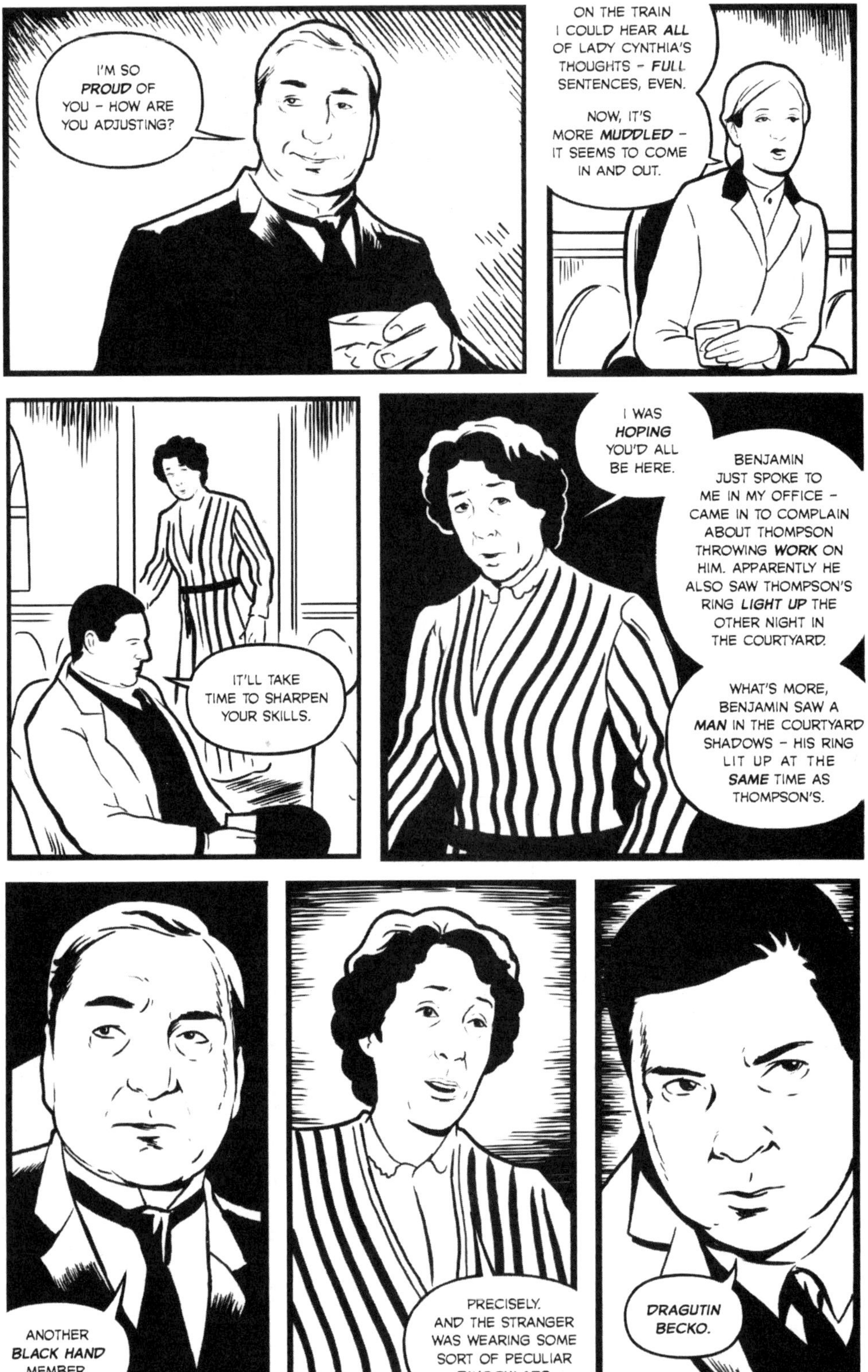

I'M SO PROUD OF YOU – HOW ARE YOU ADJUSTING?
ON THE TRAIN I COULD HEAR ALL OF LADY CYNTHIA'S THOUGHTS – FULL SENTENCES, EVEN.
NOW, IT'S MORE MUDDLED – IT SEEMS TO COME IN AND OUT.
IT'LL TAKE TIME TO SHARPEN YOUR SKILLS.
I WAS HOPING YOU'D ALL BE HERE.
BENJAMIN JUST SPOKE TO ME IN MY OFFICE – CAME IN TO COMPLAIN ABOUT THOMPSON THROWING WORK ON HIM. APPARENTLY HE ALSO SAW THOMPSON'S RING LIGHT UP THE OTHER NIGHT IN THE COURTYARD.
WHAT'S MORE, BENJAMIN SAW A MAN IN THE COURTYARD SHADOWS – HIS RING LIT UP AT THE SAME TIME AS THOMPSON'S.
ANOTHER BLACK HAND MEMBER.
PRECISELY. AND THE STRANGER WAS WEARING SOME SORT OF PECULIAR BINOCULARS.
DRAGUTIN BECKO.

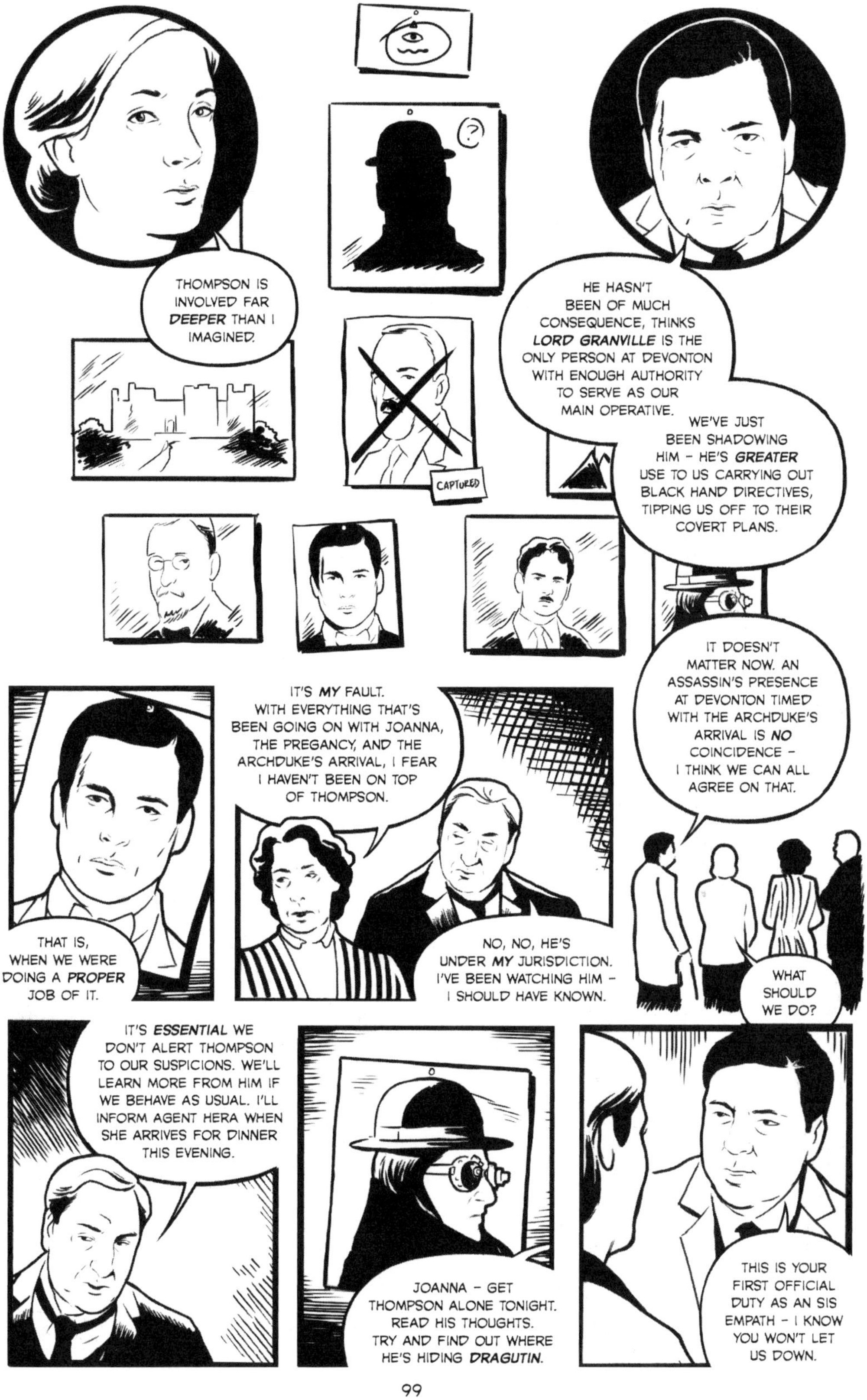
THOMPSON IS INVOLVED FAR DEEPER THAN I IMAGINED.
HE HASN'T BEEN OF MUCH CONSEQUENCE, THINKS LORD GRANVILLE IS THE ONLY PERSON AT DEVONTON WITH ENOUGH AUTHORITY TO SERVE AS OUR MAIN OPERATIVE.
WE'VE JUST BEEN SHADOWING HIM – HE'S GREATER USE TO US CARRYING OUT BLACK HAND DIRECTIVES, TIPPING US OFF TO THEIR COVERT PLANS.
CAPTURED
IT DOESN'T MATTER NOW. AN ASSASSIN'S PRESENCE AT DEVONTON TIMED WITH THE ARCHDUKE'S ARRIVAL IS NO COINCIDENCE – I THINK WE CAN ALL AGREE ON THAT.
THAT IS, WHEN WE WERE DOING A PROPER JOB OF IT.
IT'S MY FAULT. WITH EVERYTHING THAT'S BEEN GOING ON WITH JOANNA, THE PREGANCY, AND THE ARCHDUKE'S ARRIVAL, I FEAR I HAVEN'T BEEN ON TOP OF THOMPSON.
NO, NO, HE'S UNDER MY JURISDICTION. I'VE BEEN WATCHING HIM – I SHOULD HAVE KNOWN.
WHAT SHOULD WE DO?
IT'S ESSENTIAL WE DON'T ALERT THOMPSON TO OUR SUSPICIONS. WE'LL LEARN MORE FROM HIM IF WE BEHAVE AS USUAL. I'LL INFORM AGENT HERA WHEN SHE ARRIVES FOR DINNER THIS EVENING.
JOANNA – GET THOMPSON ALONE TONIGHT. READ HIS THOUGHTS. TRY AND FIND OUT WHERE HE'S HIDING DRAGUTIN.
THIS IS YOUR FIRST OFFICIAL DUTY AS AN SIS EMPATH – I KNOW YOU WON'T LET US DOWN.

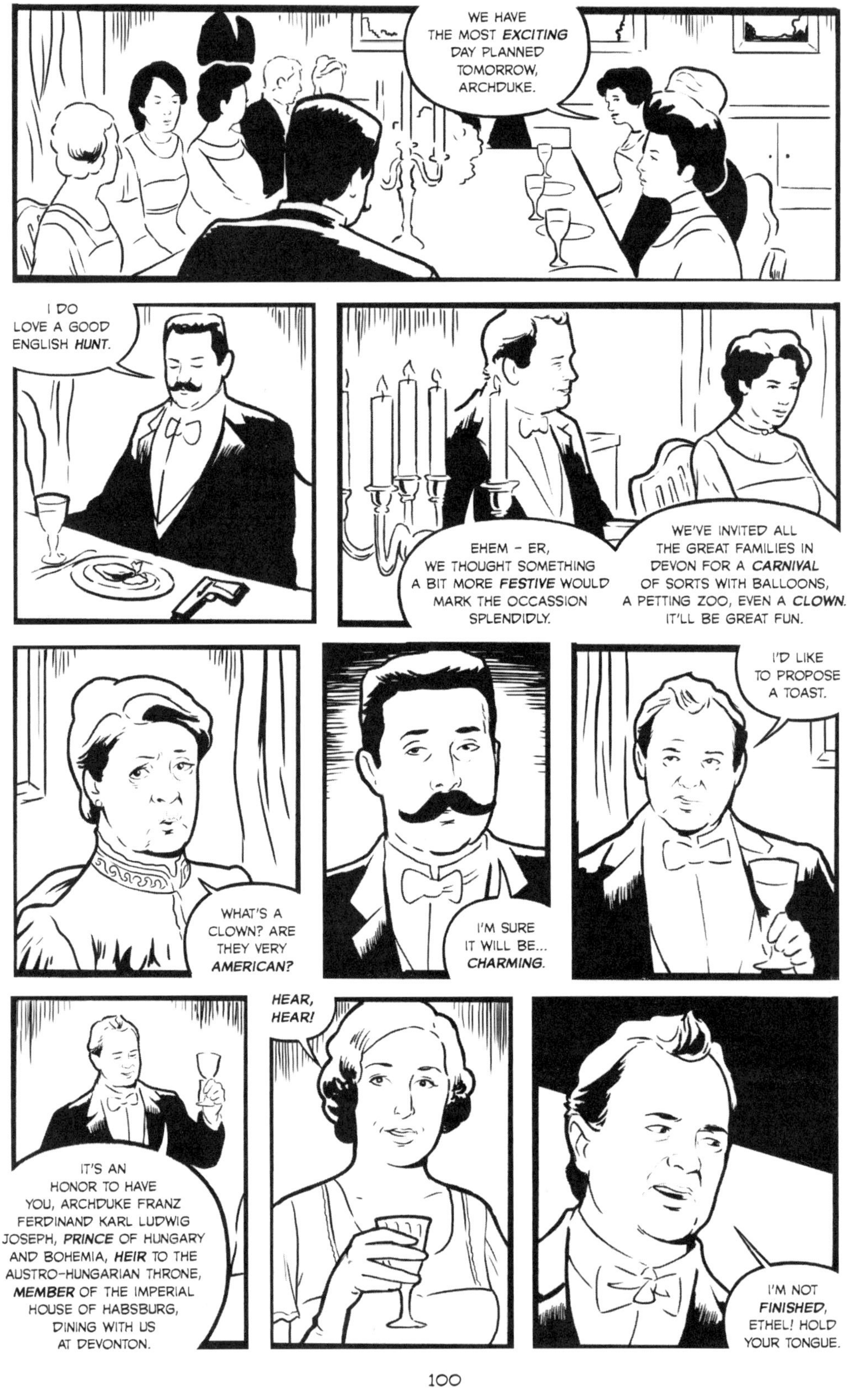
WE HAVE THE MOST EXCITING DAY PLANNED TOMORROW, ARCHDUKE.
I DO LOVE A GOOD ENGLISH HUNT.
EHEM - ER, WE THOUGHT SOMETHING A BIT MORE FESTIVE WOULD MARK THE OCCASSION SPLENDIDLY.
WE'VE INVITED ALL THE GREAT FAMILIES IN DEVON FOR A CARNIVAL OF SORTS WITH BALLOONS, A PETTING ZOO, EVEN A CLOWN. IT'LL BE GREAT FUN.
WHAT'S A CLOWN? ARE THEY VERY AMERICAN?
I'M SURE IT WILL BE... CHARMING.
I'D LIKE TO PROPOSE A TOAST.
IT'S AN HONOR TO HAVE YOU, ARCHDUKE FRANZ FERDINAND KARL LUDWIG JOSEPH, PRINCE OF HUNGARY AND BOHEMIA, HEIR TO THE AUSTRO-HUNGARIAN THRONE, MEMBER OF THE IMPERIAL HOUSE OF HABSBURG, DINING WITH US AT DEVONTON.
HEAR, HEAR!
I'M NOT FINISHED, ETHEL! HOLD YOUR TONGUE.

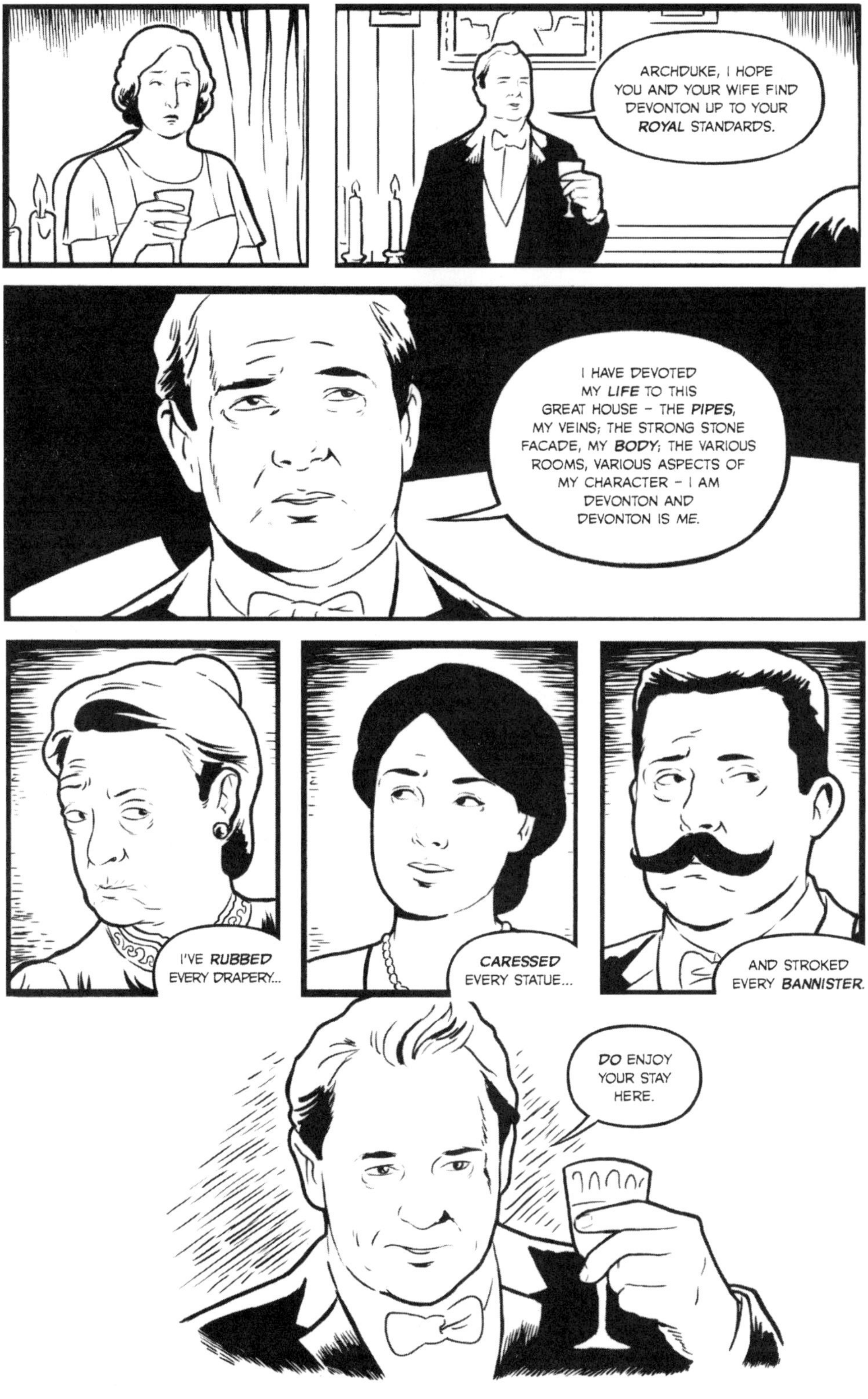
ARCHDUKE, I HOPE YOU AND YOUR WIFE FIND DEVONTON UP TO YOUR ROYAL STANDARDS.
I HAVE DEVOTED MY LIFE TO THIS GREAT HOUSE - THE PIPES, MY VEINS; THE STRONG STONE FACADE, MY BODY; THE VARIOUS ROOMS, VARIOUS ASPECTS OF MY CHARACTER - I AM DEVONTON AND DEVONTON IS ME.
I'VE RUBBED EVERY DRAPERY...
CARESSED EVERY STATUE...
AND STROKED EVERY BANNISTER.
DO ENJOY YOUR STAY HERE.

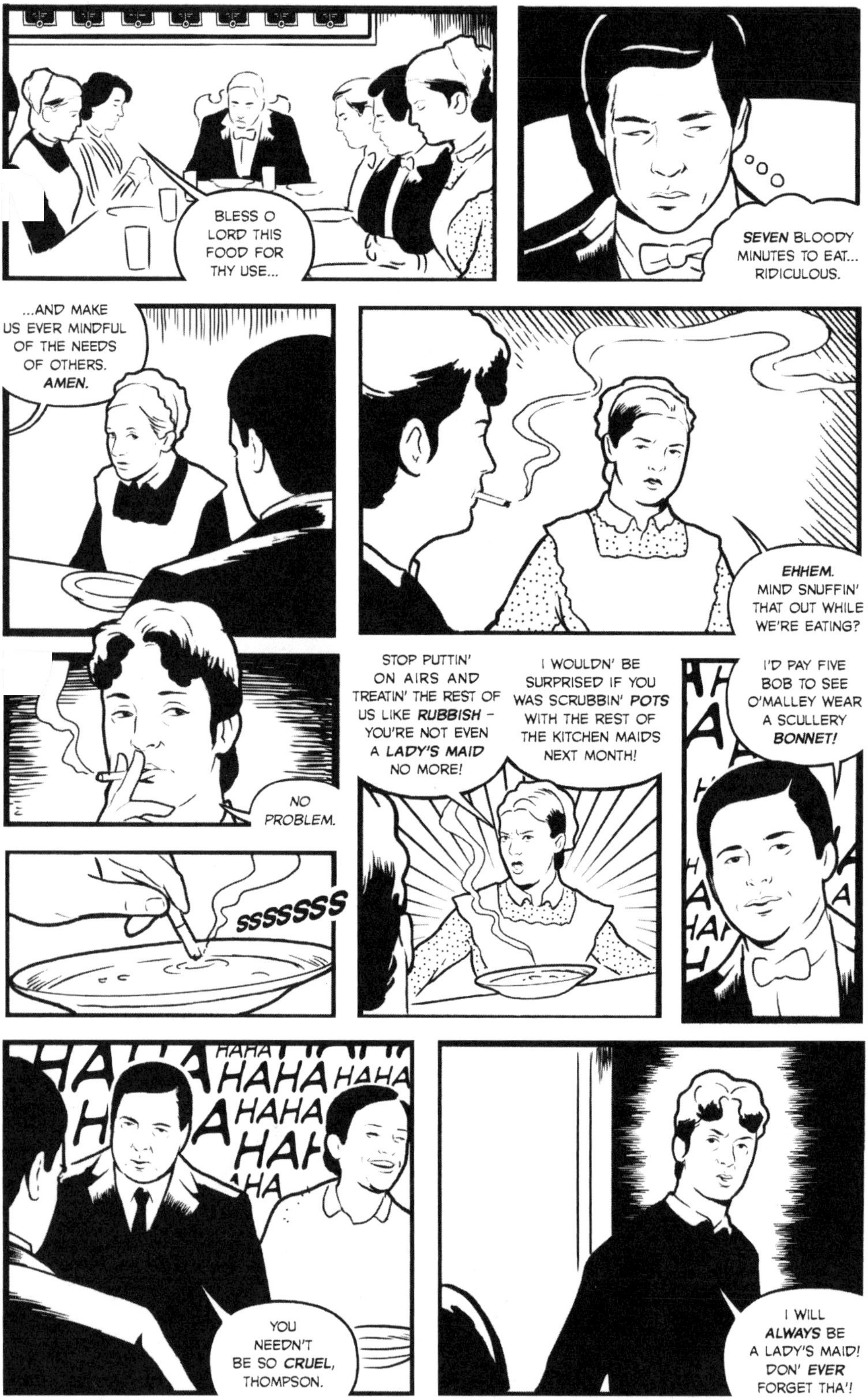

BLESS O LORD THIS FOOD FOR THY USE...
SEVEN BLOODY MINUTES TO EAT... RIDICULOUS.
...AND MAKE US EVER MINDFUL OF THE NEEDS OF OTHERS. AMEN.
EHHEM. MIND SNUFFIN' THAT OUT WHILE WE'RE EATING?
NO PROBLEM.
SSSSSSS
STOP PUTTIN' ON AIRS AND TREATIN' THE REST OF US LIKE RUBBISH – YOU'RE NOT EVEN A LADY'S MAID NO MORE!
I WOULDN' BE SURPRISED IF YOU WAS SCRUBBIN' POTS WITH THE REST OF THE KITCHEN MAIDS NEXT MONTH!
I'D PAY FIVE BOB TO SEE O'MALLEY WEAR A SCULLERY BONNET!
HAHA HAHA HAHA HAHA
YOU NEEDN'T BE SO CRUEL, THOMPSON.
I WILL ALWAYS BE A LADY'S MAID! DON' EVER FORGET THA'!

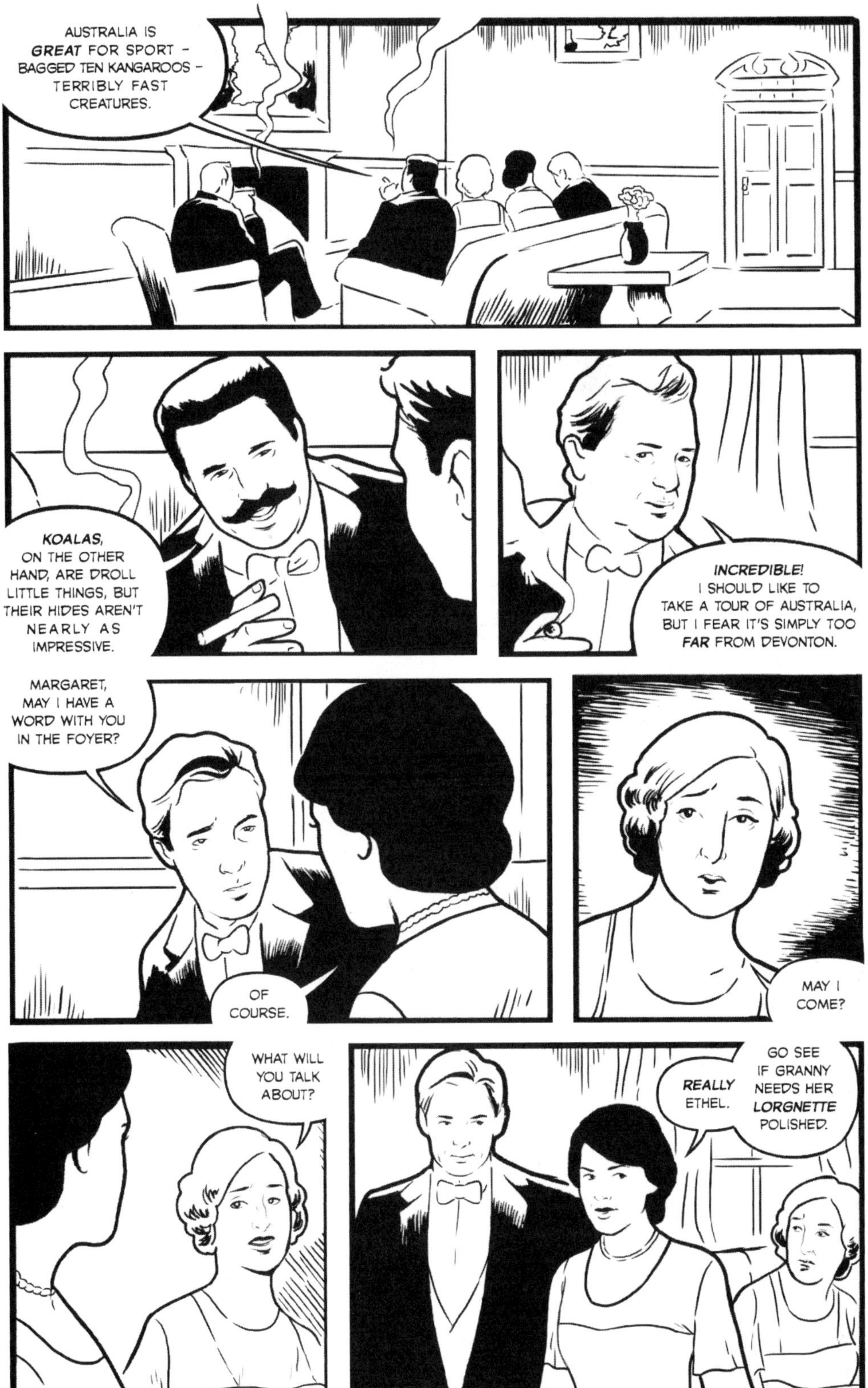
AUSTRALIA IS GREAT FOR SPORT - BAGGED TEN KANGAROOS - TERRIBLY FAST CREATURES.
KOALAS, ON THE OTHER HAND, ARE DROLL LITTLE THINGS, BUT THEIR HIDES AREN'T NEARLY AS IMPRESSIVE.
INCREDIBLE! I SHOULD LIKE TO TAKE A TOUR OF AUSTRALIA, BUT I FEAR IT'S SIMPLY TOO FAR FROM DEVONTON.
MARGARET, MAY I HAVE A WORD WITH YOU IN THE FOYER?
OF COURSE.
MAY I COME?
WHAT WILL YOU TALK ABOUT?
REALLY ETHEL.
GO SEE IF GRANNY NEEDS HER LORGNETTE POLISHED.

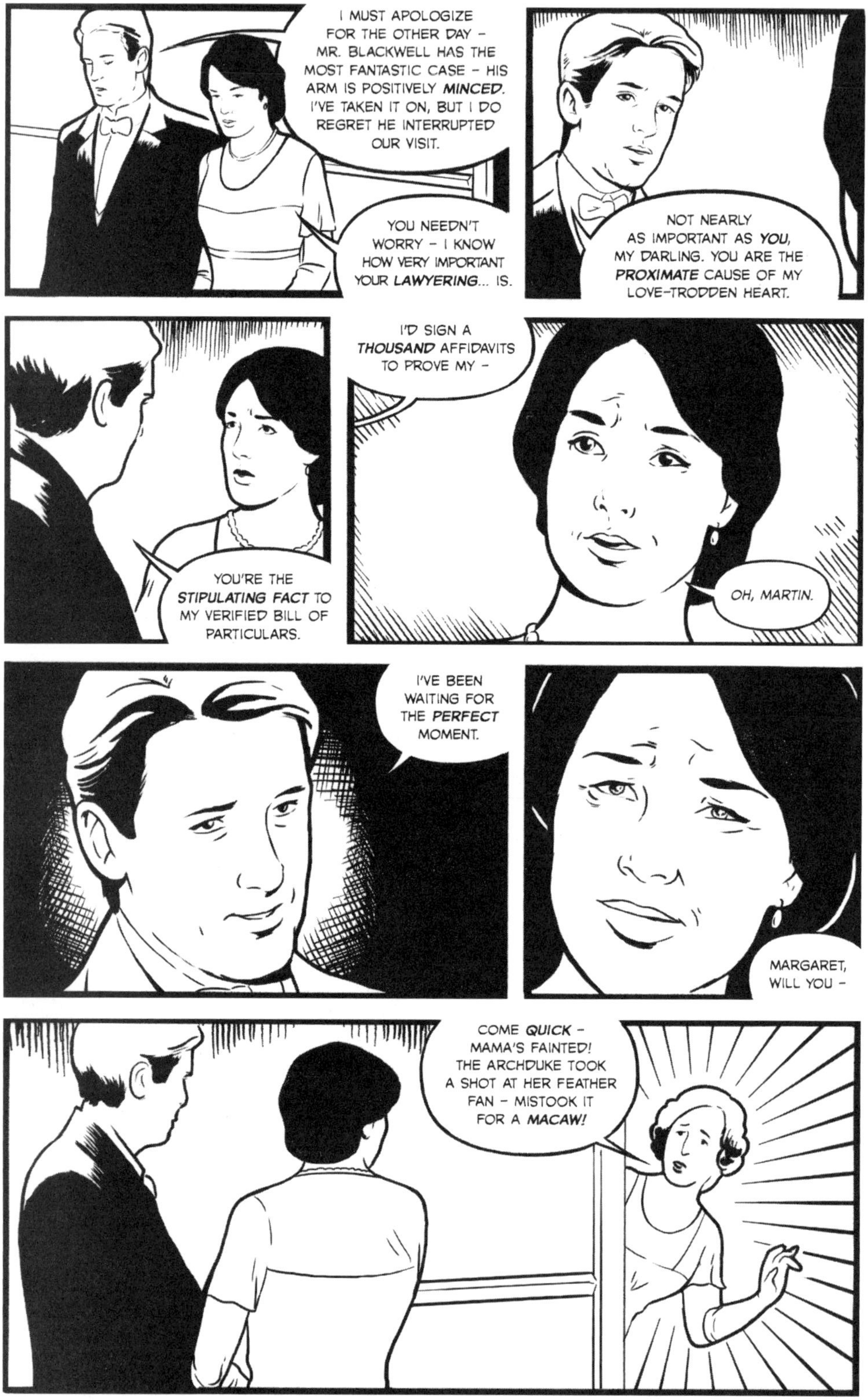
I MUST APOLOGIZE FOR THE OTHER DAY - MR. BLACKWELL HAS THE MOST FANTASTIC CASE - HIS ARM IS POSITIVELY MINCED. I'VE TAKEN IT ON, BUT I DO REGRET HE INTERRUPTED OUR VISIT.
YOU NEEDN'T WORRY - I KNOW HOW VERY IMPORTANT YOUR LAWYERING... IS.
NOT NEARLY AS IMPORTANT AS YOU, MY DARLING. YOU ARE THE PROXIMATE CAUSE OF MY LOVE-TRODDEN HEART.
YOU'RE THE STIPULATING FACT TO MY VERIFIED BILL OF PARTICULARS.
I'D SIGN A THOUSAND AFFIDAVITS TO PROVE MY -
OH, MARTIN.
I'VE BEEN WAITING FOR THE PERFECT MOMENT.
MARGARET, WILL YOU -
COME QUICK - MAMA'S FAINTED! THE ARCHDUKE TOOK A SHOT AT HER FEATHER FAN - MISTOOK IT FOR A MACAW!

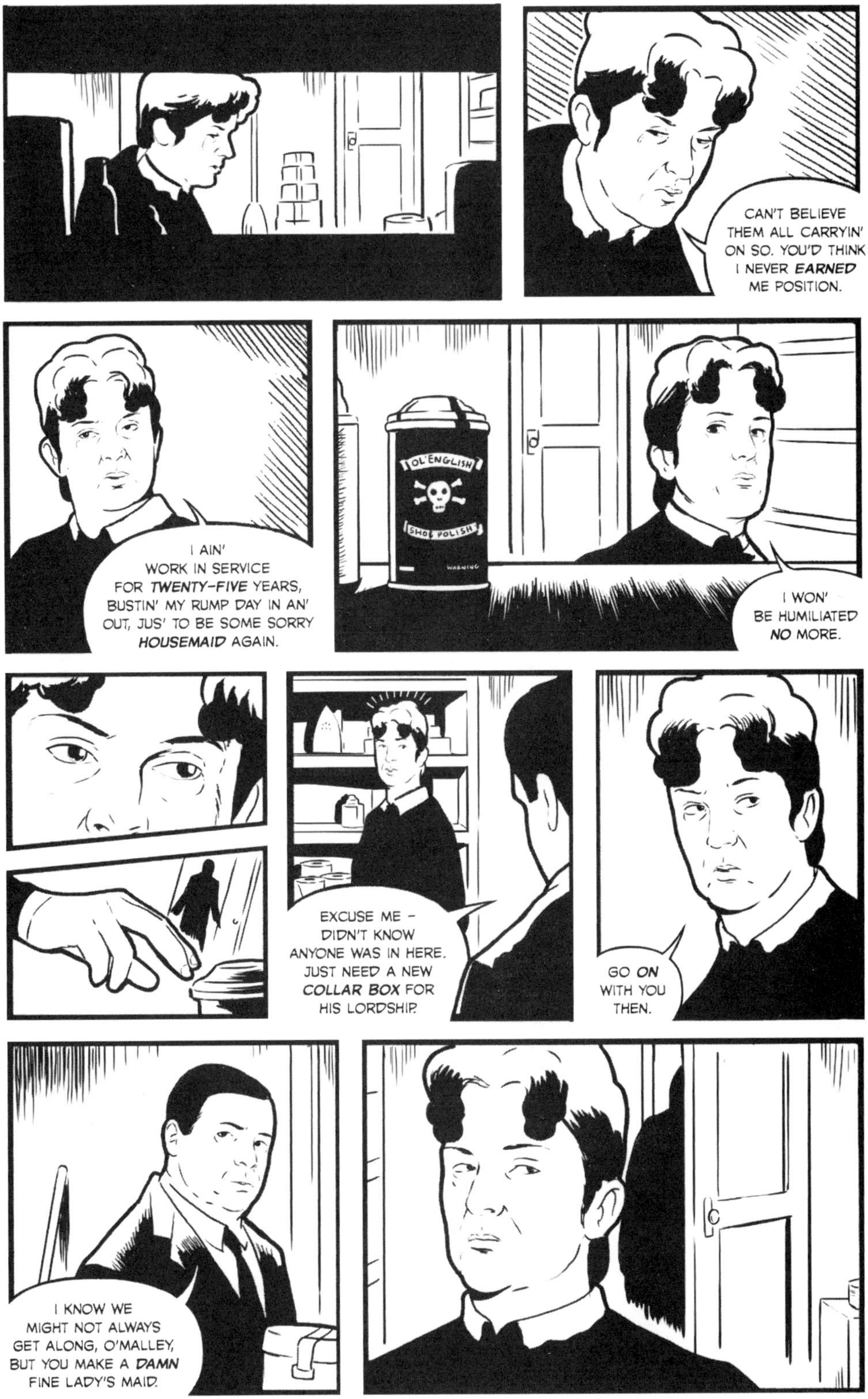
CAN'T BELIEVE THEM ALL CARRYIN' ON SO. YOU'D THINK I NEVER EARNED ME POSITION.
I AIN' WORK IN SERVICE FOR TWENTY-FIVE YEARS, BUSTIN' MY RUMP DAY IN AN' OUT, JUS' TO BE SOME SORRY HOUSEMAID AGAIN.
OL'ENGLISH
SHOE POLISH
I WON' BE HUMILIATED NO MORE.
EXCUSE ME - DIDN'T KNOW ANYONE WAS IN HERE. JUST NEED A NEW COLLAR BOX FOR HIS LORDSHIP.
GO ON WITH YOU THEN.
I KNOW WE MIGHT NOT ALWAYS GET ALONG, O'MALLEY, BUT YOU MAKE A DAMN FINE LADY'S MAID.

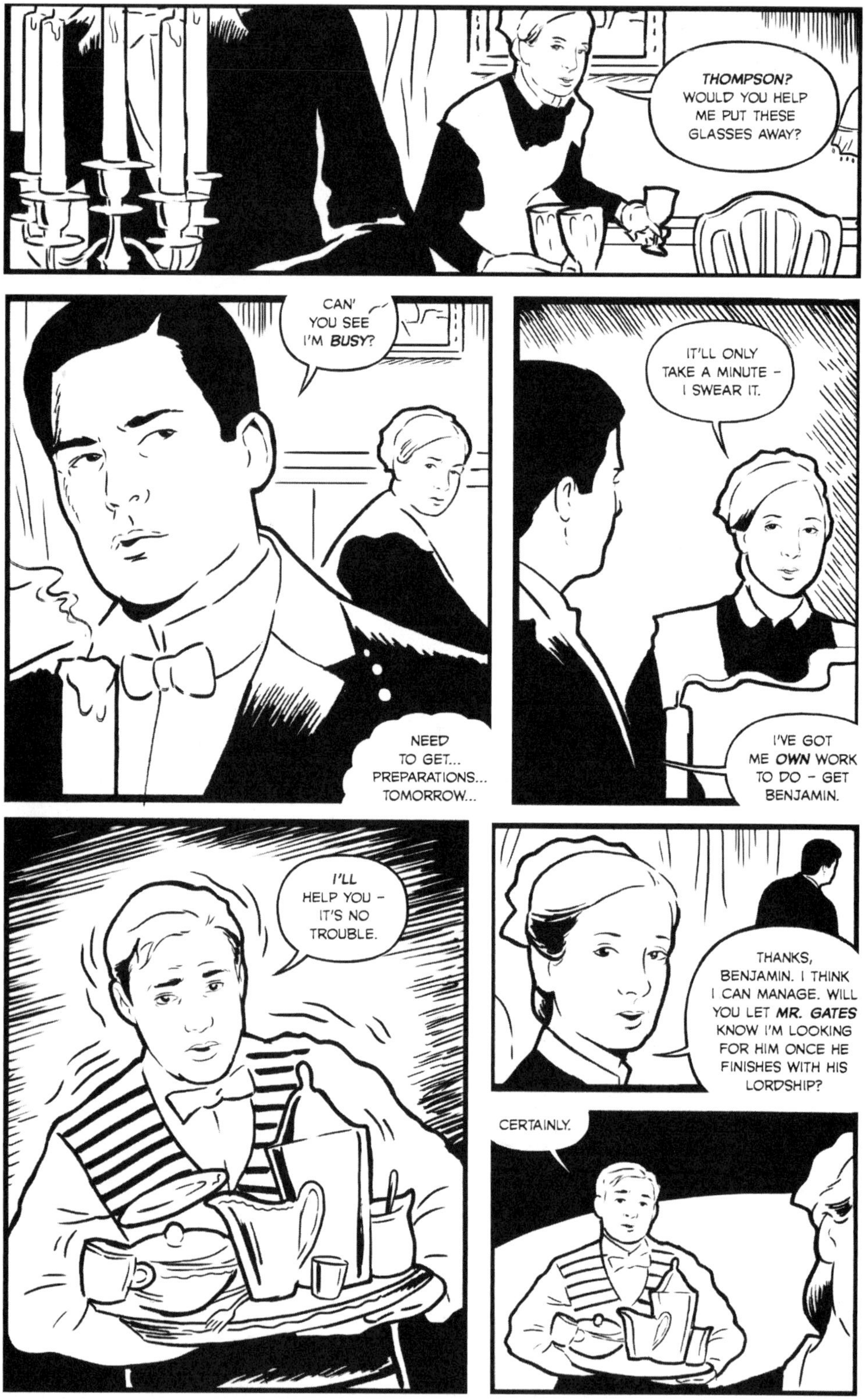
THOMPSON? WOULD YOU HELP ME PUT THESE GLASSES AWAY?
CAN' YOU SEE I'M BUSY?
NEED TO GET... PREPARATIONS... TOMORROW...
IT'LL ONLY TAKE A MINUTE - I SWEAR IT.
I'VE GOT ME OWN WORK TO DO - GET BENJAMIN.
I'LL HELP YOU - IT'S NO TROUBLE.
THANKS, BENJAMIN. I THINK I CAN MANAGE. WILL YOU LET MR. GATES KNOW I'M LOOKING FOR HIM ONCE HE FINISHES WITH HIS LORDSHIP?
CERTAINLY.

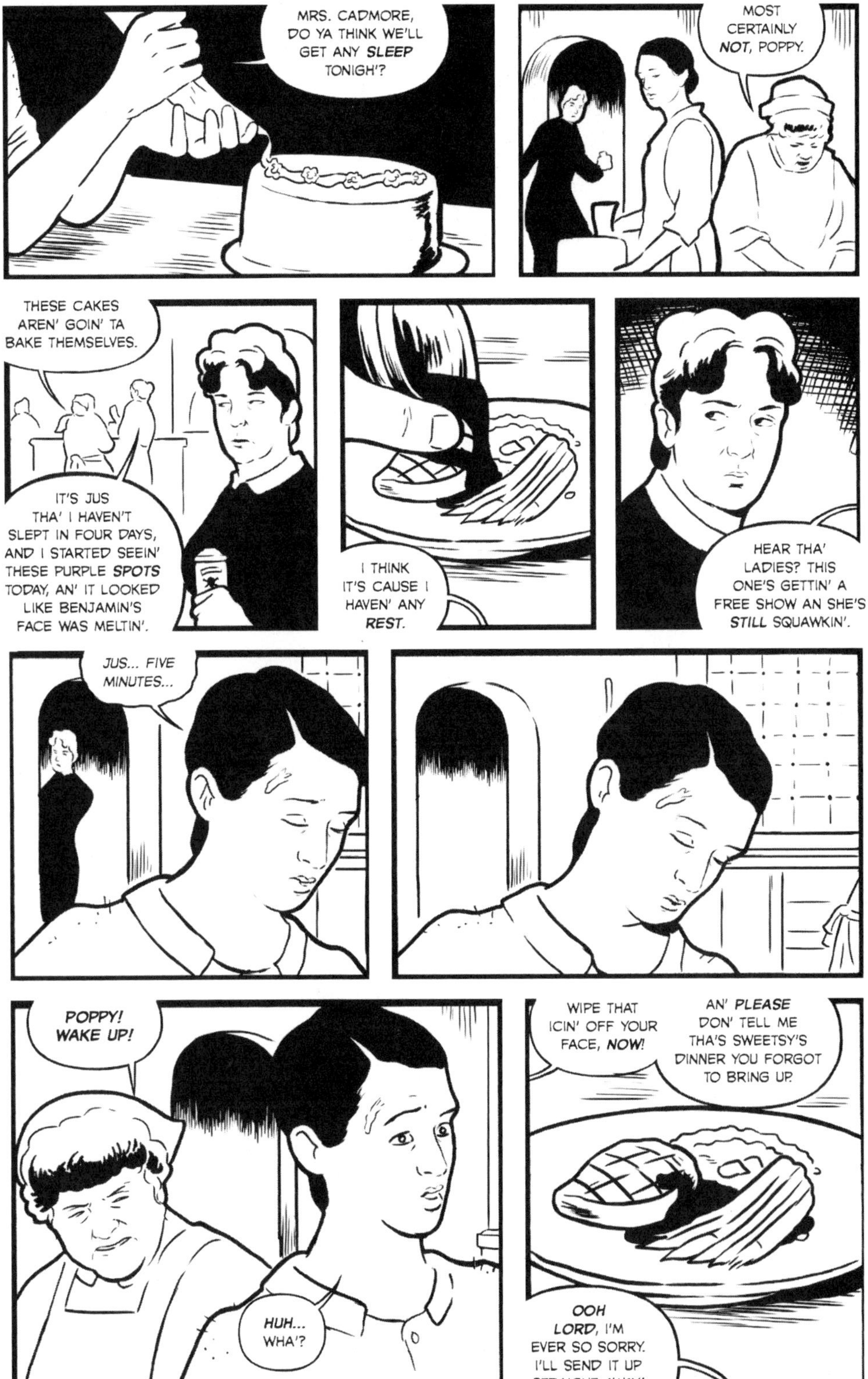
MRS. CADMORE, DO YA THINK WE'LL GET ANY SLEEP TONIGH'?
MOST CERTAINLY NOT, POPPY.
THESE CAKES AREN' GOIN' TA BAKE THEMSELVES.
IT'S JUS THA' I HAVEN'T SLEPT IN FOUR DAYS, AND I STARTED SEEIN' THESE PURPLE SPOTS TODAY, AN' IT LOOKED LIKE BENJAMIN'S FACE WAS MELTIN'.
I THINK IT'S CAUSE I HAVEN' ANY REST.
HEAR THA' LADIES? THIS ONE'S GETTIN' A FREE SHOW AN SHE'S STILL SQUAWKIN'.
JUS... FIVE MINUTES...
POPPY! WAKE UP!
HUH... WHA'?
WIPE THAT ICIN' OFF YOUR FACE, NOW!
AN' PLEASE DON' TELL ME THA'S SWEETSY'S DINNER YOU FORGOT TO BRING UP.
OOH LORD, I'M EVER SO SORRY. I'LL SEND IT UP STRAIGHT AWAY!

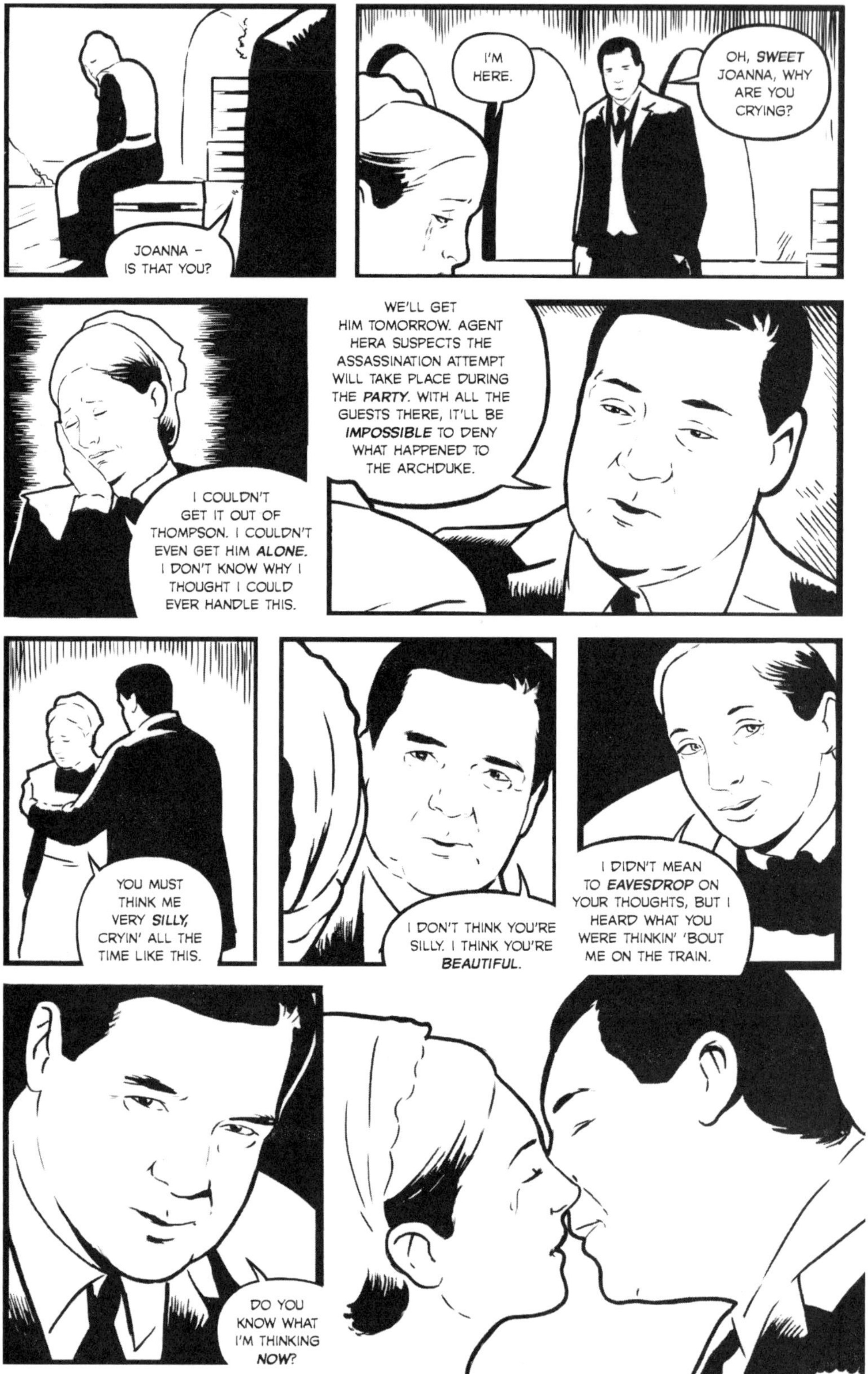
JOANNA - IS THAT YOU?
I'M HERE.
OH, SWEET JOANNA, WHY ARE YOU CRYING?
I COULDN'T GET IT OUT OF THOMPSON. I COULDN'T EVEN GET HIM ALONE. I DON'T KNOW WHY I THOUGHT I COULD EVER HANDLE THIS.
WE'LL GET HIM TOMORROW. AGENT HERA SUSPECTS THE ASSASSINATION ATTEMPT WILL TAKE PLACE DURING THE PARTY. WITH ALL THE GUESTS THERE, IT'LL BE IMPOSSIBLE TO DENY WHAT HAPPENED TO THE ARCHDUKE.
YOU MUST THINK ME VERY SILLY, CRYIN' ALL THE TIME LIKE THIS.
I DON'T THINK YOU'RE SILLY. I THINK YOU'RE BEAUTIFUL.
I DIDN'T MEAN TO EAVESDROP ON YOUR THOUGHTS, BUT I HEARD WHAT YOU WERE THINKIN' 'BOUT ME ON THE TRAIN.
DO YOU KNOW WHAT I'M THINKING NOW?

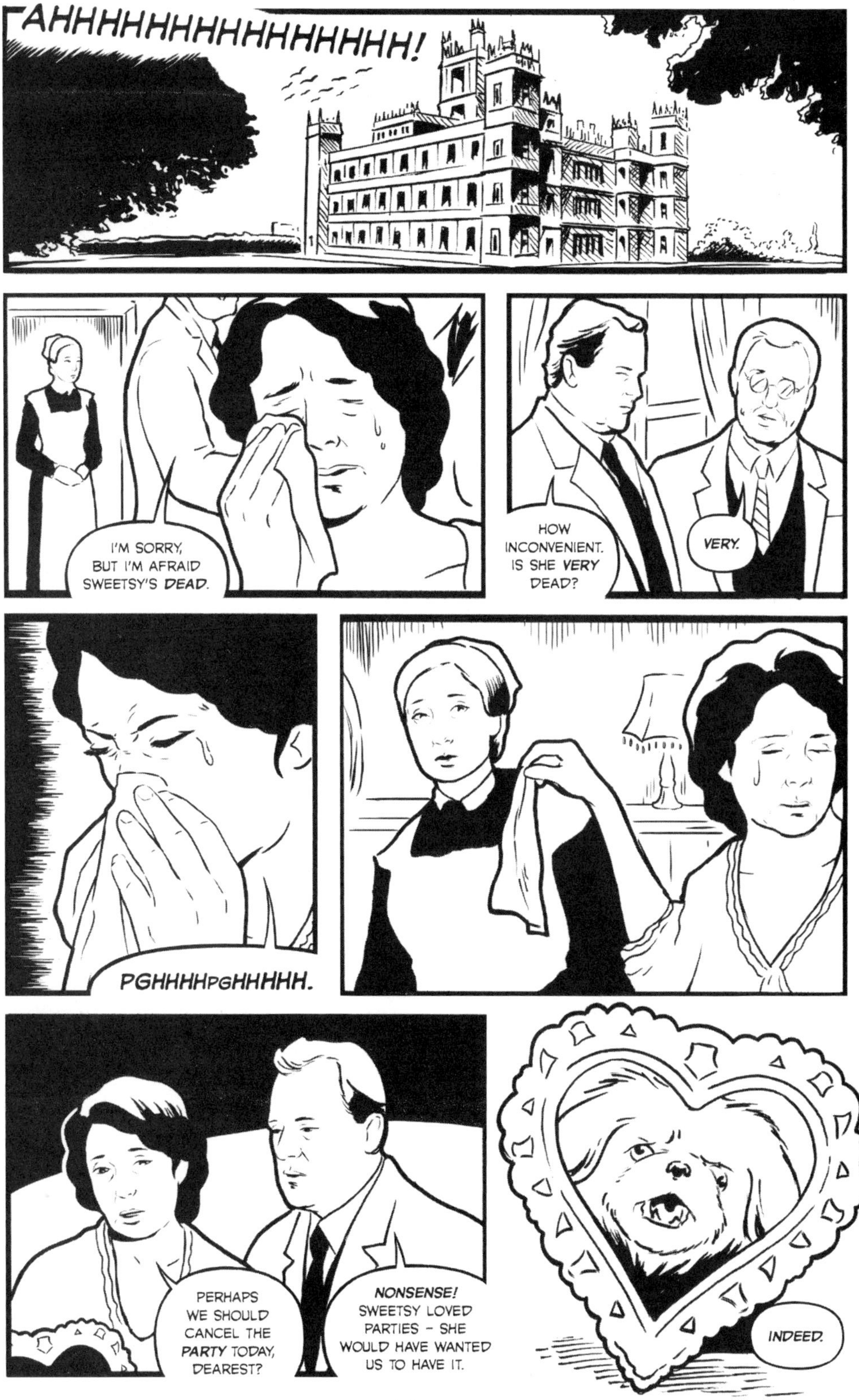
AHHHHHHHHHHHHHHHHH!
I'M SORRY, BUT I'M AFRAID SWEETSY'S DEAD.
HOW INCONVENIENT. IS SHE VERY DEAD?
VERY.
PGHHHHPGHHHHH.
PERHAPS WE SHOULD CANCEL THE PARTY TODAY, DEAREST?
NONSENSE! SWEETSY LOVED PARTIES – SHE WOULD HAVE WANTED US TO HAVE IT.
INDEED.

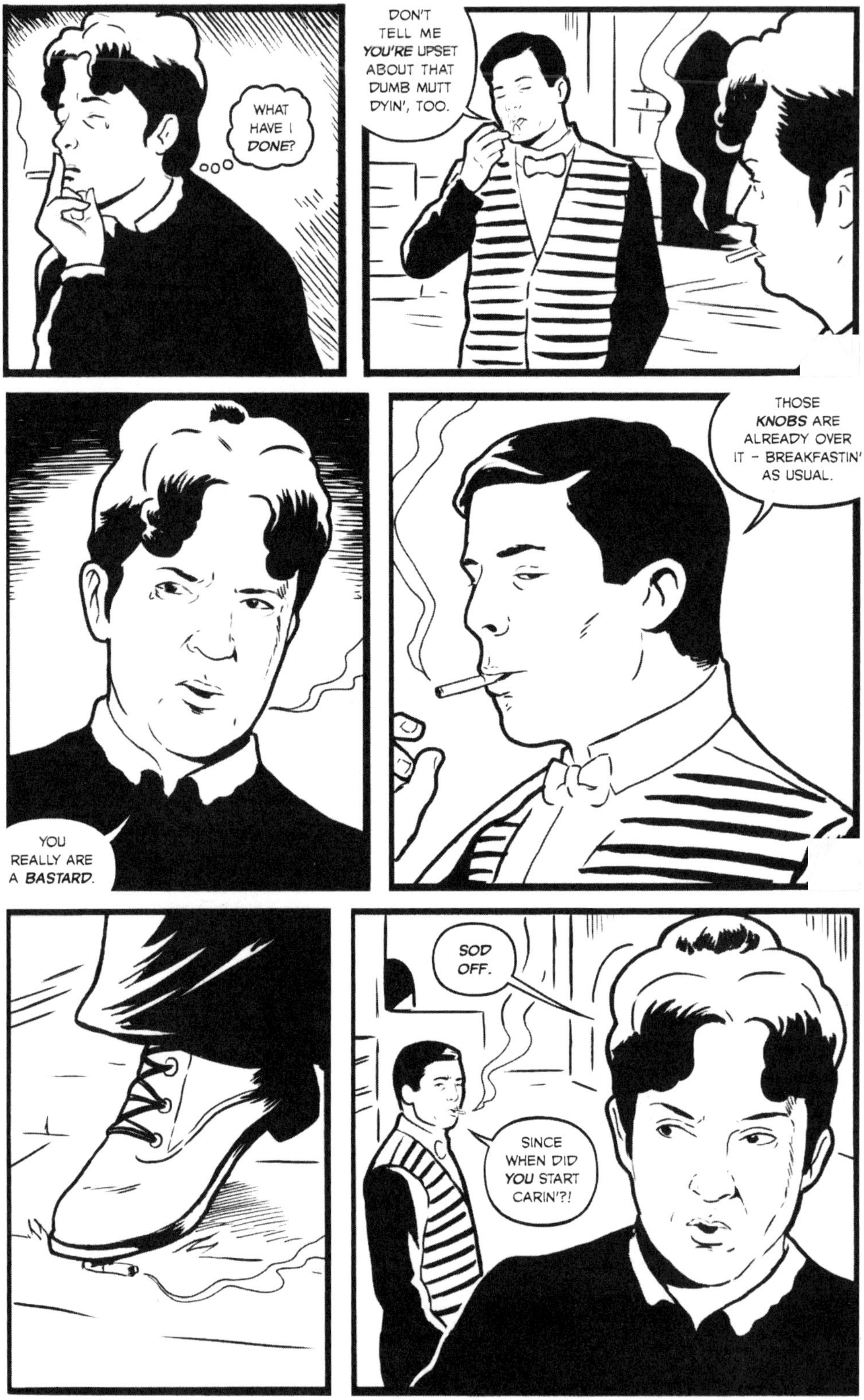
WHAT HAVE I DONE?
DON'T TELL ME YOU'RE UPSET ABOUT THAT DUMB MUTT DYIN', TOO.
YOU REALLY ARE A BASTARD.
THOSE KNOBS ARE ALREADY OVER IT - BREAKFASTIN' AS USUAL.
SOD OFF.
SINCE WHEN DID YOU START CARIN'?!

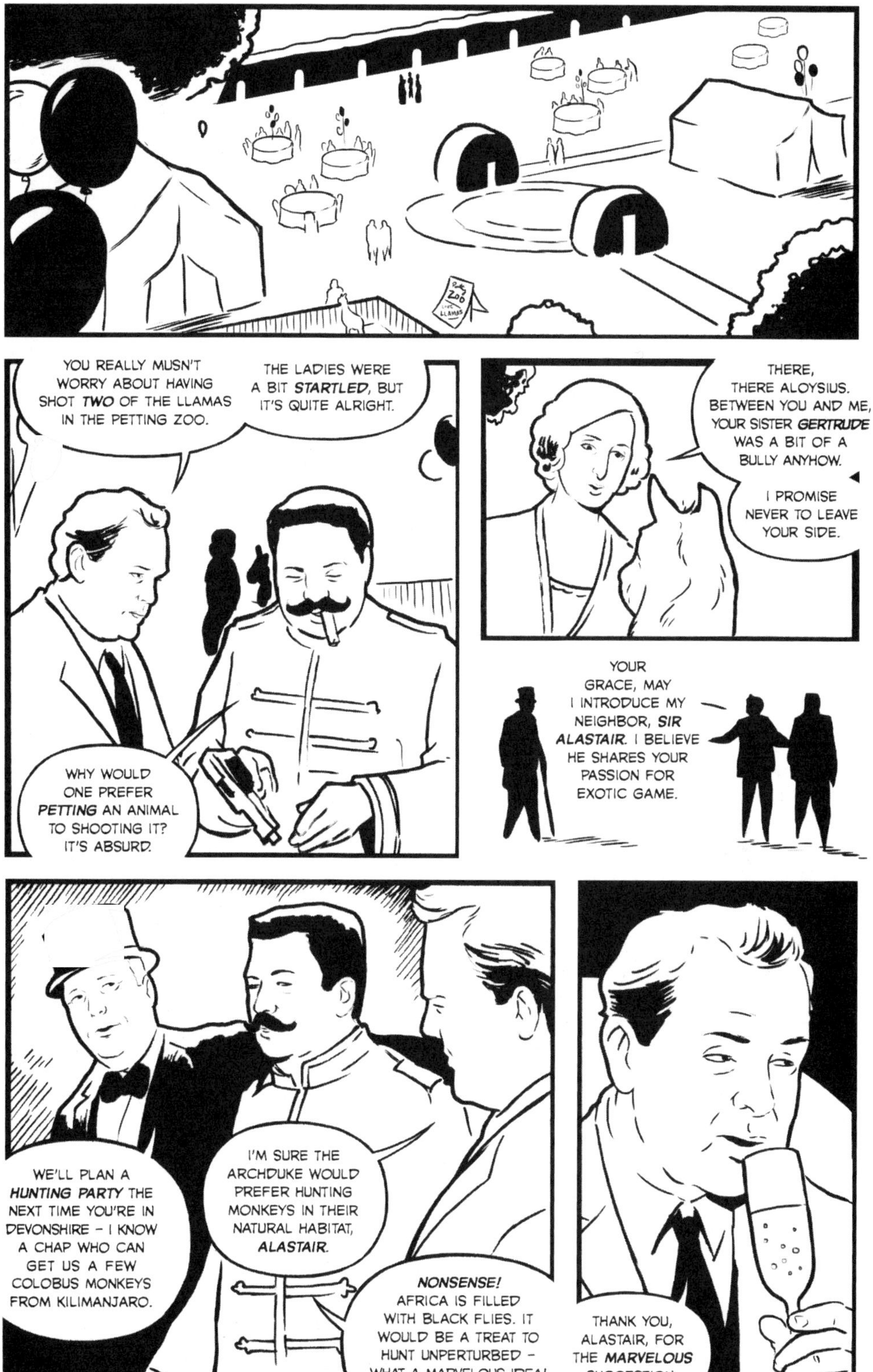
PETTING ZOO
LLAMAS
YOU REALLY MUSN'T WORRY ABOUT HAVING SHOT TWO OF THE LLAMAS IN THE PETTING ZOO.
THE LADIES WERE A BIT STARTLED, BUT IT'S QUITE ALRIGHT.
WHY WOULD ONE PREFER PETTING AN ANIMAL TO SHOOTING IT? IT'S ABSURD.
THERE, THERE ALOYSIUS. BETWEEN YOU AND ME, YOUR SISTER GERTRUDE WAS A BIT OF A BULLY ANYHOW.
I PROMISE NEVER TO LEAVE YOUR SIDE.
YOUR GRACE, MAY I INTRODUCE MY NEIGHBOR, SIR ALASTAIR. I BELIEVE HE SHARES YOUR PASSION FOR EXOTIC GAME.
WE'LL PLAN A HUNTING PARTY THE NEXT TIME YOU'RE IN DEVONSHIRE - I KNOW A CHAP WHO CAN GET US A FEW COLOBUS MONKEYS FROM KILIMANJARO.
I'M SURE THE ARCHDUKE WOULD PREFER HUNTING MONKEYS IN THEIR NATURAL HABITAT, ALASTAIR.
NONSENSE! AFRICA IS FILLED WITH BLACK FLIES. IT WOULD BE A TREAT TO HUNT UNPERTURBED - WHAT A MARVELOUS IDEA!
THANK YOU, ALASTAIR, FOR THE MARVELOUS SUGGESTION.

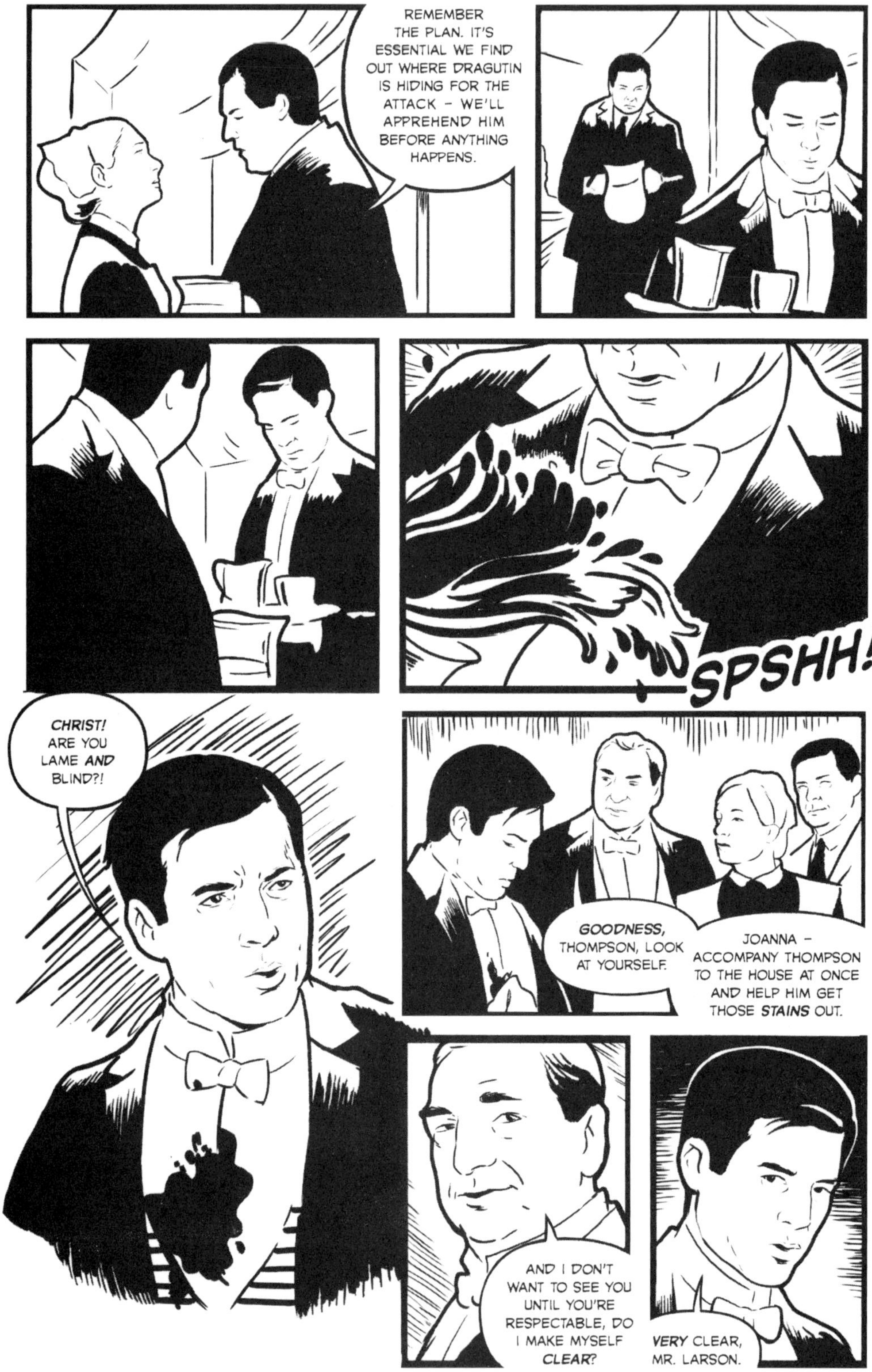
REMEMBER THE PLAN. IT'S ESSENTIAL WE FIND OUT WHERE DRAGUTIN IS HIDING FOR THE ATTACK - WE'LL APPREHEND HIM BEFORE ANYTHING HAPPENS.
SPSHH!
CHRIST! ARE YOU LAME AND BLIND?!
GOODNESS, THOMPSON, LOOK AT YOURSELF.
JOANNA - ACCOMPANY THOMPSON TO THE HOUSE AT ONCE AND HELP HIM GET THOSE STAINS OUT.
AND I DON'T WANT TO SEE YOU UNTIL YOU'RE RESPECTABLE, DO I MAKE MYSELF CLEAR?
VERY CLEAR, MR. LARSON.

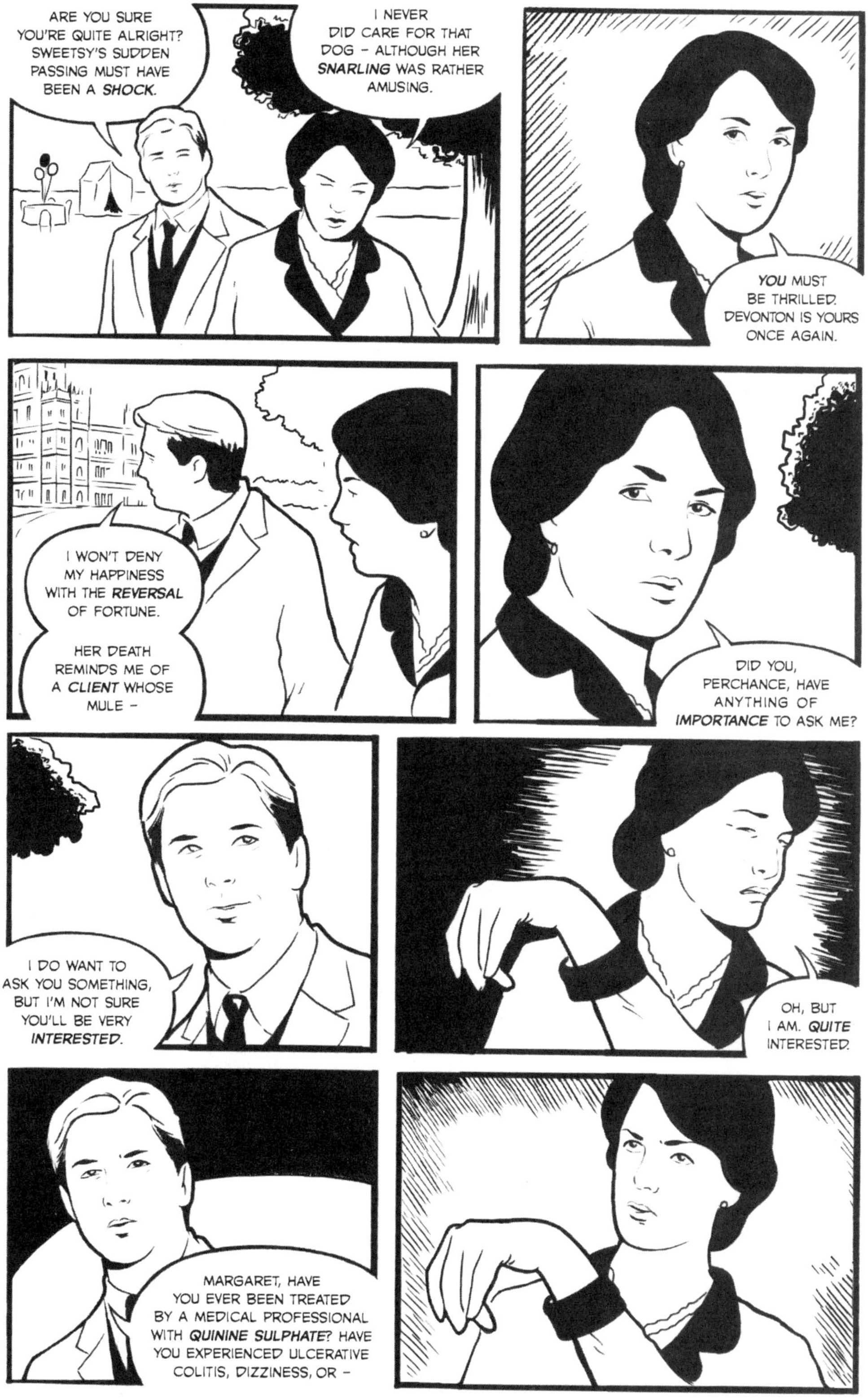
ARE YOU SURE YOU'RE QUITE ALRIGHT? SWEETSY'S SUDDEN PASSING MUST HAVE BEEN A **SHOCK**.
I NEVER DID CARE FOR THAT DOG – ALTHOUGH HER **SNARLING** WAS RATHER AMUSING.
YOU MUST BE THRILLED. DEVONTON IS YOURS ONCE AGAIN.
I WON'T DENY MY HAPPINESS WITH THE **REVERSAL** OF FORTUNE.
HER DEATH REMINDS ME OF A **CLIENT** WHOSE MULE –
DID YOU, PERCHANCE, HAVE ANYTHING OF **IMPORTANCE** TO ASK ME?
I DO WANT TO ASK YOU SOMETHING, BUT I'M NOT SURE YOU'LL BE VERY **INTERESTED**.
OH, BUT I AM. **QUITE** INTERESTED.
MARGARET, HAVE YOU EVER BEEN TREATED BY A MEDICAL PROFESSIONAL WITH **QUININE SULPHATE**? HAVE YOU EXPERIENCED ULCERATIVE COLITIS, DIZZINESS, OR –

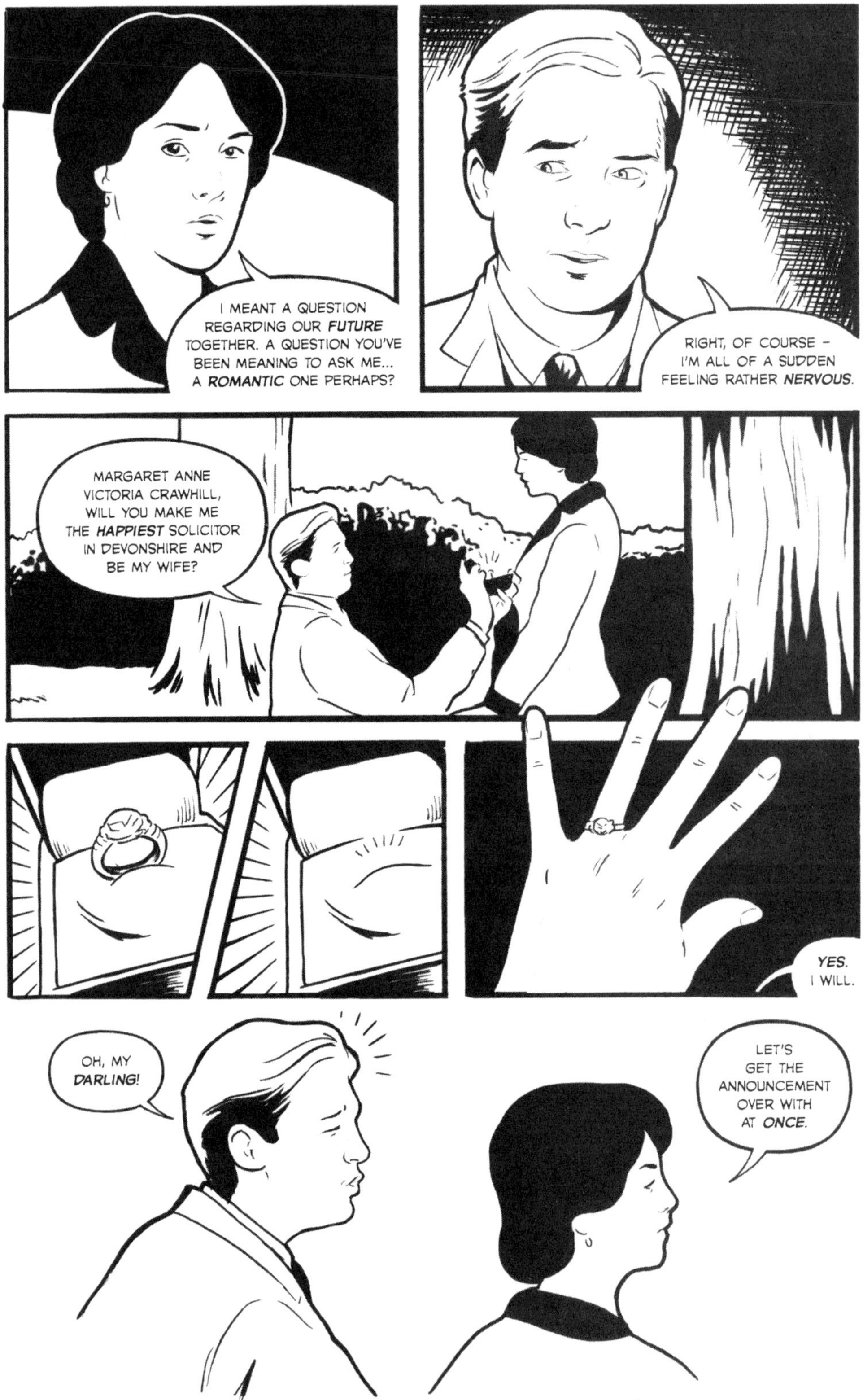
I MEANT A QUESTION REGARDING OUR *FUTURE* TOGETHER. A QUESTION YOU'VE BEEN MEANING TO ASK ME... A *ROMANTIC* ONE PERHAPS?
RIGHT, OF COURSE – I'M ALL OF A SUDDEN FEELING RATHER *NERVOUS*.
MARGARET ANNE VICTORIA CRAWHILL, WILL YOU MAKE ME THE *HAPPIEST* SOLICITOR IN DEVONSHIRE AND BE MY WIFE?
YES. I WILL.
OH, MY *DARLING*!
LET'S GET THE ANNOUNCEMENT OVER WITH AT *ONCE*.

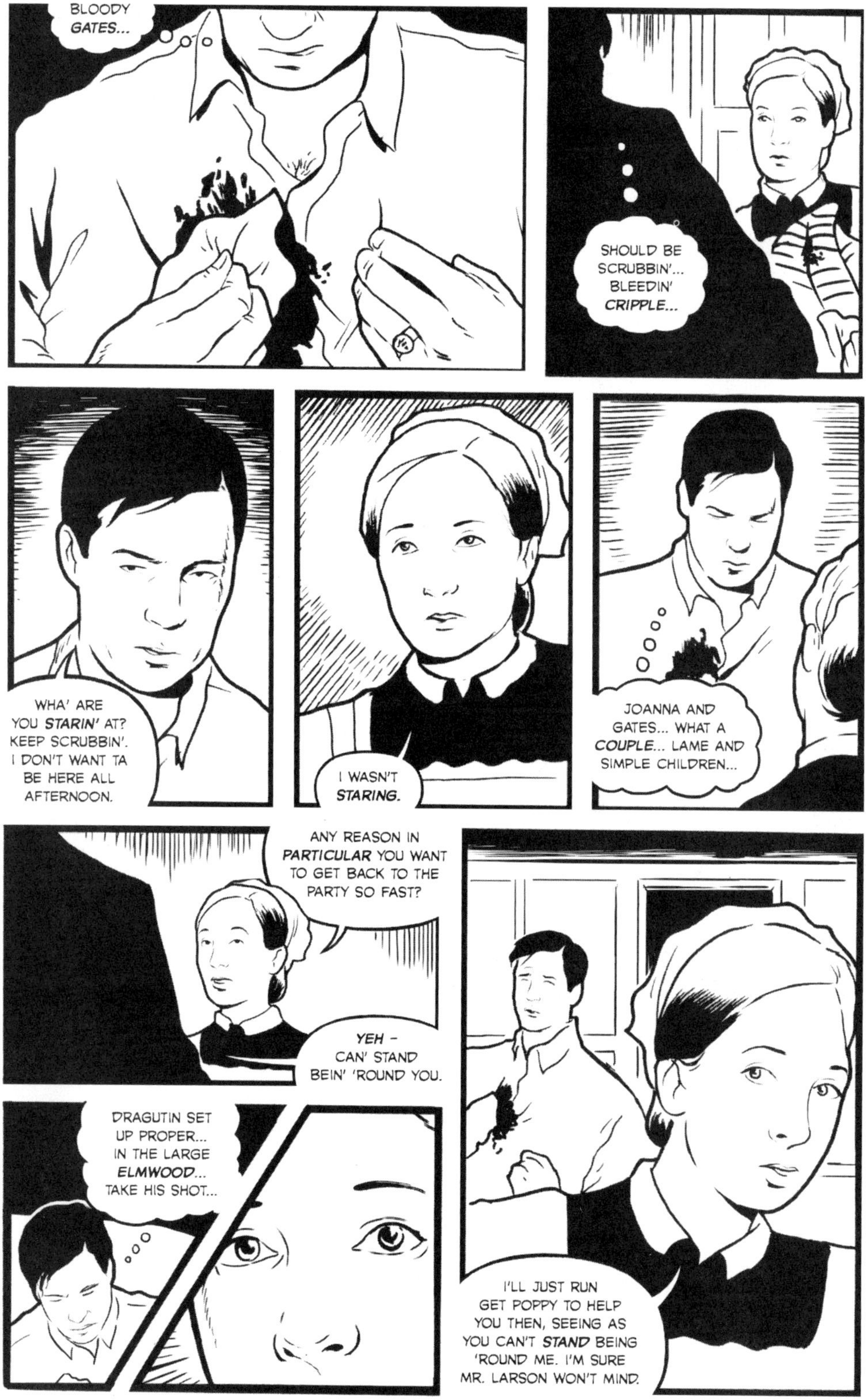
BLOODY GATES...
SHOULD BE SCRUBBIN'... BLEEDIN' CRIPPLE...
WHA' ARE YOU STARIN' AT? KEEP SCRUBBIN'. I DON'T WANT TA BE HERE ALL AFTERNOON.
I WASN'T STARING.
JOANNA AND GATES... WHAT A COUPLE... LAME AND SIMPLE CHILDREN...
ANY REASON IN PARTICULAR YOU WANT TO GET BACK TO THE PARTY SO FAST?
YEH - CAN' STAND BEIN' 'ROUND YOU.
DRAGUTIN SET UP PROPER... IN THE LARGE ELMWOOD... TAKE HIS SHOT...
I'LL JUST RUN GET POPPY TO HELP YOU THEN, SEEING AS YOU CAN'T STAND BEING 'ROUND ME. I'M SURE MR. LARSON WON'T MIND.

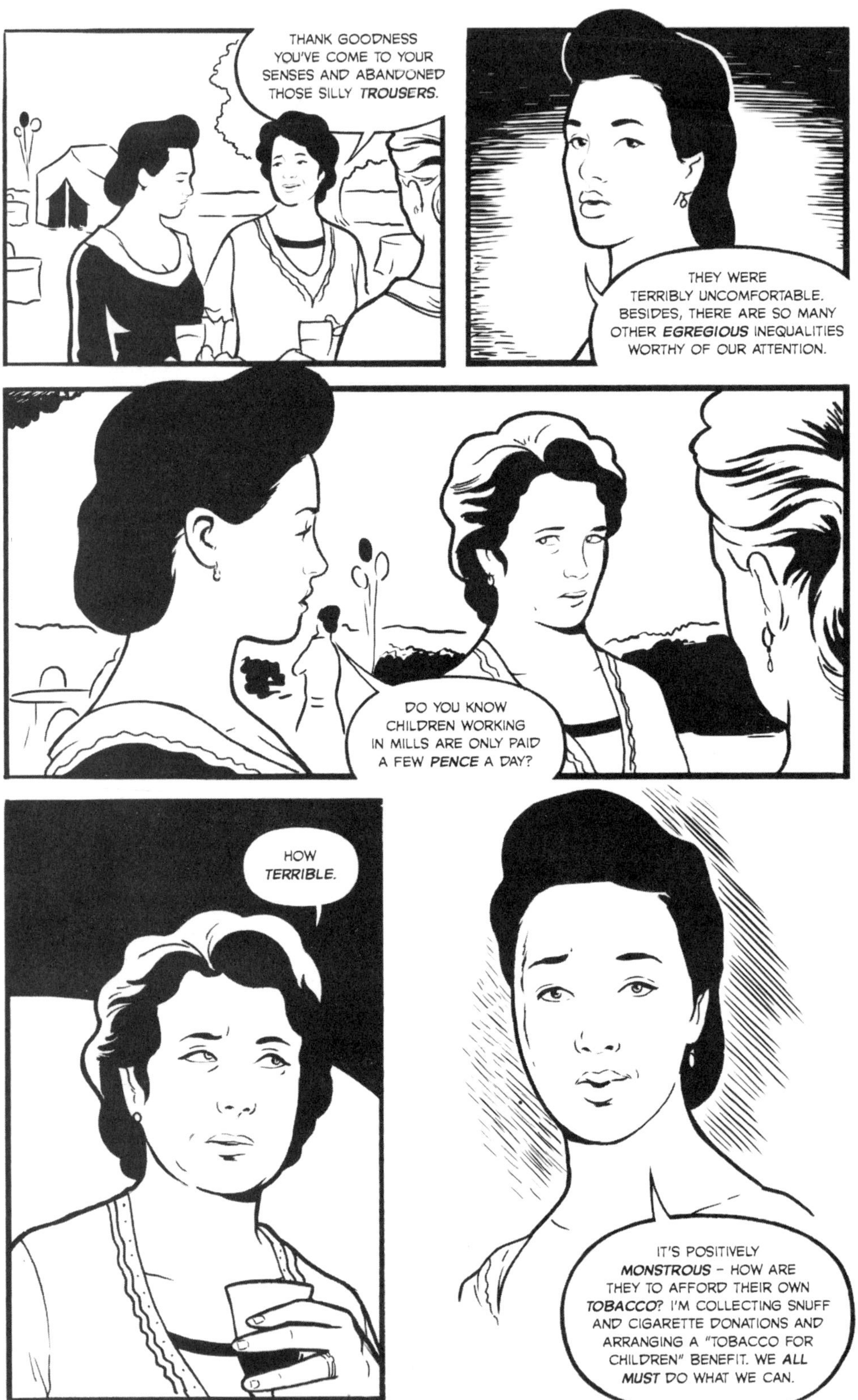
THANK GOODNESS YOU'VE COME TO YOUR SENSES AND ABANDONED THOSE SILLY *TROUSERS*.
THEY WERE TERRIBLY UNCOMFORTABLE. BESIDES, THERE ARE SO MANY OTHER *EGREGIOUS* INEQUALITIES WORTHY OF OUR ATTENTION.
DO YOU KNOW CHILDREN WORKING IN MILLS ARE ONLY PAID A FEW *PENCE* A DAY?
HOW *TERRIBLE*.
IT'S POSITIVELY *MONSTROUS* - HOW ARE THEY TO AFFORD THEIR OWN *TOBACCO*? I'M COLLECTING SNUFF AND CIGARETTE DONATIONS AND ARRANGING A "TOBACCO FOR CHILDREN" BENEFIT. WE *ALL MUST* DO WHAT WE CAN.

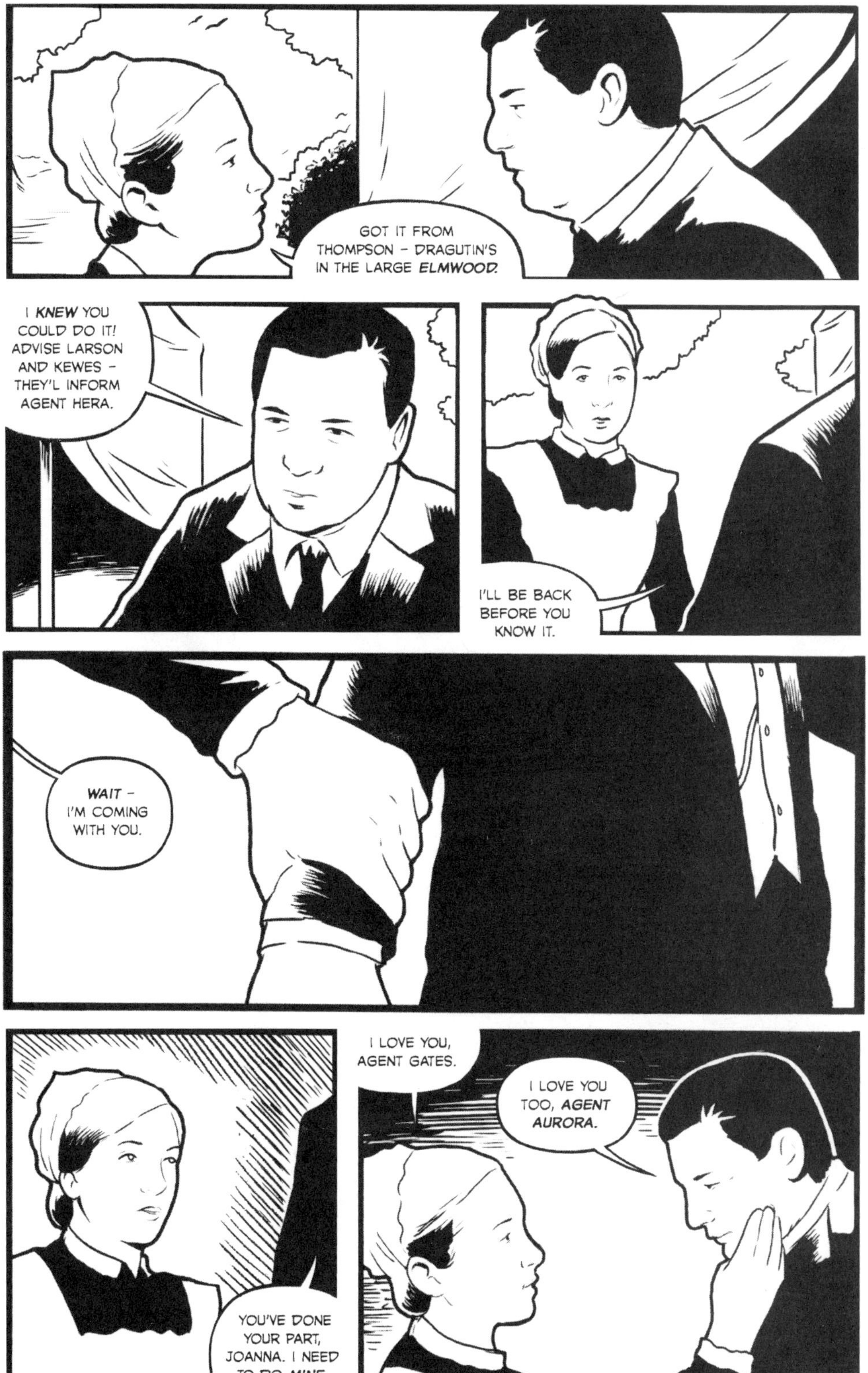
GOT IT FROM THOMPSON – DRAGUTIN'S IN THE LARGE ***ELMWOOD.***
I ***KNEW*** YOU COULD DO IT! ADVISE LARSON AND KEWES – THEY'L INFORM AGENT HERA.
I'LL BE BACK BEFORE YOU KNOW IT.
WAIT – I'M COMING WITH YOU.
YOU'VE DONE YOUR PART, JOANNA. I NEED TO DO ***MINE.***
I LOVE YOU, AGENT GATES.
I LOVE YOU TOO, ***AGENT AURORA.***

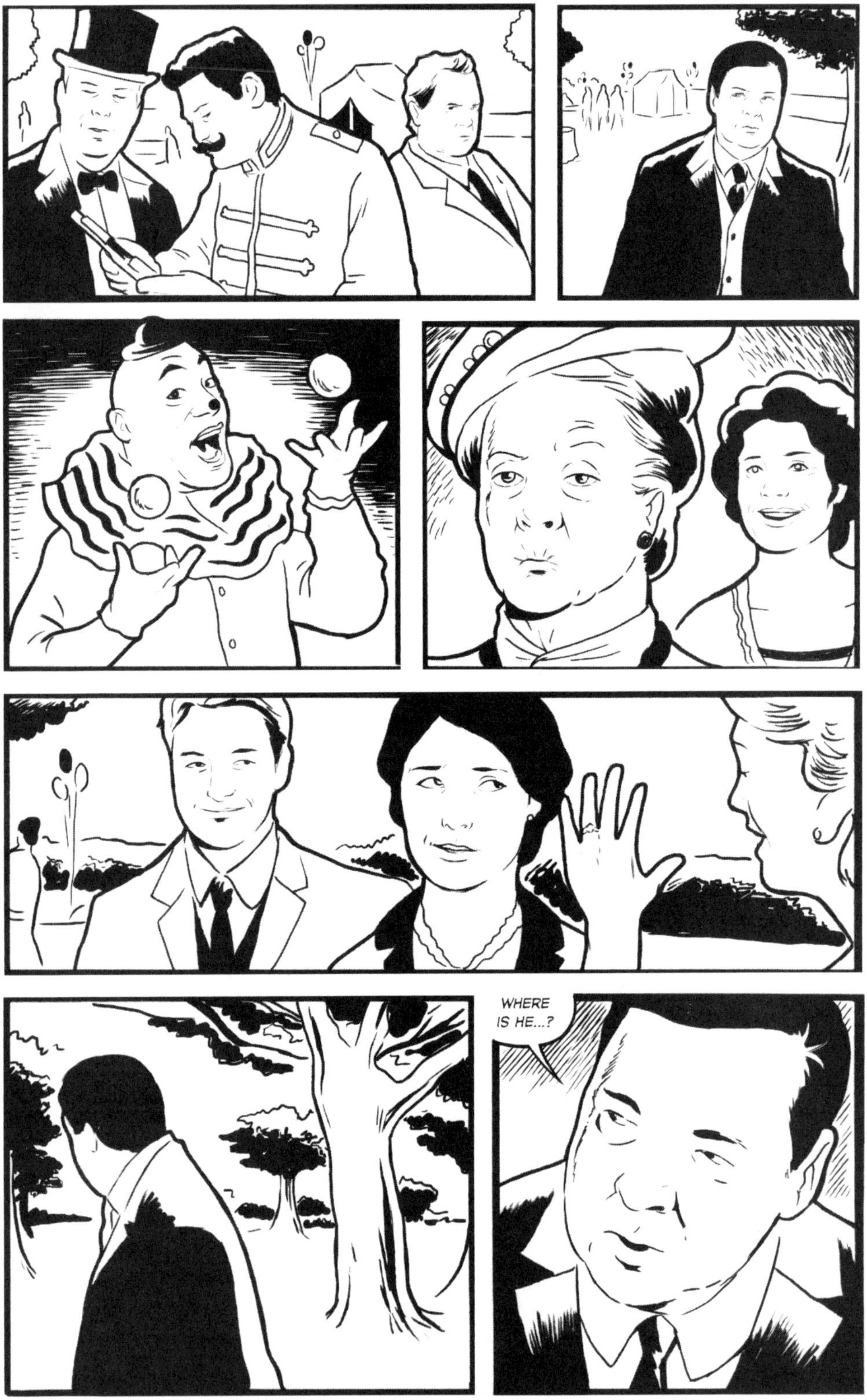
WHERE
IS HE...?

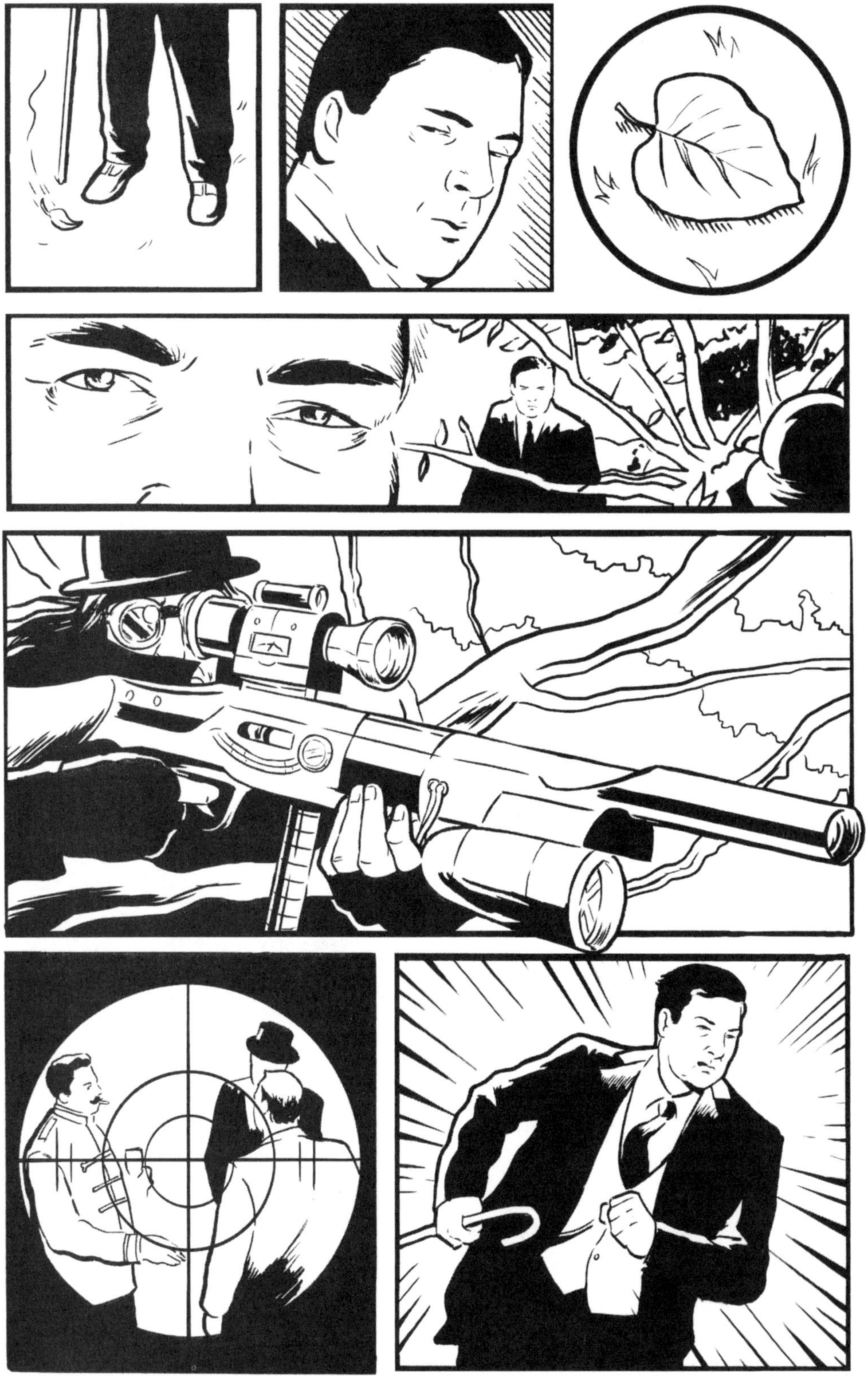

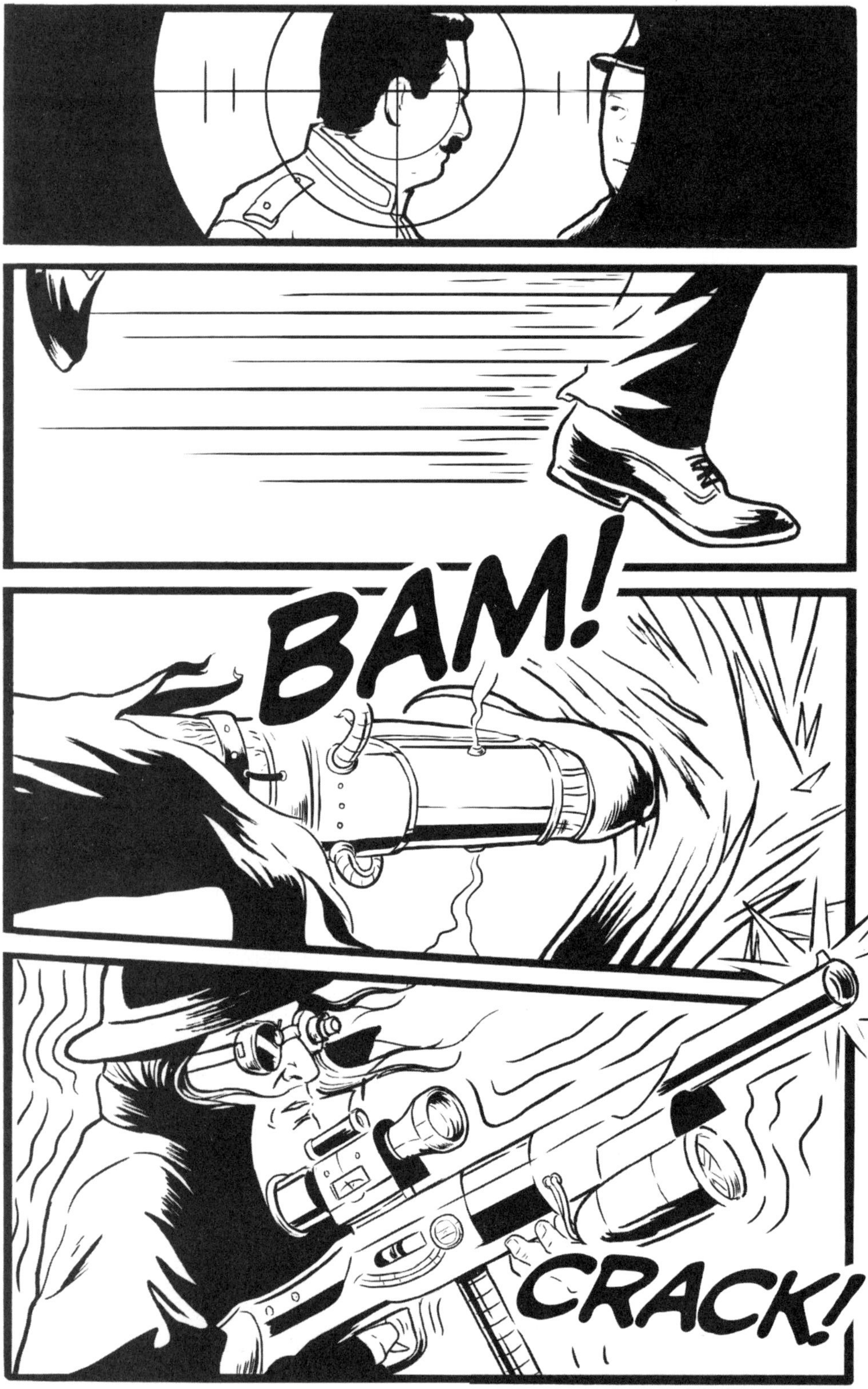
BAM!
CRACK!

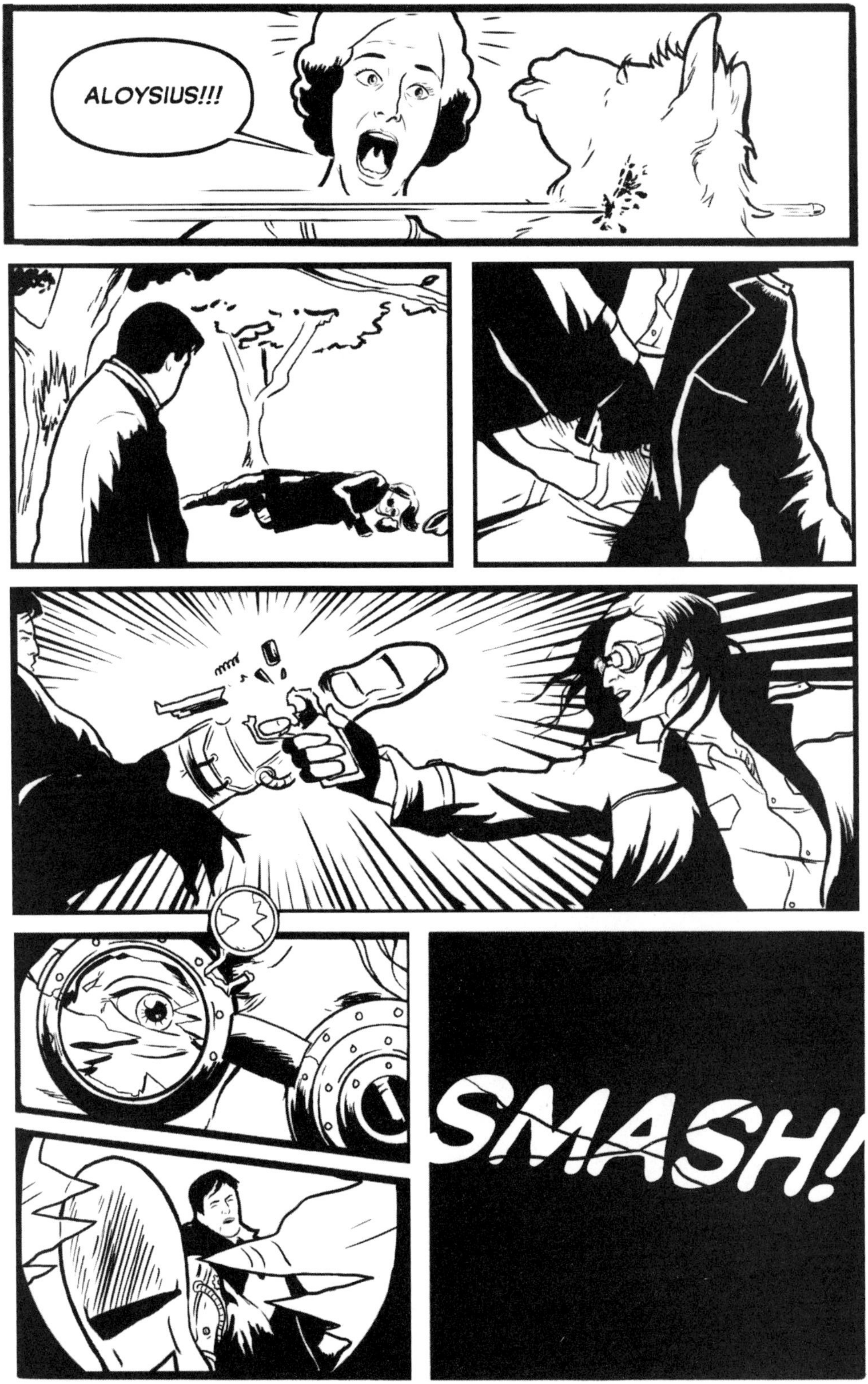
ALOYSIUS!!!
SMASH!

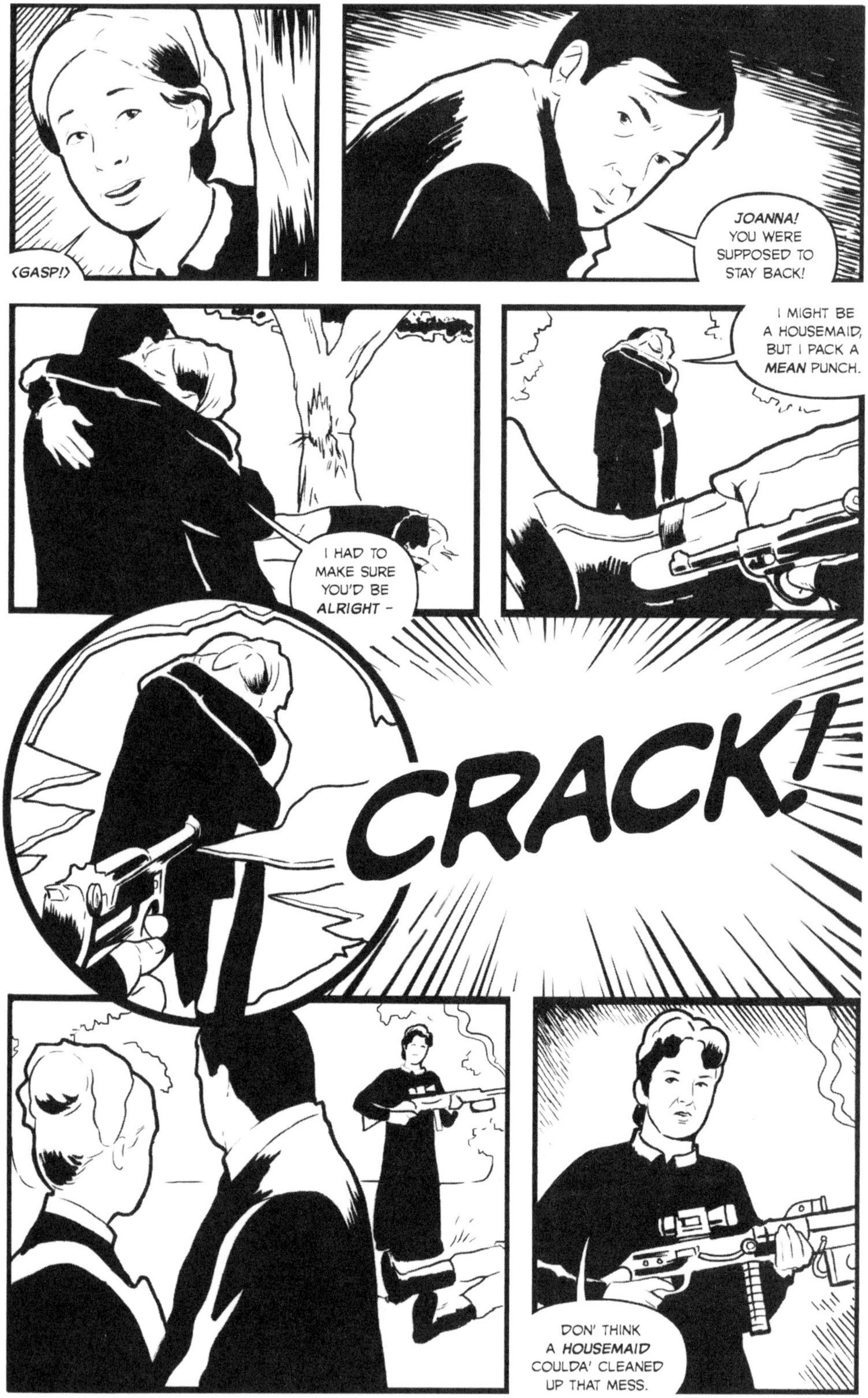
(GASP!)
JOANNA! YOU WERE SUPPOSED TO STAY BACK!
I HAD TO MAKE SURE YOU'D BE ALRIGHT –
I MIGHT BE A HOUSEMAID, BUT I PACK A MEAN PUNCH.
CRACK!
DON' THINK A HOUSEMAID COULDA' CLEANED UP THAT MESS.

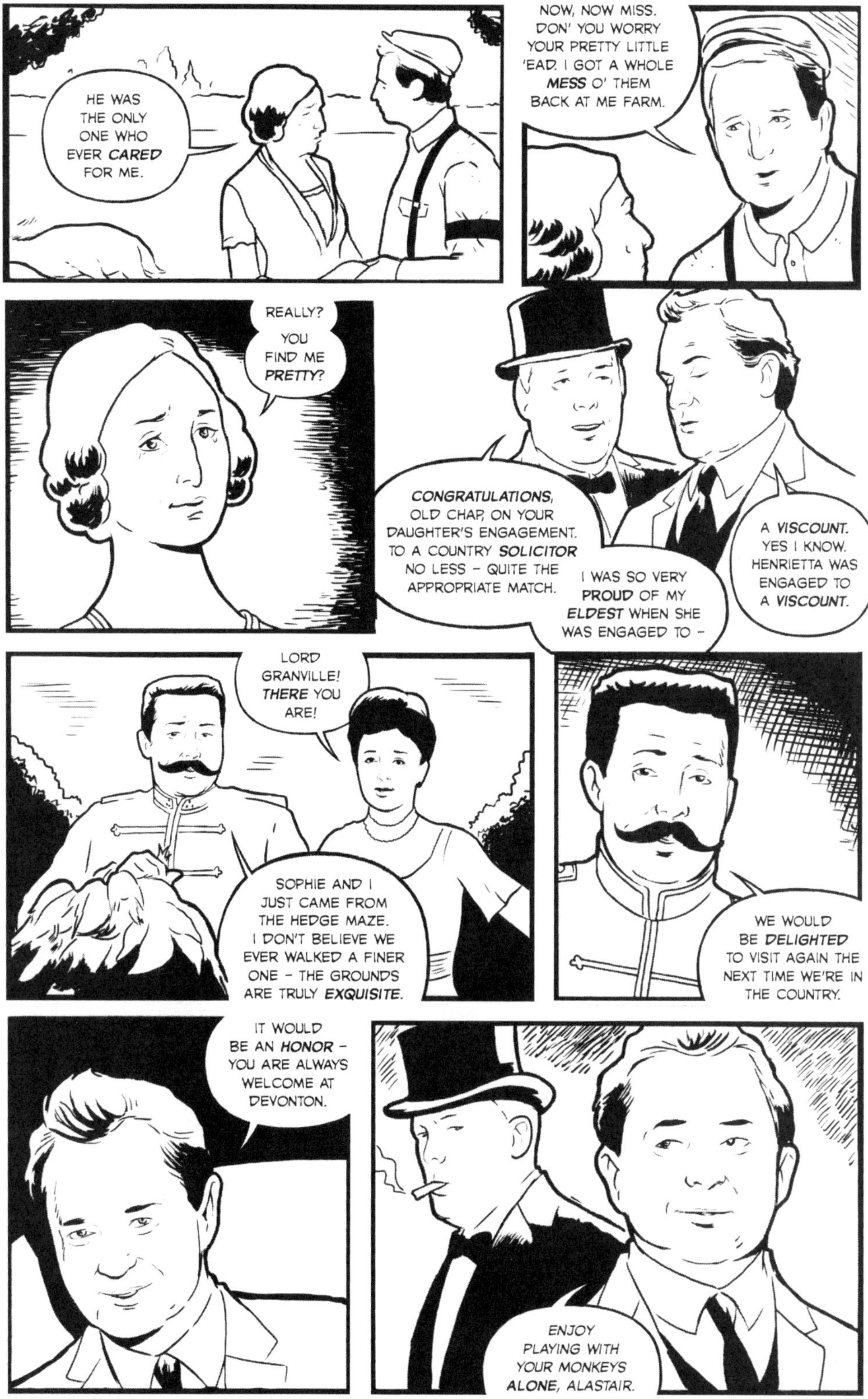
HE WAS THE ONLY ONE WHO EVER CARED FOR ME.
NOW, NOW MISS. DON' YOU WORRY YOUR PRETTY LITTLE 'EAD. I GOT A WHOLE MESS O' THEM BACK AT ME FARM.
REALLY?
YOU FIND ME PRETTY?
CONGRATULATIONS, OLD CHAP, ON YOUR DAUGHTER'S ENGAGEMENT. TO A COUNTRY SOLICITOR NO LESS - QUITE THE APPROPRIATE MATCH.
I WAS SO VERY PROUD OF MY ELDEST WHEN SHE WAS ENGAGED TO -
A VISCOUNT. YES I KNOW. HENRIETTA WAS ENGAGED TO A VISCOUNT.
LORD GRANVILLE! THERE YOU ARE!
SOPHIE AND I JUST CAME FROM THE HEDGE MAZE. I DON'T BELIEVE WE EVER WALKED A FINER ONE - THE GROUNDS ARE TRULY EXQUISITE.
WE WOULD BE DELIGHTED TO VISIT AGAIN THE NEXT TIME WE'RE IN THE COUNTRY.
IT WOULD BE AN HONOR - YOU ARE ALWAYS WELCOME AT DEVONTON.
ENJOY PLAYING WITH YOUR MONKEYS ALONE, ALASTAIR.

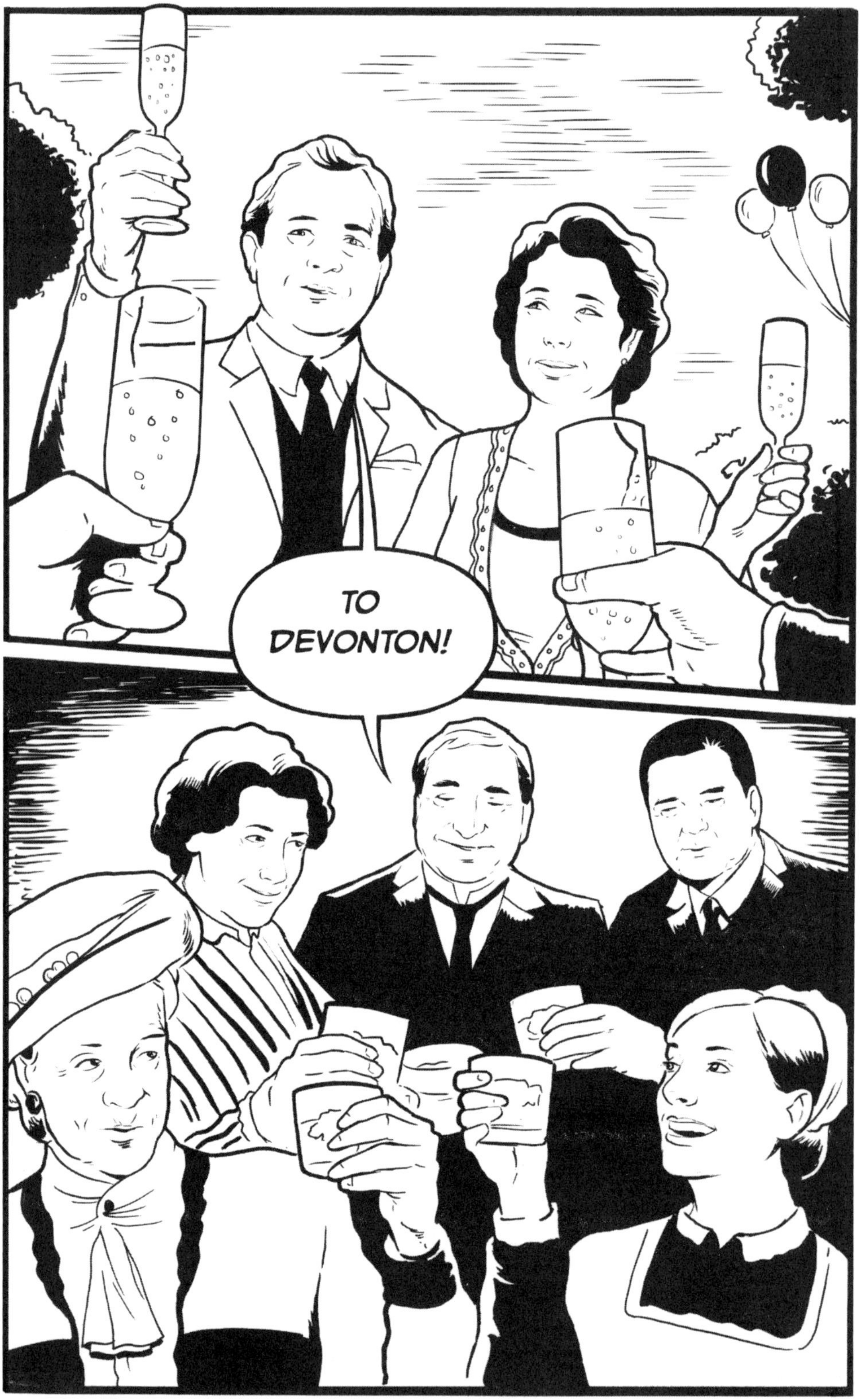
TO DEVONTON!

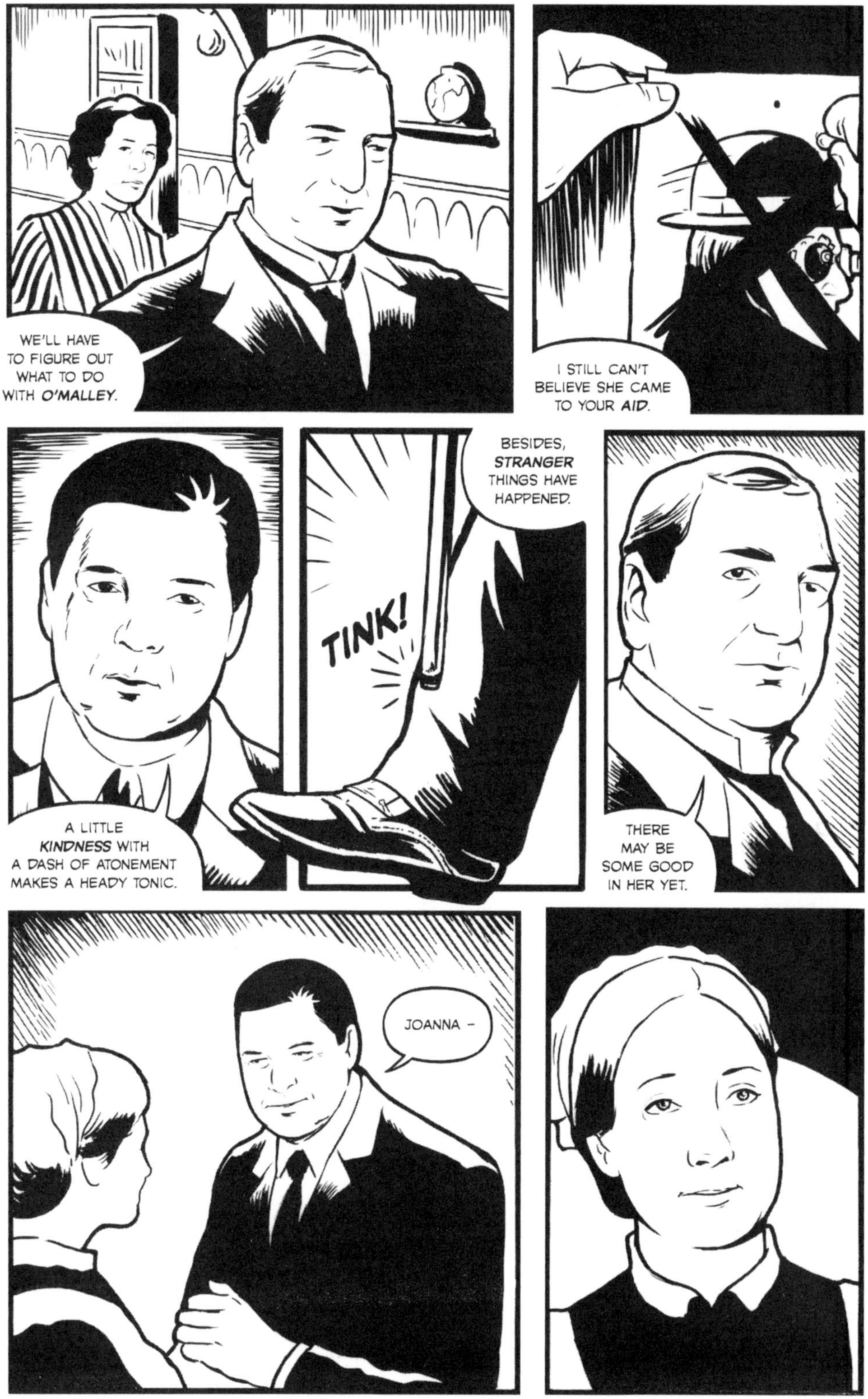
WE'LL HAVE TO FIGURE OUT WHAT TO DO WITH O'MALLEY.
I STILL CAN'T BELIEVE SHE CAME TO YOUR AID.
A LITTLE KINDNESS WITH A DASH OF ATONEMENT MAKES A HEADY TONIC.
BESIDES, STRANGER THINGS HAVE HAPPENED.
TINK!
THERE MAY BE SOME GOOD IN HER YET.
JOANNA –

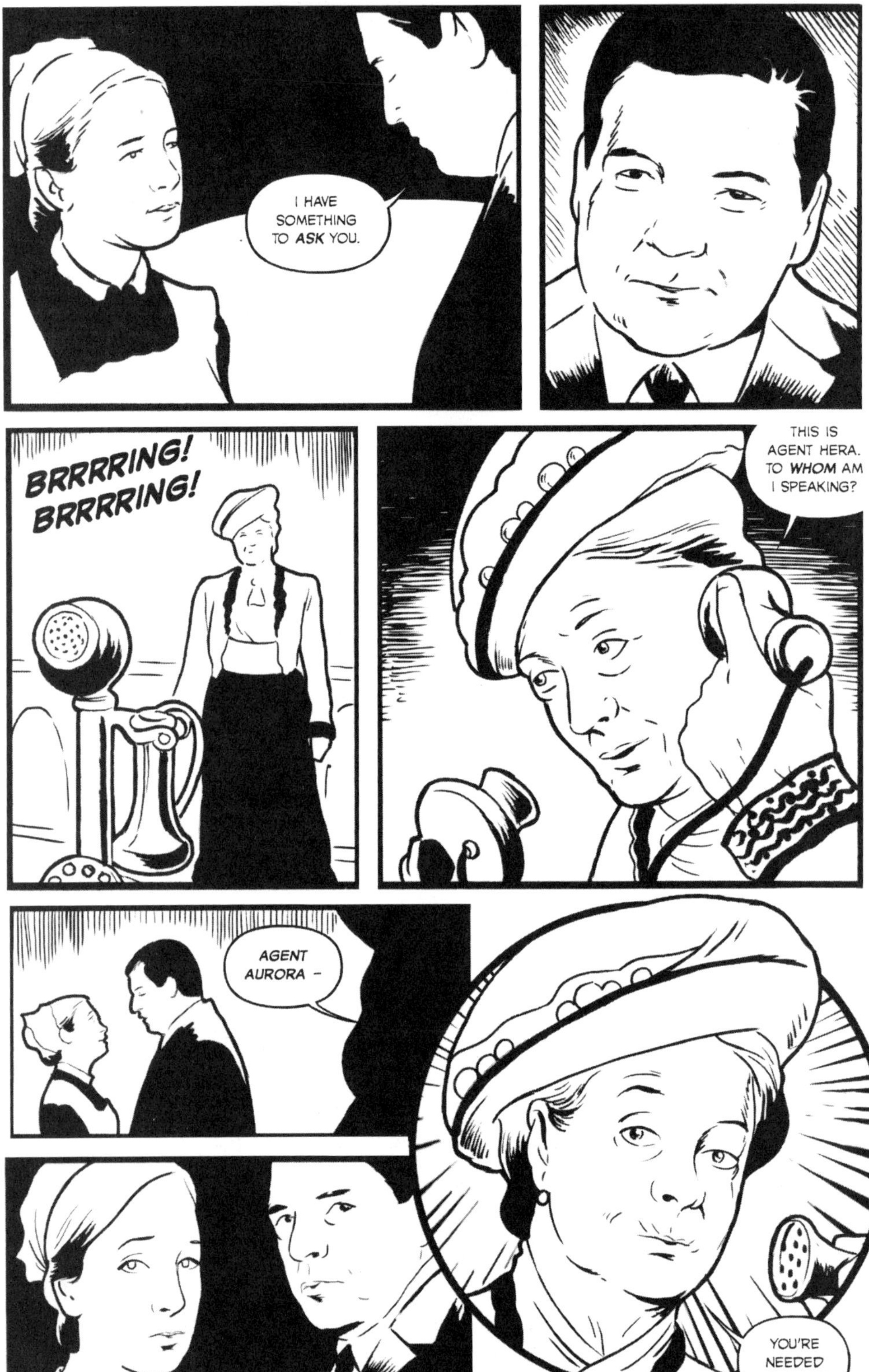
I HAVE SOMETHING TO ASK YOU.
BRRRRING! BRRRRING!
THIS IS AGENT HERA. TO WHOM AM I SPEAKING?
AGENT AURORA -
YOU'RE NEEDED AT ONCE.

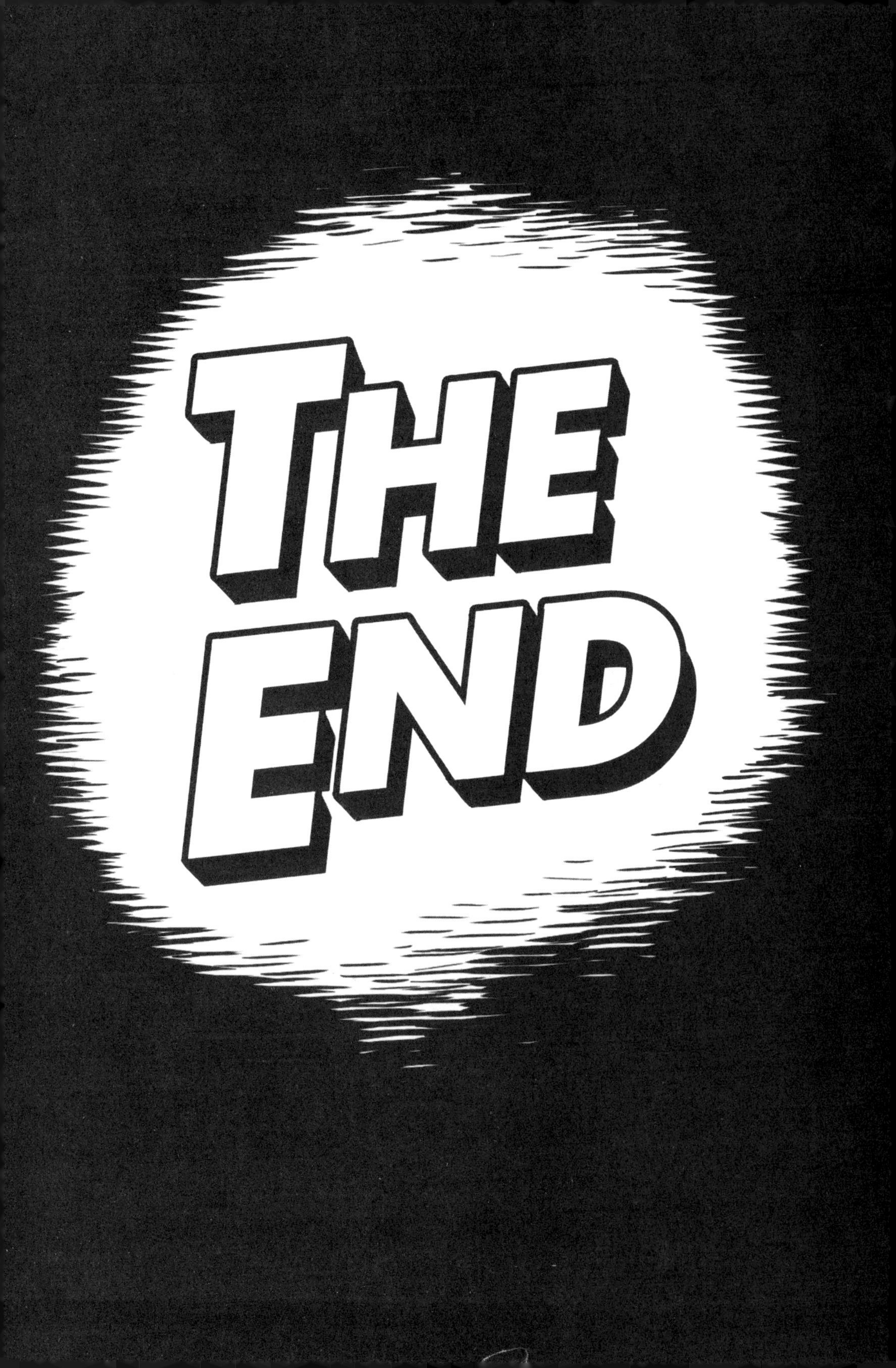
THE END

Agent Gates and the Secret Adventures of Devonton Abbey
copyright © 2013 by Kyle Hilton and Camaren Subhiyah.
All rights reserved. Printed in the United States of America. No part
of this book may be used or reproduced in any manner whatsoever without
written permission except in the case of reprints in the context of reviews.

Andrews McMeel Publishing, LLC
an Andrews McMeel Universal company
1130 Walnut Street, Kansas City, Missouri 64106

www.andrewsmcmeel.com

13 14 15 16 17 RR4 10 9 8 7 6 5 4 3 2 1

ISBN: 978-1-4494-3434-2

Library of Congress Control Number: 2012948461

ATTENTION: SCHOOLS AND BUSINESSES

Andrews McMeel books are available at quantity discounts
with bulk purchase for educational, business, or sales
promotional use. For information, please e-mail the Andrews
McMeel Publishing Special Sales Department:
specialsales@amuniversal.com